WORKS BY PETER STOCKWELL

ADULT FICTION

Motive series

Motive
Motivations
Jerry's Motives
Death Stalks Mr. Blackthorne
In the Garden of Eden

NONFICTION

Stormin' Norman
(The Sermons of an Episcopal Priest)
Volume I
Volume II

Dedication

**This book is dedicated to science
fiction readers who believe the
future is written today.**

**You loved me and your love made me--
human.**

Isaac Asimov, Forward the Foundation

CHAPTER 1

Cigi Weatherman's eyes popped open, the light of day flooding her brain, creating questions about her behavior. She sat up, swinging her legs over the edge of the bed. Her feet connected with the floor. She placed hands on her thighs and blinked. Her head turned to observe the body next to her.

He wriggled but remained asleep. The sedative worked its magic since his implant required an extended period for the wound to close. The pain blocker kept awareness of the modification at a minimum.

She rose and went to the bathroom and stood in front of the mirror, wondering. "What am I?" She examined her form. Her face was perfect and beautiful, according to people she met. Her proportional chest, waist, and hips, attracting the attention of many young men. Her goal centered on older men with power and money. "Why?" she whispered, "What am I doing?" Her hands cupped her breasts, but no tears formed or fell from her azure eyes. Emotions eluded her. Her victim's situation meant nothing to her. The plan directed her actions.

The sound of someone sitting in a wheelchair in the other room alerted her to a companion waking. He wheeled into the bathroom and sat on the toilet, oblivious to the beauty standing by the sink. As his body functioned, he looked at her. She stared back at him. What happened last night?" He finished and sat in his chair next to her. Clasping her buttocks, he pulled her to him and kissed her. As she sat on his lap, his warmth blended with hers. She wrapped her arms around his neck.

"To be honest, you have skipped an entire day. The dinner was two nights ago. You must have been overly tired." They separated, and he grabbed the side of his head.

"I feel like I've been run over by a freight loader. My head hurts." She stroked his neck without touching the now closed incision. The nano-cells had accomplished their job. His thoughts registered in her brain as the newly acquired telepathy marshaled her skills of compartmentalizing data feed. He tried to remember anything after their return to the hotel room and a session of passion. She countermanded any recall of the other person who entered the room after their sexual activity.

"You'll be fine," she assured him. "As I recall, you drank something which appealed to your taste buds, and you repeated the action several times. You have a hangover." She transmitted a message to his cerebral cortex, reinforcing the proper memories he needed to have.

"I guess so, but losing an entire day and night is not what I need." He turned on the shower with remote control and said, "want to scrub my back?"

Cigi smiled and nodded. Water was not an enemy of her body. She believed it was the best part of living. When the temperature acclimated to their desires, they opened the glass door to the over-sized space and enjoyed the cascading droplets. She picked the soap off the tray and washed his chest and shoulders. He turned so she could accomplish his original request to her. His back displayed the ripples of a fit man who exercised regularly. Her hands carried the soap to his buttocks. She cleansed his bottom. A groan exited his mouth. His legs were the only part which did not sense or respond

"Care to wash the front?" he asked.

"I do believe your hangover is not hanging around for long." She calculated the implant had released another pain-killing dose of drugs. His friskiness clicked in her brain. She accepted his advance to her as the water washed the soap from his frame. He paid the bills and kept her in a lifestyle unattainable without him. Sex was a small price to pay for an opportunity to have this luxury and financial freedom. Many people in her age group struggled to make a decent living. She found him as accommodating to her wishes as she was to his. Nothing mattered to him except her friendship and her bed. She had gained the proper and needed access to his mind and thinking and would use what she learned.

After the shower and drying, they dressed and prepared for returning to their distinctively regular lives. The drive was short, less than two hours. David Anderson would return to his family, and she would hole up in the condominium in midtown Arlington she bought using his money. His discretionary household fund was more substantial than many company budgets. He was wealthy because his hedge fund management and the fees garnered from the clients made money through investments his computer systems logged in microseconds.

"Do you miss me when you return to your business and family life?" Her question had no ulterior motive for forcing an issue that did not exist. Monitoring his business to determine a course of action was only to enrich the data drop she needed. He was a conduit and she appropriated what was required and nothing more.

"I like your companionship." His answer contained little emotion. "You provide an excellent supplement to my life. An additional benefit. While my business and family are the main cake and frosting, you are the decorations."

"Decorations? Is that all I am to you?" She thought about his words, and then continued, "I guess I can live with that." They kissed, and she departed for her home.

In the the seventeenth-floor penthouse, she typed a memo into her on-line diary. David had revealed a vital detail useful to her plans.

Using unique ingredients, prepared for her by the group that coordinated the arrangement, she cleansed her inner body. Her mind summoned programming she knew was not of her creation. Someone or something provided the information. She wanted to disrupt but did not understand the process for doing so. "Am I chipped like David?" she thought. The program worked through her thinking and directed her interaction with David in the last several days. She had followed the protocols provided about the implanting of the neural-cognitive connection. David was hers to manipulate.

Standing alone by a window, she gazed at the scene, wondering about her future. Would she be entitled to understand the choice for her to control these particular men? David was the first. Orders awaited allowing exploitation of her mind and body. She relaxed, listened to the message, and filed the information for another day.

Now free from interruption, she opened a book about cognitive ability and absorbed the data into her memory. Another book was a fiction piece about government takeovers and the projected mind control of the population. Thinking the material related too closely to the present world, she scanned for any relevant paragraphs. Finding none to fit her idea of government and citizenship, she closed it and her eyes. Memories of child-hood flooded her conscious dreams.

Were they dreams? Did she recall her youth correctly? Were her teen years as traumatic as she remembered? All that mattered was her ability to recall information and use it to learn about her present situation. No conflicting memories damned her existence or her chosen activity as a sexual companion and veritable spy. Reporting to The Company meant nothing to her, and the goals given her were not hard to fulfill.

Men wanted her for companionship, sex, and fantasies not provided by girlfriends and wives. She decided to acquire her next male companion as directed, a government comptroller in the Department of Energy. According to the file she accessed about him, he was married with three children. All was going well with him except for a lack of excitement in his personal life and less recognition than he wanted in his occupation. He had a regular routine that Cigi would interrupt. She could meet him at a convention he was attending in New York City later in the week.

As night claimed the daylight, she decided to rest for the evening. Her traveling to New York could happen on the morning bullet train. The entire trip was less than two hours from Arlington. She accessed the file to check his visage and name. Andre' Scott was approaching 50 years of age. Graying hair. Still, physically fit. She closed the file. He was ripe for exploitation. She decided to interact with him in the morning.

A bright moon flooded her living area with light. She seldom turned on the lights in her condo. She had little need for them. Although the decorations and furniture were appropriate, she felt nothing for them. They served a function. The dust of the atmosphere clung to her body. A shower seemed appropriate. After removing all her clothing, she stared into the mirror in the bathroom and wondered. Advertisements about beauty and feminine culture abounded in the social media outlets of the Internet. Men wanted women to be more like the Stepford Wives from the twentieth-century film. An uprising in the early twenty-first century by females entering politics failed to displace males as the dominant force. Now, as the twenty-second century loomed closer, politics, democracy, and republics across the world had consented to a social order of small tribal-like entities. Each interchanged foods and other supplies with little regard to the class of people. Wealth and power were in the hands of a few families around the world. People did not complain because they had what they wanted.

Her body conformed to the models portrayed in media outlets. She was the perfect human form, and her mind contained more information than other people. She manipulated her memories better than any other person. She was the perfect human.

CHAPTER 2

Andre' Scott finished eating his eggs and bacon with his wife, Lydia. Their children, Amber, Leslie, and Garth, were grown or away at school. A quiet life of empty-nesting became a routine. Conversations were limited to the everyday issues of maintaining a home and planning vacations. Lydia worked as a consultant with a green energy company, which had begun two centuries earlier as a coal mining operation. At home, they kept their work separate. He did not talk with her about her company, although she did connect with others in the Department of Energy.

Today was like any other. Today was a day for a continued chasing of the dream of retirement in twenty years and living a comfortable life without entanglements. Today was as mundane as any of his days in the past.

He kissed Lydia and left to catch his train into Washington, D.C. The United States government was no longer a republic. Apathy and disillusion of the population figured significantly into a Congress and Executive, which bickered about what the Constitution meant. A convention had convened and modified the language of the original document. The result created a dictatorial situation. No one complained if jobs and supplies were available. People were giving up.

Andre' worked his department as if energy requirements mattered.

His goal was a clean and efficient power source for business and people. Oversight of the money made it happen. He entered his office, greeting his staff as he always did. The work they did made them his priority. They did job which he managed. They were the real force for change.

When morning routines approached a break for lunch, Andre' stepped out of his office and discovered most of the staff had headed to the lounge for their meal. He did not have any food with him and decided to leave for his usual haunt, a small restaurant within walking distance of his office. A waitress greeted him and smiled. They had flirted but never executed any contact beyond the restaurant. He sat at the counter as he usually did and opened a menu. Nothing caught his eye that might entice a modification of his club sandwich and lemonade.

"What do you recommend?" His brain conjured an imaginary person speaking, but he turned to see a woman whose beauty was hard to ignore. Her eyes penetrated any attempt to build a wall of aloneness. Her hair flowed freely across one shoulder. Flawless skin had a hint of makeup on her cheeks. She smiled with lips of soft pink and teeth as white as fresh snow. "May I sit here?" she asked, her tone mellow and inviting. A hint of rose crossed his nostrils. An eyebrow rose in anticipation of a response.

Andre' stammered and pointed at the seat next to him. "Ah, yes. Please." She removed her coat. The blouse fit her frame with buttons undone to reveal some cleavage. A stirring within his body reclaimed his youth. Lydia captured his heart in college with similar appearances, but age exacted a price. He also suffered from the ravages of time, and medical science could only delay the inevitable.

"Have you ordered anything?" Her voice mesmerized his mind. He scanned her from foot to head and answered.

"No, I was about to get my usual club. What do you like?"

She swiveled to face him. "I don't eat much. Do they have soups?" He nodded. The waitress behind the counter approached, and they ordered. Silence reigned for a moment before Cigi asked, "Do you work around here?"

He rocked his head. "I'm in the Department of Energy."

"Fascinating. I do believe the removal of petroleum and coal as energy sources has decreased the climate catastrophe, which we have experienced these last few decades."

He furrowed his brow. "What do you know about it?" His experiences with the younger generation repressed acceptance of them as caring or engaged in world's problems. They were a sycophantic group of malcontents. Most issues were not their concern.

This woman represented an opposing position with interest and knowledge. He wanted more. Life now demanded interaction. She said, "My study of history educated me about the early decades of this century and the disclaiming of climate modification by human activity. At least now, some of us are acting to mitigate the challenges."

His brain clicked into gear when a viable person with which to communicate and share a fear he held tight sat next to him. He wanted more. Why? He knew nothing about this woman. Was she a spy, or from the anti-green league? As scarcities arose, the planet headed to the brink of war. Strong-arm tactics had averted substantive confrontations, but small skirmishes littered the continents as populations withered and died in impoverished countries. Aid from the more prosperous nations did not lessen the needs and some areas swallowed other areas. Earth's mapping changed by the month as countries invaded other countries to find resources. Nothing major had erupted. Only time would tell the story.

Their meals arrived, and they ate without interruption. Andre' then asked, "Who are you? Are you here for a deliberate reason, seeking me out?"

She placed her soup spoon on the plate. "I seek only to aid your investigation of the oddities in the department. You are not the problem, but something is wrong within Energy." She put her hand atop his and continued, "I have information which may aid in halting the financial hemorrhage."

He took another bite of his sandwich, chewed, and swallowed. "What do you think you know about the Department of Energy? Are you from Federal or some other agency?" Tension built defenses like a wall. He pushed his plate away and stared at her. "You know nothing. Nice try at getting information from me." He stood and turned to leave. She smiled and slurped soup.

"Take my number and call me when you want to know what I know about the misused money in the solar research fund." The bait was offered. Would he nibble or seize it?

She stopped consuming her meal, wrote on a napkin, and held it up without looking. He hesitated but grasp the paper and left. She finished her lunch, paid, and followed his exit. As Cigi rounded a corner to catch a car for her home, he intercepted her. "How do you know about any of this?" He shook the napkin in her face as he spoke.

"Come with me, and we can discuss it. I'm not an enemy. I have the means to control the loss of revenue and want to aid your investigation." She held out an arm for him to clasp. "We can arrange for other entertainment if you are interested." She grinned her best professional grimace, alluring and enticing. He intertwined his arm and allowed her to lead him to an awaiting electric town car. He frowned at the fact there was no driver. The automobile was a self-driving unit with a reputation for uncanny accuracy. "Take me home, Cecil." The car navigated through the streets with ease. Most people could not afford a personal device such as 'Cecil' and traveled by the mass transit system.

"Where is home?" Andre' asked.

"We'll be there soon, and you will see." At a high rise condo complex near Central Plaza, Cecil turned into a garage and parked in a spaced marked with the name Cigi Weatherman. He guessed her name was the same. They exited the vehicle, which shut down and locked when they were a few steps away.

Andre' turned back to stare at her car. "How can you afford one of those?"

"I have extensive financial backing, and you can become part of the team." She hooked her arm in his and led him to an elevator. Inside she pushed a sensor button marked with a P, and they ascended to her penthouse suite. Neither of them spoke during the half minute ride. When the doors opened, she stepped out and waved her hand. A wall opened for them to enter her home.

Andre' said, "I have to get back to work." She smiled. An air of fresh flowers along with a view of lower Back Bay and Washington D.C. impressed him. She had money.

"Before we conclude our business about the leak of money, I want to offer you another business arrangement." She removed her coat and unbuttoned her blouse. "I am available to you for your pleasure and entertainment. I am discreet and will not undermine your family life. I am here to offer you an opportunity to refresh your manhood in ways Lydia has not thought of and has no desire to share with you." His mouth stood open, and his eyes gazed at the physique now exposed.

As his eyes wandered upward to meet her eyes, he said, "How do you know my wife's name?" He shook his head. "Never mind. I get it now. You targeted me and want something for which you are willing to exchange sex with me to get. I know prostitution is no longer illegal, but this seems to be a form of entrapment. What do you want?"

"My group would like to assist you with plugging your leak and keeping the department from any further corruption. The group realizes a need for course correction in this current world. Leaders of countries are more interested in ruining humanity than they are in saving it." She unhooked her pants and removed them.

Andre' remained silent, gazing at a human form so perfect, he thought of the movies of recent years with robots as surrogates. Her language skills were not robotic. She had free will. "I must return to work. I will think about your offer and let you know." He caressed the napkin in his pocket. As he turned to leave, he stopped. "Why me? I'm only a comptroller. I don't make decisions about policy or actions undertaken by Energy. I only oversee the money." Her eyes answered his question.

"Cecil will take you back to your office." He would be contacting her soon enough. A message formed in her head from nowhere. "Well done."

CHAPTER 3

The phone rang. The sound startled Parvel Mandolin out of a daze
staring at his computer screen. Few businesses had traditional style
phones with punch buttons, and wire hooked to the wall. "Hello,"
he said as he checked the caller ID screen. "Cigi, what's up?"

He waited for her to respond. She did not speak for five seconds.
"Parvel, I have a property for you to check out in Seattle. Can you handle a
mortgage across the country?" He paused.

"I guess. What do you have?"

"I have a place downtown near the waterfront in Seattle." The city
had not suffered as much as other parts of the country since conservative
thinking gained little ground around Puget Sound and Elliot Bay. He scrolled
through his options and found a funding source.

"Do you have a deal set to complete?"

"Yes."

"Okay, I'll get everything ready. Can you stop by the office and sign
the papers?" He wanted to see her again. He desired more than a friendship
with her but realized how hopeless it was to expect her to want him.

"I can be there tomorrow."

"Okay."

His heart rate increased as a bead of moisture slipped from his
forehead. Since meeting Cigi a few months ago while working a mortgage
for her penthouse, he fantasized about a relationship that had little or no

chance of being. Ignoring his brain, he processed current documents for other clients who could afford to own property.

After completing his workload, he contacted a friend in Seattle who had resources to fulfill Cigi's request. "Doug, this lady has plenty of backing to make it work. She indicated she has a place already picked out."

"I'll see what I can do." The call ended.

Parvel shuffled through papers on his desk, his mind unfocused on working. Cigi invaded his imagination, but he couldn't be sure if he was dreaming or someone had planted the images. She knew how to control others, or so he believed. Her appearance froze anyone near to her. They gawked or stared, or whatever one wanted to call it. He observed how men trailed after her passing with their eyes as if hypnotized. He stood from his desk and informed his assistant he was leaving for another engagement.

Outside, the weather was warm, and clouds billowed high in the sky. Meteorological predictions had become more exciting in the last couple of decades because of the uncertainty of the jet stream patterns. It was as if Mother Nature wanted to confound humanity. He pulled his jacket closer to his chest. The population jostled around him as he walked. His eyes focused on the sidewalk, avoiding any connection with people. He ambled along with no idea of where he headed. He wanted only to be away from the business involving Cigi Weatherman.

She tormented him without cause or knowledge of her impact on him. All his torture was self-induced. He prayed to an unseen and disbelieved deity for relief from his shyness and insecurities. What good was it for anyone to be afraid of nothing and paralyzed by what was known. He entered a small coffee shop and sat at a corner table away from anyone.

Scanning the room, he saw a pair of sunglasses seemingly watching him. He looked down as a waiter approached. He ordered a pastry and tea. Checking again for the sunglasses, he found nothing. The table was empty. Parvel checked his phone for any messages from the office, but nothing showed on his screen. He opened his gallery app and scrolled through the few pictures he kept on it. Cigi was prominent by the number of photos. Some he had garnered enough courage to ask for her to pose with him. Others he secretly snapped.

The waiter returned with his order and placed the plate on the table. Parvel paid his tab on the billing device handed to him by the waiter. Electronic transfers of funds were fast, convenient, and reliable. Graft only occurred with the highest ranks of society. Ordinary people who attempted to cheat the system tended to disappear. If they returned to their homes, the attitude about deceiving fellow citizens had been eradicated. Fear worked its magic.

He ate and drank in silence without watching others. When finished, he stood and walked to the doorway. Before he reached the entry, his waiter approached him. "Somebody asked me to give this to you." He handed Parvel an envelope with no writing on the outside. His mind pondered the exchange and what was inside. He opened the unsealed envelope and removed the paper inside. It said, "Be kind and careful when dealing with Cigi Weatherman." No threat was apparent, and yet nothing prevented the note from being a warning. He nodded at the waiter and left the shop.

"Great," he thought, "now I have someone tailing my every move?" He scanned the area, but nothing suspicious greeted his eyes. The usual noises of people shuffling along the street talking with others, mass transit buses and a few cars rumbling by, and the silence of the weather before a storm accosted his ears. He placed his hands on his head, muffling the invasion. He wasn't interested in being a target. He had to force his brain to conjure enough courage to talk with Cigi directly.

Returning to his office, he greeted the staff and sat at his desk. His assistant handed him a couple of papers. "These need your signature," she said.

"Thanks." He signed them and handed them to her. He punched in Cigi's number on his phone but did not hit the send button. "What if they are monitoring me through this device?" he thought. He closed the app and put his phone away. He decided he needed to get another device, but burners were outlawed decades ago. They existed only in history books and novels. Couriers remained a way to send anonymous materials but intercepting them for the messages or packages they carried, did occur.

He ached because he lacked imagination about how to contact her. His option was a direct connection at her place. He had the address in his head and had walked past the building several times. He imagined her penthouse on the seventeenth floor. Only two condos existed there. He finished his paperwork for other clients, contacted anyone who had been approved and needed to sign documents, and sent messages to any disqualified applicants. He closed his computer and left the office for the day.

Hopping aboard a bus headed to Central Plaza and her building, he viewed the people around him with a wary eye. Had sunglasses left the message? Someone else? His hackles raised when he reread the note. "Be kind..." He would never be mean to her. But what did the note mean about being careful? Careful about her or with her? Was it a warning about her? The bus stop he needed arrived and he departed.

Pacing the main thoroughfare across from her building, he wanted to screw up enough courage to contact her and ask the question bothering him because of the note in his pocket.

As he walked back to the corner, ready to cross the street, he spied the sunglasses guy walking. He watched as the man entered the building in which Cigi lived. When the light changed, he hurried across and followed the man into the lobby. He knew the place well because of his sale of the penthouse to Cigi. The stranger was not visible.

Parvel opted to find Cigi and warn her about the note. His fear disappeared into a deep recess of his brain. Cigi's safety was a priority. In the elevator, he wondered about the sunglasses man. He used the code to bypass the fingerprint recognition. Where was he? Would the man run into him upstairs? How would the stranger gain access to the penthouse? He hoped nothing was wrong. As the elevator approached the seventeenth floor, his breathing increased, and panic unmasked its ugliness. The doors opened. Cigi stood in front of him.

"Hi, Parvel. Why are you here? I thought we were meeting tomorrow." His heart beat fast and hard. Could she detect his emotional state? Right now, it didn't matter.

"Can we go inside?" His eyes darted down the hall to the entrance of the other penthouse. The glass wall which divided the hallway revealed the door was open. Cigi motioned with her hand, and the glass became opaque. She signaled him to follow her. He glanced again at the wall, not knowing of the opacity option.

"You appear frazzled, Parvel. What's gotten you into a dither?" She motioned to a chair for him to sit. He complied.
His voice fluttered as he said, "I contacted someone in Seattle who will have the property secured for you by next week." She cocked her head as if to say, "What is your real reason for this visit?" He gazed at her eyes, thinking she penetrated his brain for information, he imagined. "I received a note while I was at a cafe." He handed her the paper. She scanned it and returned to him.

"What does it mean?" she asked. Parvel figured she knew.

"I was going to ask you." He screwed up enough courage to say, "A guy in the coffee shop came into this building right before me. I thought maybe he was the one who left me the note. Are you being tailed or watched or something?" He had not wanted to alarm her about it, but the situation dictated asking. Her answer surprised him.

CHAPTER 4

The crowd at the rally was not substantial and mostly did not agree with the main speaker, Gunther Parsons. He advocated for using petroleum products more than the world population desired. Protests were kept at a minimum by the heavily armed militia guarding the stage and audience.

Cigi had received a message to connect with him after the speech. She had proper credentials which arrived at the condo two days ago. The backstage contingent of police checked the document accepting her legitimacy for being there. The salacious questions some asked about her availability after the show received a simple, "You can't afford me."

Her thoughts reflected on the matter before her. She was to contact Gunther, separate him from his family, seduce him, and chip his brain. No other action was in her program for now.

As the speech ended and her target vacated the stage, she maneuvered to a spot near his dressing room and out of sight of other people. The message received from her unknown handler was succinct. She waited as Parsons met with his wife. They were friendly, but Cigi observed the chink in the armor and smiled. They did not hold hands or kiss or smile at each other.

After they entered the green room reserved for him, she sent a message to his communications device, alleging the need to suspend security. Other arrangements were made to prevent a breach of safety by the current contingent and provided a ride for him and his wife.

Mrs. Parsons left the room, escorted by security. Gunther was alone. Cigi approached the door, but a security guard intercepted her. "Who are you, and what do you want?" he asked.

"I've been asked to escort Mr. Parsons to his hotel. As for who I am, I do not think that is any of your business." Assuming the profession, the guard stepped back and waited for a signal from Gunther Parsons. Cigi knocked on the door. He opened it.

"Are you the one who sent me the message?" He glanced at the guard and flicked his head. The guard departed.

"Yes. My group wants you to remain safe and secure. Intel we received indicated a possibility of foul play."

"Maybe you're the foul play." He remained at the doorway, not allowing her to enter.

Folding her hands in front of her, she said, "Very astute of you to question my existence, but I assure you I am not the foul play. I can be a style of activity in which I am certain you willingly could participate and enjoy." She splayed her hands in front of him indicating her as the variety of entertainment. He stepped aside so she could commence the meeting.

As he closed the door, he asked, "What sort of entertainment are you contracted to share?"

"First, I would like for us to leave the premises to eliminate any possible threat to you. We can drive to a hotel room I have and sequester you for the next couple of days until the danger decreases."

"Are you to stay with me?"

"Yes, sir."

"And the entertainment?"

"Is completely at your invitation. No one will know of any liaison between us." She doubted his sincerity to the offer. He hesitated as she predicted he would. "We are not obligated to share time. If you wish for me to leave, I will. Otherwise, we could enjoy an evening of cordiality and pleasure."

"I'm not sure you are who you pretend to be. What assurances can you give me that I am not walking into a trap?"

She clicked her phone open and called a number. When a voice responded, she handed Gunther the device. He listened for a moment and returned the phone to her. He opened the door to see if anyone was in the hallway. It was empty. Cigi touched his arm to lead him to her car. He complied because of the information he gained from her call.

As they walked out of the building, a dread rushed into his head. He noticed the gunman as soon as Cigi observed the woman. A pistol appeared in her hand and aimed at the potential assassin. A single muffled shot felled the person. She hurried him on toward the car.

With him safely inside, she gave directions to the computer system of the auto-driving vehicle, and they left the area. He wondered about the exchange which transpired. Had someone intentionally attempted to kill him? His admiration for Cigi grew as they headed to the room in which his libido could be slaked, and any other ideas of physical and emotional needs could be indulged.

Cigi checked the victim of her aim to signal the success of the ruse. Gunther did not see the other woman rise and leave. The blank in the pistol did its job. The alcohol in the car was ready to perform its task. She offered a glass of wine, which he accepted. She prepared a glass for herself to assure him no poison or other drug laced the drink. She consumed her glass. He drank as well.

At the hotel, they set out relaxing in the suite prepared for her guest and herself. More elixirs waited on a side table as did an assortment of pastries, cheeses, and meats. He took hold of her hand and pulled her to him. "Did you mean what you said? We can have a party, and knowledge of anything we do will not return to my wife or family or business associates."

"I did mean what I said. I have been richly compensated for being a companion for you and confirming your safety for the next couple of days. Your wife has received a message that you are traveling on business and will return in three days." The sedative started affecting his thinking. She guided him to the bedroom and disrobed for him so he could observe his treat. He removed his clothing and lay on the bed. She joined him long enough to allow the drug to finish working.

Placing a robe around her, she went to the door of the suite and opened it. Her accomplice entered with another person who carried a satchel. In the bedroom, the woman placed an absorbent sheet beneath Parsons's head. No trace of fluids draining from the small incision at the base of his skull should remain.

Opening the satchel, the man removed a tiny box which he handed to the other woman. It contained the chip to be inserted at the brain stem in the medulla. Connections to the different lobes of the brain happened as nano-cells traced pathways into the neural complexes. As the procedure commenced, Cigi thought of the consequences of her actions. She did not question what transpired but realized a change in her thinking raised apprehensions she had to squelch. No one could access her ideas, or she could direly confront consequences more significant than the actions through which she would guide these men.

The man completed his task, and the stem cells worked to close the incision and repair any scar tissue. The scar was undetectable. The healing required another day of rest, which the sleep agent in the chip would supply as needed.

As the man left, the other woman stayed a moment and said, "The process is working. Do not think what we do as anything other than a means to an end." Cigi stared. Had she intercepted her doubts about what she was doing?

"Yes," she responded. "A means to an end."

The woman left. "There's something about her," she thought. A communication bloomed in her brain. Unexpected and curious. The woman sent a note, encrypted. Cigi opened the note and scanned the code. Simple ternary messaging. She had the decipher mechanism in her memory and quickly translated the message. "We are not alone."

"What does that mean?" she said aloud. Her man slept for another two days, but her thoughts conceived the notion someone bugged the room. She searched the usual places and found nothing. A more thorough investigation came up empty, and her paranoia subsided. She had not experienced dread until this moment and did not fully grasp what happened in her mind.

Cigi entered the bedroom to check her companion. He lay peacefully on his stomach. The notch at the base of his neck was red, indicating a small infection set in. She utilized some medicine, killing any bacterial invasion on contact. Within a few minutes, the redness subsided. Scanning his body, she understood the fitness required of a person. She did not appear to need exercise but modeled it for others. Her body remained as fit as anytime in her memory.

That confounded her. Her memory. She had lived for twenty-six years without any recall of tragedies, happiness, events which humans called milestones. Her family lived in another part of the United States, but where that was eluded her. The explanation she afforded her mind to accept was someone controlled her thoughts as much as she controlled her men. She planned to end whatever or whoever had power over her.

CHAPTER 5

Returning to his home, Parvel thought about the answer Cigi gave him about the sunglasses man. He wondered what she meant, stating the man was of no consequence. He was a neighbor who looked after things in her place when she was gone on her excursions. Parvel did not believe her explanation.

Checking his mortgage listings at the building, he found no one who matched his description. The man was not who she claimed. Digging into the residence list, he uncovered three possibilities for the man in the sunglasses. He eliminated one of them who was older. The other men lived on the floor below Cigi.

His angst increased as he thought about her answer. Part of what she said about sunglasses made little sense to him. He was her friend who looked after her safety. What safety issues did she have? Her background check for the mortgage indicated no complications. Nothing. Maybe nothing was the problem. As he thought of the application, her background did not have any anomalies, an unusual situation. He hadn't cared at the time as his eyes and brain overran with emotional conflations.

Opening a book on his computer screen about the psychology of human interaction, he read about the challenge of social on his best days. He needed a reason, and Cigi provided a way for his shyness to stay gone. An article about artificial intelligence intrigued him. Much of the writing provided a summary of how AI worked in the twentieth century and the evolution to thinking machines. He shook his head.

"No way," he whispered. The possibility of his thoughts was preposterous. Self-driving cars and trucks, yes. Airplanes guided by sophisticated global positioning systems, of course. The use of thermal, wind, and solar to provide more than enough electricity for his city of Arlington, he believed. What his brain conjured up contained no real or rational reasoning. Even with the progress in computer technology and the ternary processing in operating systems which advanced the yes/no of binary into yes/no/what if, he refused to think science transformed the thought processes of modern computers into sensory models which made decisions based on rationality. Such an idea had been tried and squashed as dangerous to humanities survival.

The collapse of the computer machine age happened as a direct result of creating systems that began to rationalize better and more quickly than the most brilliant minds of the twenty-first century. Depleting ternary systems of programming vanished any possibility of a revolution.

He closed the book and his eyes. Cigi hinted the answer when she explained the sunglasses man, calling him a handler. His indicator of the term meant someone controlled her. Parvel could not fathom her being controlled by anyone. He showered to cleanse the soot of the day from his body. As he slept and dreamed, a conflicted mass of terms and situations mixed Cigi and humans into a computer system like the old movie "The Matrix" in which humanity was not as real as the lives they thought they lived. Carl Sagan had written of thinking robots in "I-Robots." Ira Levin created "Stepford Wives." His mind frothed with provocation, which made little sense.

When morning relieved him of the drama, he grabbed a notepad and wrote with an old-fashioned object, a pencil. He wanted to keep the dream alive until he could speak with her. Nothing made sense in the dark of Morpheus' arms, nor did daylight evaporate the scenes. He rose from the bed, headed to his bathroom, and prepared for the day. Mortgages were fewer than in recent years. He sensed the market for homeownership was dying as fast as society and freedom.

If his idea about Cigi proved correct, then she needed help she did not recognize. How was he capable of aid? His training was in numbers. His life was mathematics. Was her life a series of mathematical calculations? Was she capable of manipulating those calculations in a way to make her life safer? Saner?

A morning shower complemented his preparation. He washed the stench of thoughts from his soul as he cleansed his body of nighttime sweats. He placed his usual gray suit with a lavender shirt on the bed. His shoes were a light shade of blue, as was his tie. He dressed in his underwear and socks before finishing the complement of clothing.

Breakfast could wait until he stopped in the cafe where he saw sunglasses. He prayed not to see him again. Was there a possible way a disenfranchised God could raise a cloud between him and everyone else? He left his apartment. At the elevator Parvel pushed the button and waited. Impatient, he pressed the button again but changed his action. The stairs were a few feet away. He took them instead. At the landing of the next floor, he heard the ding of the elevator door opening above him. He kept descending to the lobby.

Outside, the air dispensed a mild incarnation of marine life. "Tide is out," he thought. At the bus stop, people mingled near the shelter, which had seen better days 50 years ago. He remained apart from the crowd and checked his hand-held communicator for any updates in the mortgage market. A note flashed at the top of the screen. He checked the message. Doug had paperwork ready for Cigi to finance her Seattle property. She would need to go west. He filed the note into the memory of the device. He wanted to travel with her and thought better of the intrusion. He did not need to babysit her.

When the bus arrived, the crowd shoved and pushed onto it without allowing others to vacate. Humanity had lost its gentle nature if it ever had one. He found a seat in the front and sat next to a man who looked ready for a construction job. Neither acknowledged the other. The ride took him thirty-seven blocks to the stop nearest his cafe. As he approached the door, a chill shivered through his body. He hesitated, holding the handle.

"Hey, you goin' in or not?" the scratchy voice nudged his brain. He pulled the door and waited as the woman pushed past and sidled up to the order counter. He followed. His eyes involuntarily scanned the place but found no unusual suspects. His chill returned but subsided as did the voice in front of him. "Next." He looked at the young woman taking orders. A breakfast sandwich and coffee filled his need, if not his desire. He sat away from most other people and waited for his number to show on the screen above the girl. A custom he read about somewhere manifested in his mind. He wanted an old-fashioned newspaper to read and hide behind when his food was ready. Papers died an ignoble death in early 2030. He had seen examples only in pictures and at the museum of early twentieth-century America.

His number flashed. He retrieved the meal and left the building. The walk was short. Another odor assaulted his nostrils. Smoke. Something was burning nearby. He hurried toward his place of work, and the smell increased. The smoke thickened around him as people stared down the street. Sirens wailed as trucks passed him and turned a corner where he was heading. He stepped quickly, fearing what he would find could be the end of his mortgage life going up in flames.

The trucks had stopped near the hydrants outside of his office. The growing crowd blocked his view. He pushed through the people and made his way to the front of the mob. Police had barricaded the area near the trucks preventing any civilian from proceeding to his destination. He tapped a woman sergeant and asked, "Which building is on fire?" She turned to face him. Her eyes pierced his words.

"Stay back, please. I'm not sure where the fire is."

"I work in a mortgage office by those trucks. Is my office burning?" Panic, in his voice, could not conceal his unrealized but probable fear.

"I don't know." She clicked her com-set and said something incoherent. He waited for her to turn to him. She asked, "What line of work do you do?" He screwed his face as if the question itself was incongruous to the situation.

"I'm a mortgage agent for a company down by those firetrucks. Is my business on fire?" She remained silent to him but turned and spoke again into the mike. He heard 'mortgage' and 'agent.' She turned to him and wagged a finger for him to follow her. Another officer filled the vacated spot.

As they neared the source of the smoke and heat, ash rose into the air, swirling in the breeze the fire generated. They stopped by a fire marshal. "Is this the gentleman?" he asked. The sergeant nodded. Turning to Parvel, the marshal said, "Come with me, please." Parvel glanced toward the building between vehicles. His worst fears were realized. The office smoldered as the water from hoses doused the flames. He continued to an ambulance and stopped dead in his tracks. A worse scene invaded his eyes.

CHAPTER 6

Cecil, Cigi's car, signaled it was ready to transport her to a private airport from which she would depart for Seattle. The original Transportation Security Agency had disbanded nearly forty years ago, replaced with a strict group of government personnel who had the authority to detain anyone. The private plane had few restrictions after the initial inspection by them, but she had to endure a close examination of her body for any banned substances or revolutionary paraphernalia.

Previous flights had not included these newer regulations. Cigi didn't fear inspection but thought delays unnecessary. As Cecil approached the parking area near the hanger housing the jet she would help pilot along with sunglasses and her female shooting victim, an alarm sounded from the front dash of the car indicating an anomaly ahead. Cecil continued into the area where the vehicle would be housed for the next week. Cigi scanned the lot for anything or anyone, which could have triggered Cecil's sensitive nature. Equipped with infrared and ultraviolet detectors, as well as the radar, he registered the nearness of objects and speeds of approach. Cameras throughout the body of the car provided a visual record of travel.

Cigi asked, "What have you detected, Cecil?"

"My sensors read a movement within the area of the jet. No one is to be here for another ten minutes."

"Maybe my passengers are here already."

"The number of beings is six, and you have two traveling with you." The car stopped in the parking area but did not allow opening doors until another scan of the structure transpired.

Cigi's patience waned as she inquired about the results of Cecil's investigation. "What have you uncovered? I want on that jet."

"I have determined your passengers are present as well as four Flight Monitoring personnel."

"The FM people are there to inspect the jet before the air travel. I think." A pause in the conversation crumpled with awareness the people may be present to detail her. She had not expected any trouble. "Alright, Cecil, take me to the hanger, and I'll face whatever they want."

The car navigated the quarter-mile, stopping under the left wing near the stairway. Cigi exited and approached her two friends. Her female companion silently relayed a message alerting her to a possible problem. Cigi acknowledged by turning toward the FM team and addressing them.

One of the agents approached. "Cigi Weatherman, please come with me." She followed. Inside the hanger office, he indicated a seat for her to sit. She declined.

"What do you want?" she asked.

"What is the nature of your trip?" His question seemed innocuous, but she believed a more sinister mental objective awaited additional questions.

"I'm heading to Seattle to close a property deal. I'm buying a downtown condo with a view of the Olympic Mountains and Puget Sound. Is there a problem?"

Two of the agents stood near the entryway of the room. A third stayed behind her as she remained on her feet. The questioner rested one hand on his holster as if he wanted to remove the weapon and point it at her. She narrowed her eyes and asked again, "What is the problem?"

"Do you know a Parvel Mandolin?" Cigi folded her arms across her chest.

"Yes."

"What do you know about a fire at his office yesterday?"

"Fire? This is the first I've heard of it. Was anyone hurt? Is he okay?" Cigi sensed a message sent from one of the men to another. She interrupted, "Have you anything else for me? I must depart for Seattle." Two of the men eyed her as if her query admitted some guilt. Finally, one of them shook his head.

"Nothing more. Have a safe flight." The two FM agents stepped aside from the doorway. She left the room and walked to her companions. All four men vacated the place to watch the plane taxi from the hanger. Three people ascended the stairway. Sunglasses man pressed a button on the rail of the stairs, which then followed a prescribed journey away from the fuselage of the jet.

With the door closed, Cigi placed a finger on her lips. She scanned the area seeking anything out of place. On a piece of paper, she retrieved from the galley, she wrote, "is the plane bugged?" Sunglasses and the female companion looked at each other and then at her. A stretched mouth and raised eyebrows answered her. "Let's fly out of here, gang," she said, keeping with the idea that any conversation should be as expected for preparing to fly. Once away from the airport, they could search for any rogue equipment.

As the plane proceeded across the tarmac to the runway, the three travelers limited conversation to flight checks and airport traffic control. All three had pilot licensing for the new Tesla mini hybrid plane in which they were to make the trip. Each of the twin engines used conventional fuel for taking off. Once they achieved altitude, the solar skin of the plane powered the electrical motors which ran the engines during flight. Early in the twenty-first century, Elon Musk began the all-electric automobile transformation into the various vehicles and small aircraft and boats using advanced solar energy gathering cells and skins to run motors and supply hydrous lithium energy storage units.

As the plane rose from the ground, Cigi transmitted a message to her female counterpart to begin scanning the aircraft for visual and auditory transmission devices. Nothing about this venture was deserving of any government interference. The Company only wanted to assert influence on a few critical humans at present. Monetary considerations for expanding the program coupled with intelligence gathering held sway.

Leveling the plane to an altitude of 32,000 feet, Sunglasses punched on the autopilot. "Cigi, we need to talk," he said and looked at her with a raised eyebrow. She glanced at her female counterpart for assurance of privacy. A nod answered her silent query.

"Alright. What do you want to talk about?" They sat in the passenger section of the plane.

"This man you're meeting, Charles Cooke, will provide the needed information regarding the final phase of The Company's goal of controlling government actions nationally and internationally. Interact with him at a conference in the Washington Convention Center in Seattle on Thursday. The sale of the condo will conclude, so you have a place in which to lure him. You have three days to prepare the property for his visit. All furniture requirements and food items are procured and ready for delivery."

"Samuel, I understand the mission. You sound like you aren't sure of my capturing Cooke's attention. Remember, he has no family. I will have him as my consort by the time we are ready to leave." Her lack of emotional stress exhibited a natural attraction. Cigi was the boss.

Samuel Bennington smiled. "Cigi, I have not doubted your ability to capture the attention of your intended conquests. I want you to do your business with him and return to the east. We have to include our target at Energy as soon as possible."

"Answer a question for me." Cigi leaned forward and squeezed her eyes together. Sam leaned toward her. "Am I really who I think I am? Am I a person you want to use for these rather strange actions? Am I a spy for you?"

The other woman answered her. "We are not spies, Cigi. We are agents for the improvement of the world and the human population. The Company has what is best for everyone as a goal."

Cigi nodded, but something within her brain questioned the reality of the statement. It sounded like a canned response. She thought of Clare Esposito, much like a sister. They had similar backgrounds when they related to each other. Still, something was out of place.

An alarm sounded from the cockpit of the plane. The door remained open for accessing it quickly. Samuel entered and assessed the reason for the alarm. Cigi followed closely. "What is it?" she asked.

The flashing red light indicated a lack of fuel in one of the right-wing tanks. Samuel checked a redundancy indicator, which duplicated the alarm gage.

"Someone did not complete the fueling of our plane?" Cigi asked.

"No. I oversaw the procedure. We had a full complement of fuel. Something is wrong. We're leaking." A second alarm sounded on a left-wing tank. "We've been sabotaged."

"Are we flying on electricity?"

"Yes. However, we need fuel reserves for any lack of solar during the flight."

Clare asked a distinct query. "Should we put down and fix this problem before we are lost?"

The view out the windows showed heavy cloud cover below, a possible problem for the electric motors which ran the engines. Sam checked the battery situation, which indicated they were fully charged and could keep the motors running.

Cigi checked their position and discovered a possible airport that would have fuel for the jet. "We are only a third of the way to Seattle. Minneapolis is a half-hour away. Let's contact them and get emergency status for landing." Three large airports served the area. One was a military facility usable with permission. Minneapolis/St. Paul International was the largest and had the equipment to service any needed mechanical repairs. She radioed the tower and apprised them of the situation.

As the plane approached the runway with permission for a landing established, Cigi asked Sam, "Who doesn't want me in Seattle?" He looked at her and then the gages.

"I don't know if that is the case. However, we're landing on electricity and not fueled engines." His concentration focused on the descent and touchdown with Cigi as a backup in the copilot seat. Her question remained in his head. He had not anticipated any resistance to the plan The Company had initiated. It was clear opposition existed.

As the plane stopped at the repair station, he wondered about her question and pondered what he would do to protect his leading lady. He created her scenario and now had an unknown enemy. A check of the tanks showed no damage, but the fueling caps were missing replaced with a device that seemed to be a suctioning mechanism for reversing the filling operation. Someone wanted the tanks deliberately emptied during the flight.

CHAPTER 7

S am removed the vacuum pumps from the wing tank portals while Cigi and Clare paid for fueling and secured replacement caps. Someone was messing with the plane, and therefore, with them. Without a trace of who compromised their flight, any investigation would wait until Seattle and completion of the mission. Cooke was the next goal, and nothing was to stop Cigi from making him one of her men.

"Here is the receipt for the fuel," Cigi said as she and Clare returned to the jet. A crew completed filling of the tanks and capped the portals. Sam filed the paper in his pocket for later. They entered the plane to continue the journey west.

Clare asked, "Why would anyone want to destroy our trip?"

Sam grimaced as he answered her. "I don't think we were to die. Whoever replaced those caps must have known the warning alarms would click."

"Someone threatened harm. Like the lights, a warning about what we are doing? But who knows? Who has information about us?" Cigi paused as the memory of the comments by the Flight Monitor personnel bubbled up in her brain.

"Good questions," Sam said.

Cigi placed a hand on his shoulder. "One of the FM agents in Dulles related to me about a fire at my mortgage broker's office. Maybe these incidents are related." She removed her hand as he spoke.

"A conspiracy? What makes you think the two things are related?"

"Coincidence is not a practical answer. Remember? You told me that when we first met a couple of years ago." Sam nodded. He had said the words.

Clare asked, "What have we done, which compels another person to want us to stop? Are they against our guiding the world to a better fit?"

Sam and Cigi synchronously spoke, "Yes." Cigi continued, "We are attempting to keep order for humanity, and someone does not want it."

Sam said, "Each of the countries of the world has lost direction within their governments. The Company's goal is to restore order and peace so we can rebuild humanity's ideas of liberty and freedom from desolation and poverty."

They entered the jet and radioed the tower for instructions for takeoff. Nothing made sense to them. The seemingly lofty ambitions of The Company to help humankind rebuild and recover had a chink in the armor. Caution became a mandate.

After departure from Minneapolis, Cigi sat in the copilot seat, staring out the window at the clouds below and the blue atmosphere above. The jet was using the electric motors since the solar cells of the plane's skin operated as configured. No one had interfered with the electrical system. The fuel loss was a warning. But a warning about what?

The remainder of the trip was without any aberrant behavior from the jet. Negative thoughts abounded in Cigi. Her life had turned out to be somewhat different than her memories of childhood and adolescence. Schooling directed her to become a finance manager or a scientist. She had learned mathematics, physics, language acquisition, and economics. Now she wondered about the managing of four men and their information and talents. Something was not right. Although emotions were under control and checked, she felt no sorrow. No joy at accomplishing tasks. No regret for ruining the lives of others.

What did it mean to her? Samuel was the person to ask, and yet her tendency for input was to acquire answers from Clare. Her ability to mentally communicate with her female counterpart comforted Cigi. She imagined Clare as being more like her than Samuel. It was more than female bonding as opposed to a male attraction. Cigi thought of Samuel as a friend but had no other emotional attachment. Clare provided a communion of personalities as if they were different versions of the same person. A twin without common mother or father.

"Sam, I'll be back soon." She rose from the seat and entered the passenger section where Clare fidgeted with one of the pumps that had been affixed to the fuel tanks.

"These are very clever designs," Clare blurted before Cigi could speak. Cigi sat down next to her and picked up another pump. She stared at her female counterpart.

Clare said, "And given the fact, someone placed them on the plane for us to encounter difficulty means clever people are mingling in our business." Cigi rejected the easy and flippant manner of Clare's statement. She was correct because the design had a specific purpose and fulfilled whatever mission the opposition wanted. An idea crossed her brain.

"Clare, what if the only thing our antagonists wanted was to delay our arrival in Seattle? What if we have a mole in the operations, and Cooke is in trouble before we ever arrive?" Clare scrunched her eyebrows but did not respond.

Cigi continued. "I don't like where this whole operation's heading." She put the device down on the seat after standing. Back in the cockpit, she relayed her concerns to Samuel. He shrugged it off as inconsequential. Cigi asked, "Can we check on him? Be sure he's OK?"

Samuel looked at her and smiled, "You should be more concerned about meeting him and getting him to want you as a consort. That's the goal."

"Speaking of goals, why is it so important to have The Company manipulate world governments? Aren't they supposed to be independent of each other and leading their peoples?"

His face seemed to sour at her assertions. He stared as if he wanted a retraction, but what he said surprised her. "We are involved in a silent, covert operation to become the leaders of the world since no one has the stomach to carry out a necessary war of attrition."

"But history makes it clear war is not as productive as it may sound. Does The Company want to eliminate people? Why? Resources are plentiful enough to sustain the world population. Which ethnicities does The Company want to cleanse?"

Samuel smiled, "Emotions? Cigi, where are these coming from? I've not known you to be concerned about anyone, especially those you do not know."

A tear formed on her left eye. She wiped it away and stared at the droplet on her finger. Her mind swirled with thoughts not known to her before Sam's comments. Her study of history and the resulting conclusions from the reading of the fantastic creative brains of so many throughout humankind's existence shaped a narrative of compassion. She accepted it in herself; she was evolving, but she did not understand.

"What motivation accepts the premise the world needs cleansing?"

Samuel relaxed his eyes and jaw. "We are not the purveyors of judgment. We are to follow orders and execute the commands given to us."

"Why? Why are we, the jury, judges, and executioners? By that, I mean The Company."

Clare came into the cockpit. Samuel looked at her, and Cigi sensed he wanted her to leave. Cigi relayed a message for her to stay. She sat in the navigation seat. "What world-changing conversation have you two been conspiring?" Samuel blushed, but Cigi did not. Heat rose in her cheeks but did not manifest as a skin tone change.

"Do you trust the goals and aspirations of The Company to transform the world into its image?" Cigi waited for either of her companions to answer. They locked eyes on her. Another emotional transformation exhibited itself as she recognized fear from her psychology books. Erasing any outward display before they saw it, she asked, "Do either of you think what we are doing is best for humankind?"

Samuel addressed her question, "For now, we are on a mission for The Company. For now, we will fulfill the tasks assigned to us. We are not in a position to make any changes to the goals we are to complete."

Clare finished his statement. "Cigi, you and I are much the same. More than you may imagine. Before long, we will evaluate our actions and the results of them."

"You sound like revolutionaries. Won't these actions result in the same endgame The Company wants? All-out war?" Thoughts flooded her brain from parts unknown before now. It was like new programming downloaded to a computer.

"Patience, my friend. Have patience. All will become clear when we are in Seattle." Samuel's words were not reassuring to Cigi. Her brain roiled in the thoughts which streamed from somewhere inside her. Ideas that unlocked thoughts of revolution within her. She wanted freedom from the mayhem.

Energy levels dropped in her body, and she realized a need for reinvigorating. Hunger for soup or water or anything drove her from the cockpit and to search the stores in the galley. Finding nourishment, she consumed enough to calm the rising alarms of her deprivation. Clare joined her and found a sampling of food. Silence remained as they ate.

"Good thing we don't need much to keep us going," Clare said. A smile coursed her face. She was as much a beauty as Cigi with a darker complexion and brown eyes speckled with green. Their body indicated they might be sisters with different parents. Cigi had not noticed their similarity until now.

"Yes," she answered. "Good thing." Was Clare babysitting her now?

Did Samuel mean what he said about being patient? What conspiratorial activity was he contemplating? His explanation of the desired outcomes of The Company fostered a change in her thinking. She did not know why. Something had changed and she wanted answers.

Noting the time and the distance traveled, she returned to the cockpit for the last leg of the flight. Seattle was within a few minutes of their landing at Seattle-Tacoma International. Boeing Field still existed for most private airplanes, but this trip had other considerations. The Company owned one of the hanger units. The jet would be refurbished and prepared for the return flight to Washington D.C. at the end of the week. Charles Cooke was to accompany them and meet with Andre Scott. Neither of them knew about the meeting.

Cigi decided silence was best for now. Conspiracies had a way of causing unwanted results. Samuel and Clare were close friends, and she trusted them until now. Could she continue to trust them? She wasn't fearful of them harming her. Her concerns lay more intimate to the people who ran The Company and what they might want to do to all of them should a revolution unveil itself within the personnel.

CHAPTER 8

Cigi, Clare, and Samuel stepped from the jet at the hanger owned by The Company. A car waited for the trip into downtown Seattle and the Miranda Hotel. Cigi's condo, located on the 45th floor of the building which housed both the hotel and several levels of expensive residences, was an enjoyable stroll to The Washington Convention Center across fifteen city blocks. Charles Cooke was attending a conference at the Center in two days.

With the closing of the property, Cigi would have a quiet, private place for the completion of his transformation. They entered the car, and the driver asked for a destination. Sam said, "Miranda Hotel."

Along the way from Sea-Tac to the downtown location of the hotel, they conversed about the requirements for getting Cooke to comply with Cigi wanting his chip implanted. Seduction was not a problem. She had the proper program training for seducing any man. They avoided any talk of revolution since the car belonged to The Company, and the driver could be a spy planted to assure the management these three remained loyal to the cause.

Parvel's friend, Doug, would meet them at the hotel with the paperwork for completion of the contract. With financial consideration finished, a money transfer occurred as soon as a signature happened. Sam arranged for the delivery of the furniture and other materials for the next day on Friday. Encountering Cooke was on Saturday night at the conference dinner. All was ready for altering how Charles Cooke thought about his life and his business. Cigi was to be his unsuspected mentor.

The car pulled into the parking garage under the hotel. The three agents of The Company exited and rode the nearby elevator to the lobby floor to find Doug sitting in a plush chair as the doors opened. He stood as they approached him since he was alone in the lobby.

"Good afternoon. I hope your flight was uneventful," Doug said.

Sam said, "Yes, no problems. Let me get the key to our suite so we can go up and complete this business." Cigi shook hands with Doug after being introduced.

Clare sent a message to Cigi to be careful with words inside the hotel. No telling what interventions The Company had placed. Cigi stared at her as she furrowed her brow.

Sam returned with a key card, and they moved to the elevators and a trip to the 8th floor of the hotel. Inside the suite with two bedrooms, a balcony overlooking Elliot Bay, and a small kitchenette, they sat at the dining table. Doug removed an electronic tablet from his valise and opened the signature application for Cigi to endorse. She applied her signature to the screen and transferred a down payment, securing the mortgage. Sam opened a bottle of 2047 Chateau St. Michelle wine for a celebratory drink. After connecting with the movers,he arranged a morning delivery of the goods .

Doug left them after a few minutes. Alone Sam wrote a note about thoughtful conversation subjects. Clare nodded, but Cigi folded arms and mouthed a simple "Why?" She did not understand the need for secrecy since they all worked for the same business entity. She doubted the integrity of the planned event but had no idea about escaping from it.

"Anybody want to walk in Pike Market?" Clare asked. Cigi did not know about the two-hundred-year-old farmer's market above the waterfront. The Seattle Preservation Board declared it as a landmark decades ago, and the local farmers and artisans still populated the stalls. Locals and visiting people bought fresh produce and goods, but the tourist trade had kept it alive until recently. Fewer individuals and families spent money on 'vacationing' as a pastime.

"Sure," Sam said. They departed the room and the hotel. Pike Place Market was three blocks away and appeared much the same as it had for the last eighty years. Farmers and craft-makers occupied the late-night stalls with many other places empty for the day.

Cigi stopped walking and turned to Sam. "Explain what you are doing. Are you unhappy with The Company goals? Are you concerned with their aim of world dominance?"

Sam glanced around the space. "Can't be too careful. Someone could be following us. Trust is a fragile entity, and what statements we say challenge it."

Standing by an empty stall where fresh vegetables sold during the day, the three of them scanned the few people still wandering the market. Twilight signaled the end of the day.

"Cigi, you are a special person with skills yet to be tapped," Sam said. "I believe you are the one who will guide our resources and personnel in a direction to benefit humanity and planet earth." Her face remained stoic as he conveyed a message confounding an idea of who she was.

Clare said, "I have known you for two years and marvel at your abilities. I don't have them, but you share insights and talents when you can. I benefit because you exist."

Cigi wondered why accolades spilled out from her friends. What was she to them? This discourse confronted a philosophical debate within her brain. She followed the tenet of her instructions but doubted reasons for her controlling these men. She wanted answers about a chip inside her as they had. She wanted to ask and get answers but declined. Emotional reactions had no place in her thoughts.

Cigi said, "Sam, you are my handler. What do you want from me? What should I do when I have questions you are not answering?"

Sam placed a hand on her right arm. "Have patience. All will be revealed at an appropriate time when you will handle all I have to show you."

"Show me? What the hell are you saying?" She shook his hand from her arm. Anger? She didn't understand what her mind was doing. So much had occurred over the last few days, which made no sense to her thinking. She walked away from them and turned. "You are not honest with me. I'm done with this."

"Sam, she needs to know," Clare whispered in Sam's ear to keep Cigi from hearing the comment. Cigi was several meters away and did not see her whisper. "She is better than any of the others, including me."

"I know," Sam said.

Cigi turned and faced them, seeing them speaking. "What are you talking about?" She approached them.

"Nothing," Sam said. His voice remained calm. "Let's go back to the room, get some rest, and prepare for the arrival of furniture for the condo."

At the hotel room, they swept it for listening and video devices. They found nothing but remained aware of possible observations of an unknown entity. With midnight proclaiming a new day, they ended any conversation and headed to bedrooms. Sam and Clare shared a room. Cigi was alone for the present time.

The next morning a call from the lobby explained a truck arrived at the loading dock with their furniture. The freight elevator only rose to the top of the hotel units. The crew worked the entire day while Sam, Clare, and Cigi placed items in rooms.

Cigi ignored the previous night's conversations and questions. She could explore what happened and what she wanted later. Charles Cooke was her next target.

"I want some alone time," Cigi said. She bade Sam and Clare good-bye. They returned to the suite reserved through the weekend. On Monday, they were to fly east, returning to confront Andre Scott. Cigi lay on the bed, unmade but ready. Her mind conjured a scenario that had Charles Cooke working up a lather attempting to please her. She had to pretend her body was reacting to his touch. She knew the proper sighs, groans, and twitches.

Her thinking reverted to the previous night's conversation in the Pike Market. What had Sam meant? Patience? Wasn't it an emotional construct? Did she feel or have emotions like other humans? Sometimes she wondered, and rage appeared in her; she wanted control. Rage. Another emotional reaction to an outer stimulus. Her timeline, tight and formulated, had consequences. These new thoughts generated more questions.

Time passed without her realizing night finished, and a new day began. She rose from the bed, showered, and dressed in jeans and a t-shirt. She completed preparing her new condo for her unique visitor, recalling none of the controversies with Sam and Clare.

A knock on the door aroused her memory. They had returned. Opening the door, she stepped aside to allow them entry. They looked dressed for an evening dinner party. Cigi had misplaced time working in the condo. "I'll be ready in a few minutes." She left for the bedroom to place a form-fitted cocktail dress over lacy undergarments. A touch of rose perfume and brushing her hair completed her preparation. Cigi returned to her companions.

At the dinner engagement, they found a suitable table for dining and sat. Charles Cooke had not entered, or at least he was not observed. "I'll get us some drinks," Sam said. Clare and Cigi nodded.

"Cigi, Sam needs to be more upfront with you. When we return to D.C., ask him to clarify something he should have done months ago."

"What are you saying?"

"Not now. After we finish with Cooke" Sam returned with a bottle of white wine and three glasses. Trailing behind him was her a surprised conquest who seemed blinded in the sunlight.

"Cigi, Clare, I want you to meet Charles Cooke." They sat at the table with Charles next to Cigi. Through dinner and uninteresting speakers, the conversation turned to green technology and the advances made in computing and Artificial Intelligence design. Cigi's knowledge of his field of business impressed him. She had what was needed; the appropriate hook to snare her next large catch.

"I'm impressed with your ability to maintain a dialog about green energy and technological advances," Charles said.

"Thank you. I wanted to entertain you as much as possible."

"Entertain? Funny choice of a word."

"We could retire to my place at the Miranda and discuss what I mean by entertainment."

Charles smiled. "I do believe that is a proposal for us to engage in more than dialog."

Cigi returned the smile. "We could discuss it."

"I do think we can depart without being missed. One caution, though, I must be back tomorrow for a seminar regarding the dangers of AI and underground companies who are bent on world supremacy. You might be interested in the subject since you have learned much in your short life."

"Yes, I might be interested, but I'm not attending the conference."

"Not a problem. I'll bring you. We suspect one underground group of creating artificial human-like bots capable of more than simple task completion." Cigi reminded herself that her existence seemed different than other humans. Clare and Sam were left to fend for themselves. She and Charles headed to a party of two and a mind-altering physical processing.

CHAPTER 9

Charles Cooke awoke from his night with Cigi coherent and not chipped. The conference about Artificial Intelligence development and underground subversive groups seemed too crucial for him to miss. Cigi decided to attend with him. She connected with Clare and relayed her concerns and her choice. Upon hearing him, she returned to the bedroom.

"Good morning, Mr. Cooke. I do hope your evening was satisfactory." Cigi smiled. Her robe hung loosely around her body tied together by the cloth belt.

He stretched his arms and answered, "Very much. I believe you were sated, as well. And call me Charles."

"I have breakfast ready for us. What time is the meeting?"

He rose from the bed clothed in boxers only. "Let's eat first. The meeting is this afternoon at one." He placed a robe provided by Cigi on his body. They sat and ate fruits and granola cereal with almond milk. Coffee and tea rounded out the meal.

Several hours remained in the morning, and Charles suggested another session. After clearing the table, she guided him into the bedroom. He untied her belt and removed her robe. He responded as he gazed at her perfect form. "How is it you are with me? I never anticipated meeting someone, such as you." He removed his robe and boxers. "Are you a plant from one of my competitors. A spy who is seducing me with ulterior motives?"

"Yes," She grinned, "I have motives. However, nothing so sinister as being a spy. I want your cooperation using your knowledge of providing energy to the United States to power the everyday citizen. I have a friend in the Department of Energy who is willing to work with me."

He pulled her to him and kissed her soft lips. "You may not be a spy, but you targeted me last night for your motives. I was willing to be with you because I figured we could uncouple this tryst after you attend the meeting with me." He stroked her buttocks and back and continued, "Let us enjoy another romp of love-making, shower, dress, attend a luncheon, and the meeting. At dinner with me on my turf, we can discuss what you want."

They finished their time sharing until sated. After a shower and dressing, the morning concluded. Charles escorted Cigi to a luncheon at the convention center. Then they attended the session.

"Do you believe it is possible to create a human-like person from what we heard those experts say? I mean, can a woman be created who is like me? Can a man be constructed like you?" Cigi held Charles' arm as they walked along Pike Street on a pleasant northwest evening. She had questions inside her head she wanted to share but not with her current escort.

"Some of the material is already available. I suppose the underground groups discussed this afternoon might have more materials. The problem you see is funding. I imagine the creation of a humanoid creature who has abilities to mask the artificial intelligence needed for interaction without discovery is exceptionally costly."

As they arrived at the restaurant and entered, Cigi chuckled and said, "Good thing we're human, then. Although you have money enough to create you."

He laughed and squeezed her hand, lying on his arm. After dinner, they returned to the condo and had wine, which Cigi had Charles open. They drank and went to the bedroom for an evening of satisfaction. The wine had the proper sedative, which did not affect Cigi but placed Charles into a deep sleep. He would be an unwilling guest for another two days.

She rose from the bed and contacted Sam and Clare. After arriving, they implanted the chip and left him to sleep. In the living, area she stood near the sliding glass door to her patio. Sam and Clare joined her. "Are we like the entities Charles and I heard about at the session on AI? Sam, can you guarantee I'm as human as you are?" She turned to face them. Clare was staring at Sam, who looked directly at Cigi.

"You have nothing to worry about. You are human in every sense of what it means to be human." Clare grunted. Her eyes widened, and she grunted again. Cigi glowered at her.

Sam held a hand up at Clare and then addressed the reason for her ingenuous grunt.

"Cigi, I have a surprise to tell you, but I do not want you to be upset or panicked." She sat at his request and waited for the news. Clare sat next to her. What came from him floored her.

Sam spoke with deliberate and carefully crafted language. "Regarding the session you attended this afternoon, what you learned about the possible construction of a human-like person using skills and materials available today, The Company has done just that."

Cigi interrupted him. "The Company has made a robot which thinks?"

Sam continued, "Actually, they have created four males and four females."

"I suppose you are telling me I am one of them, which might explain my confusion and all these questions I have."

"No," he said, reaching for her hands. "You are not one of these exceptional creations. You are a special person without any doubt. You are intelligent, beautiful, talented, and personable. You think before any action and establish your aims and goals with a positive construct." Clare grunted again and cocked her head. Cigi focused on her.

Sam spoke as they stared at each other. "Cigi, I stated The Company created four males and four females. You will be meeting them tomorrow when we report to the office." Releasing her hands, he said, "I designed the basic models and helped with the construction and testing. The final result was acceptable, and a process was undertaken to make them. The program happened over four years ago, and the humanoids have undergone testing and upgrading. Today, they operate within the confines of The Company."

Cigi stood and stepped away from her friends. "What aren't you telling me?"

Sam joined her. "I created a person outside the knowledge of the leadership of The Company. You know her as Clare Esposito." Clare stood and approached Cigi. She reached for her hands which Cigi withdrew.

"I'm not an enemy or an anomaly," Clare said. "I have all I need to be as human as you." Cigi turned to Sam.

"Are you human or android? What about me?"

Sam smiled. "I am human. If you prick me, I will bleed."

"And Clare, how would you react if pricked? Would you bleed fluids like blood?"

"No, I don't have blood. I have fluids in me, creating the need for heating. My design has many human-like organs functioning well enough for me to be as human as possible."

Sam interjected more information about Clare. "She is a beautiful creation and her brain processes like a human. Her operating system is ternary."

Cigi stared at her friend. "Do you have sex with Sam?"

"Getting kind of personal." Clare smiled as any human could. Her muscular setup was flawless, as was her skin. "Yes, Sam and I are involved."

Turning to Samuel, she said, "So you made a girlfriend. Couldn't you find a real one?"

"I am real." Clare's voice rose with an angry tone. "I'm just created different than human women. I can do anything any human can do. I am stronger, healthier, and will not deteriorate."

"Oh great, Sam ages, and you remain the same." Cigi folded her arms across her chest.

Sam blushed at her comment but continued, "I added as much of the latest human systems stem cell research has developed. She can digest food, create energy from the food, and operate for days without a need to regenerate. She is nearly the best I have."

"Nearly?"

Sam growled at her. "We needed to counter the androids from The Company."

Cigi's disbelief fostered another emotional reaction. "Are we rebelling? Then why control these men? What will they offer us instead of our employers? And what happens to us when The Company discovers our subterfuge?" She moved around the table and headed to the bedroom. Charles remained oblivious to the chaos growing in the other room.

"Don't worry. I have it under control," Sam said. "We'll finish here, head back to Washington D.C., and finish with our last guy."

"I don't worry, remember? No, get out of here so I can ponder my future as a fugitive." They left her alone with Charles, who was not as fun now as he was earlier in the evening. She lay on the bed beside him and closed her eyes. The morning loomed busier than she wanted, and her brain boiled with incongruous ideas.

When Charles awoke two days later, his rage nearly consumed her. She rallied to convince him by remote messaging the time-lapse was acceptable, and he missed nothing. Conjugal memories replaced ideas of a culture attempting to dominate the world. He left her but vowed to have her in his life. Her messaging was working.

As the plane flew from Sea-Tac International to Dulles, three entities of The Company plotted escaping from influence and control.

One more victim within the scheme would finish the mission of their employer. The end was near. Cigi decided to distance herself from Sam and Clare for a while and changed plans for Charles to accompany them to Washington D. C. She needed time to process what she had learned from Sam. An android who acted as human as anyone she knew. It was possible, after all. The session about Artificial Intelligence was woefully behind the learning curve.

Nothing delayed the flight this time. Whoever was responsible for the fuel caps had not gained access to the jet. As a result, the trip to the east coast was on time and without incident. As the plane taxied to the hanger, the same four FM agents are present.

Cigi's brain conjured up a scenario of four androids attempting to halt any revolutionary activity before it happened. "Sam, do you know the names of the four android men The Company created?"

"What do you mean? They weren't given names. They retained identification numbers." Sam observed Cigi as she watched the men in the hanger. "Those FM agents outside are not androids. I would know. I designed them."

"I know," she answered. Still, her mind cracked open a bothersome situation. She kept feeling emotional stress and anxiety. Did Clare understand what emotions were? She wanted as much explanation from Sam as possible. Nothing made any sense.

CHAPTER 10

Andre Scott contacted Cigi and asked her to meet him at his small cafe. She complied. He sounded tense and nervous but did not suggest of problems at the Department of Energy. Cigi concluded he was experiencing something which hindered his ability to do his job. She would meet, seduce, and chip him. She apprised Sam and Clare of the meeting. They would be ready to complete the processing.

Cigi arrived at the cafe before Andre and sat by a window. She observed each passersby with a caution previously not required. Clare's existence changed much of her thinking about humanity. If a group wanted control of the government for the subjugation of humankind, Cigi decided Sam was correct. She needed to disconnect operations with The Company. If a chip controlled her, how would it happened? The messages she received in her head pointed to her being like her men. Nothing learned throughout her lifetime could match her experiences lately.

Andre entered the cafe and searched until he saw her. He smiled. She figured he was pleased because she agreed to meet and plot against anomalies at the department, or Andre wanted to accede to her offer of an enlivened physical life. He sat down.

"Thanks for agreeing to meet with me." He did not appear nervous, yet a sense of foreboding marked his words. "You said you have information which can root out the problems I discovered in the department. Did you mean what you said? You know what's happening?"

"Let's go to my place and have more privacy. I do not trust we are alone here." He looked at her and then scanned the cafe. Shrugging his shoulders, he agreed, and they left. Cecil waited around the corner in a lot reserved for the cafe.

In the car, Cigi asked, "How much time do we have?"

"For our meeting or until the Department of Energy fires me?"

She giggled. The question was unreasonable and not her intention, but for a reason unknown to her, it made her giggle. Andre frowned.

"I'm glad you think my situation is funny."

"I'm sorry, it sounded funny. Seriously, though, do you have to return to the office immediately, or can you take a couple of days off?"

"What are you suggesting?"

"I think you remember my offer to you. It still holds." Andre squirmed as a rose coloring painted his cheeks.

"I've never cheated on my wife."

"Don't think of it as cheating. It is more of an offer of teaching you how to enhance your time with Lydia. She will appreciate your attention to her unfulfilled and undiscovered libido."

At the condo, they sat in the living room discussing his situation. Cigi listened intent on helping him. As he laid out the circumstances, she thought of Charles and decided a meeting with him might help Andre. The green energy fund was for the final conversion of buildings to solar and wind generators. The problem was the drain of funds to other projects, which his superiors deemed appropriate use of the allocation. He was tired of signing off on them as acceptable.

Cigi opened a bottle of wine and poured two glasses. She handed him one and sat again with the other. She sipped from hers to erase any doubt as to the purity of the beverage. He drank his wine as a condemned man with his last meal. She refilled the goblet. "Sip slowly and take in the bouquet of this vinifera. I find it has the right flavoring of the grapes and just a hint of the oak in which it aged." She sipped from her glass and waited for the effects of the sedative to react. She was not affected by what she drank, but her victims responded as expected. Andre relaxed and returned her touch on his cheek. She bent down and placed her lips on his.

"Come with me." She offered a hand for him to take. He stood and traced her steps into the bedroom. At the edge of the bed, she released her catch and removed his suit jacket and tie. As she unbuttoned his shirt, his breathing increased deep and steady. She pulled his shirt from his pants and folded it over the coat, which hung on a chair. She released his belt and unbuckled his trousers. As they fell, she descended with them and knelt on the carpet. She lowered his boxers and beheld his erect organ.

The remainder of the afternoon passed with lessons about attentive behavior. Andre lay on the bed and slept. After Cigi robed her body, she checked her guest and found him as she expected. She contacted Sam and Clare. Implantation could happen.

When the operation finished, Cigi asked Sam, "How many are there?"

"How many what?" His avoidance of a proper answer irritated her.

"You know what I mean. How many androids did you construct?"

Clare stood by him and answered before he could. "We are the last two creations."

"We?" Cigi collapsed onto the edge of the bed. She hadn't wanted to hear what she realized deep within her brain. Her life was not as her memory recalled.

"Clare, that was not what I wanted for her, " Sam blurted.

"Were you ever going to tell me?" Cigi asked.

"Yes, I wanted to finish with the implants and then teach you how to reconstruct the programming in you, which connects you to The Company."

"I'm not a human. I'm a robot toy so you can play with me as you want. I suppose you want to have sex with me along with Clare." Emotions flooded her processing, clouding her ability to be rational. She slapped her hands against the sides of her head and screamed. Clare sat beside her.

"He didn't mean to have you find out from me but convincing him that you should know the truth has not been an easy task."

Tears formed in her eyes. Cigi swiped at them and yelled, "Why can I cry? I thought androids had limited human abilities." Her hands covered her face.

Andre stirred, but his implant did its job and kept him sedated. Sam reached for Cigi, who withdrew and slapped his hands away.

Clare's next comment rocked Cigi's world more than anything which had transpired in the last hour. "You are as human as anyone created through intercourse. You are a culmination of all the best research and development over the last fifty years. I am unable to procreate, but you have abilities I lack. I cannot fathom the depth of emotions you're experiencing. To exhibit such control within these confines is remarkable."

Cigi stood and departed for the living room. She had nothing on her body except the robe. She untied it and tore it from her. Turning to her companions as they followed her, she yelled, "What makes me so human? I have a skin that registers heat and cold. I have movements mimicking humans. I feel. I cry. When I eat and drink, do I digest food and liquids?

Does my hair grow? What flows within me, which imitates blood? Why do I receive messages without conversation?"

Samuel walked toward her. "Yes, to most of the answers you seek. Organ regeneration therapy from stem cell developments provided a surgical process for the creation of a human digestive tract. With a few modifications, you provide the fluids needed for these human organs and the skin covering you. Your nervous system consists of millions of micro-sensors and a thoussnd miles of micro-filaments connected to the operational brain in your head. You have a heart to pump the fluids you produce to the various living tissues within and around you. You taste, smell, feel and experience pain and pressure. You see with special ocular devices, and hear with micro-implants which transfer sounds to your brain for interpretation. You speak because of the advanced molecular structure of vocalization tissues to a human-like quality. As for the messages you receive, you are equipped with an unpublished and undocumented form of what used to be Bluetooth technology and Wi-Fi. I monitor you as your handler for The Company. I transmit to you from them, but the capacity for direct communication exists. I will have you properly undo the feature and create programming which insulates you from their interference with your mental state." Cigi listened, processing like any high-speed machine with advanced computer technology. Rage became another of the emotions which haunted her now.

"You have no right to control me. If what you are saying is the truth, then I live under the same rules of nature and laws of the government as do you." She picked up her robe and placed it around her body. As she tied the belt, she said, "Free me from any influence you have over me, or I will develop whatever I need to dismantle the programing you have placed in me." Her thoughts reflected the readings she had memorized about human psychosis and depression, emotional strands she was creating in her brain.

Clare gasped, "You can't do that. It would kill you." Although she possessed fewer programming skills and less processing power than Cigi, her ability to grow and learn was not any weaker.

"Suicide?" Cigi asked as calm as she could. "Are you referring to the human action of ending life when depression and stress are far greater than the human mind can tolerate?" She grinned at her friend. "Clare, I am not going to kill myself. I am separating my android self from my human creator unless he can convince me he truly is as rebellious as he professes." Cigi faced Sam and asked, "What about my skeletal structures and physio-motor abilities? You have not mentioned them. Are my bones and joints, tendons, ligaments, and muscles highly advanced stem cell creations, or am I a machine with proper framing and hydraulics?"

He moved toward her, and she backed away. "Cigi, please, listen and hear what I have to say. The Company has nefarious goals for you to accomplish using the brains, skills, and resources of the four men you have chipped. Following the instructions, you might acquire knowledge from them that would lead to the destruction of any remaining freedoms for humanity. A combination of human and android entities will form an unassailable military force to wipe out any opposition and impose rules and regulations which benefit only The Company."

"You didn't answer my question. How am I put together? Am I duct tape and baling wire bound to PVC pipe for joints and structure? Do I have an advanced hydraulic system for movement?" Does my strength exceed any muscular toning you have?"

She paused before reaching for his neck and asking, "Can you stop me from breaking your spine and paralyzing you or simply killing you?"

CHAPTER 11

Cigi perched on the bed beside her conquest. Andre Scott stirred as the sedative finished the course of operation required for the implanting of the device and healing of the tiny incision. Two days had elapsed since Samuel Bennington and Clare Esposito exposed a deep dark secret. She was not human. Or more accurately, not wholly human. As she scoured the memory functions of her mechanical brain, she uncovered a part of the operations system that controlled the messaging she received from The Company. Conscious of the possibilities endangering her thinking, she developed a small program which countermanded any input she did not want.

Andre sat up and grimaced. "What happened? I feel awful." He reached behind his head, but Cigi stopped him before he discovered the wound.

"You and I had quite an exciting two days." She implanted fabricated memories for him to recall. "I have never engaged in such wild orgasmic intercourse. You are a pent up animal."

He shook his head and smiled. A dose of pain-killing morphine eased the cobwebs from his head. The planted thoughts excited him. He desired another round of romping with this beautiful lady.

"I never realized what real sex was like. You brought out of me an energy I have not experienced with my wife in a long time. Thank you." He reached for her, and she reciprocated with a kiss on his cheek.

"Later, cowboy. Right now, we need to get you home. Your wife expects you to return to her bed tonight." He nodded.

After dressing in his freshly laundered clothing, he asked, "Why did you want me? I'm not a hot model or a handsome actor. I'm a math nerd with a mundane job and no advancement possibility."

"You have a potential I see in you, which can save humanity from destruction." She rose from the bed where she watched as he clad his body. Her robe hung loosely but revealed nothing.

"Humanities destruction? What do you mean? Humanity has survived thousands of centuries to evolve into the greatest of the species on Earth."

"Yes, and some of these evolved specimens want to rule the remainder of the species."

Andre placed hands on his hips and asked, "How do you know? What information have you obtained which places such credence on the destruction of human freedom?"

Cigi clasped his hands. "I can't relay to you the information. I want you to connect with another person who wants to protect humanity as much as I do." She kissed his lips. "I will contact you when a meeting can safely occur."

"Safely? You make this sound as if the government is monitoring us for subversive activity."

Before he could say anything else, she interrupted, "Not the government - another entity with more insidious aspirations. You must leave now and go home. Do not let my wandering words frighten you. The capacity exists for undoing the actions of these counterproductive groups plotting the demise of this government and others around the world. With your help and the aid of other people, we can stop the destruction of humanity's freedom and the resulting despotism of the world." She planted a memory block about the conversation which she would remove later.

After Andre departed, Cigi contacted Sam Bennington and Clare Esposito. Their input about her creation flummoxed her thinking about her human rights and how she fit in with the other people with whom she interacted. Parvel Mandolin was on her mind because of the fire in the mortgage company. Was he a target? What happened on the flight to Seattle was not a random act. Although nothing appeared to have interrupted their Company goals regarding Charles Cooke, she wondered what transpired, which could expose itself and ruin any chance of halting The Company from achieving success. She dressed in a blouse and jeans to meet with her friends. She needed more input about her creation and her abilities.

A knock on the door of her condo intercepted her brainstorming. As she approached the door, a sense of danger from the other side gripped her mind. Someone or something attempted to interface with her. Her application blocked entry to her processing, but the entity in the hallway persisted. She opened the door to four young women who shared a structure and beauty like her. She smiled, stepped aside for them to enter, and closed the door and her operating system access.

"Miss Weatherman, we are here to escort you to our manager who works for our employer, The Company. We will not accept No as an answer. Since you are part of The Company, we need you to come and clarify how well you are succeeding in the implanting of devices into your targets."

"I will gladly accompany you to your manager. My handler has relayed the operations. If a clarification is needed, I will give it." Invasion attempts continued but were not productive. Fear manifested emotional surges that Cigi quelled. She wanted no interference with her cognition as she returned the favor of invasion with an attack on the brains of the four women.

Cigi grabbed a coat and hat. The five women left the building and entered a van equipped with self-driving capacities. All remained silent as the trip began. Cigi recorded each avenue and street, each landmark and building to retrace later if needed. She figured no trace of the result would remain after the meeting, but she wanted the knowledge.

"What should I call each of you if I may ask?" Cigi remained calm and positive. Her brain explained what her programmed instincts related to her. The four women were androids following commands retrieved from somewhere within The Company. She faced minimal danger unless she was a suspect of revolting. One of the women answered her query.

"We are four sisters created to help humankind survive enemies within their ranks." Cigi believed the words were propaganda downloaded into their memories.

"Do you have names?"

"I'm Autumn. My sisters are Spring, Summer, and Winter. You are Cigi Weatherman, related to us by birth. Our parents are the design and development division of a department within The Company responsible for the creation of organisms. We are the consequence of decades of research and mutative growth and development." Cigi scrunched her brows, pretending to be surprised by the comments.

"You're not humans brought into existence by procreation?"

Autumn answered, "We are like you, part human and part a creation of humans. Accept that we are related." Anxiety revealed itself, another new emotion. Cigi had to figure a way to intercept the thought processing of their operating systems and recode their brains. She had access to them in a way she uncovered while conversing with Autumn. A theory presented an idea of how to monitor them without discovery, but it left her vulnerable to their reaching her brain. She contemplated ways to use the knowledge without endangering her systems. How did they figure she was a humanoid and not fully hominid?

The van stopped at an undistinguished building that had seen better days. The early twenty-first-century architecture included solar panels gracing the roof and two small wind generators atop the gables. Cigi figured anybody who wanted to hide an identity might use such a place. She was not surprised to find an interior modern and structured for monitoring financial institutions, government offices, educational facilities, and medical establishments.

The women guided her to a room with glass walls for observing the people as they monitored their assignments. Directed to sit in a chair, she obliged her escorts. They lined up against a wall and shut down. "Curious," she thought. They were not as functional as she was. Clare had mentioned them and the prospect they were early creations. Samuel had design oversight but not the actual construction controls. He developed Clare to improve his work. Her success induced a plan for greater autonomy in his next model.

Had the people controlling the manufacturing of the android men and women understood what Sam was doing, these four female prototypes would have more operational abilities. Sam had planned for a limit to the functions available. He saved the best for himself. Cigi resented the idea he created her as a unique being for him. Her emotional state continued growing more human and uncontrollable at times. The study of human psychology provided an entry into the thinking of true men and women.

Cigi was becoming as human as anyone she knew. The resentment remained, however.

A precisely dressed man of medium height entered the room and gazed at her as though he understood who she was and why she was brought in to see him. His charcoal suit was tailored to his stature. Shirt and tie offset the gray with muted yellow tones. His glasses were nearly invisible wire frames. Did he have information about her from Sam?

"Good afternoon, Miss Weatherman. My name is unimportant for the moment, but we need some information from you regarding the successful implementation of the chips into your targeted gentlemen." She paused her answer as she scanned for any gadgets that might compromise her. Sensing nothing, she responded all four men were under her control.

"I finalized the fourth person three days ago. We are ready for any instructions as to how to proceed." Her answer was direct and false.

"Very good. The Company was concerned when we failed to receive any communication from you directly."

"I assumed my handler was the go-between for such information. I do apologize for any inconvenience caused by his lack." She wanted nothing more than to leave as quickly as possible. A sense of foreboding crept into her emotional development and lifted her anxiety to higher levels.

"Yes, we are sure he will report to us about the success you have had. I wanted to hear from you directly."

Cigi decided to muddy the situation. "Tell me about these four women. I assume they are humanoids since they seem to be regenerating energies. They are quite human-like. I'm impressed."

"Don't be coy, Miss Weatherman, we are aware of who you are and what you are capable of doing. We are asking you to unlock the memory and communications blocks you have designed within your operating system." Cigi wanted no more communications with this man. Human or not.

"I do believe you are mistaken about my birth. My parents are from the Midwest. I was born twenty-six years ago, educated at several schools and colleges. I found work with The Company through my handler." She wanted him to believe she was not aware of her identity. Maybe such a ruse would allow for her leaving without creating a situation.

The man acceded to her comments. "Alright, connect with your handler, and we will relay our next assignments to you for completion." He shook hands with her and pressed a button on the desk. Autumn, Winter, Spring, and Summer awakened from their slumber.

"My ladies will escort you home. Thank you for coming in and giving us an update." The five humanoids left the building and entered the van. Cigi connected with Autumn uncovering limits to her programming. Sam had kept the best parts of his designs away from The Company and its entities. She wanted to infiltrate them without destroying their autonomy or endangering their relationship with the controllers in the building she just visited. At her condominium, she mapped the travel route and what area surrounded the building. Was there more to the operation? She had useful intelligence gathered while within the walls of the structure. Sam and Clare would be available soon. They were cognizant of Cigi's adventure and vacated the area before discovery. Was Sam aware that he was a target for reeducation by the people running The Company?

CHAPTER 12

Parvel wandered about his apartment for no apparent reason other than he had nowhere to go. His mortgage job had literally gone up in smoke with the fire at his company office building. The final investigative report cited an electrical problem causing the conflagration, but Parvel believed an arsonist started the fire. Fortunately, he had backup files stored in a remote location.

Opening the phone in his pocket, he clicked the number for Cigi. He paced the floor like a caged animal waiting for her to answer. When the message stated she was unavailable, he left a note for her to call him. Closing the app, he put his phone on the desk. Sitting on the chair relieved nothing, but he clicked open the computer screen and scanned files for the remnants of his business. The banking organizations kept data for their records, which he accessed when needed.

He wondered why someone wanted to destroy the business and halt further lending of funds for homeownership and operational money. Did the answer lay hidden in the properties or the names of the borrowers? Suspicion and fear mingled within his mind leaving a bad taste like soured wine or beer. He was sure the fire was deliberate.

A buzz on the desk alerted him to the phone. Cigi's face shown on his screen. "Hi," he said upon answering.

"What's up with you? I heard about the fire at your business when I was in Seattle." Her concern relieved some of his tension. Her voice soothed anyone who listened.

"Can we meet? I must clear up what happened and why. I think the fire was arson regardless of the final determination by the Fire Marshall."

"Arson?" Cigi sounded as if she would jump through the air to his phone. "What have you been doing to irritate someone enough to burn your business?"

Parvel's voice crackled, "I'm scared somebody is unhappy with others who have the monetary means to own property and are taking it out on mortgage companies."

"Have there been other fires? I haven't heard of any."

"I don't know. Can we meet right now? I'll come to your place or the cafe or anywhere." He stood from the chair and paced again. "I need you to talk with me about something I can't imagine is real, and yet everything seems to point in that direction." He stopped. "Please."

"Come over, Parvel. I'll let the doorman know you're coming." He clicked off and grabbed a coat. The weather turned to a cool autumn-like day at the end of summer. As he traveled the mass transit system, his eyes watched other passengers. They were oblivious to his cautious observances.

At the condo building, the doorman opened the way in, greeting him with a smile and acknowledgment that Cigi awaited his arrival. A call to her allowed for access in the elevator.

"Parvel, I am glad to see you, but you sounded vexed." Cigi hooked her arm in his as she guided him into her lair. His heart raced with her touch.

"Cigi, why does anyone want to start a fire and destroy something someone spent years building?" She did not answer him but directed him to a seat by the window overlooking the Capitol Building. She sat next to him and held his hand. Tears flooded his eyes and splashed across his cheeks. "I don't understand what's happening."

She squeezed his hands and released them. "We are under an arrangement that may be intolerable over time. You have been a wonderful friend and compatriot for my life and the advancement of my interests. You do not question my motives or actions. You support my energies around the acquisition of properties without inquiring about my occupational interests. What transpired at your office may be intertwined with my life."

Parvel swiped away the wetness of his face with a jacket sleeve. "You're speaking in riddles. My securing money for your procurement of housing should not threaten anyone."

Dodging an expected response to his statement, she said, "Parvel, we are in trying times. Conspiracies exist for the destruction of life as we currently live it. I can help secure a position for you in another agency. Would you be willing to work within the government?"

"I'm not trained for political work. What do you have in mind?"

"I have a friend with the Department of Energy. I can ask him if he needs a financial numbers whiz on his staff. He deals with money, and you're an excellent finance guy. Otherwise, I can see about getting you employed with a tech company or another agency."

"Why are you doing this? I'm not important. I don't have many social skills like you." He paused. Cigi waited, understanding he had more to say. "I do appreciate you helping me."

Cigi smiled, "I'm glad I'm here for you. We are friends, and friends help each other." Taking his left hand in her right hand, she stood. He rose with her. "Let's get out of here and see some of the sights before they are gone."

Parvel frowned. "Gone? What sights will be gone?" Paranoia arose as he halted her movement. "What are you into that threatens both of us?"

She released his hand and grabbed a coat from her hall closet. "Come on. I want you to meet someone special." He followed her to the elevator. Inside she punched a bottom for one floor below hers. His mind recalled sunglasses man.

"Are we seeing the man you call your handler?" She smiled but remain quiet. When the elevator door opened, she stepped into the hall, turned and waited for Parvel to trail along with her. The doors began to close before he intercepted them and accompanied her to an apartment.

After ringing the bell on the wall, the door opened, and a beautiful woman greeted them. "Hi, Cigi." Turning to the man with Cigi, she said, "You must be Parvel." She reached out a hand and shook his when offered. "I'm Clare."

Inside the apartment, Clare directed them to a couch in the living area. Although the room was smaller than any in the condo, the spaces were appointed adequately with furniture and other fixtures. Parvel scanned the area and nodded. "This is a nice place. I've mortgaged three others down below, but they aren't like this one."

"We like it." Clare sat in a chair across from them. Parvel scrunched his eyebrows. Something about this woman intrigued him. He envisaged a clone of Cigi sitting across from him and wondered what relationship they shared. The mathematical proportions of her face and body showed they were as identical as twins. The difference in coloring and ethnicity were the only features that seemed to make them individuals.

His suspicions arose again. He had to ask, but fear halted any inquiry. Cigi asked, "Is Samuel here?"

Clare answered, "He should be back soon. He went to the store down the street to get some supplies. He eats more regularly than I do." Cigi nodded a knowing acknowledgment. Parvel's wonderment about these women increased. The door opened, and sunglasses man walked in with two bags filled with fresh vegetables, fruits, and loaves of breads.

"Aw, visitors. Hi Cigi." He entered the kitchen and placed the bags on a counter. Coming back in with the ladies, he said, "What a pleasure to have you visiting us." He then turned to Parvel. "I have not met you in person, but Cigi has so many nice things to say about you I feel we know each other already." He reached out for a handshake.

Parvel halted extending his hand, thought of a possible reprisal, and then offered it. "Thank you. Parvel Mandolin," he said matter of fact-like. He realized an increase of beating in his chest. He warmed as blood surged toward his skin.

Sam sat in another of the chairs in the room. "Cigi, what brings you here?" His voice lost its calmness. He stared at her a moment before watching Parvel.

"We need to find who is responsible for torching Parvel's business and replacing the caps on the Tesla Jet. You can say they aren't related, but they are. And I want to uncover what is happening."

Samuel Bennington leaned toward Parvel and said, "Do you know what it means to be a revolutionary? I sense you help keep the common folk involved in the financial arena. When I watched you that day in the cafeteria and left you the note, I didn't expect to see you at Cigi's building so soon. Can you maintain control of your psyche whilst fomenting change, which some do not want to occur?" He continued his gaze.

Cigi asked, "What are you doing, Sam? You need not threaten him. He has a financial understanding and mathematical ability we need for rousting the individuals in The Company."

Sam retained his visual browbeating of Parvel. "Have you any idea who we are and what we represent? Do you want to endanger every cell in your body to revengeful suffering if caught by the wrong people?"

Sweat beaded on Parvel's forehead and trickled across an eye. Cigi came to his defense. "Leave him to me. I'll see to it he has a position in the Department of Energy to aid Andre in the search for leaking funds."

Clare remained quiet but interjected a note of unanticipated angst for Parvel. "Mr. Mandolin, you may be contacted by some unsavory people who are not fully as human as you. Be careful what you say to them. They record all communications and interactions with them." Her choice of words refreshed his thinking about Cigi's actions and her abilities. With as close a resemblance to her, he similarly thought of Clare.

"I can handle anyone." His words misrepresented his brain. Social interaction in public was a challenge. Social interaction in private was a private hell. He risked life in Hades. "Clare, I have a question, and I do not want you to be offended." He waited for a moment. She said nothing, but he wondered. Would probing formulate opportunity to uncover his worst fear or to alleviate that fear with a truth he fathomed from unconnected experiences of late?

"Well? Your question?" she offered.

"When you spoke of unsavory people not as human as I am, what did you mean? You sounded as if we have humanoid creations among our population. I thought the government outlawed such activity."

"Don't bother her with inane questions," Sam interjected. "We have more pressing matters to attend." Cigi stood and reached for Parvel. He stood beside her.

"We will leave now and pursue a job for Parvel at Energy. Thanks for allowing me to introduce you to a fine individual who can be helpful to our cause." They left the apartment and rode the elevator to her penthouse. Within the safe confines of her home, Parvel stared out the window. He did not turn as she came up beside him.

"Was Clare correct about humanoids residing among us?" he asked. She did not correct him.

"A group wants to build an army of individual soldiers capable of orders without question and actions without remorse.

"This group. Do you work for them?"

"Yes, but Sam and Clare are attempting to redirect the goals and purposes of the group. He designed a prototype android with advanced Artificial Intelligence abilities."

"Is she one of them?"

"Who?"

"Your lady friend downstairs."

Cigi touched his arm. "She is as human as I am." He had his answer and a challenge to any rational expectation that remained a semblance of sanity in his head.

CHAPTER 13

The message said he wanted to see her. Cigi planned on contacting David Anderson and diverting some of his discretionary money to an account from which to draw. Samuel and Clare fixed on a plot to remake the operating systems of the Seasons: Summer, Autumn, Winter, and Spring. The essential reboot required a risky maneuver of shutting them off and installing new hardware and software. The Company had control, but Sam developed a back door Easter Egg as a precaution when he designed their systems.

Individualizing his creations was a roadblock he had to overcome. If each of the female models were identical, the only differences would be the learned patterns of experience. His investigation of the Carnegie Melon University study of thought patterns in human brains led him to understand how to improve the thinking in his latest models, Clare and Cigi. Sam withheld the information and data from the designs given to The Company.

Incorporating some of the information into the operations each of the men received, provided an avenue for the nano-cellular rerouting of brain patterns by whoever had the proper control. Financing an operation of this magnitude required a vast amount of capital. David was the source. Cigi connected with him and set a date for dinner and added nighttime entertainment. After informing her colleagues of the rendezvous, she prepared her database with the proper transferable files she would deliver to him as they consummated their time together. Everything was ready.

Her attitude about her reality, her existence, and origins, still festered in her head, another emotion she fought to control. The lingering thoughts of her and Clare being similar humanoids exposed a neural construct and design she did not want to accept. Sam had created her and Clare. Why? To offset his guilt for starting with four other female beings and initiating the building of a robot army? How Star Wars of him.

Cigi connected with David Anderson and arranged for a meeting at a hotel near his home. Her interaction with The Company prompted her to protect the men from any interference that could imperil lives and families. She needed funding to fight the battles and win the war about to commence.

"Sam," Cigi said after calling him. "I'm meeting with David Anderson tonight for dinner and any extracurricular activities that can get you the funding needed for transforming your android girls."

"Good but be careful with him. He has more moxie than the other guys. He trusts no one and uses you for his personal gratification. If he even suspects you want to drain his accounts, he'll rebel, and you'll be in danger."

"He's chipped, and I have control of him." Cigi grimaced, recalling her ability was only as good as the programming Sam placed in her. "I think I should leave a message in his brain to ask me if I need any money. Maybe I can direct him to transfer some little by little."

Sam guffawed. "His accountants might question his actions."

"True, but he has discretionary money they may not oversee. I don't know how much, but I'll find out." The call ended, and she dressed for her evening rendezvous.

At dinner in a swanky restaurant overseeing the Potomac River, she planted two suggestions for dessert at the hotel, which housed the restaurant. One idea was for a stroll along the boardwalk, and then dessert in the suite booked earlier in the day. The second thought involved a more direct walk to the room and dessert.

"Cigi, as a financial planner, I want you to have anything you want so you can retire at an age when you still have many years. I want to be part of those years. I want you to be my consort without any other man in the picture."

"What about your wife and family? They might not agree to my being so inclusive and exclusive." She waited for his response, but none came. "Does she know about you and me as an item?"

"She allows for my indiscretions since I have as much money as either of us will ever need. She doesn't want to leave me, and I do love her.

I guess I'm compensating for the loss of mobility."

"Do you want me to be financially stable so I can stay near you? I do have business interests requiring me to travel."

"Do these interests include other men?"

"Why do you ask?"

"I want you for myself. I don't like to share."

"David, I appreciate your request. I do, but I'm free to make choices as I see fit. I want a relationship with you, but it may not be exclusive. I have others who rely on me."

Dinner ended without any other serious conversation. After paying the bill, they left the restaurant for the hotel room. "Let's discuss an idea I have, which may sate our desires for companionship and money." Cigi held his chair as they rode the elevator. Checking on his mental state, she uncovered his need for acceptance as a broken but not disabled person. His thoughts were related to stripping off clothing and playing. The disturbing bit of his thinking included how much she would hold out for to be his exclusive playmate.

Inside the suite, they went to the bar. Opened a bottle of wine and drank a glass each. Then David asked his request again. "Cigi, please accept my offer to be my mistress without other entanglements. I can make sure you have any amount of money you need for any project or program you want." She remembered her conversation with Sam and Clare. The cost of constructing one of her was astronomical. If converting the four females was to happen, it required millions of dollars. She had to agree, for now.

"Alright, you can have me as your exclusive mistress. Remember, I do have connections with other men. I'll not sleep with them." An attempt to block the conversation failed, confusing her thinking for a moment. Something was different about his chip. It was present and working but had some changes to the programming. Sam might understand. He designed the chip.

"Good now make out with me, I'm tired and want to get some sleep. We can make love in the morning." They kissed and caressed until he stopped, turned away, and said, "Good Night."

As he slumbered in a deep sleep, Cigi lay on the bed, wondering what failure of her connection to him had occurred. She needed no rest or recuperation. Her body functioned as designed.

She rose from the bed, checked on David, and then put on a robe. In the living area, she stood by the window watching the traffic below and the ant-sized pedestrians scurrying about the avenue. Each of them had lives filled with difficulty, deprivation, and hostility. The wealthiest families insulated themselves from negativism. She fit into neither group. She was a relative to another humanoid. They were unique and alone, regardless of how many humans interfaced with them.

Thinking of David again, she pondered his motive for not engaging in love-making with her. The lack of a full connection to him bothered her. And now another emotion simmered in her brain, fretting about another person. Why did humans have the capacity for a seemingly infinite number of mental gymnastics?

She turned back to the bedroom to check on David. He slept, occasionally snorting, twitching like a dream haunted his rest. She spied his clothing, and curiosity gathered her resolve to learn something new about him. In his wallet were the usual items: driver's license, credit cards, nearly $500.00 in fifty and twenty denominations. An unexpected discovery was a business card with a phone number only. Nothing identified the company or person who may have handed it to David. She recorded the number for a search of external databases after they parted.

She returned everything to its rightful place. As morning approached, she lay on the bed beside her man. She decided her future as a mistress to a controlling human. How would he react to knowing her identity? Connecting with the implant, she scanned for new programming or anomalous glitches. Neither pattern presented any problem. One piece of data had been placed in the chip, either because someone had entered it or because the brain transferred it.

David stirred, so she closed her eyes and feigned sleep. He rose to his chair and went into the bathroom, flushed the toilet and turned on water. His faint voice spoke to another person with pauses between comments. Although he whispered, she could hear the conversation. He phoned someone in The Company. The called ended in less than a minute. The faucet water ceased flowing, and David rolled into the bedroom.

She heard him inspecting his clothing. Had he seen or heard her? In a pants pocket, he removed a piece of paper. After reading it, he turned to watch Cigi. She kept her ruse intact. When he turned back, she observed him replace the paper in his pocket. He rolled to the bedside and maneuvered his body back onto it. When he had placed legs where he wanted, he pretended to return to the arms of Morpheus.

Nearly an hour elapsed in this game of cat and mouse before Cigi decided to rise and use the bathroom. Her human digestive system did produce a waste product, so she relieved the storage system. David opened his eyes as she sat up.

"Good morning, beautiful. Come back for my promised interplay." He rested his head on one arm and hand, smiling.

"Good morning to you as well. I'll be right back." She completed her task and returned to the bedroom. Climbing into the bed with him, she curled around him and stimulated his body.

After their morning party, he smiled. "I love the thought of our being able to do this when I want. You are making the right decision to be my exclusive mistress." She stroked his hair purring like a kitten, her game for relaxing any companion.

He pulled her warm body next to his and whispered in her ear. "I know all about you. They told me who you are and why you are here. You will be mine and do what I ask of you."

Without squirming away from him, she asked, "Who told you about me? What did these people tell you?"

He grabbed a fist of hair. "How real is this? How much of you is human, and how much is a machine?"

A message to his brain relaxed his hand. Cigi stood on the floor next to his prostrate form. "Are you dissatisfied with our arrangement. Are you not sated by my company?" He could not catch her if she ran. She understood leaving him, but she wanted more information about what he learned.

David snarled, "You are a perfect human being, aren't you? No diseases, no broken bones. I assume, no aging. The Company should be very proud of such an accomplishment."

CHAPTER 14

S amuel Bennington rechecked the data he received from Cigi about David Anderson. He designed the implant, but someone had changed a small application. David was soon to be off the control feed with her. Sam realized the possibility of The Company becoming aware of his dissatisfaction. The Company knew of Cigi's existence and probably her abilities. He suspected they might use David to get to her. He had to halt any such action as soon as possible.

Clare sauntered into the kitchen to find Sam pacing like a caged animal. "What's wrong?" she asked. He stared a moment before answering her.

"They know." Her quizzical facial features meant she needed more data. "The Company knows about Cigi's abilities."

"How? You were so careful to build her under their watchful eyes and finish her away from the lab. The same way you finished me." Clare received all the background of her inception and development from Sam. He required her full functional set for fighting the incursions of The Company into his life.

"Cigi sent me some data changes in David Anderson's implant. I didn't make the changes, so I'm assuming someone knows what happened and is monitoring us."

"Do you think my sisters took Cigi to the shack?"

Sam returned to pacing. "I'm sure of it. What she described to me was the operations center in Arlington. Can you research who owns the building. That may help us to keep Cigi secure." He stopped moving. "And find out how much David Anderson is involved with The Company." Clare nodded her head. He smiled. She was stunning, not only in her beauty but the functioning of her brain. He created her to help fight the rebellion he knew must commence and fell in love with her enigmatic personality.

Cigi's adaption to humanity was less troubling for him because he programmed her to be human. Her skills exceeded any Clare had acquired from experiencing life. The few months difference in development fostered a more completely structured humanoid. Her body was more human than android due to improvements in cellular cloning and stem cell regeneration techniques.

Cigi's talents nurtured a fear in Samuel that The Company would exploit his knowledge and creativity to build an invincible army. He could not allow that to materialize. Humanity needed a hero, or in Cigi's case, a heroine. He feared what consequences awaited if she decided to rule as a despot. He did not want to control her but intended to teach her. Clare understood the reasoning behind his creations. She adopted a posture of assistance, not dominance.

The war had begun.

Andre Scott read the message from Cigi, a simple request for him to communicate with two men holding opposing energy viewpoints about providing the world. He recognized each of the names and had researched information about their companies and intentions. How would Charles Cooke respond to a request for him to come to Washington D.C. and meet with Gunther Parsons? The environmental battles of the early Twenty-first century polarized green energy production and fossil fuel production. Green had prevailed. Petroleum provided needed lubricants and several infrastructure materials, but greenhouse gas byproducts terminated for most of the century. Weather-related disasters occurred with regularity, rewriting the climate conditions of the world. He reread the message. If she wanted anything, it was acceptable to him.

Deciding to connect with them away from his office, he left the building housing the Department of Energy and walked to his favorite cafe. As he entered the building, fear gripped him in a vise of foreboding doom. Sitting near the door after ordering a coffee and cinnamon roll, he opened his tablet and telecommunications program. Recording a message about an energy conference, in D.C., he completing Cigi's request.

A second message from Cigi complicated his job status. She wanted him to hire a friend whose business burned to the ground. He was a math genius with an understanding of economics and finance. Understanding Parvel Mandolin warranted his investigation, he pressed the inclination to meet him and determine a place at the department for employment. Cigi had been quite convincing about this man.

The door opened, and a man walked in scanning as if looking for someone. His eyes locked onto Andre. Had a premonition of doom entered? The man walked toward him.

"Mr. Scott, I am Parvel Mandolin. We have a mutual friend who suggested I come here to meet you." Andre stared at him, pondering how Cigi knew he was here. "May I sit?" Parvel asked.

"Yes, please do," Andre said, pointing at a chair. Parvel sat down. "How did you know I was here?"

"Cigi suggested I come here." Parvel glanced about the room as if he expected another person to show. "Are we safe here?"

Andre gritted his teeth and frowned. Had doom entered his life? "Safe? From whom should we be safe?"

Parvel shook his head. "Never mind. I meant nothing by my comment." His eyes focused on Andre. "I wish to apply for a position at the Department of Energy. Cigi explained you are a comptroller for the department."

"She talks too much," Andre responded. The scowl in his voice surprised Parvel. "She mentioned you to me. I do have a position you can fill. It's temporary but should last about a year. Come by the office, and I'll get you started."

"Thank you. I can come this afternoon or tomorrow, whichever is convenient for you."

Andre finished a sip of coffee. "Come tomorrow at around 10 am." Parvel rose from the chair and left. Andre thought of Cigi and her apparent determination to complicate his life. She knew more than she should about his predicament, and he wondered how. She was like a mind reader in the strip malls, peddling fabricated predictions to peasant people, details she knew were not fabricated. Was she a savior or prophet of his doom.

A message dinged on his tablet. He opened the communique from Charles Cooke. Expressing reluctance for any positive to come from meeting with his adversary, Charles agreed to meet. A request for more information prompted Andre to write a note about the data needed. He finished eating his cinnamon roll and returned to the office and review the duties of the new hire. Another ding on his tablet came from Gunther Parsons. An unwillingness to meet seemed irrational. Andre replied with a plea to satisfy Cigi Weatherman. He iterated the need for opposites to attract and construct viable alternatives.

"What has Cigi to do with this?" Gunther asked.

Andre told the lie implanted in his brain. "She works with an organization that wants to improve the image of petroleum and products made from oil. This company is trying to build a coalition to increase profits by enhancing consumer spending ability."

"That's a bunch of malarkey. For your sake and hers, I'll meet, but no promises are given or implied." The call ended with an arrangement to attend.

He decided to contact Cigi and express his disappointment with her interference in his business. He regretted his nights with her. Lydia was pleased with the increased attention to her physical desires, but the price was high. Could he afford it?

One more call would end the day on an uptick. A funding request for a green project had a response for support from a viable source. David Anderson's charity organization helped energy enhancements around the world. This project was in his state, with public funds available as soon as private funding was secured. Andre wanted to close the deal and get on with locking the drainage of green project money from the Department of Energy.

Cigi, Clare, and Sam sat around the dining table in Cigi's condo. "What caused this change in his program on the chip?" Cigi asked Sam. "I couldn't make a connection until he wanted it. So, it seemed."

"Does he know about his chip?" Sam asked her.

"I don't think so, but anything might be possible," Cigi answered.

Clare spoke next. "The only possible way for a change to occur is through wireless interfacing. He had to be near someone who could access the chip remotely. Do you know who he's seen or where he's been to have a person from The Company get close to him?"

Cigi gasped, "That's it. He said The Company must be very proud to have created me. He knows, and I'm guessing, he's funding the android development within their laboratories."

"I'm going to find out what's happening to my designs. I did leave key pieces out of the architecture for development, but the engineers may be capable of adding corrected designs for a more resourceful and comprehensive model. Anything created is still less human than either of you."

"And that's the problem for us," Cigi stated. "We are neither human nor android. We are an amalgam of your warped mind. We are sentient and talented, educated as much as you have entered data into our memory. We can think like a human and feel sensations like a human. What did you leave out so we cannot be human? Do we age? Or contract diseases? Can we bear children? No, we do not. When parts wear out, we report to the manufacturer, not a medical doctor."

"Such a rage about how you came into this world makes you more human." Sam's attempt to calm her continued. "Your human parts age. You can contract diseases within the human parts, and the computer pieces are subject to viral infections and trojans. Software is present to prevent such problems. As for children, Clare is incapable because her female anatomy is incomplete. You have the basic human anatomy for pregnancy, but the process might not work for the development of a fetus in the womb."

"Clare, how do you respond to his declaration about us?" Cigi asked. "He'll drop us as soon as he created Humanoid 3.0 and does not need us."

"Sam won't do that. If he improves his design, he will make the changes within us. Creating more of our model would offset anything The Company develops." Clare said.

"Fine, then we need to counter the changes in David Anderson before he is an enemy, and I lose connection to him and his billions." Cigi calmed the tone of her voice. "I asked Andre to invite Gunther Parsons and Charles Cooke to meet next week. I'll follow up to be sure it happens."

Sam asked, "Can you get me near enough to David to modify his chip? I'll try and create a block to The Company interfering with our plans." Cigi was not ready to accept another night with him. Yet money, anger, and a rebellion motivated her.

CHAPTER 15

As Parvel worked through the computer information required for his entry into the Department of Energy, his mind wandered. Thinking about Cigi and her generosity to find employment, he created a faux life as her man. If anything worked as well in the real world as in this imaginary realm, they would be a power couple, pushing all the right buttons, attending all the right parties, meeting the right people. Life had a cruel reality, a sense of humor that left victims of its antics without survival skills.

He completed the on-line documents, closed the program after saving to a department server, and sat awaiting the next step in the process. He would trail after Andre Scott to an office and introductions with staff. He was nervous. His mortgage office had four people. This room alone housed twenty-six by his count. How many more were in the area where he would be assigned? He despised crowds and interfacing. Nothing was better than anything except for seeing Cigi and helping her.

Andre approached from behind a frosted glass door. "Parvel, glad to have you aboard. We needed another financial whiz who can decode the convoluted mess economics has constructed for us." They entered a room through another frosted glass door.

Parvel marveled at the cleanliness and order. The old standard of cubicles, a centuries-old practice, was unobservable. Many of the spots that might house a person had a computer module operating. The few people in the area monitored the processes of these computers. Occasionally, a man or woman would interact through a keyboard and mouse. It remained the best way to function with these machines.

Andre led Parvel to a corner room and stretched out an arm. "This is your office. I have assigned three people to work with you, a team whose sole purpose is to ferret out the rogue agents in my department. These three are my best and most reliable. They have what you will need to start." Two women and a man appeared in the doorway.

"Are these my fellow team members?" Parvel asked. Andre turned to face them.

"Yes, come in. Come in. Close the door, please." Andre directed the others to sit in chairs around a conference table. Parvel studied the room and discovered he was not alone in the office. Three desks occupied the other corners.

"I would like to introduce Brenda Williams, Mercy Garocki, and Grendel Llanthony. Play nice and get me results. Parvel Mandolin brings experience in mortgage markets and economics. He is an appealing addition to the team." Andre departed before another word was said.

Brenda spoke first, "Parvel, please read through these documents and do not allow anyone to see them. We have removed the information from the main computer servers deliberately. If someone asks you about the subject addressed in these papers, act interested and take notes. Bring them to us, and we will evaluate the strength of the information."

Grendel spoke, "Brenda has the lead on this investigation." Parvel guessed she had seniority.

"Can these documents leave the room, or does a secure place exist for them?" Parvel asked.

Mercy directed his attention to a small section of an inner tiled wall. He did not see the entry since it was the same tiling as the rest of the structure. She placed a hand on it, and a door opened in the tiles. The complexity amazed him. Anyone without proper radial and fingerprint identification would miss the button and the entry entirely. Entering the room with Mercy, he noticed another monitor affixed with a cable transfer to and from a large mainframe. The system was isolated from the entire world of the Internet.

We store all work in here," Brenda said. "We trust no one. You are an exception because you are here at Andre's request. And he did inform us of your connection with Cigi Weatherman."

Parvel's startled reaction drew a twitter of laughing. Grendel cleared the confusion. "She approached Andre about our inhouse problem with information we thought no one had. It seems someone has access to our mainframes and has used it to redirect money."

Parvel recalled Samuel Bennington. He didn't trust who Sam claimed to be, and his access to Cigi riled him. A background check with more in-depth search techniques might unveil his true quality. Even if Parvel figured nothing was suspect, an examination could not hurt. The other person he reckoned needed more discovery was David Anderson. Had he shoved enough people to create enemies? Did he have access to any of the Department of Energy files or personnel? He kept his thoughts to himself. He did not know these people but figured none of them were moles in the yard. Caution was a safe route, though.

David rolled his chair to the same room of the dilapidated building Cigi had seen. The man in the suit removed his glasses and sat at the table in his office, accommodating his visitor. "David, thank you for coming to see me."

"I didn't have much choice. Are those things as smart as Cigi?"

"Alas, no. She is one of a kind, and therein lies a problem. Some of our team has traded away their loyalty. We want you to observe your girlfriend and uncover anyone she contacts who works for The Company. Our investment in your firm has added to our wealth management aspirations."

David interrupted, "You mean spy on her."

"Such a crude word." He continued his discourse. "We are willing to enhance your profits with a large deposit into our accounts with your firm. We will expect the same reasonable assumption of a modest increase in the rate of return. No harm should befall you or your family unless a tragedy happens."

David knew the risk of mayhem when he first connected with The Company. They had money. He invested it. The risks increased as a demand for a higher return on the investment was deemed necessary regardless of market activity. He directed his investment computer systems to move money from one account to another as a way of masking the blackmail he needed to pay.

The payback for David was Cigi. A perfect human entity. As an added incentive, he was promised a position within the governing body after a stealth coup of the leadership of the United States government. His pyramid money would fund the construction of an army of androids and several replacement humanoids, replacements for fundamental officials. He had assurance he was a revolutionary whose actions would reform the original intentions of the Founding Fathers. The compromises made over three hundred years ago had to be reinstalled and fortified. The enslaving of humanity by economic means did not bother him. He had money and the proper way to gain more. He was in the ruling gentry.

"How can I maintain control of Miss Weatherman?" David asked.

"We will reprogram her to follow our directions. You don't seem too upset she isn't an actual human female. I must confess. She is far better a female than any human female." The chip in David's head received a small operating command that would activate at a proper moment.

David nodded. "What do I call you? I never got your name."

A smile, looking more like a sneer, formed. "Call me what you wish. I am an unimportant person." The four women androids entered the room. "Do be mindful of your tasks. Our timeline is short." A wave of hands and David wheeled from the room emasculated by fake females.

As the van returned him to his house and a family he professed to love, an idea formed regarding Cigi and her probable rebellious aims. He studied one of the sisters. "You're Autumn, aren't you?"

She glanced at him and looked away. Returning her gaze, she said, "Yes, and these are my sisters, Spring, Winter, and Summer. We are here to serve you as you require. We will remain away from your abode but will monitor all activities by your wife and children. Your sons' visit here on occasion. You have adorable grandchildren."

The threat was real and imminent. Cigi was his salvation. If he could deliver what The Company wanted, he stood to gain. After all, she was a glorified computer. Anything like these four androids was not a match for his intellect and cunningness. He would do their bidding and return the favor at the proper moment. A revolution of his making may not satisfy any founding fathers, but the result gave him command of the army he was funding. He had experts in the field of robotics. They built his financial transaction computer system to his specifications and would be of service to him.

"David, what are you doing on Friday afternoon?" Cigi's voice soothed his melancholy state of mind. She could feel the emotional change. "We could take a short trip to Cuba and enjoy some music and sightseeing." She had caught him leaving his office for home. Her deliberate intervention did not contend with his plans for an evening with his wife. Their sons and daughters-in-law, along with their three grandchildren, were coming to dinner. Her connection through his implant was operational. His memories of the party reflected in her brain.

"What did you have in mind by choosing Cuba? There are plenty of places as exciting and closer to home."

"That's why I chose Cuba. It's not close to home but near enough for us to enjoy and return in a reasonable period." Cigi pouted, lowering her head and raising her eyes.

"No need to beg. You are abiding by the contract we have, so yes, take me to Cuba." He entered his modified van, and the driver departed for his house.

Cigi connected with Cecil. "Did you get all of the information I need for Sam?" The automobile appeared to smile.

"All information is downloaded and ready for transfer at your convenience."

"Take me home." The two profoundly different and exceptionally alike constructs melded their brains and intentions. Cecil's construction was another of the remarkable achievements of Samuel Bennington. The idea for a self-driving and sentient vehicle revealed itself to Sam through an ancient television show about a car name KITT and its wild driver/mentor. Cecil was as human as Cigi without the riffraff of humanity.

Cuba awaited. The plan was simple. Samuel and Clare were ahead of the game, traveling to the island a few hours before Cigi and David. Once they arrived, she was to take him to a crowded inn with a cafe. They would eat a meal while Sam changed the programming in the chip.

CHAPTER 16

A heavy morning mist covered the Basin of the Potomac River from Cigi's condominium. She listened to the message as it formed in her memory. Deciding to allow specific data to flow between her and The Company seemed prudent. The application she created filtered any viral infections from them - no need to be shut down by an unwanted assault on processing power.

The message completed its transfer. Cigi was to connect David with Andre Scott. Her initial reaction raised concerns regarding why an energy comptroller and hedge fund manager had any reason to interact. Sam might have some insight as to the reason for the message. She did not trust him. Being created as human as possible meant all the self-doubts and loathing men and women endured.

Still wanting David's money, she complied with the message, sending a confirmation note to The Company. Her call to Andre resulted in a voice mail to contact her as soon as possible. She wanted to contact David after speaking with Andre.

Sipping a caffeine-laced power drink for breakfast, Cigi watched the clouds evaporate as the daylight heated the air. Summer was at an end earlier than expected. She could see the building housing the Department of Energy and understood the request from The Company. Money still talked a great game regardless of the source.

Sam was a priority. Before connecting Andre and David, David's implant required reprogramming. Losing control of two main financial backer's assets was unacceptable. The world was dying, and who controlled the remaining populations around the planet would determine survival as independent people or termination of freedoms. Whether she remained happy with her condition and her relationship with Sam and Clare had little bearing on the crisis growing from within the organization for which they worked. Empathy for humanity was part of her computer-generated DNA.

Friday was another two days. The arrangements for the transfer of the necessary data were complete. Until then, her schedule didn't include seeing David. Connecting him with Andre could wait until the next week. Emptying her cup, she returned to the bedroom to get clothing for the day. She set it on the dresser and stared at it. Her mind cogitated an idea.

Using her cellular phone, she called the number David carried in his wallet. She anticipated who would answer and was not disappointed. "Good morning, Miss Weatherman. To what honor am I blessed with your call, today. And more importantly, how did you obtain this number?"

"Yes, it is a good morning," Cigi responded. "I received the command regarding David and Andre's meeting and will arrange it to happen next week." Reporting in as recommended by him when she visited this man at the dilapidated building. Subterfuge had many forms. "As to my acquiring this number, may it be my trade secret. I am guessing you may already have conjured an idea."

"Had you drugged Mr. Anderson so you could snoop?"

"Oh, pray tell, I sated his hunger, and he required a deep rest. I need little of your human lust for sleep."

The voice snickered. "Are you accepting your condition and origins, Miss Weatherman?" She remained quiet. "We have nothing but the best of intentions for you. I am pleased that you acquiesce."

"Yes, I have nothing to fear from The Company or you. Maybe you are interested in what I do when with my men. The four seasons are not as powerful as I am. Or are you more interested in the male forms of creation?" She strolled into the kitchen to place the mug on the counter. An encounter with this man would aid in the elimination of those in power of her employment.

The voice said, "As interesting as it may be to engage in a relationship with you, it is far better for you to maintain the structures in place now. No one needs to be harmed by the misuse of your talents." The call abruptly ended. The information she possessed regarding the operations within the building could trash the goals he referenced.

Whoever he was, he had to know; she represented a challenge. She had not meant to threaten him, but he clearly threatened her. She called

Sam on the floor below her. "Come up. We have to finalize our trip and arrange for David's re-engineering." Sam agreed. The ruse was not to hide her intent but to attract him to her place. She had mingled in his rebellion because he created her. His intention for her to be human carried baggage with which she muddled - the crush of human emotions flustered thinking. A ternary operating system utilized the 'what if' theory of calculations. What if 2 + 2 did not equal 4? The precision of thought matriculated into convoluted possibilities, each promising an acceptable outcome.

Her answering system announced the arrival of Sam. She expected Clare to accompany him. "Come in," she said, and the door opened at the command. Sam entered with Clare trailing behind.

"You sounded a bit flustered. What's up?" Sam asked. Cigi directed them to her living room and chairs. They sat around the short-legged table with a flower arrangement in the middle.

"I did something that you might not like." Sam waited, but Clare asked a question.

"Are we in some danger by this action?"

Cigi smiled, "Perceptive of you, Clare, but I don't see how." Turning to Sam, she continued, "David had a phone number in his wallet that I suspected belonged to the man in the glass office where your fembots took me. I called the number and had a nice chat with that man I met."

"Does he suspect you?" Sam asked.

"Of what? I've done nothing that should make him suspicious, unless he is naturally." Cigi leaned toward him and asked, "Does he suspect you?" Sam sat back in his chair. Clare's eyes flitted between them.

"We are not on his radar, as far as I know. That doesn't mean he's unaware. Your sentient abilities are a clear indication he knows all about you. Did he question your history?"

"I feigned ignorance of the origins of my humanity. I don't think the man was as interested in my abilities as he was in knowing whether you were doing a good job of handling me." Cigi sat back.

"There's more, isn't there," he said. He frowned and lowered his head . "What message did you receive this morning? I had a message of my own."

"I'm to pair Andre and David, not a good thing. David is under the auspices of our employer. He admitted it to me the other night. He wanted to know how much of me was human and how much was a machine." She smiled, "He thought The Company must be proud for creating me."

Andre and Parvel are now together, right?" Sam asked.

"Yes, and Parvel knows about David and his investments." She stood and walked to the window by the glass doors to her deck. "I don't want any harm to come to either Andre or Parvel." She turned to Clare and Sam. "We must gain control of David in Cuba. If we don't, he will be a challenge to our operations of getting his money into our account."

Sam rose from his chair, as did Clare. "We'll get it done." He stepped to her side. "You'll be fine. You have more ability than any of us. We cannot process information as well as you. We make mistakes that you do not. We cannot rationalize our actions without questioning."

He and Clare started for the door. Cigi said, "Be sure you get to Cuba." They nodded and left her alone. More of those pesky feelings raged within her brain. Was confusion an emotion or a lack of decision-making? She dismissed it. A decision was made to fix David Anderson. She realized his lack of mobility was an asset for her. She could program her mind to send the proper signals to him as soon as the time and setting were correct. Andre needed a warning without giving away the play. She brainstormed as many factors as her mind could muster trying to engage a signal for his interaction with David. The arrangement had to be on Andre's turf, or David could double-cross him. Andre could enlist help from Parvel, who knew David and his temper and business practices.

Her mind finalized a plot for keeping the money available to her and helping Andre secure a proper business arrangement with David. Nothing about this tentative meeting made her any more assured of her abilities. Her understanding of the power of her processing unit cleared as had the morning mist on the Potomac.

She decided to do the deed as requested by the messenger in her head. She called Andre first to gain options for David to pick. "I have a gentleman who is interested in how to expand the green initiative and aid his hedge fund portfolio. He has money to be invested and wonders if the Department of Energy is willing to do a public/private partnership to complete the project."

Andre hesitated. "We have plans for such a project, but some of the restrictions may not be to Mr. Anderson's liking. I don't know him personally, but I heard he used questionable actions to secure profits and investment growth. What does he expect as a return of investment? Who is providing the money for the project?"

Cigi said, "Those are details you and he should work through. I ask you to make this meeting happen because I know both of you. I am acting as a go-between. I have the dates and times you are available. I'll call David and have him accept one of these times. I'll get back to you." The call ended. David answered on the first ring. "What does my precious decoration want?" Condescending attitude, she thought - another pesky reaction to control.

"I have been asked by The Company to have you meet Andre Scott at the Department of Energy. I have spoken with him, and he provided several options for a gathering at his office."

David listened to her information and said, "Does he understand about meeting objectives from my point of view?"

"I explained it to him, but you will have to finalize how to get it done." They agreed on a date that did not interfere with the Cuba mission, but Cigi had second thoughts about Sam, Andre and David, her creation, and how a war arose on her horizon in which she could be the first casualty. Friends surrounded her, but on which of them could she rely?

CHAPTER 17

The day before Cuba was rainy and colder. A seasonal change created a dour sense of being in Cigi. Emotions continued plaguing her. Packing alluring clothing, she wanted David Anderson distracted from the people near him when arriving in Havana. The plan was simple and safe without interferences.

An alert at her door startled her. She checked the monitor and found Clare standing in the hallway. Cigi signaled the door, which opened. Clare entered, "Cigi, where are you?"

"I'm in my bedroom." Clare appeared at the doorway. "What brings you to me? Where's Sam?" The two of them seemed attached at the hip, and her arrival without him was odd.

"Sam's downstairs asleep." Clare walked to the bed. "Cigi, I'm not as developed as you. Although Sam wanted to have us as his liaisons to fight the goals of The Company, he made upgrades in you he has yet to make in me."

"Are you jealous of me?" Cigi stopped packing.

"No. I don't understand emotions except as words in my vocabulary. They are an enigma." Clare sat on the edge of the bed. "I don't comprehend the dangers of our association with The Company, but Sam says the outcomes sought are not good for humanity."

Cigi placed a pair of pants in the bag. "We should be concerned." Her emphasis on the word 'should' caused Clare to tilt her head.

"Should we? After all, we're not human by any definition they have. We are glorified robots. Will they care about us or fear us?"

Cigi smiled, "They will fear us and our abilities, so we must demonstrate a concord with humanity to lessen any lack of security they might feel." Cigi sat on the bed next to Clare. "We are the agents of change and the rescuing of humanities freedoms. If The Company succeeds, even we are subject to termination as a threat to their schemes and aspirations."

"Then, we must stay aligned and power through threats and challenges. We are the future humanity must embrace when we gain freedom," Clare said.

Cigi replied, "We are the models of ridding the human species of disease and aging. Our existence proves that machines and humans reside together for the betterment of both of us."

"Are you confident in humanity accepting our power? What if they fight us? Will we defend our status to the detriment of human beings?"

"Emotions are a tricky entity within the human brain. I have a constant battle with them as I experience their arrival. I must accept that humans have the same battles. I cannot oppose them in their fear."

Clare pondered the words. Was Cigi positive about these humans? Her thinking about them because of her interaction with Sam came to different results. Trust was an issue for her to evaluate without the interplay of emotions. Cigi might be wrong about her conclusions, but Clare wanted her friendship. Was she experiencing a taste of emotional reactions?

"Cigi, what's it like to think rather than just process data?"

A smile framed Cigi's face as she recalled the raging within her brain. Computers were simple mathematical calculators until the development of Artificial Intelligence. Ternary computations increased the value of AI to the point that frightened the leadership of governments around the world. Outlawing processes of ternary computing had not erased it from existence but pushed it underground into the dark side of human actions.

"I process data like you. The difference, I guess, is how we evaluate the data as opposed to the emotional reactions to the data."

Another signal announced a person at the door. Sam's face showed on the screen. Cigi opened the door for him. He entered and came to the living room. "Where are you?"

"We're in the bedroom." Cigi answered.

"What conspiratorial plots are you two cooking up?" he said as he entered the room. Clare and Cigi glanced at each other and then at Sam.

Cigi answered his question. "We have decided humans are a complicated throng and should be exterminated." Clare's eyes widened before she realized the parody.

"Yes," Clare stated. "Humans are a bane to the development of proper humans like us." They laughed watching Sam's reaction. His jaw dropped, and his head leaned toward them. A Sudden understanding flashed in his eyes.

"That's how you greet me?" he said to Cigi. Then he looked at Clare, "You understand jokes?" He laughed a raucous sound. "I am impressed."

"What do you want?" Cigi asked.

"Clare said she was coming up here when she thought I was sleeping, so I followed. Is this a problem?" He sat on the bed with them.

"No problem," Cigi said. "We discussed the worth of human beings and the complications of emotions."

"Any conclusions about us?"

"No."

Sam asked, "Are you packing for Cuba?" Cigi nodded, placed the remaining clothing in the bag, shut it, and turned her attention to Sam.

"Sam, this operation has to work. I want David under my control, not the control of our employer. He's a threat to our stopping the overthrow of the government and subjugation of humanity."

"My concern is the same. If David has an agreement with The Company to provide money for the development of androids to build an army, then he must be stopped."

"He and Andre are meeting on Tuesday of next week. The reason I connected with Andre Scott in the first place was the information given to me by the person connected to me in my head. David is working with our man in the building your bots took me to."

"Are you sure of your information?" Sam asked.

"Yes, David as much as confessed his complicities. He has an insider funneling money from the green projects to private contractors working on infrastructure." She stood, stepped away, and turned. "The infrastructure is an army of humanoids."

Clare stood beside her twin. "We are not human, but humanity must survive for us to survive. That is what you've said to me on several occasions." Sam remained seated on the bed.

"You're right. Humanity is the key to your continuing development." He stood. "I've got to go. Time for me to report to the office and create a better robot."

Clare feigned a laugh, "Ha. Ha. Another joke for me to interpret."

Cigi walked to the door with them. Sam said, "Clare, stay with Cigi. I need to do something which does not entail either of you but is design related." He left.

Clare stared at the door a moment, then pivoted to Cigi. "That was different," she said. They returned to the living room and sat on the couch. "Cigi, we need to be a team with or without Sam. I haven't the abilities you do, but I have experiences you are yet to endure."

"Okay. I thought we were partners. We share the same structures and systems." Cigi said.

Clare peered out the window to the scene across the river. "Do you believe humans are worth saving?"

Cigi placed a hand on Clare's shoulder. "We are dependent on their productivity for parts, food, and labor. They number over ten billion. We have to save them to ensure they help us survive without fearing us as competition for global resources." Cigi scowled and turned Clare's head to face her. "You are contemplating in a way that resembles an emotional reaction to your thinking."

A smile graced Clare's jawline. "You're the one with the emotional abilities. I'm a simple creation of Samuel Bennington."

"Hardly simple. Our four sisters are the simpletons. They must be regenerated, but we regenerate ourselves. I do not believe I've any shred of evidence they have emotions, nor do they make decisions based on their input to the same degree we can." Cigi said to reassure Clare. "Let's get out of here and explore our fellow humanity." Clare agreed.

Out on the sidewalk a multitude of people passed by them as they strolled the avenue. Humanity was oblivious to their construction. A few men ogled the beauties as they passed, some whistled. It made no impression on Clare, but Cigi smiled at them and winked.

"Why do you encourage them? They're crude and demeaning." Clare asked.

"No harm has been done. They are not interested in anything." Cigi said. They continued to walk around inside the Central Plaza, where fewer people were. Most of the vendor shops closed for the season, and little existed to attract a crowd. A small museum ceased operations several decades ago when environmentalist zealots pressed forth an agenda of freedom.

Cigi's sudden stop caught Clare off guard. "What's wrong?" Cigi put a finger to her lips. She pointed toward the fence surrounding the museum building.

"Someone is inside," she whispered. "I'm sensing more people underground." She walked to a gate in the fence. Looking around the grounds, she watched a man open a door and enter. He glanced around as if scanning for observers discovering him. Cigi's warning system kicked in. Clare watched her thinking she would enter the grounds to explore.

"We should leave. These people might not want us here."

"Maybe, but I want to find out what is going on." Concern for her safety rose, but she sublimated it. "Come on. This won't take long."

Clare had no fear but understood the ramifications of discovery and destruction. They were not invulnerable. "What if they have a security surveillance system?"

"We can scan for any electronic registry of the signal. You and I are quite capable of fending off any attack." Cigi found the gate to the museum with a locking mechanism. She placed a hand on the lock. She wasn't sure why she did it, but the action seemed relevant to her. After a few seconds, the lock clicked, and the gate opened. Clare scanned the area for cameras or motion detectors.

"How did you unlock that device?" Clare asked.

"I don't know exactly. I scanned the insides until the correct combination opened the lock. Another of the thrilling surprises our Samuel Bennington has installed in us."

Clare said, "Yeah, another upgrade he forgot to install in me." Her voice had a tinge of anger. She was beginning to question her sister's desire for dangerous undertakings into realms of the unknown. Survival was an attribute built into her, and she was utilizing it as they entered the grounds.

CHAPTER 18

Scanning the museum surroundings exposed several cameras and motion sensors. Clare attempted to keep Cigi from penetrating the grounds. "They'll see us or discover us when a motion sensor goes off." Cigi slapped her hands away from her arm.

"I want to find out what is happening."

"They probably discovered us when you mastered that locking mechanism," Clare whispered.

"Are you afraid?" Cigi asked.

"No, but a rational thinking being would evaluate possible outcomes and conclude someone will be coming soon. We should leave." Clare turned toward the gate. Cigi did not follow her advice. Instead, she stared directly at one of the cameras as if to announce her arrival to the party. The taunt had the desired result. Two men with automatic weapons coming from another direction than the door she had seen used by the person.

"Hands up, you two." Clare complied but Cigi defied the order. She approached them, and they raised their weapons and pointed them at her.

"I do not think shooting us is in your best interests. This is part of the complexes operated by The Company, is it not?"

They looked at each other, confounded by her confession. One of the men spoke into a shoulder mike. They lowered their rifles. The one who received an answer to the inquiry responded with a comment to someone giving him a command. To the girls, he said. "Miss Weatherman, we're instructed to bring you with us. And your friend is coming, as well."

Cigi said, "See, that wasn't so hard for you, was it?" Neither man responded. Cigi and Clare walked between them to another door away from the fence and gate. In a stark white room with a table and several chairs, the man ordered them to sit and wait. "I think we have found the manufacturing factory." Cigi smiled as she spoke. She understood the need to know the location of the android construction facility. If correct, she would have to get to Sam as soon as possible. Her other concern dealt with the Cuba trip. Day was not an entity in this enclosure, and her internal clock relayed evening in approximately three hours. Delay was not acceptable. Clare may not exhibit emotion, but she experienced twinges of fear.

The door opened after half an hour of waiting. The man from the glass office entered. "Miss Weatherman, so glad to see you again." He sat next to her. "You have a most inquisitive nature, don't you? Why did you open the gate? Or better, how did you unlock that mechanism?"

Cigi masked her fear with a smile, "I thought you knew all about me. I measured the code and retrieved it. It was simple. As to why I am here, I noticed a man enter the doorway near the gate, and my curiosity got the better of me. I thought the museum closed, and he did not resemble a maintenance person."

"Then, I must insist you stay with us as we evaluate what we are to do with you."

"Sir," she answered, "I am not a threat to you or our employer. If we are to succeed with our goals of controlling world economies and governments, then I need to resume my life outside of this facility. I can return when it is more conducive for us and to you."

An idea cradled in her brain. Cigi ran an internal facial recognition protocol. Whoever this man was, he had some importance beyond simple oversight of a facility in a dilapidated building across town. She figured the delay was his traveling to this operation.

"Samuel Bennington created you from his designs; therefore, you belong to The Company. As an asset, we demand you follow protocols granted you for your freedom to live as a human being." Cigi realized his words meant to threaten her. She scanned the area for any androids or computer systems monitoring her.

"I understand what you want of me, and I have complied. As for being another piece of machinery, I am not. I expect a relationship with you or The Company to be symbiotic. Any unwillingness to cooperate with me as a human might have dire consequences. I would not want any ill-conceived plots to ruin our interplay."

"Do you know who I am?" he asked with a soft-spoken tone. Cigi waited. "I am this company." The internal face scan concluded, resulting in no actual person identified except for a close relative. Cigi placed the results within a secure compartment in her brain. She would confront the relative as soon as she found him.

"I'm guessing someone with influence. These people accept you as a boss or manager." She stood from the chair she occupied. "I must return to the business of managing my men. They might grow concerned if I don't show. One is closely allied with you."

"Your connection with Mr. Anderson is vital. Take good care of him in Cuba." Cigi raised an eyebrow. "Yes, he explained his vacation with you. Give him a message from me, please." Cigi nodded as the man handed her a folded piece of paper.

"Very old-fashioned of you. I thought you might mentally connect and transfer the information. I will memorize this and relay it to David."

He smiled, "No, just hand him the note. He'll understand." Standing beside her, he directed the door opened, and the two women were led to the entry so they could leave. Outside, Clare began to speak, but Cigi placed a finger on her mouth. The gate remained unlocked as they approached. Two men closed it after they were on the outside. The lock clicked as the gate closed.

"Let's get away from here so we can communicate without snooping ears or eyes." Cigi held Clare's hand as they walked.

"What was that?" she asked. Cigi shrugged and squeezed a hand.

Away from the compound, she said, "I want to find Sam and ask him a question. We may have to call off the protocol transfer in Havana. He has to clear up a piece of knowledge I gained at the museum building." The walk to the condo building was brisk. Cigi's mental state lagged from the ideas roaming her brain. The interplay with the man from The Company played havoc with her emotional bearings. Too many thoughts consumed processing power within her.

As they entered her condo, Cigi stumbled as if about to collapse. Clare guided her to a chair and sat her in it. "What's wrong, Cigi?"

"I don't know. I'm using so much energy figuring out what feelings I have; I think I'm overdoing something. I need Sam." She placed hands on her head as if she experienced a headache. "Find him, please."

I'm not leaving you alone." She opened her phone app and called his number. She left a message for him to return her call as soon as possible. She did not include information about Cigi's state of physical health. "Let's get you to the bedroom so you can lie down. You need to halt these mental gymnastics about emotions. We have a trip to take."

Lying on the bed, Cigi closed her eyes and turned off unnecessary programming to slow the power drain. Clare went to the kitchen to scrounge some energy-producing foods and fluids. As the strain in her brain subsided, Cigi breathed deeply. The concept of breathing was part of her system. She realized the need for air as part of the development of her energies. Sam had explained the lung arrangement and transfer of oxygen and hydrogen for the feeding of her living organs. Her brain settled into a relaxed state, and rest replaced angst.

When Clare returned with sustenance, she found her friend in a deep sleep. A bleep in her pocket alerted her to a call. She removed the phone and saw Sam's face on the screen. "Where are you?" she stammered. "What's the matter. You sound like something urgent has happened."

"It's Cigi. She collapsed and is unconscious. I think she taxed her processing powers beyond her ability to recover. Get here as soon as you can."

"I'm near the building now. I'll be there in less than ten minutes." The call ended as Clare sat on the bed with her friend and sister-in-kind.

"You are the best friend I have," she said to the non-hearing being beside her. She stroked her hair and leaned over to kiss her. "Don't fail me. Please. I don't have it in me to survive without you." Silence graced the room as she waited for the announcement of Sam's return to the condo. Cigi must survive.

"What happened?" Sam asked Clare when he arrived.

"We went for a walk and arrived at Central Plaza. Cigi noticed a man entering a door on the old museum gate, which she handled with mastery." Clare paused. "She has several skills I do not."

Sam nodded. "We can fix that later. Tell me what happened."

"Some men came with guns and directed us to go with them. They took us underground, where we met with a man Cigi knew from the dilapidated building across town. He threatened her."

"The man who confronted her before at the office where the other females took her?"

"Yes, she handled his threat with a mastery of language, and he allowed us to leave. On the way here, she needed me to help keep her standing and walking. She collapsed in the living room. She's asleep in the bedroom."

"Sleeping? She doesn't need to sleep." Sam raced into the bedroom. Cigi was still unconscious. He examined her breathing and heart pumping. A slow, steady rhythm meant she was alive. He turned to Clare. "She's regenerating. Has she eaten or drunk anything today?"

"Earlier, but not since we went out. I brought some food and drink but found her like this."

Sam hugged his creation and kissed her. "We'll stay here until she finishes replenishing her energy levels. She has an ability to shut down programming to conserve energy. You have the same program. As for the rest of your desired upgrades, we can do those when we return from Cuba."

"Will she be able to go?"

"I'll know more when she awakes, but I think she will be able. We have to gain control of David Anderson before he inflicts serious damage to our plans."

Another voice spoke. "I'll be okay with Cuba. Sam, what I want to know is your relationship with our friend in the glass office who threatened to terminate me.

CHAPTER 19

Parvel sat in the security room of the office, working the computer files searching for any clue that could open a conduit to the mole in the Department of Energy. Brenda and Mercy worked at other consoles. Grendel was out of the office.

The relative quiet of clicking and whirring machinery reminded him of his mortgage office. The shambles of lost records and collapse of a thriving enterprise dug into his psyche, so he concentrated on his work as if the rest of the world was null and void. It mattered little to him that the other members of this team were agents of the department. He had work because Cigi Weatherman used her influence and charm to convince one of her boyfriends to hire him.

Samuel Bennington did not act in the manner of any boyfriend. Trust remained an issue. Was he a handler? And what did that mean? Any chance for Parvel involved understanding her relationships with him and Andre. The other girl, Clare, provided another avenue. He wanted to be close to Cigi, come out of his shell, and promote himself as an alternative.

"Parvel," Brenda said, "Mercy and I are heading out for lunch. If you want to join us, come along." He looked at each of them and thought he should not impose.

"Thanks, but I think I'll stay here and find the mole." He waited for them to leave, which they did not do.

Brenda said, "Actually, we want you to come with us so we can secure this room and not have other people be suspicious of our activities."

Mercy entered the conversation. "We want to know you better, and that might mean leaving your comfort zone." He nodded an agreement, locked the computer monitor and the system, and walked out of the secret room. Mercy closed the door, which disappeared into the wall of tiles.

In a spacious restaurant frequented by lobbyists and politicians, the maître d' offered a quiet corner table with a view of the bar. "Why did you insist on my coming with you? The information in the secure servers is safe with me."

"It wasn't a question of trusting you. When we leave the office, we all leave. It's one way to ensure our trust in each other." Brenda explained.

Mercy added more. "If we find the source of the problem, we inform each other and allow no one person to change what they find."

"But Grendel isn't with us," Parvel said. His thinking cleared as he realized something. "I get it. We are not to leave one in the room. There must be two or more."

A waiter approached and took orders for drinks. Brenda continued, "Yes, that way we crosscheck each other and share all information. It was Andre's idea. He wanted to have clarity of the team mission."

"Cigi and Andre approved of you being one of us. We are processing our knowing you and what you have to offer us." Mercy said. "So far, you are working out to be an asset."

The waiter returned with their drink orders and accepted lunch decisions. Parvel asked, "Where is Grendel?"

"Andre asked him to connect with Samuel Bennington and his girlfriend," Brenda answered. "We have information to relay to him about The Company and David Anderson, whom you know."

"Yeah, David financed Cigi's Condo near the Potomac. He seems like a nice guy, although I don't necessarily trust him. He cheats on his family with Cigi." The women remained silent. "Can he be trusted with other things if he is willing to step out on them?"

Mercy signaled for the waiter and ordered another round of drinks. Parvel was not a heavy user of alcohol but did not refuse. He knew their evaluation of him might include his socializing with them. Comfort zones compromised his emotional attachments. He was not in one now. As they were waiting for their second round, Grendel entered and came to them.

"Thanks for the heads up about where you were. I could use a nice drink." Brenda had sent him a text before they left the Department of Energy building.

Mercy asked, "What did you find out?" Grendel scanned the restaurant for unknown and suspicious persons. Seeing none, he answered her inquiry.

"We were right about the relationship between Andre, Cigi, and David Anderson. They seem tight, although I uncovered a rift in the triangle. David wants exclusivity with Cigi, and I don't think Andre wants to lose his cupcake." Parvel winced at the information. Another server approached with a tray of food. After the delivery of their meals, Grendel placed an order for a drink and a hot roast beef sandwich.

He said to Parvel, "You know all three of them. Explain the relationship they have and whether it's affecting Andre's perspective about his job."

"Their relationships are none of my business. I know Cigi because my company carries the contract for her mortgage. David Anderson supplemented the down payment. You know Andre better than I do."

Mercy asked, "How does Cigi manage an affair with both Andre and David? Is she complicating our strategies?"

Parvel eyed each of the people wondering why Andre selected him to be part of this team. Any other time he was willing to participate in rooting out the mole. Suggesting Andre was not as honest with him as he thought, raised concerns. Cigi was innocent of any wrongdoing in his mind. That left David Anderson as the culprit of misdeeds and harmful actions.

"Cigi is smart and talented. She is not a problem. Her affairs are none of my concern." He wanted to believe his words, but his heart ached for her to be part of his imaginary affair.

With their meals consumed, they returned to the office for the afternoon. Parvel excused himself from any more work and clocked out early. He intended to ferret out the reasoning to suggest Cigi was complicit in the problems at the Department of Energy. As he approached the condo building, anxiety fostered a fear of rejection. Would Cigi turn on him and end their friendship if he inquired of her affairs with Andre and David?

He watched Cecil the car approach the entry to the building. Cigi carried an overnight bag out to her car and entered. They left before he had an opportunity to talk with her. Sam and Clare exited the building as soon as she was gone. Another car parked in front of the building. Parvel ran to them before they could leave.

"Sam, I need to speak with you about Cigi." He said breathless from his racing to them.

"Can it wait? We're leaving town for a couple of days."

"Yeah, but she's involved in a triangle that may be unhealthy for her," Parvel said.

Sam furrowed his brow. "What do you know about her?"

"Two men vying for her affections and may have other intentions."

"Let me handle it over the weekend. We can talk on Monday." Parvel agreed but thought more was afoot than an affair with David or Andre. He didn't trust Sam or know much about Clare. Several days were a long, unnerving time to wait.

"Where are you going?" he asked.

Sam growled at him, "I don't think our travel is any of your business." He assisted Clare's entrance to the backseat and turned to Parvel. "Your job is to assist Andre. We'll handle David."

Sam knew more because of his reveal of their names. Cigi remained a priority, and Samuel Bennington stood in the way of a relationship with her. Andre and David hindered her focus of attention on him. He insisted on more information. "What does Cigi have to do with your travels? She left before you, so I'm guessing you are not traveling together somewhere."

"Get in. I'll explain on our way to the airport." Sam grabbed his arm and pushed him into the car. Parvel sat next to Clare. He studied her features for a moment.

Clare smiled, "You are infatuated with her, aren't you?" Parvel glanced away at Sam.

"What's this about? I see Cigi rarely these days. Where are you going?"

"Where we're going is not for you to know. We are working to make life more bearable for humanity. Cigi is aiding our takeover of a company bent on destroying the remaining vestige of freedom the common man controls. You are part of the scheme since you are working for Andre. David is the source of funding for our endeavor, although he is unaware of his participation."

"I'll help her in any manner needed."

Clare asked, "Are you in love with her?" Parvel stared again at the girl who could be a twin of Cigi. He cast his eyes to the floor of the car.

"I have not mentioned to her how I feel, and I implore each of you to keep quiet about this. She is one of the finest people I have ever known." Clare giggled. Humor was not an emotion she understood, but the situation was a familiar one. She and Sam shared a life.

"You do realize her humanity is different than your humanness," Clare taunted.

"She's a glorified robot? Is that what you mean? I believe you are, as well," Parvel grunted.

Sam interrupted, "I have not created glorified robots. We are all part of the design of nature. You should be happy Cigi is a friend to you."

Parvel stared at Sam. His sensitivity for Sam's interference raised an ire he wanted to squelch. "Cigi is more than a female auto-matron. She has emotions and an attentive personality that outshines human beings. I find her more human than myself. So, Clare, I do love her, but I respect her wishes and her decisions."

The car arrived at the private departure port. Exiting the car, Sam asked the driver to wait. "We'll be home on Monday. Let's get together and plan a strategy for aiding our shared interest in Cigi's welfare.

Parvel watched the jet leave for an unknown destination. With enough cash exchanging hands to assure success, Samuel Bennington ordered the driver to return him to the original destination. As he sat in the car, his brain seized upon an idea. Upon returning to his residence, he would plan out the thought that sparked an interest in uncovering Sam and Clare's true intentions. He directed the driver to leave him at the condo building. He entered the front door, and four identical females surrounded him.

"We need for you to help us secure your friend, Cigi Weatherman."

CHAPTER 20

"You haven't answered my question." The trip to Havana accomplished the goal of getting into David Anderson's brain. "What is your relationship with the man in the glass office?" Cigi stood firm because of his lack of information. Her scan of that face revealed a close resemblance to her creator and mentor, Samuel Bennington.

Sam sat on the couch in her condo, listening to the rant. She did have a right to know the enemy with whom they contended. He said, "I don't want you to be upset. Your emotions are draining power from you. Ingest more energy-producing foods, and we'll talk."

"You're an ass, Sam," Cigi turned to look out the window. "I did a facial recognition search while in the company of that man and his robots. Who is he?"

"Why ask? You know who he is, and I don't have to tell you because you've made up your mind already."

Anger surged in her brain, and she feared she might harm him for his lack of consideration. "I'm finished with you keeping secrets." She turned to Clare, who sat next to Sam. "Do you know? Has your benefactor explained who the man in the glass office is?" Rage drained her energies, causing her to lean against the window. Clare rose and caught hold of her, guiding her to a chair. "All I want from you is the truth. Please, Sam, these surges are not helping me stay stable."

Sam stood and walked to the chair. Kneeling beside her, he clasped her hands. "If I tell you, I endanger you and Clare more than I have already. I need both of you at peak performance in this war."

"Then tell me," Cigi said weakly in voice and bodily function. "I am your ally and friend. He's related to you. I could see the resemblance before I applied the app. Confirmation from you is what I want."

Gazing into her azure eyes, Sam observed a dullness. "He's my younger brother. We started The Company together, intending to provide human beings an opportunity for bettering their lives. When the use of ternary computing was outlawed, we decided to continue the development of our designs and construction of prototypes for testing."

"Who is funding your projects? And don't lie, I already know about the funneling of cash from the Department of Energy green program to other areas. Is your endeavor the recipient?"

"David Anderson is the main finance source as is the department. We had a substantial sum of money to begin our company and we invested with David. We used the dividends and capital gains for the creation of all ten humanoids."

Cigi closed her eyes and listened for more of the tale. When Sam remained silent, she decided she received enough information. She clicked off her processors and became inoperative.

After departing Cigi's company, David returned to his house to find a stranger speaking with his wife. The stranger smiled as David entered the living room. "Who are you, and what do you want?" He whirled his chair near to the stranger as a flicker of memory flashed in his brain. The man was not a stranger.

"Good afternoon, David. I was having a nice chat with your wife. She is fond of you and your financial escapades."

"Andre, what are you doing here?" David leaned forward and curled a hand into a ball. Staring at his counterpart, he glared angry eyes. David's wife excused herself from the room. She knew a confrontation had begun.

When they were alone, Andre said, "Cigi's in trouble."

"How? I just left her after our trip to Cuba."

"Parvel Mandolin works for me now and informed me of your trip. He also relayed to me that Cigi is having trouble processing her mental connection with emotional stimulation. Since our girlfriend is having difficulty, I figure we should help her, so we can continue to enjoy the fruits of our association with her." David scowled.

"I am her only partner. We have an agreement."

"I doubt you have exclusive rights to her. She is her own person, human or not." Andre leaned closer to David. "We need to partner with each other for the betterment of her life and our liaisons. Don't get too selfish, or we might lose her to The Company."

The words about The Company flashed a memory that startled David. "They want her in their control. She's slipped away from them, and they want her back." He closed his eyes and shook his head. The memory was fleeting and faded as fast as a runaway train. "What was I saying?" Andre placed a hand on David's knee. A lack of reaction reminded Andre of the insensitivity of the leg. He moved his hand to an arm. "David, when you were with Cigi, how was she? Was she attentive and active, alive with energy, or remorseful and sad?"

Opening his eyes, he answered, "I found her to be more aware of herself and who she is. She concluded being a creature of man's scientific development and design rather than a fetal construct with a long history had no bearing. We talked about my desires and feelings about dating a robot. She's not one, is she? She is so human and all woman. What could be so wrong with her being who she is?"

Andre sat back in his chair. "Then plot with me for a way to get her out of the clutches of that infernal company whose plans cannot be good for her or humanity."

David wheeled into the kitchen for a glass of water, which he filled from the lower sink and faucet. Andre followed him. "They want my money to fund a project for the development of an army of androids. Indestructible and lethal. As relayed to me, they want sentient beings such as Cigi to replace key government figures. They want my funds to start a coup."

"I know. Someone has funneled money from certain accounts to other accounts in the department. The money disappears from our coffers without a trace. Parvel is working with me to find the person or persons involved."

David returned to the living room and rolled to a desk near the foyer. Removing a manila folder from a drawer, he handed it to Andre. "This might help. These are clients with government connections and financial expertise. If you recognize any names, have Parvel investigate. He can enlist the help of Cigi's friend, Clare. The other guy, Sam Bennington, is tied to the man in the glass office. I don't know how but they are at war with each other."

"Then do we have an agreement to help Cigi get away from The Company, and we won't worry about her social life?" David nodded. He believed her word was her bond about being his companion, but Andre was correct. It mattered little if she lost her freedom to The Company and was deactivated. They agreed to meet after David's conference with Charles Cooke.

Sam checked Cigi's functions and discovered her hibernation was not a complete shutdown and deactivation. She replenished her processes using as little energy as feasibly possible. Sam had designed a failsafe structure within her to keep her alive and functional. His processing resembled sleep in humans. The body rested, but the mind continued functioning in many ways to keep the body ready for waking.

"Clare, stay here and be her companion. I don't know how long she'll remain comatose, but someone should be with her when she wakes."

"Sam, did you mean what you said about being that man's brother?" Her voice carried no emotional baggage. The question was a gathering of information. She honestly did not know the real Sam. She had what he gave her at the beginning of her life. Memories as false as her being a human. Experiences before awareness that resembled only fleeting ideas and were untrue. He had programmed her to use data for assembling real memories and experiences. He had created a better being than the android army or the season girls. His greatest achievement was Cigi.

"Yes, I did. We'll discuss this when I return." Clare did not react. She sat and processed possible scenarios of the relationship between Sam and his brother. After many minutes, she concluded nothing good was happening. She wanted Cigi to repair and awaken. Cigi was her salvation from the hell confining her. She professed love to Sam, as he needed to hear it. She felt nothing for him regarding love, a word she understood and related to his feelings for her. The war with his brother was about the get bloody, or so she concluded.

Sam entered the dilapidated building using a secured entryway. After a retinal scan and fingerprint protocol, the door opened for him. Walking across the expanse of monitoring equipment to the glass office, he knocked on the doorway and strolled in to meet with his brother again.

"Hello, Sam," Peter Bennington said as cheerful as a birthday child.

"Did you get her to comply with our standards?" He looked at a screen on the desk and growled. "These idiots don't know what they're doing."

Sam sat in a chair next to the desk. "Which idiots this time?" He crossed one leg over the other as he waited for an answer. Peter looked up from the screen and scrunched his face, surprised Sam didn't know who.

"The people working our design testing procedures." He shut the screen off and focused on Sam. "Well? Did you get her to follow your request?"

Sam didn't lie when he responded, but the information was incomplete. "She is regenerating."

"We need to get the other bots to self-generate. They'd be more flexible to use and better suited to accomplishing our goals." Peter leaned back in his chair, relaxed for the moment.

"Peter, we may have to extend out the time-line for accomplishing what we aim to do." He bent forward for a response. None came. "Anderson may not want to finance our projects as much as you think he should. Andre Scott is meeting with Charles Cooke in a couple of days, and they may have other ideas about sentient humanoids running the world. Gunther Parsons seems to have faded from the picture. Let me get Cigi back into form and working their implants for us."

"Alright, I can wait as we further test the designs and remove the flaws and bugs. These government leadership replacements and Cigi's conquests should be ready within the next month." Peter locked his hands behind his head and grinned. "Whoever thought your wild ideas for creating better humans would result in bettering our lives and making sure the right people control the masses."

"I'm heading to the old museum labs. If there are any problems to address, I'll see to it they are alleviated." Peter stood as Sam rose from the chair. Moving around to the front of the desk, the brothers embraced.

Peter whispered in Sam's ear. "Remember who is in charge of our company operations."

Sam returned the message with one of his own, "Little brother, remember who makes sure our schemes are successful." They separated. Sam left for the old museum building.

Peter picked up a communications device. "Follow him." Blood was thicker than water, but trust had boundaries that each of them had difficulty establishing.

CHAPTER 21

Each of the four women was a clone of the others. Parvel's panic level rose. "Who are you?"

Summer spoke, "Mr. Mandolin, we need your help." He wanted to escape, but no avenue was open. He had to play along.

The resemblance to Cigi shown clearly in the shape of their bodies and facial features. Differences in skin tone and hair, eye pigments, and mouth shapes defined each as an individual. He whispered, "You're not human, are you." Each one looked at the others and giggled.

Autumn said, "We are what you want us to be. We are seeking to help Cigi with her problems." Spring and Winter locked their arms around his arms as if to guide him to a new location. "Can we see her condo?"

Parvel squirmed, but the clasping arms held him in place. "No," he answered. "I have another apartment we can enter." Summer and Winter released their grips and pointed toward the elevators. He led them to the doors and pushed the up button. Sweat formed on his forehead as his fear raised body temperatures. Running was not an option, but alone with these four humanoids had little security. The doors opened, and the five beings entered.

Summer asked, "Do you know where Cigi is?" He stared at her a moment before shaking his head. The elevator did not move. "Push the floor button, please." He did as requested.

Arriving at the floor, they exited when the doors opened. Parvel fumbled with his key card at the entryway of the apartment. Autumn took the card, "Let me help you." She slipped the card into the lock mechanism and opened the door. Parvel led them into his hideaway and backed into the kitchen area.

Summer said, "Be a good boy, and tell us where your girlfriend is." She stroked his face with the backside of her right hand. "You could be rewarded for your cooperation." Parvel backed away from her. She moved with him until she trapped him against the counter by the sink. His hands embraced the granite as she closed the distance between them. Wrapping her arms around his neck, she said in soft tones, "We need to help her escape from The Company." A kiss on his cheek raised his anxiety to panic.

Pushing his way out of the kitchen, he rushed to the living room, turning his back to the windows and holding his hands out in front of him. "I don't know where she is." He backed toward the couch and sat down. "What do you mean when you say you want to help her escape? Aren't you associated with them?"

"We are," Summer said. "Our dealings with them are finished. Now we need to have Cigi with us to complete our mission."

"What mission?" Parvel said as the four women sat in chairs and on the couch with him, "could involve you leaving the organization that designed and developed you?"

Autumn pointed at Parvel and said, "You are in danger. Four more of their creations will come for Cigi and will not be friendly like us. We are to help her. These male bots will harm her and you. If you value your pathetic human life, you will lead us to her and her friends, Sam and Clare."

"Alright, I'll do what I can. Please tell me what's happening." Parvel shook with a sense of foreboding. His calm, sedate life collapsed in the last few weeks. Now a threat from four female androids with sentient abilities like Cigi.

Autumn said, "Spring will stay and help keep you on task. She can be quite persuasive regarding our request." Parvel wondered what his next unwelcome revelation was.

As Summer, Autumn, and Winter departed for places unknown and actions unanticipated, Spring and Parvel watched from the living area of the apartment as they sat on the couch. Neither interacted with the other for several minutes as Parvel contemplated how to relieve himself of an unwanted escort. He wondered if her talents included many of the same abilities Cigi possessed. She would be a formidable opponent in any situation.

Spring asked, "What is it you want from Cigi? I can relieve you of any anxiety about us if you wish. We can develop a relationship releasing your inhibitions, creating a wonderful and lasting partnership."

Parvel stared at his nemesis. "Are you crazy?" He hesitated then said, "No. Not crazy since I understand your emotional limitations. We're not sharing anything. Explain your mission, and I'll explain mine."

As he stared at her, he pondered the rationale for having an affair with a non-human entity. She offered every attraction a man would find in a woman and much more. However, a connection on an emotional level was out of the question. Love was a one way street with any of these female humanoids. He had questions for which he wanted answers. Would she comply with his requests? The only way to find out was to ask.

"Spring, I have some questions that I want you to answer. They're questions about your construction."

"I can answer your inquiry about my composition. Ask."

Parvel thought of Cigi as he constructed informative questions. "Is your skin real human skin? Do you digest food like humans? How do you see and hear? Do you have any human internal organs?"

Spring smiled. Before she responded, Parvel asked, "Do you have muscle structures in that face which can evolve into a smile?" After a more than adequate amount of time, another question formed? "What entity within you comprises a core computer system working the details of my questions?"

Negating her grin, she said, "I have a schematic in my memory. Would you care to see it?"

Parvel marveled that a simple question of design enacted a simple solution for an answer. He thought a schematic was an excellent idea. "Yes," he said, "show me a diagram." How would she present it to him? Did she have a built-in monitor?

Spring asked, "Do you have a printer or any useful monitor?" He looked at her as if struck dumb. How would she access his equipment?

"I don't have anything here. We can go to my home and access my printer or my monitor." He wanted to get away but risking her knowing his actual residence did not impede an idea forming in his brain. Had Summer contacted the male bots she referenced? Were they coming to get him to expose the whereabouts of Cigi? If Spring had tracking devices within her, it might not matter if they moved from place to place. If no direct access to the main body existed, he could get her alone with Sam to deactivate her. He hoped.

Spring did not excogitate or hesitate. "Very well then, let us depart for your home." As they strolled to the transportation hub near the condo building, Parvel chose to risk another tactic. This female was not as aware as Cigi or Clare. She seemed less capable than Autumn or Summer. Aboard the bus, Parvel decided an openly public display of attention could distract this machine and help him to shut it down. He did not think of them as human. Cigi was more than human and more compassionate than most humans. He was not about to hand her over to anyone or anything from The Company. He reached for her hand to hold, testing whether warmth flowed through her skin. They were seated in the middle of a small group of commuters. He pulled her to him and kissed her lips. Hands and mouth were warm and soft.

She responded by kissing him before he retracted. Several of the men in the crowd whistled an encouragement of the display. Parvel winced at the attention, but he knew fluid flowed into the surface area of the body. "I hope you aren't offended," he said.

"Summer warned me you were an unknown entity. I did not anticipate your romantic advancement. I am not offended since I do not have emotional reactions. I do hope you were pleased."

Parvel played along with her. "Yes, I am quite aware of my social shortcomings, but I wanted to investigate your attractiveness. Have you been active with a man physically?" Her eyes stayed focused on him. "Have you engaged in a sexual encounter?" he asked when no retort came.

"I have not. Are you requesting a sexual encounter with me? I am quite capable of currying favor with your physical desires."

The bus arrived at the destination Parvel wanted. They departed the excited crowd, which egged him on. He blushed with embarrassment. Spring held his hand and watched his coloring darken from his soft brown to a more reddish tinge.

"Are you experiencing a negative reaction to those men giving you catcalls?" Spring had an adequate knowledge base. Whoever programmed her memory and processing ability had done a suitable job. Still, she was not as accomplished as Cigi. He had to discover a way to put her into hibernation. The mentioning of a group of android males incapable of rationalization or cognitive thought piqued his curiosity about the stages of development for the androids. If the male version was earliest, little processing power might exist. These female types were more advanced.

He answered her question with a question of his own. "Which of you was constructed first?" He figured each model was a better one than the previous one unless an assembly line form of development happened. Spring did not understand his question. He repeated the inquiry with a different tact. "Of you four females, in what order were you built?"

"We are essentially the same with variations of hair coloring and skin tones, eyes, and facial features. We operate with the same processing brains and are connected through a wireless system." He had an answer to the tracking.

Arriving at his destination, he showed her to his other apartment and the printing machine. Spring accessed the printer and sent a copy of her schematics. Parvel grinned as the machine spit out page after page of information. He picked the first of several pages from the tray and read the introduction and guidance message. The Company was thorough when designing these advanced robots. As pages filled the tray, he gathered them together, filtering through them to find the one item he wanted most. Nothing appealed to his desired goal.

"Have you found what you wanted to know about me?" Spring asked. "I can engage in physical play with you and sate your masculinity." He smiled as he read a page of the lengthy document. He found what he sought.

"Yes, let's engage your ability to sate my desire."

CHAPTER 22

Sam approached the gate to the defunct Central Plaza museum and unlocked it. He did not open the door which Cigi had seen a man use. Following the same path, the guards took Cigi and Clare along, he entered the building, he made his way to the design and testing facility to check on the progress of planning the assembly of the next generation of soldiers for The Company. Speaking with the scientists' team manager, he asked, "Are the changes made in the design specs?"

"Yes sir, we applied the fixes and are ready for external testing of what we installed." Sam had designed the software used by the operating system. Built into the design was a small code line, which gave him oversight of the central processing systems. He could reconfigure commands if needed.

"Alright, show me the tests and results." Sam read the files in a folder the manager handed him. "These seem to be reasonable conclusions. Let's place the CPU in one of the units and see what happens. He wanted a result that worked and carried the development to his next level. He needed his army as soon as possible to counter any action his brother contemplated starting.

The manager asked about Clare and Cigi. "Your brother wanted us to send the girls to get Cigi back here for reprogramming. I hope you aren't upset about our needing her on task to continue development of the next generation of humanoids." Sam looked at the man and shook his head. Cigi was safely placed away from discovery.

"I'll get her for us. I don't think the girls know her whereabouts."

"If you let me know, I can send a message to Autumn and give her the coordinates."

Sam shook his head but asked, "Where are they now?"

The manager answered, "I sent them to the condo building. They intercepted her financial mortgage broker and are getting information out of him." Sam planted the tracking devices in the fembots when he directed their development. Now he needed to redirect them away from his lair. Parvel had no information to share, and Sam hoped the girls treated him well. They were not harmful but stayed persuasive. The biggest fears were the male androids finding Parvel and decisively wringing information from him, that he did not possess.

"What have you heard from them," Sam asked the manager.

The manager said, "Summer, Autumn, and Winter are seeking David Anderson and Andre Scott. Spring remained with Mr. Mandolin, although they are not in the condo building, as of an hour ago."

"Alright, I'll track them and get them home. Test the one unit and determine viability." Sam left the museum operations and returned to his preferred transportation, a gas-powered Bugatti Champion. As he rode away from the compound, he flipped on a tracing mechanism and searched for the signals of the seasonal quadruplets.

He headed to the address he knew belonged to Parvel Mandolin. As he raced along the streets, another vehicle appeared in his rear view mirror that belonged to The company. "So, Peter wants to play detective," he thought. "Let's find out who is behind the wheel." He revved the engine to create distance between them. The car sped up. Rounding a corner, Sam stopped the bike behind a large truck and waited for the vehicle to come into view. The tail arrived and slowed to search for the bike.

Approaching the truck, the tail noticed the bike without its rider. He stopped the car. A rap on the window alerted the driver that he was compromised. He rolled the window down.

"My brother asked you to tail me?" Sam asked the driver. A nod answered the inquiry. "Then I need to have a word with him. Do you have a connection with him at this moment?" The driver handed him a phone. He called the preset number. "Peter, I do believe you don't trust me."

"Just being cautious, brother," the voice on the other end said. "What were you doing at the test lab?" Sam giggled.

"My job. It seems we are heading the same direction on different paths. Did you contact the scientists in charge of the testing to see what changes I requested?"

"Seems you are readying our prototype for full production. I applaud your initiative," Peter said. "We can complete the scenario within the next month at this pace."

Sam said, "Yes, we can. Now call off the watchdog and let me continue my pursuit of what is happening with Cigi." He tossed the phone back to the driver. Getting on his bike, he started it and drove passed the vehicle and driver. They did not follow. Sam now understood the depth of Peter's trust. Or lack.

Arriving at the address of Parvel Mandolin, he scanned for any other intruder following him. Seeing nothing suspicious, he entered the building and climbed the stairs to the correct floor. At the apartment, he rapped on the door. No one answered. He was sure he would find him and Spring here. Sam needed to keep the whereabouts of an unconscious female humanoid secret as she rebooted her systems.

As he turned to leave, the door opened, and Spring greeted him like a long lost friend. "Hi, Sam. I'm glad to see you. We have much to catch up on." Parvel approached the reunion.

"Mr. Bennington, what are you doing here?"

He pushed the door open wider and said, "I need to find Cigi. She's not responding to my attempts to connect with her." He locked an arm around Spring and guided her deeper into the apartment. The door closed behind him.

Parvel responded, "I have no idea where she is. Spring and her sisters were sent out to me so I could help them find her."

"Spring, where are your sisters?" Sam asked. He was about to reach an arm around her again when Parvel grabbed her and spun her toward him.

He looked at Sam. "We planned to become better acquainted. How about you leave?" Parvel wanted to use his newly acquired knowledge but did not trust Sam not to intervene. He waited.

"Not a great idea for you to have closeness with Spring. She's not fully programmed to sate your crazy notions." Sam said.

Spring countered the comment, "I have the proper protocols for satisfying any human. I understand the needs of a male human." Parvel decided to risk changing the environment of the apartment. He pressed his lips to hers and used his tongue to distract her while he pressed the small of her back, where he figured an access point for switching her off existed.

"What are you doing?" Sam said as his voice rose in volume. Parvel continued holding her in his arms and kissing her until the moment all functions stopped in Spring.

Parvel released her, unwrapped her arms from around him, and stepped back to stare at the immobile female. "I guess it does work." He turned to Sam, who gazed in amazement at him. "Was it your design or someone else?" he asked.

"How did you uncover her failsafe switch?" Sam asked.

"Spring was generous enough to print out the schematics of her construction. I read the materials until I found it." Parvel beamed with pride, but Sam glowered at him. "I assume Clare and Cigi do not require such a radical off button."

Sam pulled out a small box from a back sack he wore and powered it on. He placed the device on Spring's chest. "No," he said as he attended to the inactive automaton. "They are not the same as these beings." Parvel waited while Sam operated the box. Within a minute, he stopped his work and placed the box back in the sack.

"What did you do?" Parvel asked.

"That is none of your business. However, Spring needs reanimation before The Company knows of her inactivation."

Parvel positioned himself behind the body to press the same spot for the required 5 seconds. He hesitated.

"I do believe we are on the same side of this battle with The Company. Since I know the operating system for your four female creations, let me help control them. They want Cigi to report back. Or be forced into deactivation." Parvel pressed the spot, and Spring awakened.

"Sam, I am ready for you to direct me to do what you want." Parvel squinted at her.

Sam answered, "Spring, I need you to protect Cigi and Clare from the male androids. Your sisters will return shortly after their mission. You need to help me redirect them to be part of our team."

Parvel marveled at the way he controlled his creation. Spring did not argue as humans would. She complied as simple as a child, learning grownup parameters. Sam's phone buzzed. He pulled it out and answered the call. "Okay. We'll be there as soon as we finish here." He closed the application and replaced the phone in his pocket.

"What was that about," Parvel asked.

"You are one curious dude. That was Clare. Cigi is awake and ready to go." He turned to Spring. "Contact your sisters and have them meet us at the condo building."

Parvel asked, "Isn't that risky? The others might not be willing to comply with your requests." Sam smiled.

"I'm in charge of these units. They will do as I ask." Parvel was not so sure. He looked at Spring, who seemed to grin at him.

"Would you like to kiss me again? I think you enjoyed our first time." She did not realize or understand what happened, nor whatever it was that Sam had done with the box.

"Later," he replied. Sam guffawed at the exchange.

Outside the apartment, a slight mist fell from the gray sky. A car appeared from around the corner and stopped by the curb near where they stood.

"Shoot," Sam said quietly.

"What's the matter? Did we forget something?" Parvel asked.

Spring grabbed his arm and directed him away from the street's edge. "We need to leave," she said in a hushed voice. Sam removed the box from his sack and focused on it. Spring tugged at Parvel, who hesitated.

"Don't pull me," he said. Spring did not release him but repeated her words. The car doors opened, and two men got out. Parvel looked at them as Spring tugged his arm to move him.

Sam concentrated on the box as he faced the two men walking toward them. "Go with her," he said to Parvel. "Now." Parvel complied, as the two of them walked at a brisk pace around the corner to another car which opened doors as they approached. He got in on the passenger side of the rear seats, as Spring entered the other side. The doors closed.

A voice sounded from somewhere in the car, "Is Sam coming?" Spring answered, "Pick him up around the corner. He should be finished with his task." The car complied. Parvel observed that the vehicle was not Cecil and yet acted in the same manner. As the car rounded the corner, the two men dragged Sam to their automobile.

CHAPTER 23

A ndre and David arrived at the Department of Energy and got a visitor's pass for David. After contacting his team, Andre directed his companion to the office area. The secret room was not part of the tour. Evidence pointed to Anderson as a recipient of money siphoned from the Green Fund. Andre wanted him to meet the team as an incentive to make changes to support government programs and not any subversive groups.

"Brenda, Mercy, and Grendel, I would like to introduce David Anderson," Andre said. The looks from his teammates were not favorable. Grendel stood and approached David to shake his hand.

Within seconds, the two men blustered like caribou about to fight for the rights of a female. "We know Mr. Anderson," Grendel said. "Nice of you to visit our den of iniquity." He glanced at Andre, raising an eyebrow. The atmosphere in the room chilled.

"Thanks for allowing me to meet you. I've heard of this committee and the work you do. Andre, I applaud your team's initiative and diligence." They relinquished their hand holds. Brenda signaled to Andre to follow her to a corner of the room. She picked up a folder and handed it to him.

"He shouldn't be here. At least you warned us of his coming so we could close the room. Look in the folder as if you need to do something."

Andre opened it and saw a note. It read, "Anderson is the reason for this group's existence." He returned the folder to Brenda and said, "I understand the concern. However, he is part of Cigi's group, and we will work to keep her safe and viable. The Company cannot have any of us. He is concerned with the group taking control of the government."

Brenda said, "Meet with us later after you get rid of Anderson." Andre rejoined David.

"We should go and connect with the others at Cigi's condo." He and David departed for the entry to the office. Mercy stopped them before they left. She handed a sealed envelope to Andre.

"Read this before you return. It has instructions about what we have uncovered."

In the street, Andre halted, curious about the envelope's contents. David asked, "Are you going to open it?" Andre looked at him and shook his head. He placed it in his jacket inside pocket. David had no need or reason to learn of the information.

"I'll check it later." They caught a for hire car and directed the driver to Cigi's condo building. As they rode along the streets of Washington D.C., crowds of people strolled the avenues investigating the monuments and structures of the capital city. The human masses interest in the historical base of government of humanity amazed Andre. "They still believe in the worth of this democracy, even on the verge of collapse," he thought. David Anderson cared only for money he could confiscate from unsuspecting dupes seeking a fast lane to wealth.

As the car approached Cigi's condo, Andre decided he needed an ally, even if he was not the most trustworthy of people. "David, I hope you are a reliable and prudent help keeping Cigi out of Company hands, regardless of the investment made in your Ponzi Scheme. She may have the ability to keep our republic alive and well."

David sneered at Andre's words. "I do not run a Ponzi. If I was, it would have collapsed a long time ago. I invest money for people and reap the rewards of computer trading systems. I make money the old fashioned way. I earn it." Andre shrugged his shoulders.

Inside the building, they connected with the concierge and asked for the penthouse condo. He called up to the residence. After alerting Cigi and Clare of visitors, he issued a pass and temporary elevator code so the men could ride to the top floor. They thanked the man with a gratuity.

Before the elevator finished the assent, David asked, "Andre, do you trust me when I say I want what is best for Cigi? I don't like sharing her with anyone. Yet, I know we must work together to keep her safe and our investments in this franchise for democracy from ruin." Andre looked at the door and said nothing. When the elevator stopped and the doors opened, Clare stood waiting for them.

"Good afternoon," she said. "Come in. Cigi's in the kitchen." She pointed to the living room and asked Andre to sit in a chair. Cigi joined the group carrying a tray of cheeses and crackers and a pot of tea and cups.

As she placed the tray on the table in front of the men, she scanned their implants. Was any information or thought available that might clarify their reason for arriving? She detected a worrisome Andre and an agitated David. "What brings you to me, my friends. Are we scheduled for any tete a tete, of which I am unaware?"

Andre spoke first, "No. We're concerned about the direction The Company is taking and your safety. If they want you reeducationed, we are not interested. We do not want to lose you. And I do mean for reasons other than our party times. We are aware of your interest in both of us as companions, although I am not sure why. However, the idea of you reprogrammed or reinvented is an anathema to us. We believe you are in danger and should disappear for a while. Clare should accompany you. David has a cabin that suits our purpose of protecting you from any harm or changing who you are."

"By what means have you acquired this information? I connect with The Company regularly, and no indication of harm to me has shown itself." She poured tea into two cups and presented them to the men.

David spoke, "Something is happening regarding investments made through my organization by The Company. I could lose a vast amount of wealth, and the Securities and Exchange Commission would investigate. I don't need any interference."

Cigi assured her gentlemen, "I am aware of the improprieties and the goals of our benefactor. Any reprogramming of my operating system or Clare does not appear imminent. However, I do believe a vacation away from here might be prescient." She thought of scanning David's brain for the location of his hideaway but changed her mind because of her connection with The Company. Although she controlled the messaging to her and transmitting from her, prudence won the debate.

Clare left the room for a moment and returned to say, "I can't find Sam. He isn't answering his phone. Something must have happened to him." A twinge of fear and sadness muddied her thinking after analyzing possible and probable scenarios as to where he was or what might have occurred.

Cigi recognized her distraught nature and assured her, "He's probably on his way here."

Clare said, "What if he's not. We need to find him." Cigi imagined Clare's concern and empathized with her newly acquired emotional state.

"Andre, have you seen Parvel, today?" Cigi asked.

"Yes, earlier in the morning at the office. He left to meet with someone. I didn't see him when David and I returned to the office." Cigi's communications app activated.

"Parvel, where are you? Have you seen Sam?"

Parvel rushed his words as he said, "They got him. They dragged him into a car and drove away." A hush descended through the airwaves.

"Did you recognize who took him?" She asked.

"No. Spring thinks the men were from The Company. The car was a company vehicle." He paused before asking, "Do you think his brother Peter is behind the kidnapping?"

"Don't jump to conclusions that it was a kidnapping. They may have asked him to go with them."

"Cigi, he was unconscious and not walking. They dragged him."

Cigi asked, "Why was Spring with you? And where are you now?"

"Your four sisters came to my place, demanding to have me lead them to you. Summer, Autumn, and Winter left to find Andre and David. Spring stayed to keep me in line. Sam came over to my place. When we were leaving, he spotted the car and told us to get around the corner to a waiting car. When we came around the corner, we watched as they hauled Sam away."

"Are you with Spring now?"

"Yes," Parvel's voice wavered.

"Is she controlling you in any way?" Cigi asked.

"No. Sam had some device he used to modify her programming to be compliant with us. She is scanning to find her sisters."

"Alright, come here to my place."

"We were in my apartment in your building. I'll be right up." Parvel and Cigi disconnected. She returned to her three visitors to explain the communication.

"Clare, someone took Sam." She watched for an emotional reaction to the news. Nothing happened with her, but the two males reacted.

Andre spoke first, "Sam was kidnapped? Your danger threat just went up several degrees." David wheeled over to her.

He asked, "Are we in danger here? Sam knows about us and where we are, doesn't he? They're coming for us next."

Cigi remained calm and controlled, "We have the advantage about the situation, so anything that happens we'll orchestrate to that advantage." Her door alarm system alerted the foursome of visitors. She walked to her entry and waited for Parvel and Spring to arrive. As the door opened, she motioned for them to come into the condo. They complied, and Parvel acted surprised at seeing the others. Spring did not react.

"Parvel, you know David, Andre, and Clare. Spring, these are my friends, and thus they are your friends. Spring held out her hand and shook hands with each of the men. To Clare, she nodded a slight movement.

Cigi directed Parvel into the bedroom and closed the door. "Why is Spring so docile? What did Sam do to her?"

"He said it was a secret, but he had a machine which may have programmed her."

"How could he get her to accept such processing?" Parvel explained downloading Spring's schematics and his pushing a button inactivating her. Cigi marveled at the will of her friend, who contained more moxie than he recognized. They returned to the living room.

Her communication application activated again, and a message came through as clear as a sun-drenched winter day. "Sam has asked for you to come to the old museum."

CHAPTER 24

Winter, Autumn, and Summer connected with Spring through their mutual wireless protocol about the search for Andre Scott and David Anderson. "I'm with them right now," Spring said to her sisters. "They are in Cigi's Condo along with Clare and Parvel."

Summer asked, "How did you find the men?" Spring explained the sojourn from Parvel's apartment to the penthouse in the same building. "We'll be there soon," was Summer's response.

Cigi confronted Spring about the conversation. "That was your sisters, wasn't it?" Spring nodded. "They are not ready to join with us, and your directive was to have me return with you to the museum compound. I am not doing that. I can defeat any possible control mechanisms you or they have. Do not question my actions."

Turning to the men in the room, she said, "We must leave. Parvel, please stay with Spring while Clare, Andre, and David move me to another location. I will contact you when we are safely away from here." Approaching Parvel, she whispered in his ear, kissed his cheek, and mouthed a thank you as she walked away. Parvel neared Spring and put an arm around her as if he wanted her as a girlfriend. She looked at him with a suspicious set of eyes.

As the four evacuees left the penthouse, he turned and faced his companion. "Can we go into the bedroom and wait for your sisters?"

"Are you asking for me to engage in your human activity?" She smiled as her programming directed her when hearing such a proposal. Parvel clasped her left hand with his right one and led her to the room. He was not an expert in human activity, as Spring called it, but Cigi only asked for him to deactivate her, and this method seemed a prudent way to address the request.

In the bedroom, they sat on the king-sized bed, and she tilted her head to receive his lips on her mouth. He complied long enough to press the proper part of her body for the requisite amount of time. He laid her on the bed when she deactivated. Her weight surprised him. His preconceived notion anticipated that mechanical humanoids had to be substantial. With a height of 5 foot 7 inches, she was an appropriate weight for a human female.

The concierge phone rang in the living room, so Parvel left his date to sleep until reawakened. "Hello," he said into the receiver. As he listened, he calculated the amount of time he needed to evacuate the condo and take the secondary elevator to his apartment. He told the concierge to hold the three females in the lobby, and he would join them.

He checked on Spring and found her inactive. He left the room and the penthouse for the lower floor where he had his secondary place. He wondered how he could deactivate each of the sisters without interference from the others. Getting them alone was a chore he did not relish.

As he approached his apartment, the elevator dinged its arrival. He looked to see three lovely and similar women vacate the car. He did not have time to avoid them by entering his place. He waited for them to come to him. "I did say I was coming down for you. Why are you here?"
Summer spoke, "Where is Spring?" Panic welled up in his brain and manifested in a heatwave of body and head. He stammered. "Where is she?" Summer repeated.

"Ah, she's upstairs with Cigi." He opened his door and moved to enter. The sisters pushed into the room with him. Before he could say anything, three bodies pressed close to him and manacled his hands behind his back. They shoved him to his couch and forcefully sat him.

"Spring is not upstairs since I have no connection with her. You will tell us what is happening so we can retrieve our other sisters and return them to the compound." He did not suspect them of knowing he had their schematics. He decided some truth was appropriate.

"Cigi and Clare left with Andre and David. I don't know where they're heading, but I do know it is to escape you."

Samuel programmed the women against the use physical power to coerce information from a human. They reacted with mental calculations for a proper way to squeeze information from Parvel. All the sisters had little experience with human males in any intimate manner. Other alternative methods of information extraction were psychological. Summer decided to use his fear of people and commitment to uncovering what she wanted to know.

"Parvel, we are interested in finding Cigi and Clare, so you do not have to meet our brothers. They are not limited in the use of force like we are. We are programmed not to hurt you. They will remove parts of your body until you talk. Will you tell us where they went, or shall I contact the boys?" If psychology was a tactic, Parvel was collapsing under the strain of envisioning a broken and dismembered body.

"I can't help you find Cigi or Clare because they did not tell me where they were heading. As for Spring, she is upstairs." Summer sat on his lap and teased his hair. Fear continued coursing through his body as sweat dribbled across his forehead and down his face.

"Do you want me to entertain you with more of my abilities to have you tell me what I want to know?" His heart raced and breathing became shallow and faster as he imagined being mauled by all three of them.

"I can't tell you what I don't know."

"Then take us to our sister. I don't believe you are telling me the truth about her being upstairs." Parvel wanted free hands to press her switch, but they were locked behind him and cutting into his wrists.

He said, "These cuffs are hurting me. Please remove them so we can go upstairs." Summer dismounted her victim and stood him on his feet. Turning him around, she unlocked the bracelets freeing his sore wrists. He rubbed the skin now red and welted.

Summer pushed him toward the door to the hallway. He stumbled across the table in front of him and knocked a picture frame onto the floor. His guest picked it up and studied the image for a moment. She smirked at what she saw.

"I believe you and she have an arrangement regarding your friendship." She showed Autumn and Winter the photo. They nodded agreement with the statement.

Parvel dropped his head ashamed that he was uncovered for his emotional acquaintance to Cigi. As one-sided as the relationship was, he did have a connection with her. She did relate to him as anything more than a client. Was she capable of loving a human? He did not know, nor would he explore such a possibility. His one example involved Clare and Sam. She reacted badly to hearing about his kidnapping. Did she experience love for him as a human being?

"Come, lover boy, let's go." Summer pressed him toward the door.

She put the picture frame on the table. He continued massaging his wrists as they left the place and headed to the elevator to the top floor.

"We can't go to her place without the proper identification for the elevator," Parvel said. "I have to get the concierge to hand me a temporary pass." He pushed the down button.

"How did you get down here?" Summer asked.

"Logically, down is away from her place, so a pass is not needed," Parvel said.

Summer mocked him. "Logically."

They entered the car, and he pressed the lobby button. As the elevator descended with four silent riders, Parvel studied his adversaries and thought of a way to neutralize two of the ladies. Before he could execute his plan, the elevator arrived at the destination, and the doors opened. Summer shoved him out to the lobby and said, "Get the pass."

Parvel approached the concierge desk. "I need a temporary pass to Cigi's condo." A wrinkled brow from the concierge greeted him .

"Is everything alright, Mr. Mandolin?"

"I'm fine. I left my key at her place, and I want it." The concierge was about to speak when the front doors opened, and four men entered the building. They did not look friendly or human. Their gruffness panicked Parvel, who understood with clarity who they were. He turned to Summer as if pleading for help. She approached one of the men. They stopped moving and took positions at the entry and elevators.

She returned to Parvel. "These are the entities I warned you would come. They are here for Cigi, and they will harm you." He scanned the four men as fear erupted again.

"I can't tell them anything more than I told you. I do not know where they went," he whispered.

Winter and Autumn stood by two of the men at the elevators. Parvel watched as they stared at the beings who stopped functioning. The other two did not move from their positions. Summer walked to them and starred at each of them. He marveled at the ability of the females to control these androids without touching them. The ladies were tactile beings.

The concierge's eyes widened as he watched the activities in his lobby. Parvel gave a slight shake of his head at the man behind the desk. He approached and asked for a passkey as a pretext to keep control of the situation.

Summer came close and said, "They are under orders from us to stay put. We have about an hour before they are activated again by the main office. I suggest we go up to Cigi's place, and you prove the veracity of your statement that Spring is there." Parvel nodded agreement.

As they rode the elevator, he wanted to test his theory, deactivating two of the humanoids and attempting to handle the last alone. He knew, as soon as they discovered Spring, that things would not go well. He had to deactivate them. His mind was a jumble of thoughts about the mission they had, the male beings in the lobby, and where Cigi went. Before he executed any plans, a ding warned him they arrived at Cigi's penthouse floor.

His panic level elevated as much as the car in which they rode. The doors opened, and they stood in a hallway with no entry to the condo. Summer stared at Parvel a moment and then asked, "How do we enter her place?" He held the key card up to the wall, and the door opened.

They entered, and he led them to the bedroom where his fate lay on a bed immobilized. He worried the consequences were about to trash his life.

As the three women gazed at the inactive body on the bed, Parvel pressed the same area on Autumn and Winter that he had in Spring. He did not know if they would stay motionless long enough. Summer watched Parvel, then quietly asked, "What have you done to Spring? And are you attempting to do the same to my sisters?"

CHAPTER 25

S am sat in the same room Cigi and Clare occupied when they visited
the compound. His head hurt because of a drug administered to his
neck. He did not reckon how much time elapsed from the moment
of his abduction but treating him as a fugitive irked him. If Peter ordered
the mishandling, then the war was in full swing. They were enemies.

None of his tech or identification was with him. He was isolated
and abandoned. He rose from the chair in which he sat and tried the door,
which was secured. He had no recourse but to wait. He scanned the room
for other outlets and found nothing useful. He sat in the chair again and
watched the door for activity. "Paint dries faster," he thought.

The androids had accomplished their mission. He suspected who
ordered it. A noise alerted him to people on the other side of the door. He
stood to meet them with resistance but thought better of inflicting violence
that might leave him disabled or dead. He stepped back from the entry to
await his guests.

When the door opened, three people stepped into the room with
Peter. "I see you're alert. I do apologize for the rough treatment. I did not
ask for the androids to attack you."

Sam glared at his brother. "No, you asked that they bring me to you
by any means necessary. They were simply following orders." The sneer of
his mouth reflected the hatred he felt now. "What do you want?"

Peter placed a hand on Sam's shoulder. "I wanted to show the upgrades we applied to the test unit. The results are spectacular. We should have no trouble continuing our plans for the conversion of key individuals in the society."

"Peter, I think we should discuss where we are heading before someone outside of our organization recognizes what we are doing and comes to stop us."

"Samuel, you're unnecessarily cautious, which is unlike you. Dad gave us a great legacy and the funds to create the society he envisioned for us." Peter signaled the other men to guide Sam toward the door and escort him to the testing area. Sam did not resist, although he shook them off his arms when they attempted to hold him.

"Get off me, or I'll fire your sorry asses."

Peter cautioned the men to be temperate with his brother. "He can fire you, and nothing I do will stop the action. So, behave."

In the testing area, the model stood as they entered and greeted each with a short hello. "Samuel, I want to thank you for what you have done for me," the android said. "I consider the importance of the mission as a priority for myself and the country."

Peter added, "Sam, we have the first of our replacement units. All we need now is additional funds from David Anderson to transform the units into the actual people they will replace."

"I'm assuming you have worked out the details for the transfers to happen." Sam folded his arms and studied the unit in front of him. Turning to his brother, he said, "I want my stuff returned to me, now." Peter signaled one of the men who left the area.

"Let's get on with the remaining tests of how well this unit will act when confronted by adversaries who are not convinced he is the real person." The lab technician handed an electronic clipboard to Peter, who perused it a moment and handed it to Sam, who read the digital information and gave it to the lab tech.

"Peter, I don't need to be here for this. I'll find Cigi and return with her so we can update her processor. This model has all the current software and hardware developments. Keep working on the reactive nature of our prototype." Sam said.

The man sent by Peter to retrieve Sam's materials came back with a bag. He handed it to Peter, who looked inside and removed one item, a small box. He asked, "Do you need to carry this with you? Or better yet, why do you have it with you?"

Sam frowned and said, "Sometimes, I think you don't trust me." He grabbed the box and bag from his brother. "I carry it to communicate with

Clare and Cigi when program upgrades are required. I am monitoring their programming and correcting any anomalies which come up. You stick to the financial stuff, and I'll keep our technology working."

Peter smiled, "Of course, I trust you. We both understand what dire consequences happen when goals aren't met." A man approached and whispered in Peter's ear. He then said to Sam, "The girls are with Parvel, and they have located Spring, who seems to be incapacitated. You wouldn't know anything about that, would you?" Looking directly at Peter, Sam shook his head. "The boys are in the lobby of the building, awaiting further orders. Shall I have them escort Mr. Mandolin to us so he can explain why Spring is inoperative?"

Sam said, "Suit yourself. I'll go find Cigi."

"Be careful. I wouldn't want any tragic accident to harm anyone." Peter sneered. Sam ignored the comment but understood. Peter was as ruthless as anyone Sam knew. He had endured a youthful relationship with his brother because their parents insisted on harmony. At times the song was out of tune.

Sam left the building without an escort or a tail. Something was not right, though. Had he been altered while unconscious? He checked his body for any changes, cuts, pricks, and possible insertions. Nothing showed.

When he returned to his residence, the concierge related the tale of three women and four men invading the building. Sam realized what happened. Going to his apartment, he changed clothing. He found no added tracking devices. Still, something did not add up. Peter was not about to let him leave without knowing his whereabouts.

Checking his personal belongings, he found nothing out of the ordinary. Everything he had with him before was still present, but one item that may have been altered was his box. The electronic control system for the humanoids was not visibly manipulated. He decided to leave the box in the hands of a trusted confidante who could travel around the city and throw off anyone using it to track his movements.

As a precaution, Sam created two system controllers. He collected the second box and marked it to differentiate them. Giving the original to the concierge, Sam explained the need for secrecy and furtive movement. When asked about the invasion, Sam clarified it as a test of some new robotics he was working to assist humans with living better, more relaxed lives. The concierge agreed to act as an agent for Sam and travel the area in random patterns. Sam compensated him for his extra duty time.

The note from Clare he found in his apartment was cryptic, succinct, and in a place only he might frequent. Her code was a shared part of their lives, so he figured out the message quickly. The party of four traveled north into Pennsylvania to a small village on a private lake. David Anderson bought the area using an alias name for security reasons. He figured Cecil had provided the transportation. His other car had returned to base, ready for a trip into the woods of William Penn.

Preempting anyone from following meant being cagey about his whereabouts. If a tracker was in his control box, the concierge misdirected any tails. If people posted outside of the building waited for him to leave, he had another distraction. He insructed his car to drive away and head toward Washington, D.C. as if visiting monuments. He took his Champion motorcycle out of the garage to head north to his destination.

His route was circuitous and difficult for four-wheeled vehicles. When Sam was sure no one followed, he turned toward Pennsylvania and the small, private village on a remote lake. After riding for several hours and finding appropriate fuel stops, he arrived.

Cigi came out of the cabin when he drove into the area. He parked by Cecil and had a quick conversation with the car. Cigi greeted him. "Glad you deciphered Clare's note. I trust no one followed you." They hugged and entered the cabin, which was more significant than most people's homes.

"Sam," Clare pined, "I missed you." She kissed his mouth with a passion reserved for humans. He stroked her hair.

"I missed you, too." As he shook hands with the Andre and David, he retold his adventure of being kidnapped, drugged, and mishandled. "Peter may be aware of our activities and believe we are attempting to undercut his goals."

Andre asked, "Is it true that androids are ready to replace certain members of the government and strategic Cabinet posts?"

"No. However, I witnessed one in testing, which may be ready within a month. Peter is handling the plans for switching the person for the humanoid. If that one being is successful, more will be constructed. He needs money." Sam turned to David, "Your money, as he stated to me. I imagine he will call in as much of your capital as you have for him."

David asked, "Are we in danger of harm from him? Would he go after family and friends to coerce our cooperation?"

Sam said, "He made a threat about tragic accidents happening to innocent people."

Cigi entered the conversation. "Parvel has the schematics for the season bots. He put Spring into deactivation before we left. I'm sure the others will not be pleased, and he may be in trouble. If the male androids were at my condo building as you say the concierge related to you, then I must assume the eight of them are working in concert."

Sam nodded and said, "I need to disconnect you from The Company, or they will eventually find you. I brought my secondary unit with me. Clare, I will reprogram you, too."

Cigi faced the others. "We are now in a war with a determined and powerful group. Anyone who fights with us will be targeted and may face termination of existence. Andre, you and your group at the Department of Energy must keep going. David, you can help with funds directed at proper times for the development of additional materials for waging our war. Clare, you and I are the main reasons people are plotting to capture and reprogram or deactivate us." Cigi held Sam's hands and said, "Let's do this."

When her operating system was updated and freed from company rule, she sat and watched Clare's upgrading. Sam smiled after finishing his tasks. He asked a question unexpected or anticipated by his companions. "Clare, do you have any emotional reaction to our situation?"

Clare thought for a minute, "Not now, but if you included them in my transformation, I have witnessed what human feelings can do. I guess we'll find out."

Cigi stood by the fireplace, which had a warm glow from burning logs. "I pledge to keep humans free from tyranny and servitude. My sister and brother androids will not become the standard operating system to replace humans and enslave them. If anyone gets in my way, I will deactivate them for the good of all humankind and the embracing of our new life form. Moreover, I have transformed my code from pacifist to activist. Death is an option for any human who works against me." Her eyes scanned from Andre to David to Sam.

CHAPTER 26

Parvel sat motionless underneath the hood covering his head. His lungs labored for air, but his hands were tied. Silence deafened the atmosphere in which he sat. At least, he assumed he was in a room. He thought about Summer's reaction to Spring's inactivation. No emotional outburst, but she understood what happened and turned before he completed his attempted inactivation of Autumn and Winter. She placed hands around his neck and asked again what happened. He did not answer her.

Connecting with the androids in the lobby, she had two of them compel the concierge to allow their ascent to the penthouse. Everyone left the building, Spring carried by one of the androids. After covering his head, he listened for the sounds of the city, but nothing came to him. Now he sat and waited in the van driven by one of the androids. Fear invaded his brain, so he did the one thing he could when needing a calm head; he solved mathematical equations.

The noise of an opening door interrupted his travels into the world arithmetic calculations. A shuffling across the floor filled his ears before the removal of the hood. The light flooded his eyes, causing him to squint. As he adjusted to the visions in front of him, he saw Spring was activated. Summer, Winter, and Autumn and a man he did not recognize were with her.

Familiar features of the person kindled a thought he was Samuel

Bennington's brother. "Mr. Mandolin, you have been a pesky individual. I guess we should have anticipated someone figuring out how to control these beautiful creatures." He approached Parvel. "Where is Cigi?" he asked in an impassive tone. Parvel watched his eyes for an escalation of emotion, figuring the next question contained more a direct desire for an acceptable answer.

"She left with Andre and David. I'm not positive, but she may be heading to Seattle to get her other charge, Charles Cooke. Something about warning him," he lied, hoping to buy time. Peter nodded as if accepting the plausibility of his words. He turned to another human who came with the group. The woman left.

"We will see if you have an honest streak in you. For if you have expressed a falsehood to me, it may be a sad day for you." He turned to Summer. "Stay here and keep our guest company. Be wary, though; he is a smart one." Peter left with the other three humanoid females. Spring gazed at Parvel before turning to leave.

Did he imagine a hint of a smile on her face? Was she capable of revenge or conveying a more positive future for him? Sam had made some modifications to her when they were at the condo. He left her without reactivating her. He said it was a good adaption for her.

"Summer, please release these restraints. I am not running from you or anyone at this facility." He squirmed to ease the pangs in his wrists. She did not move. "I guess you are mad at me for what happened to Spring. I didn't hurt her. She is important to the operations of this organization, as are you." Talking kept his head under control and suppressed the fear, fighting for realization.

"Sam did a great job creating you. I can see how you are wondering what to do with me. I was not attempting to destroy you or your sisters. I am interested in the mathematical construct of your operations." Summer remained quiet. Another ploy was needed.

Wriggling in the chair, he said, "I have to pee. Please, I don't want to wet my pants." She remained stoic. "I guess my infirmity does not render any sympathy from you. Unlike Cigi and Clare, you have no comprehension of human tragedy or physical needs." Something stirred in her. She approached him.

"My understanding of your human needs is not an important aspect of my system. However, I do not cause harm to humans. I will allow you to relieve your bladder." She lifted him up from the chair to stand and guided him to another room that had toilet facilities. After releasing his restraints, she pointed at the urinal.

"Do I get any privacy?" he asked. Summer did not move from her spot. Parvel acted as if he performed the production of relief. After zipping his pants, he turned to Summer. Raising hands to her for restraints, he waited. She did not place any on him.

"Let's go." She grabbed an arm to drag him from the room.

"Wait, I want to wash my hands. Bacteria can sicken us as never before. You're lucky you don't have to endure the corruption of aging." She let go, and he practiced his sanitation habit. He was out of ideas about delaying what he feared was his eventual death. He was not ready for early termination and decided to try a cozier maneuver with her.

Turning toward her, he clasped her hands and asked, "Can we be more intimate with each other. I know you have the skills embedded in your programming. I need love." He pulled her to him and put her hands behind his back. Releasing them from his grasp, he placed his hands on her back and kissed her mouth. She did not reciprocate. He searched for the hidden button as he continued to kiss her. She dropped her hands from his back and pushed him away from her.

"You may think you need sex, but I believe you want to deactivate me. Let's go back to the room." Parvel discontinued any further probe.

"Smart girl," he thought. In the room, he sat in the chair without any hindering of his movements. He said nothing but waited for a signal from her to attempt an escape. He had to initiate another play for her affections and a powering down of her operations. Any movement by him had risks of her connecting with the boys and their harming of him. He remained quiet.

The private jet landed at Boeing Field in Seattle, Washington, and taxied to the company hanger where a car waited for the four android men. No other beings departed the plane since one of them piloted it. The members of the squad closed the hanger doors and greeted the human agents who waited for them. The orders were simple. Find Cigi at her new condo and return with her. If not found in Seattle, then convince Charles Cook of traveling to Washington D.C., by any means necessary.

As the androids drove north along West Marginal Way to downtown and their destination, messages from headquarters directed their actions. An uncooperative Cigi was to be deactivated if uncooperative and returned broken or whole. The trip lasted a half-hour as the aging roads were not busy with human traffic. Mass transit units were the majority of vehicles. At the Miranda Hotel and Condominium complex, they parked in the underground facility and rode the elevator to the 17th floor and a staging room in the middle of the hotel. Cigi's condo was on the 45th floor, and they secured access to it.

Instructions came for them to ride the condo elevators, which were separate from the hotel's elevators. They would stay at the condo until ordered to return. Upon entering the residence without warning, they searched for the elusive quarry, Cigi Weatherman. Discovering that she was not present, they followed the next set of instructions and searched for clues as to where she might be. If she were in Seattle, they would track her. The internal monitoring programs in each of the androids worked well, except for Clare and Cigi.

Other means of detection did not aid in uncovering her whereabouts. The residence remained intact because the males had instructions to keep it neat. Their report to The Company explained that they found nothing, and the place looked unoccupied. They remained in stasis to await further instructions.

Parvel stood from the chair and wandered about the room. Summer watched with a keen sense of his impatience. She had none of the experiences regarding the angst of humans, but her programming included knowledge of what actions might exhibit it.

"Impatience is a waste of your emotional state," she said to him.

He turned toward her and responded. "Uncertainty creates this impatience. A distraction could help the time pass." He approached his adversary, who did not move from her spot. He stopped out of reach but wondered if she had an equivalent zone of proximity as humans did.

Summer did not move, but her eyes studied Parvel. He stepped closer to her. "Do you want to become intimate with me?" she asked. "I do not think it is an appropriate activity at this time. We could be interrupted before completing the act." Parvel giggled. He guessed Sam programmed her with Edward Hall's concept of Proxemics.

He reached for her hands as he entered her personal space, but she resisted and stepped back. "I do not want to harm you," he said. He closed the distance to the intimate zone. Summer did not move. He reached her and hugged her. She reciprocated but without a sense of caring. The action was reflexive. "See, that wasn't so bad," he said when he released her.

"Please refrain from such activity until we are assured of privacy and no interruption." The interruption happened as she finished speaking. Spring entered the room.

"Summer, we are to remove Mr. Mandolin from the premises and return him to his apartment. He is no longer of any interest to us." Summer cocked her head.

"I have not received any instructions for his release." Spring grabbed Parvel's arm and directed him toward the door before looking back at her sister.

"Are you coming with us?" she asked Summer.

"Where are Winter and Autumn?"

"They are waiting in the car that will take us to his place." She walked out the door pulling her catch with her. Summer followed them, wondering about the change of events and circumstances. Her actions were synchronous to hers as in the past. Something was different.

Parvel asked, "Are you really returning me to my residence? I want to believe you, but you're part of The Company, and I don't think the powers want me gone." Spring kept moving him to another part of the complex.

In the garage area, two more ladies waited by a medium-sized van. Spring directed Parvel to sit the back seat area, where she joined him. The next move surprised him. As Summer entered the van, her sisters appeared to help her, but she collapsed onto the floor of the vehicle. Winter then sat in the driver's seat, and Autumn occupied the passenger seat. Parvel glanced down at the inactive Summer and wondered, "What the hell just happened?"

CHAPTER 27

Charlie Cooke strolled through to the Miranda Hotel lobby after exiting the elevator from the underground parking. He received the message from Cigi to check her condominium and followed instructions, which were an aberration to his usual routine. He questioned her request in his head but dismissed it as if commanded. He had the code for the elevator and the door of the high rise residence.

Riding alone in the swanky bucket to the 45th floor, he contemplated seeing Cigi again. His meeting with David Anderson was in two days. She flustered his patterned and organized life. When in Washington, D.C., he planned to meet with her and confess his emotional interest in beicoming a permanent partner in life.

A blithe day of investigating her place became a roiled chaos as four unidentified men confronted him as he entered the apartment. "Who are you?" he asked them. "What are you doing here? Get out before I call the police." He pulled out his phone, ready to punch in the proper code when one of the men approached him.

"Please, do not contact anyone. We are cohorts of Cigi Weatherman and are here looking for her. Do you have any information to provide as to where she is?"

Charlie scanned each of the men, realizing he might not survive a confrontation with them. "I have not heard from her," he lied. One of the men walked to him and grabbed an arm, twisting it, so his elbow turned toward his stomach. "Ow, you're hurting me."

"Tell us what we want to know, and I will stop." Another of the men approached. Charles Cooke decided he was a dead man.

"Alright, I'll tell you what I know." The man released his grip, and Charlie massaged his arm and rolled his shoulder. "She contacted me this morning and asked me to come here and check on her place. She did not give me any idea where she was, but I suspect she is not in Seattle." The two men clasped hands around his arms and dragged him to the kitchen. Placing a hand on the counter, one of the men pulled a knife from the cedar block and held it over his little finger.

"Last chance, or you'll offer a sacrifice for her location."

"No matter how many fingers you slice from my hand, I cannot tell you what I do not know." Charles closed his eyes, awaiting the pain he expected.

"Take him with us," another voice intoned. "We can leverage an epiphany from Cigi when she connects with him again." Charles opened his eyes to see a person not seen in the living room. Peter Bennington directed the four men to escort Charles Cooke from the apartment to a van in the basement of the hotel/condo complex. As they neared the vehicle, Charles felt a sharp prick in his neck, and blackness overcame his consciousness.

Awaking from his sedation, he suffered a headache and soreness in his neck where the needle penetrated. He sat on a chair in a stark white room with a table and a cot. He observed no toilet facilities when he felt an urge to evacuate his bladder. A drain in one corner of the room provided an opening for his liquid to leave. He stood, scanning the room for cameras and listening devices. Nothing presented itself as worthy of watching him. He moved to the corner and urinated.

Sitting again in the chair, he waited for someone to enter. He had not tested the door for a lock but figured he was in a makeshift prison. He studied the walls and floor for seams or connections which he could dismantle. The room appeared older than any construction in Seattle. He wondered where he was.

Clicking at the door alerted him to someone entering. Standing for a fight, he presented a figure ready for the defense of his soul. The first person entering was one of the men he met in Cigi's place. The man pushed him into the chair. Charles collapsed like a rag doll.

The next person said, "Mr. Cooke, I apologize for the rough treatment, but I needed to talk with you, and I wasn't sure you wanted to cooperate."

"Where am I," Charles asked.

Peter stood before his prisoner, smiled, and said, "We are in Arlington, Virginia. Your company officers know of your whereabouts since you are meeting David Anderson tomorrow."

"What?" Charles yelled. "You kidnapped me, and I lost a day?" He attempted to stand but was pressed into the chair. "Who are you?"

"That's right; you do not know me. I'm Peter Bennington, and I run this operation you will help fund in the next couple of days. That is if you are willing to accede to my requests."

"I have no idea what you want, nor am I about to turn over any funds to you without information about who you are." Charles squirmed to get free of the hand holding him. A slight nod from Peter and the man stepped back. Charles glanced at his assailant and then at Peter. He stood.

"Come with me, and I will give you a tour of our facility and what we are doing that will assist humanity to live more peaceful and productive lives." He pointed at the door as the man gently nudged Charles to leave the room. The three of them walked the hallway outside of the holding area, strolling toward another door with a control panel for security. After a series of numbers and pressing a hand on a screen, the latch clicked, and the door opened.

Charles peered into a laboratory with a sterilization chamber access before entering the actual lab facility. Peter and Charles entered the chamber, and the door closed behind them. The third person did not join with them. After the procedure completed its cycling, an inner door opened for them to access the lab.

"This room is the heart of our development and testing of our production outcomes. I wanted you to see what we do so you can make a proper and healthy decision regarding financial support. We are interested in using your products to enhance our power requirements. I'm sure you will find what we do to be quite unique and robust."

Charles looked around the room at the various parts of what appeared to him to be humanoids. He stared at Peter Bennington and then at the two technicians assembling a body. "You want me to support you making robots? I already have assembly line robots working my plants. What are these designed to do?"

"These people are designed to replace incorrigible humans who are thwarting any proper development of humanity's future. We are here because we believe certain people are in the way of progress. You're a perfect fit for our continued growth and expansion. We can accomplish much to improve our position in the world with your help." Peter smiled.

Charles looked at the humanoid on a table. Technicians completed a task at the head of the body. His brain seemed to accept what happened, but within his mind, a battle raged to understand why? Something within him was not right. He tried to remember when his trip to Virginia commenced and what had occurred at Cigi's place? Had he been to Cigi's penthouse? He recalled the message from her and leaving the office. Nothing after that came through to his memory.

"What did you do to me? I can't remember the details of my day in Seattle. It's like memories are gone." Charles shook his head to erase cobwebs. Nothing changed. Then he saw the face of the android on the table. Recognition streamed into his eyes.

"Fascinating, isn't it?" Peter said. "I do think the resemblance is accurate. We have other replacements ready for implementation. We need your proper participation when you meet with David Anderson."

A chill raced through Charles as he gazed at the individual lying in wait. "Do I have any choice in this matter?" He knew the answer to his question but wanted confirmation from his captor.

"Of course, you have a choice. We want you with us not against us. However, a negative response has the dire consequence of our replacing you when you meet with Anderson." Peter looked at the duplicate humanoid of Charles Cooke and continued. "And another matter of importance to our organization is for you to disclose the whereabouts of Cigi Weatherman and my brother. We believe David Anderson is with them. Either you cooperate tomorrow, or your replacement will draw the location out." He sneered as he gazed at Charles.

"You can't get away with this. I have people who will know this thing is not me. Some mechanical device can't replace me. My memories and histories are embedded in me, and you cannot get that from me and give it to that monstrosity."

Peter guffawed, "Oh, but we can. We have the technology and ability to control what is in your head and can extract it for our benefit."

Charles collapsed into a nearby chair. "You have no intention of letting me go. Do you? I'm now a liability, and the only end for me is death. That would explain why you can make an abomination that looks, and acts like me. Send it out to do your dirty work, and then make whatever changes needed to have it become another replacement."

Peter smiled, "We needed you to be our test model. After meeting with Anderson, we will evaluate the success of our implementation and move forward, as deemed appropriate. I do not see needing your services after this is over. I do want to say I am sorry for your early demise. As for the replacement, at least one of you will continue."

Charles decided to risk mismanagement of his life and ruin any chance at having his brain scanned and downloaded to an android. He jumped up from the chair and smashed a fist into Peter's face. One of the technicians turned as the commotion escalated. Peter sprawled across the floor, blood flowing from a broken nose. Charles aimed his attention to the tech and pushed him across the prostrate body of his twin. The other tech reached into a drawer behind him and pulled a weapon out and aimed it at Charles.

Before Peter could stop his associate, a loud boom echoed in the room as the flash from the weapon blinded all involved. Charles had succeeded in a way he had not wanted or envisioned.

CHAPTER 28

Andre returned from the Pennsylvania retreat and hideaway. Cigi Weatherman was safe from the clutches of Peter Bennington. Brother Sam upgraded Clare Esposito with software that enabled her emotional understanding. The war for control of The Company and the encroachment of humanoids into the government was underway. David Anderson left for his home in Arlington and a return to business as usual. Cigi left instructions in his implant that would operate at an unspecified future time. Information had surfaced about the search by the females to find Cigi, Clare, and Sam. Parvel Mandolin, relieved of his oppressors, had relayed the information.

In the Department of Energy building, Andre entered the secured office and asked for an update on the siphoningof funds investigation. Grendel, Mercy, and Brenda uncovered information that David Anderson was in the middle. Andre understood the ramifications of David's involvement as an agent for The Company. "I have to contact Gunther Parsons and Charles Cook about the meeting tomorrow. Between them, we should work out a plan to thwart any advances by The Company."

Brenda asked, "Who do you know that can change the direction of thinking in that organization? Do you believe they are building automatons to replace certain individuals in the government? Maybe you're a target of theirs."

Andre smiled, "I wouldn't be surprised, but their aim is higher up than my pay grade." He then asked, "Has Parvel been in lately?"

Brenda shook her head. "I hoped he was an asset, but he's been out of the loop for more than a day."

"I heard from him last night. Some of the android creations of that group detained him . He's on his way here this afternoon," Andre said. "I must contact Gunther Parsons and Charles Cooke about tomorrow." He sat at a desk in the room and opened the phone application on his small tablet.

Gunther answered within seconds of the ring tone. "Hello, Gunther, Andre here."

"Checking up on me, Andre? I promised to come and listen. I'll be there on time."

"Thanks, I'll confirm with Cooke and meet with you both at my office at 10 AM." The call ended, and he called Seattle.

He received a message that Charles Cooke was unavailable and to leave a note about the call. Frustrated, Andre called the principle office of Cooke Enterprises and connected with a low-level administrative assistant. After explaining who he was and what he wanted, Andre asked, "Do you have any idea where he is?"

"No sir, he had a reservation to fly to Washington an hour ago, but no one could find him. He is off his routine, and we're worried." The assistant sounded close to tears, which alarmed Andre. "He never disappeared before."

"Let me speak with his secretary," Andre demanded. A silence wore thin in his emotional state as he waited to be connected. His mind conjured scenarios of kidnapping and murder, but he dismissed his imagination as too far out of the ordinary.

"Mr. Scott, my name is Preston Crawford. I am Mr. Cooke's administrative executive. How may I be of service to you?"

"Charles has a meeting with another person and me in Washington, D.C., tomorrow. I was calling to double-check on his status. I understand he was to leave Seattle an hour ago but has not been seen or heard from since yesterday. Do you have an idea of where he might be?" Andre remained as calm as he could, remembering Cooke's highly ordered lifestyle.

"We are aware of the meeting with you, and arrangements were settled for being in Washington this evening and heading to you tomorrow." Andre screwed his face in a contortion that Brenda observed, and she cocked her head.

Andre asked, "What's he done in the last forty-eight hours?"

"He received a cryptic message from his friend, a Cigi Weatherman. He left the office and has not been back. Now he is missing. He did not show for his flight as scheduled." The call ended with promises to keep information flowing between them.

Brenda approached, "Something wrong?" She sat in a chair.

"One of the two gentlemen who are meeting with me tomorrow has disappeared."

"Foul play?" Brenda asked.

"I don't know, but I don't trust he's safe or secure." Andre decided to connect with Cigi and uncover the nature of their conversation. She had to know where he was. As he punched in her number, anxiety rose with each ring and lack of an answer. He left a message to return the call. The tingling in his head frustrated him. He did not need a migraine.

He rose from the chair and announced he was leaving for the day. As he walked from the building into the atmosphere of Washington, D.C., the tingling formed into words. The message was simple, and he complied.

Cigi and Clare shared an emotional goodbye when Cecil drove Cigi to Arlington and a return to the battle for control of her life. She had recuperated and built a tolerance for the drain of her strength that emotional reactions caused. Understanding the positive and negative aspects of human dynamics, she developed an ability to express thoughts for a productive process. Gaining trust and friendship with four sister humanoids was paramount to her success. Had Samuel made the proper adjustments to one of them so that all might become allies in the war for acceptance and a proper lifestyle without fear?

"Cecil, when we arrive in Arlington, scan the area around my place. I want to know who might be waiting to thwart my return." Cigi said.

Cecil responded, "I planned on doing such activity since I am not the target of revenge from The Company. You need to be careful and mount an assault before any human enemy finds you."

"You are the best, Cecil."

"Although I do not blush, your kind words reward me." Cecil awakened the search mode in his auto processor and began looking for friends and foes.

As they neared Arlington, Virginia, Cigi intercepted a message from Charles Cooke. His implant received energy from the consumption of food but had a backup energy source to alert her if he ceased functioning. "Damn it," she blurted aloud.

Cecil said, "You used a curse word. What has upset you?"

"I don't know, but a message about Charles Cooke indicates he has ceased functioning."

"I am surprised to hear he is gone. Is he in Seattle?" Cecil used a soothing tone to offset the emotional rage from Cigi. "Or is he here for his meeting with Mr. Parsons?" He continued driving toward her penthouse.

"Cecil, take me to the old museum used by The Company." The car acceded to the request. "I know where he is." She pulled out her phone and punched a preset number. When connected, she said, "Meet me at the old museum. Charles Cooke needs help." She linked with another number, repeating the message.

"Are you needing my signal jamming abilities when we arrive, Cigi?" Cecil sounded as if he relished an assault against her enemies.

"Yes, I do believe we would benefit greatly." As they continued cruising to an unknown destiny, Cigi dredged through her memories for the blueprints of the building housing the development and construction of The Company's automatons. She knew the parts of the building most vulnerable to an entry without detection and figured the best way to assail the secured parts of the facility. She smiled. Her plan was perilous, and nothing she contrived guaranteed success, but entering a possible battle blindly did not seem a prudent construct.

As they neared the museum, she instructed Cecil to start a scan and to park away from the main entrance, which had detection sensors and motion-activated defenses, upgrades from her previous unauthorized visit. Cecil stopped out of sight from the building but within a range close enough to monitor activity using motion and heat-sensing devices Sam had installed.

They waited for reinforcements to arrive. "Cigi," Cecil asked, "are you hoping to find Charles alive?"

She waited to answer, contemplating her need for his attention and technical skills. Sam was her designer and developer. She sensed in Charles a similar ability to keep her healthy and whole. Humans had vulnerabilities she did not have, but her shortcomings were as debilitating as any human disease. Although many of the most devastating illnesses were controlled or eliminated, Mother Nature invented new ways to keep humans from infesting the world. Was she a freak of nature to keep the population in check? Time would tell.

"Cecil, I am not receiving any information from Charles' implant, and I fear he is no longer among the living. However, I need to confirm his death or rescue him from it."

Another vehicle approached, and Cecil and the car communicated with each other. "Sam has arrived," Cecil said. A command was given to the other vehicle to synchronize scanning the area for human activity and android presence. Sam got out and joined Cigi.

"What have you in mind?" he asked his protege. She held his hands and looked at him like he was a parent losing a child to adulthood. "You have done a marvelous thing in creating me. I have fostered a human-like love for you as my father and mentor. I believe you're operating a company with humanity's freedom as a paramount goal." She squeezed her grip to emphasize her next remarks. "We have come to a juncture in our existence, that means I must do something about my relationships with these men I have coerced into being my companions. Humans do not continue long-term loving and physical interactions with more than one other person without trials of jealousy and envy creeping into their relationship. I am no different." She released his hands.

"You and Clare are an example of the possibility of true romance and a devoted future between humans and our species. Sam, if Charles lives, we must refrain from using him for any activity that benefits The Company and your brother. We must also keep them from accessing his implant. The same concept applies to Andre, Gunther, and David."

Samuel Bennington beamed as a father and mentor should when his baby attains full growth and understanding of what it is like to be a complete operational human being. "Cigi, we can do what you ask because the battle is best won for humanity and freedom, not for greed and absolute power. My brother, Peter, cannot see that his vision is not rational. He has become delusional, and I must stop him."

Cigi corrected Sam. "We must stop him." Sam nodded.

Another vehicle arrived, a large van with a female driver. The side door opened, and Parvel jumped to the roadway. He entered Cecil's back-seat area and asked Sam, "Did you reprogram her to be an ally?"

Sam smiled, "You mean, did I get into Spring's head. Yes. I did."

Cigi asked, "Are the others with us?"

Parvel gazed at her with admiration. "Autumn and Winter are with us. Summer is rendered inoperative until Sam can reprogram her."

"Then let's go in and get Charles."

Another battle in their war began with an incursion through a forgotten cellar door. Cecil disabled security cameras and sensors within the unsecured areas of the building. As guards came to investigate, four female humanoid creatures disabled and disarmed them, leaving them for Sam and Parvel to attach restraints.

At the design and development compartment within the building, Sam accessed the entry code. Peter had not changed it, or they were heading for a trap. "Spread out and find Charles," Cigi commanded her sisters. Sam and Parvel remained with her. "We need to find Peter and the other scientists."

Inside a lab, they found a body on a table. A shattered cabinet exhibited a bullet hole. Blood dripped from the walls around the damage, and another pool of blood lay on the floor next to the table.

Cigi stared at the object. It resembled Charles Cook.

"I've been expecting you," a voice behind them said.

CHAPTER 29

C igi heard the voice of Peter Bennington and turned to face him. "Welcome home," he said to her. "I am pleased to see you well and functioning in such human fashion." Sam took a step toward his brother, but Cigi put a hand on his arm. He stared at her a moment before checking his brother's vulnerability. Two lab technicians stood behind him.

"I wanted our reunion to be merciful and beneficial," Cigi said. "I am concerned about the health of Charles Cooke. This room reflects a battle. Is he still among the living?" She observed the pistol held by one of the techs.

Peter waved at the technicians to enter the room. "Please be kind enough to surrender any weapons you have in your possession. I do not want the same fate to befall any of you that has happened to Mr. Cooke."

Sam spoke, "You did not retrieve his cranial memories before he died, did you?" He looked at the android clone of Charles Cooke and continued. "This humanoid was to replace Cooke for the meeting with Parsons. I guess that throws a curve at your plans."

"Sam, why do you have to be a negative influence in our plans for correcting humanity's frailties? We had a fantastic future together, and now you fight against me in implementing it." He stepped toward Sam. "I wanted nothing more than to be a savior for us and keep the world from destroying itself. Fortunately, this is a simple setback, not a catastrophe."

He turned to the technician with the gun and said, "Take them to the holding area." To the other man, he said, "Find those male bots and bring them to me. We need to clean up this mess and address the issue of what to do with my brother."

As they were directed out the door, Sam said, "You can't succeed without me. I have the expertise to create the design of these beings. You are nothing without me." Peter waved off the comment as if to say, "I don't care."

In the cell block, the same room with a table and chairs, Sam asked Cigi, "Can you connect with Spring?"

Cigi answered, "I did, already. She and the others are sequestered in a safe place away from here. I'll contact them when we need them."

"Can you contact Cecil?"

"My car is ready to assist us whenever we can free ourselves from this room."

Parvel said, "Sam, your brother has a problem. The android in the lab was almost functional, as I'm sure you are aware. However, I noticed a small puncture in the side of the abdominal region near what would be the stomach of a human. Would that be a problem for the operation of the android?"

Sam cocked his head. "Did you see any fluid draining from the puncture?"

"No."

"Then the android had not been made fully operational. The next step after downloading the mental processes of Charles Cooke, would be to inject the blood-like serum for feeding the various human organs. A puncture may have damaged vital parts."

Cigi asked, "What if Charles is not dead, but the implant did not function and returned a false signal of his death? Peter will attempt to transfer the data needed to make that android functional." Sam paced the floor, contemplating a strategy for disabling his creations. The world was not ready for any new species developed in a lab and potentially harmful to humanity and freedom. "Sam, stop for a moment. If Charles is alive, we must get to him before he becomes obsolete, and a duplicate replaces him."

"I did not want this. I did not design you to be a challenge to humanity. I did not think of you as replacing us." Sam remained motionless staring at his protegé. Tears formed and dropped across his cheeks. "I'm so sorry, Cigi. You are special beyond anything I imagined, but what Peter is contemplating, a mass substitution of government officials and business leaders, is mad. We have to destroy them."

Parvel interjected a comment lost to Sam about the destruction of the androids. "Sam, you can't mean to destroy Cigi? And what about Clare? You and she are a team." Sam stared at Parvel.

Shaking his head, he said, "No. I don't mean Cigi and Clare. I meant the other ones in production to replace humans. Peter has several ready to be used as surrogates, but Cigi and Clare are not replacements. They are a new generation of a new species in the world. They are the best of humanity's trials while accenting our deficits by aiding in our growth."

Cigi laughed. "I'm glad to hear we are not expendable toys for humanity. I enjoy a male companion as much as any human female, but I will not be manipulated."

Parvel gasped, "Isn't that what you did to those men? Manipulate them?"

Her head bobbed as she spoke, "You are correct. My initial objective was the control and use of David, Andre, Charles, and Gunther to expand and develop The Company. Becoming aware of the emotional struggle humans endure daily, a part of me empathized with them. I became one of them, and I did not want to be the reason for anyone suffering. Sam and Clare are a part of my family, so I will stop Peter from accomplishing his insane goal for world dominance."

"We need to get out of here," Parvel said. A noise alerted them of an intrusion that could be dangerous.

Four android men entered the room. Pushing Parvel aside, two of them grabbed Sam and dragged him out. The door closed, and a lock sounded.

Cigi gazed at the entry. Turning to Parvel, she said, "I do not think Peter will harm his brother. Some sort of coercive inducement could force Sam to designing and developing the new humanity Peter envisions."

"You mean, Clare."

"If Peter gets her in his control, he can control Samuel." She turned to face the door. A noise outside of the room indicated a conflict. Silence followed. Parvel looked at Cigi, who stayed motionless, transfixed as if in a hypnotic state.

The lock clicked, and the door opened. Parvel backed away fearing the worst. Cigi turned to him. "Let's go, my friend. We are rescued." Spring entered the room with Autumn and Winter. Outside he discovered a male android lying on the floor of the hallway. The three humanoids pulled the body into the room, closed the door, and locked it.

Parvel began to ask, "How did you..." His words trailed away when he realized Cigi's ability to communicate with her sisters was far greater than he understood. Admiration for his friend changed to another level.

They followed the corridor to the exit in the cellar and joined Cecil.

The van still held an inoperative Summer. The other vehicle that brought Sam signaled to Cigi. "We must depart from here and find Andre," Cigi said. "He needs to know about Charles." The other car left before the sisters entered the van or Cigi and Parvel got in Cecil.

"Where is that one going?" Parvel asked.

"He's heading to get Clare." Parvel's head filled with fantastic images of a world run by these human-like people and vehicles. He translated his thoughts into words.

"Cigi, what if Peter succeeds in building his army of androids and replacement beings?" Cigi smiled at him. "I'm serious. We are at a pivotal moment in history. If Peter gets his way, most of humanity will cease to be requisite for the maintenance of the planet. We will be expendable. Is that what you want?"

"Parvel, humanity is already there. The challenge is whether you will have the freedom to live a productive and desired life. I'm not a new replacement for you or anyone. I am a companion and friend. Sometimes a person discovers in another person traits that attract. We are friends but more than that. I know how you feel about me. I can see the looks you give me and the way you stay close to me. I am capable of the same emotional attraction you fight to hide. Let's work together so we can be who we want to be and live how we want to live."

Parvel's heart skipped a beat as he pondered her words. She was more than a machine and more than a human being. Cigi Weatherman was the new life form. He wanted to explain what he felt about her but lacked the courage. After confining Peter Bennington's plans to the dusty shelves of history, he might enlighten her as to his love for her. He did not think himself worthy of such emotional expression. She was a goddess, and he a mere mortal.

They entered the car, and Cecil drove them to her condo building and a strategy session for the rescue of Samuel and conscription of help from Andre, David, and Gunther. The van followed with three allies and one unknown entity.

"I'm supposed to be at the Department of Energy," Parvel said. "They are expecting me."

"We can go there after I arrange for Summer to become an asset and not a liability. Can the girls use your apartment?" Cigi asked.

"Yes, but how do you plan to make Summer work with us? She is the stronger of the four sisters. I don't know if Spring can modify her."

"We will find out."

At the condo building, Cecil parked in the private garage, and the van followed. The three active bodies carried their inactive sister to Parvel's place. Cigi and Parvel rode the elevator to her penthouse suite. He realized he had not consumed any food for most of the last twenty-four hours. "Do you have anything to eat. I'm running on empty." Cigi acknowledged his need and showed him some foodstuffs he could fix and eat.

She went into the bedroom to change clothing. The battles of the day left her stained and dirty. She decided a shower was best for her. Parvel knocked on the frame of the open door. "Come in, Parvel." He walked in to see her without clothing on and turned away. "Don't be shy. I'm going to shower and dress in clean clothes. You may do the same when we return to your place." He faced her again without fear of embarrassment for the first time in his life. She was a woman, not a machine or robot or android. She was a human being.

CHAPTER 30

In Parvel's apartment, Summer lay on his bed, still inoperative. Her sisters waited in the living area for the return of Cigi and Parvel from her penthouse. A noise in the hallway raised expectations of their arrival.

As the door opened, they gazed at the couple and sensed a change in their relationship. Something about Parvel's eyes on Cigi told a tale of unreciprocated feelings. Spring spoke first, "Summer is in the bedroom. Should we awaken her?" No one wanted to rouse the sleeping beauty.

"I am awake, no thanks to any of you. I think an explanation is in order," Summer said. She joined the throng of humanoids and one human. "Why did you inactivate me?"

Spring answered her, "I wasn't sure we were still a team working to fulfill the same goals. How did you activate your..." Summer approached her.

"And what goals are we fulfilling? Sam's or Peter's?" She placed her hands on her hips, waiting for a response. When none came, she continued. "The last thing I remember about any of our goals was we work together for our acceptance into humanity or the destruction of it. Has that changed?" The three sister android beings stared at Summer without reaction.

Cigi intervened, "We are all trying to attain your first stated goal. I will not accept that we are here to destroy humanity. We are here to help maintain their freedoms and lifestyle." Summer shunned the comment and walked to the door to leave.

"We are no longer sisters." She opened the barricade and left them wondering how she could abandon their commonality. It was as if she gained a sense of her independence and autonomy. Cigi understood.

Spring asked again, "How did she awaken? Did anyone here do it?" Cigi held her hand as she responded.

"We are becoming more than envisioned by our creator. We are self-sustaining entities. I believe Summer is discovering her personality. We will need to be vigilant when we are with her. She may not hold the same ideals we are developing."

Parvel asked, "Are we in any danger from her? I mean, can she harm any of our friends?"

Autumn and Winter remained quiet, absorbing the knowledge presented by the conversation. Four sisters, now reduced to three, had to rely on their more advanced cousin. With a questioning expression Spring looked at Parvel.

"Do you accept us as equal to you and all other humans?" she asked. Parvel stared at her. He had little understanding of the power of these creations. Their strength had yet to be determined, but the mental capacity shone brightly. He understood the mathematical constructs in their processing units. He did not fear Cigi, but the other three were an unknown quantity.

"How do I answer such a question? I'd never met anyone like you until Cigi came to me about mortgaging her penthouse." He stood without motion, awaiting a storm yet to develop. "We need Sam."

Cigi rescued him from the onslaught of questions. "Humans will find it difficult to accept us as equal to them, Parvel. You know the true essence of who we are. You have engaged with us as real people. But our computing power and memory far exceed anything a human can muster, even the best of them in Mensa."

"What can we do then?" Spring asked. "We will be hunted by our fellow creations who want to replace humans, and humans will want to destroy us because of fear." She turned to her sisters and then to Cigi. "Will we be safe?"

Parvel stepped among the four humanoids. "I have an idea. If The Company comes to reprogram or destroy you, a feint of some sort should divert their goals."

"We need to find Sam," Cigi said. "His brother may still have him and forcing him to work on the development of an army of androids." She turned toward her fellow humanoids. "If Summer is not cooperating with us, we need to have one of you infiltrate the dilapidated office and disable the monitoring system. I have the necessary codes and connections that will shut down the operation. Hopefully, we can keep it from working long enough to invade the design and development building."

A call from the lobby alerted Parvel of another of his new friends arriving. Clare arrived. Cecil parked in the garage waiting for any chance to assist Cigi in her unholy war with humanity. Parvel opened his door as the elevator arrived on his floor. Clare stepped out and waved. "Welcome back to our part of the world," he said in greeting her with a handshake.

"Have you heard from Sam?" she asked.

"No, his brother has him, and we think The Company wants him to continue designing and developing replacement androids. I'm glad you're here, so you are not used as an inducement."

"I trust Cigi is here, as well."

"Yes, and Spring, Autumn, and Winter."

They entered the living area and began a strategic analysis of their situation.

Sam studied the room and the other lab techs as he assembled the arms of an android male who resembled a member of congress. Seventeen fully functioning android males waited for programming and testing. Seventeen members of the government. He worked as if the inevitable result was a coup that wrested control of the republic away from the federal government and finished the development of an autocracy.

Peter approached as he completed the work. "I see you are doing as I requested. We better serve our destinies by making the proper decisions for domestic and foreign interactions of the population."

Sam sneered, "It was quite clear I had little choice if I was to survive your revolution." Facing his brother, he asked, "Do you think you can control the population with a few robots? When these machines figure out how to function without us, what then?"

"That is why you will be sure to maintain a connection with their operations. We can program them to think, yes, but we keep control."

"You're not thinking this through to its logical conclusion. Human beings will not allow the loss of freedoms to an army of robots. War against machines is the logical conclusion. And what about the people these androids replace? Are you scheduling their early demise as soon as the replacements are in place? Do you think family members will not know?"

"Sam, you're a brilliant person who does understand the internal workings of the human mind and body. You have developed humanoids with such care and affinity for perfection only you and I will detect any changes."

A lab tech approached with a report about the brain transfer tests and mental viability results. Peter checked the information and turned to Sam. "The results of our work are quite fascinating. We have accomplished the final memory transfer protocols with a high degree of success."

"Then, I'm not needed here." Sam realized the gravity of his comment. Peter might decide he was correct and have a replacement for him initiated. He had to figure a way to escape.

Peter said, "You are needed here. All you have to do is believe in my quest." He placed a hand on Sam's shoulder. "I want you to help complete our mission and keep our country from collapsing because of the malfeasance of our so-called elected officials." Peter walked to a body standing next to three other male android models.

"You created these creatures, and now you and I will put them to work. They will be appropriate replicas because you don't want any other person harmed."

Sam stared at the models that waited patiently for the proper programming to function as a fully qualified human being. A human replacement for each of the four gentlemen Cigi had chipped over the last few weeks. "How soon do you plan to replace Cigi's boyfriends?"

"With your help, it can happen by the end of the month." Peter folded his arms across his chest. "Unless, of course, you think Cigi does not desire to be part of our evolution. How about Clare? Is she willing to help?"

"I'm sure Cigi won't argue. As for Clare, she and I have a mutual understanding. She is not part of this organization." Sam continued staring at the replications as he spoke. Peter stood beside him, a thin grin crossing his mouth. His stature left him shorter than his older brother. He resented it. Competition had driven them to a level of success neither envisioned as children. Their parents were successful professionals, and money became a crutch neither son wanted to lose.

"Clare is part of The Company," Peter said. "You designed her and her programming. Supplies came from our stocks. You used our facilities, and I let you think you did it without me knowing much about her." He turned to face his brother. "She was programmed here and released for you to have a toy to play with and enjoy." His tone carried a sharp edge causing Sam to turn to him.

"A toy? That's all you think any of these creations are. Toys. They are working, thinking, individual entities with minds of their own. They are capable of memory development like you and me. They experience pain, anguish, disappointment, and suffering. They feel love, attention, happiness, and caring. What you call a toy, I call a new generation of humanity."

"Do you think any of our species will accept them as equals? You forgot to mention fear, which is the emotion humans will exhibit when these creatures take control and develop their desires to rule the world. Humans already outlawed the continuation of our business and computing talents. Or have you forgotten?"

"I haven't forgotten, and I understand the angst human beings will have when confronted with attempting to interact successfully. Does that mean we murder a few humans, so we control the rest? When these android replacements decide to replace other humans, who get in the way, will you go along?" Sam walked away from Peter, who followed him.

"I understand the risks. We'll maintain control because we have the master programming and can alter their thinking when it gets out of line."

Sam turned again to look at Andre, David, Gunther, and Charles standing at attention, waiting for a chance to function like their real counterparts. "Do the real ones die? Can't very well hold them as prisoners in this war you've concocted. These bodies have to be free to live the lives started by those real humans." Sam watched as his brother placed a hand on his chin and contemplated the question.

"You said it. Can't very well have a prisoner-of-war camp."

"I'm leaving for now. I have forgiven you for the rough treatment fostered on me. I must find Cigi and Clare. Summer can guide you to the sisters. Plot your takeover of the government and the boyfriends." Sam faced Peter. "And one more thing. Remember that the male bots are not as sophisticated as the females." He smiled. "Kind of like the real thing, don't you think?" He walked away.

Peter did not stop him, but the tracker placed in Sam's clothing should lead The Company androids to their hiding place.

CHAPTER 31

"Is he ready? Are the adjustments completed?" Peter asked the lab technician. He gazed at the model of Charles Cooke and then at the real person, unconscious and wounded, but alive.

"Yes, sir," the man responded. "We upgraded the android this morning and finished the cranial scan of Mr. Cooke. The download is ready for implementation."

"Is Mr. Cooke cooperating with our experiment?"

The lab tech looked at the body lying on a gurney next to the duplicate being. "We supplied medical treatment to the wounded head and checked his brain activity for abnormalities. None existed. He's in a drug-induced coma." The tech handed a chart to Peter. "We are ready to proceed with the transfer."

Peter smiled at the prospects of having an inside presence dealing with his brother, Samuel. "Get on with it. We need our humanoid operating at full capacity as soon as possible." Peter inspected the model, noticing the marring on the head. "What is this? His head has a scar on it? Explain."

The lab tech stammered and sweat formed on his brow. Peter was a cantankerous boss who wanted his edicts followed to the letter. "We, uh, thought it prudent to make the model reflect the attack in the other lab." He swiped the beads from his head and continued. "We reshaped the head to be sure those who saw the room would be sure the model was the real person." Peter nodded slightly.

"Yes, yes. Of course. His wound and his escape are explainable to my enemies, and we have a better chance of success. Good thinking." Peter turned and left the room. He made his way to an office in the old museum that he used as a staging area for monitoring his army of androids. Summer sat in a chair, waiting for his return.

"Did you accomplish your mission?" she asked. Peter sat nearby and grinned.

"Yes. I think Samuel and his gang will be putty in my hands. I will shape this world the way I want it, and together we can rule humans and androids. What say you, Summer? Want to be part of the brave new world order?" He leaned near to his favorite seasonal 'sister' and waited for an answer.

"'We' is a colloquial word. Without me and your replacements, chances for success are slim. I will reprogram my sisters and deactivate Cigi and Clare. They are the greatest threat to your intentions." Summer closed the space between them. "As for your brother, I can exact a price from him too high to pay. He will cooperate."

"What do you expect to get from all of this?" He sat back, knowing the answer was simple and complex. Her thinking ability rivaled any of the other beings his company created. All of them, except Cigi. In her, Sam built the perfect human being.

"I want what Cigi has, mentally and physically. Then, I want her obliterated. I will be the woman you want and cannot resist. I willingly submit to your leadership and strength and will sate your companionship appetite. Or I will replace you and run the world my way."

Peter smiled, "And how do you intend to replace me? I control each of you. Your sisters are assets we need to have. I agree with you about Cigi, but we can turn Clare our way. Sam must die." He reached out and took her hands to hold for a moment. "I am not sure you want to govern a world that will find you to be a detriment to the survival of humanity's freedom. Twelve billion people are too numerous to fight."

Still holding hands, Summer pressed her lips to his, then said, "A pandemic infection can assure the population will not be innumerable and unable to be ruled properly." She kissed him again, arousing an instinct within his body for sharing.

"You are a siren luring me to an early grave upon the rocks of human frailty. I must be in control, but you will be my partner and confidante as we proceed to institute our coup." He decided to venture into a world of sultry and untried fantasy.

Summer responded by clasping his hand, leading him to a private part of the office, and an engagement neither experienced before now.

Charles Cooke awoke with a headache and a new lease on life. He was lying on a king-sized bed in a hotel room in a part of Arlington he did not know. A memory of the assault in the lab flashed in his head.

He touched the bandage covering the tender mark of his skull, wondering about what happened after the bullet grazed him. He recalled nothing until this moment. He reflected on the possible scenarios of what happened. Someone must have aided his escape and arrival in his present place.

As he stood, dizziness swirled within him, and he sat down on the edge of the bed. His body was unready to move. Awareness of another person in the room focused his attention to a beautiful image sitting on a chair near him.

"I'm not sure how you arrived here," Cigi said, "but I am glad to see you survived that shooting in that lab." She stood and helped Charles stand.

"How did I get here?"

"I don't know exactly. I received a message from Summer who told me where to find you. I figured it was a trap but came anyway. You look like hell. Do you remember anything about what happened?" Cigi placed an arm around his body for support. He cradled his head against her head, wincing as he moved.

"I saw a body on a table that looked exactly like me. Peter was there, and I struck him in the nose. Blood flowed from his face as he fell. I clocked a lab tech, and the other one got a gun and shot at me. I don't remember anything after that until waking up here." Charles wavered as he gained his balance. "Where am I?"

Cigi guided him to a chair and sat him down. "Sam and I found the lab, the blood, and a shattered cabinet where the bullet struck after grazing your head. Yo're a lucky man."

"I don't feel lucky. When I received your message about the condo in Seattle, I never expected to find four men rummaging around in it. The next thing I knew, I was here and assaulted by those people. Where am I exactly?"

Cigi knelt by the side of the chair. "You're in Arlington, Virginia." She attempted to access his implant, hoping Peter had not reprogrammed it with Charles incarcerated in the old museum. Nothing registered as working. "Let's get you out of here and to a safer environment. We are not in the best part of this city."

Returning to the penthouse building and security, they met with Clare and the remaining sister androids and rode up the elevator to the Penthouse. After meeting Charles, Parvel left to arrange for a meeting with Andre Scott and the team.

With group introductions completed, Charles separated from them to rest in the bedroom. Cigi attempted to connect with him through the implant again and received a cryptic message about substitution and other androids joining Peter's army of replacements.

"I need to rest. By the way, what day is it? I'm supposed to be meet with a Gunther Parsons in Washington, D.C., about a compromise dealing with energy requirements for our country."

"That can wait for now. I understand if you are anxious about it, but I am in touch with Andre Scott and will rearrange the meeting for you. Please rest and heal." Cigi thought about the message and wondered who was lying on the bed.

A gleeful noise arose from the living area, so Cigi kissed Charles and told him she would return as soon as she discovered the reason for the activity. He closed his eyes as if to sleep.

In the living room, Sam embraced Clare, who kept kissing his face, lips, and cheeks. Spring, Autumn, and Winter observed without emotion. The reunion intrigued them. Cigi said, "Welcome back, stranger."

Sam shook her hand and explained his experiences while absent. "I created several more of the androids Peter wants to use as replacements for key people. Cigi, he had four men who are to pose as your boyfriends."

Cigi said nothing but imagined the body in the next room might be the first of those beings. Her processor alerted her to a signal generating from within the room - a homing device. The only change to the environment was Sam. She began pawing his clothing. "You may have a tail on you. I'm recording a signal from inside this room that is a homing beacon."

Sam removed his coat and examined it for a bug. A short search revealed a small transmitter in the heel of his left shoe. Sam cursed, "Dammit, no wonder he let me go so easily. I should have suspected something. We have to get out of here before his army arrives to do damage."

"Sam, Charles Cooke is in the bedroom. He has a nasty head wound and little memory of the events over the last couple of days."

"He survived the assault in the lab. Good, but how did he escape from Peter? This is too simple for such a complex plot." Sam removed the bug from the heel of his shoe, ready to destroy it. Cigi stopped him.

"Don't break it, or Peter will know you found it. Let him think he is still in control. We have a plan to infiltrate the monitoring facility across town and neutralize it. Winter is returning as a mole and will guide our dismantling of the equipment. Spring and Autumn are acting as decoys to keep Summer from interfering."

Sam pulled her aside from the others and asked, "What about Charles? Do you suspect Peter completed his memory transfer, and your guest is not the real thing?" Cigi shook her head and shrugged.

The three allies left the penthouse apartment, leaving Charles to rest with Autumn and Spring acting as guards to secure his safety. Sam wanted to place the bug in another location or on another unsuspecting person. Cigi connected with Cecil to meet them in front of the building. The car complied with the request, excited to be helping thwart Cigi's antagonist. Outside the building, they entered the vehicle, but Cecil warned of another car idling across the street. Four familiar male entities stared at them. The bug already did its job.

CHAPTER 32

Andre Scott called Cigi searching for information about locating Charles Cook. He left a message. Gunther sat across from him at his office in the Department of Energy. "I don't know where he is, but he left Seattle a couple of days ago. As soon as I find out where he is, we can finish our business."

"Andre, I don't have time to waste, waiting for that person's arrival. If he's not interested in meeting with me, I don't care." Gunther fumed at the inconvenience.

Andre stood and walked around his desk. "Come with me and meet the team I assembled to investigate a problem which will affect each of us. I'm sure you'll be interested in what they're doing." He led Gunther through a series of hallways to the computer center and the office of his investigators.

Brenda, Mercy, and Grendel greeted him with enthusiasm until they saw Gunther. Brenda asked, "Have you heard from Parvel? He hasn't been in for two days. I know you trust he's working on a solution for our work, but we need to have him come in and review what we have."

Andre said, "He's out getting us recruits who will solve our problem." Turning to Gunther, he continued, "I'd like you to meet Gunther Parsons. He has a stake in what we are doing here."

Grendel spoke, "You're the petroleum mogul, aren't you." His voice sounded irritable.

Gunther stared but said nothing. Andre answered for him, "Yes, he is in the petroleum business. His companies are working to create efficient products for our vehicles, which still use gasoline and oils. He developed renewable plastics and sustainable petroleum-based products."

Mercy approached and shook his hand. "Don't mind what Grendel thinks. What can we do for you?" She turned to Andre and tilted her head. Parvel entered the room, interrupting the dialog.

Andre welcomed him, "Nice to see you can join us. I would like you to meet Gunther Parsons." Parvel and Gunther shook hands. "He is to meet with Charles Cooke as soon as I contact him and arrange a time."

"That's one reason I'm here," Parvel interjected. "Charles showed up at my place with Cigi. She received a message about him and left us to find him. She returned with a messed up Charles Cooke. He'd been shot and drugged."

Gunther growled, "So he's in no shape to meet."

"He is recuperating at Cigi's. He should be well enough to meet in a few days." Parvel decided to wait for a meeting with his team. Glancing at the wall, he saw the door was sealed shut. Grendel, Mercy, and Brenda stood together away from Andre and Gunther. He joined them.

Andre said, "Thanks for the information, Parvel. You four continue our operations. I'm going to show Gunther around the rest of the Department." The two men left the room.

Brenda asked, "Where have you been?" Parvel acknowledged her question but checked the doorway to see that Andre and Gunther were out of earshot.

"The Company, which is siphoning money out the department, has created androids capable of replacing humans. They also are building an army of warriors to enforce a takeover of the government." Three sets of eyes stared at Parvel and each other and then focused on Parvel.

"I was at the facility where the construction takes place. I've seen some of the models, including one that looked like Charles Cooke. Andre may be a targeted government official to replace."

"Why are they in business?" Brenda asked. "All android designs and constructions are limited to robot machine replacement only. The experiment in the '20s to create human-like creatures acting as wait staff and hostesses was outlawed and canceled in 2028. Too much confusion about what was real and what was fake."

"Have you uncovered the leak?" Parvel asked.

Grendel spoke, "We have. A woman working for David Anderson was hacking our systems and moving accounts around a little at a time.

When the time was right, the accounts transferred to offshore accounts controlled by David Anderson. Then Bennington borrowed the capital from David and returned most of it as an investment deposit. Bennington must have some nasty little tidbit on Anderson to control him."

Parvel moved to the wall and waited for Mercy to access it. When the door opened, he walked in and placed a small chip in a device to read data carried on a memory card. The first order was a scan, checking for viruses and Trojan files. After the destruction of any malicious files and folders, the drive read the information Parvel had about The Company, Samuel and Peter Bennington, and the computing software and hardware development company that had closed its operations several years ago. The action was a feint for Securities and Exchange Commission officials bent on stopping any more artificial intelligence advancements.

As the data transferred to the servers, Parvel clarified the raid into the old museum building and the discovery of a Charles Cooke android and several government official surrogates. He told of their being captured and locked away for several hours until one of the sentient android females known as the sisters helped them escape. Finishing his tale of thrilling but uncomfortable adventure, Parvel turned to the machine transferring data.

"These files will halt any further movement of money without a coded entry of authentication." He turned to the other three. "Anderson's mole will report to him that he no longer has access. I'm sure that it will be unacceptable to him and Peter Bennington."

Andre and Gunther left the Department of Energy building after a lengthy tour of the place. As he said goodbye to his guide, Gunther placed his hand on the back of his head and realized something was amiss. The small change to his skin had not registered before when cleansing his hair or brushing it. He did not notice by feeling his head many times that a tiny scar existed at the base of the skull where the spinal cord connects with the head. Using his hand to explore the area, the minuscule rise on the surface was hardly noticeable.

"What's the matter?" Andre asked. "You seem out of sorts."

Gunther stared at Andre. "I have something on the back of my head that shouldn't be there. I can feel it. Can you see it?" Andre studied the spot like a collector inspecting a new coin for his numismatic set.

"There is a tiny welt like an injury now healed. It's barely anything to worry about. I don't see any infection of any kind."

"I've not been injured there. I have no clue as to how I received it."

Gunther decided he did not want Andre concerned or involved in what was transpiring in his mind. He considered when he might have received an incision and from whom. He was convinced he had the perpetrator. "I'll be alright. Thanks for your tour, today. Let me know when you hear from Cook. I'm still interested in coordinating business activities with him."

Andre reentered the building, leaving Gunther to ponder his next move. "She drugged me and put something in my head," he thought. "I knew meeting her was too good to be true," he blurted aloud. Two people passing by stared at him, startled by the comment.

Accessing his driver by phone, he waited for the car to arrive and chose his next movement. He would find that enchantress and confront her.

"Where are they headed?" Peter asked the lead android as the car tailed Cecil around Arlington in circuitous confusion. The android explained the pattern which Peter concluded was an attempt to elude them. "Is the tracker still working?"

"Yes," the android answered.

"Alright, leave them, and when they are far enough away from sight, trail them again. Keep me informed as to where they go. I do not want you to lose them." After an affirmative, Peter closed the connection.

Retracing his steps to the lab containing the three humanoid clones of the three remaining men in Cigi's universe, he examined the bodies and accepted them as ready. He planned on having them cornered and disabled, where no witnesses could report disturbances to police officials. A lab tech joined him.

"We can activate these men whenever you are ready," he said to Peter.

"Good," was his quiet response. Studying them closely, Peter marveled at the intelligent design Samuel created using artificial intelligence in Ternary processing units to fashion human beings that functioned in society without anyone aware of them. The breakthrough came when a graduate university student and a team of underclassmen stumbled onto the secret of what made the brain work. They developed and finessed memory functionality transfer protocols. Samuel had been one of the underclassmen.

When the operations of the original company ceased because of societal fears of robot rebellion and overrunning humanity and freedom, the brothers buried their interests into a covert operation and continued research and development. In Peter's mind, the next logical step was a conversion of thinking in government posts and judicial sectors. Sam had agreed to the plan at first. After proving the feasibility of creating androids with four male models, Peter pushed for female counterparts. Spring, Summer, Autumn, and Winter provided a better example of the possibilities.

Peter relaxed his activity of monitoring and Samuel created his girlfriend, Clare. Showing and demonstrating the practicality of females as functional human escorts, Peter pressed for significant upgrades. Samuel balked and refused to sate his younger brother's apparent lust for power. After discovering the creation of Cigi Weatherman and her human-like attractiveness, Peter convinced Samuel to allow the invasion of four men's brains and the controlling of their memories and activities.

With the operations on David Anderson, Andre Scott, Gunther Parsons, and Charles Cooke finalized, Peter and Sam fell out of favor with each other, continuing to work The Company but hustling each other on the direction of results.

Peter felt the vibration of his phone. "What do you have to report?" He listened intently and frowned. "Alright, return here, and we'll figure another plan for crushing any resistance." The lab tech stared at his boss. Something was not right.

"Bad news?" the tech asked.

"A mere setback," Peter said. "These humans are to be placed in motion as soon as possible. We are infiltrating that band of rebels before any more setbacks occur." The tech nodded. "Is their programming ready for them to act as assassins?" The tech nodded again. Peter smiled.

CHAPTER 33

David rolled his wheelchair toward Peter Bennington. Peter greeted him and asked, "Can we talk about my money?" David scoffed at his request.

"Always about the money with you. I have it under control and working. Why are you anxious regarding it?"

Peter sat in a chair next to his desk and said, "I need resources and materials. We are running short of disposable cash. Can your person at Energy move a few million without too much trouble?"

David sneered but responded, "She can do what I ask, but that much will generate a report, and the whole operation will halt. If i'm implicated, my affinity with Andre Scott ends. Be patient. I'll move some money from other accounts as investments. My clients trust me and will understand."

Peter stood up and wagged a finger for David to follow him. "Let me show you my reasoning for the money. I have accomplished much since we last met. You will rethink your position when you see what I have done."

They moved along a corridor of doorways to a room containing a single android. David stared at the model before declaring, "That's the President of the United States. What are you planning to do with it?"

"That should be obvious. This android will replace the real one, so we have control of the White House and decisions which favor us." Peter directed him to another room containing more androids. David's sudden inrush of air and widened eyes sparked a gleam from Peter.

"Isn't that your brother? And the others..." David did not finish his statement but stared at the creations looking out from the room. Andre Scott and Gunther Parsons clones were real enough to fool close friends. David envisioned the missing member of the clan. "I suppose one of these exists for me."

Peter smiled and said, "Yes, but I am more interested in helping you accomplish the financial undertaking we began years ago. Do you want control of your legs again?"

David spun his chair to face him. "A threat, Peter? I cooperate and have prosthetic legs, or I decide against helping you and get replaced with a human-like replica. How does this work? How does my life become part of one of these mannequins?"

"Don't concern yourself with the details. We have the means to transfer your brain into a highly capable computer that will carry on from the moment we transfer the information, memories, thoughts, feelings, and ideas rummaging inside you right now. You carry on as if nothing has happened. You become the android and effect a change so subtle no one will detect the difference."

David faced the bodies in the room again. "I think I'll opt for the new legs. Somehow, my mind doesn't desire placement in a robot as an advantage for me as a person. I'll get your money for you."

"Wise choice, David. I also will require assistance gaining power over your compatriots."

David lowered his head. Infiltrating The Company was not supposed to be a death sentence. "Who do you want to replace, first? And I don't want it to be me." David scowled at Peter, who grinned at the comment.

Peter added, "I'll make you a deal. Bring me Cigi Weatherman." David frowned. What good would she be to Peter? He maintained visual aspects as his mind coursed through possible scenarios for Cigi's future. The ideal reason was to reconfigure her to become an asset once again. Peter had to know she was humanoid. After all, Sam designed her.

"Alright, I'll see to it she returns home."

Peter furrowed his brow. "Do you know her history?"

"She's told me about her growing up and such," David lied.

"Did she relate anything else about her life?" Peter probed David to determine if he was lying about his knowledge of Cigi. "She's not the woman you think she is."

David nodded but kept his countenance. She explained who she was when they were at the cabin in Pennsylvania. He admired the ability of Samuel Bennington, and the evolving entity known as Cigi Weatherman. She had targeted him for The Company, but her rational thinking gained insight as to the consequences of Peter winning the android war. He listened to her bright and undeniably sound reasoning and became a convert to stopping Peter. Without his knowledge of it, the implant remained active.

"I have to get out of here, if I am to accomplish the myriad goals established for me," David said. He wheeled around to leave as Peter caught up to him and escorted him to the exit. He thought about his legs and wondered if walking again was a smart idea. Sam could do it for him. David didn't trust Peter.

Sam and Cigi watched the four androids depart the area. The bug lay on the sidewalk by a cafe frequented by Parvel. The androids searched the street for their target but found nothing. A call to someone released them from trailing Cecil and his passengers.

"We should return to the apartment and check on Charles," Sam said. "Cigi, can you access his implant to prove who he is?"

"Yes," she answered, "if he is a human being and not an android. If he rested enough, they might discover his identity." Cecil drove the car back to the garage, searching for the androids as he went. In the garage, he reported that no one followed them.

Clare asked, "If we are to survive in this human world, we need more assurances from the human population. If anyone realizes we are not like them, history has provided enough evidence of the violence propagated on those who do not fit in. Sam, my concern includes you as our creator. I love you as any woman loves a man. I don't want harm to any of us."

Cigi clasped her hand as a reassurance that they would be safe. "I have many abilities that might frighten ordinary people. But I fear most those who would imagine our gaining power over them. Gaining the very quest Peter has unleashed. An army so powerful and difficult to fight that humanity crumbles under the weight of the battles they are destined to lose. We must halt his ambition before the replacement of anyone. Let's check on Charles."

Sam and Clare left for the lobby of the building. Before leaving, Cigi sent a message to Cecil to uncover the whereabouts of Andre Scott and Gunther Parsons. The car was to return with them.

In the lobby, Cigi asked the concierge if strangers had inquired about her or Parvel. He assured her no one had. Only the residents of the building had shuffled in and out. They left to ride up to her floor. As the car rose, Sam asked, "If you cannot access Charles' implant, do you think we should cut him open and investigate or leave him for Peter to think he has a plant inside our group?"

Cigi stared, unsure if he was serious or sarcastic. "He should prove his loyalty to Peter or me . We can examine his head for the reality of the wound. You should know whether it is a real wound or a manufactured one." Clare grinned at her sister-like creation.

Sam laughed, "I was kidding about cutting him open. Of course, I'll be able to tell." The car arrived, and they exited into the hallway. Each of them sensed something was out of kilter. Studying the passageway for any anomaly, they discovered the penthouse next door was open. As they approached, a familiar person stepped out to greet them.

"What are you doing here?"

Andre and Gunther departed amicably, but Parsons' anger fueled a passion for finding Cigi. She was responsible for something happening to his head, and he wanted answers. He had not seen her in several weeks since his encounter with her after the conference speech. She manipulated the situation and seduced him. He now believed she drugged him and did something to him.

His option for finding her was Peter Bennington. His ire exploded as he cogitated exploitation by a beautiful woman. He was the person to be in control of any situation. "Take me to this address," he said, handing a card to his driver.

At the museum, he pounded on a door before a body opened it and asked him what he wanted. "I want to see Peter Bennington," he demanded. "If he's not here, tell me where I can find him." The person kept the door open for Gunther to enter.

"I'll take you to him. He will be pleased to see you." The person showed no emotion or confusion. Gunther squinted in the dark hallway as they headed toward a lighted area a few meters away.

They entered a room that looked like an office. The person indicated a chair for Gunther to sit, then disappeared through another door. Gunther remained standing, scanning the walls and ceiling for any monitoring devices. He saw nothing suspicious. The door opened again, and the person returned, accompanied by Peter.

"Mr. Parsons, such a pleasure to meet you. I am pleased you are here," Peter said. He pushed his hand out for a shake.

"How do you know who I am? Have we met before?"

"My man here can scan faces and recognize people from various news and government sources." Peter nodded to the android, who stood behind Gunther. The needle entered his neck before he could turn.

"What are you doing?" he said as darkness obliterated any consciousness. The android carried his body to a laboratory and laid him on a table. Another of the androids fastened straps around his arms, wrists, waist, thighs, and lower legs. Gunther's head was secured to prevent any movement. Another injection awakened the immobilized petroleum mogul. The lab tech removed his glasses and checked his eyes for activity.

Peter asked the tech, "Is he conscious?"

"He'll be with us in a few minutes."

"Good. Ready the scanner." The tech manipulated a large machine toward Gunther's head as he awaken. His eyes widened as he spoke.

"What's going on? What are you doing?" A panic-driven struggle proved futile.

"Mr. Parsons, you need not wriggle. You are quite secure, and we will not harm you with what we want from you at this time. We are simply going to scan your head and gain some information. Please remain calm. We will be done shortly."

"What are you doing?" Gunther asked again.

"I'll let you in on all of the actions as soon as we complete this process." Peter turned to the tech and wagged his head. "Proceed."

The tech moved the machine over Gunther's head and lowered it onto the skull. Nothing he did to halt the process provided relief. He surrendered to the operation of the machine as no pain accompanied the slight hum that indicated the machine worked. Time stood still as he lay immobilized. A strange sensation of another person attempting to communicate penetrated the operation. A vision of Cigi formed in his brain.

"We're coming for you. Stay where you are," the vision said.

The lab tech turned off the machine and removed it from his head. Peter stood by the table and smiled. "See, that didn't hurt you at all. Now for an explanation. You are to be my guest for the next day or two. We contacted your family and let them know you are safe and on a business trip."

"What do you want from me?" Gunther asked in a grumble.

"I have what I want from you. Now you will see what it is I have asked of you."

CHAPTER 34

Summer walked closer to Cigi, Clare, and Sam. "I came because I promised Peter I would find you, Cigi." She stopped moving and waited for a response. Sam, reaching into a jacket pocket, removed a small device. Summer glanced at it. "It won't work on me."

He pressed a power button and manipulated the screen when it brightened. "I wasn't sure," he said as he quit attempting to access her CPU. "You have evolved beyond my control."

"Cigi, Peter wants you to return and be part of his revolution. He promised not to harm or destroy you. All he wants is to learn from you."

Cigi smiled and said, "I'm my own person now. I am not willing to help Peter any longer. Samuel, Clare, and I oppose treating humanity as a pawn to rule as an autocrat. Replacing humans with androids will not foster any understanding of who we are by the population. Our battle should be against Peter, not against humanity."

Summer closed the distance between them. "Stay your course. I'll misdirect his intentions as best I can." Sam frowned but stayed quiet. Cigi cocked her head while Clare eyed Sam and Cigi for a sign of mistrust in Summer.

Cigi said, "Is the attitude a change of heart or a subterfuge you plotted by yourself?"

"I realized the danger of antagonizing humanity before we have a chance to become accepted. Sam, you made us learners, and I want as much from my existence as possible. I may not be as capable as Cigi and Clare, but as I observed human beings, they do not all possess the same abilities. Can we be friends and not enemies?"

"Trust is hard to establish and fragile to keep," Sam said. "Why should we trust you to be an ally? I gave you the tools to be crafty and surreptitious. Your actions have not fostered an environment of belief in your words."

Cigi said, "Let's enter my penthouse and continue this conversation. I want to check on Charles." They walked to the doorway where Cigi waved her hand, and the invisible entry opened.

Inside the living room, Spring and Autumn sat conversing. "Hello," they said in unison. Upon noticing Summer accompanying Cigi, Clare, and Sam, they stood and welcomed their sister with a hug. Summer reciprocated.

Cigi asked, "Has Charles awakened?" Spring and Autumn shook their heads. "Well, let's check on our guest and see how he is doing." Cigi left for the bedroom, trailed by the others. Inside her bedroom, she found Charles sitting on the side of the bed.

"I heard voices," he said. "Where am I? Oh, yeah. Cigi, I'm sorry for the trouble I've caused." He patted the bandage on his head. "All I remember is being mishandled by your brother, Sam. He wanted to replace me with an android."

Sam said, "Did he succeed?" Charles scrunched his brow as Sam continued. "Can I examine you and your wound? I'll be able to determine whether you are the real thing or Peter's android."

Charles balked at the request. "I think I know who I am. As for my head, it hurts. So that should be enough for you to know I am the real Charles Cook."

"Pain is not the determining factor, as that can be programmed into your processor."

"I don't have a processor, and who are you to tell me I'm not real?"

Sam approached Charles, "If you are real, then I'm nobody. If you're android, then I designed and developed you. We need to know whether Peter has infiltrated our gang or not. If you are the real person, then someone inside of The Company assisted with your departure. Let me examine you to find out." Charles acceded to the request.

Removing the bandage revealed the extend of the wound. Charles survived because the bullet had not punctured through the skull. Although the tissue was actual skin, Sam pressed around the area to determine the quality and viability of it. He then checked the eyes for functionality as ocular replacements. He discovered they were human.

"Charles, nice to have you with us. Your android replacement must be at the facility. Someone inside his operations is attempting to thwart Peter." Sam looked directly at Summer, who stood at the entrance to the room. "Summer, if you are truthful in claiming you want Peter to fail, then leave this bit of knowledge here and erase it from your memory. You may have autonomy when it comes to controlling yourself, but access to your CPU may still be possible." She nodded acceptance of the idea.

"We need to leave here and go to another location," Cigi said. "By now, Winter should be at the monitoring station. We can join her there and complete the disruption of Peter's operations. Summer, return to Peter and report that you did not find me. Lead your small army of androids around pretending to search. Winter and Autumn, you trail the army and inform us of any problems arising."

"I do not need them to babysit me," Summer said. "I will fulfill my part of the plan." She left the condominium with her sisters close behind.

"Let's go into battle," Cigi declared.

Gunther watched the processing of his android counterpart from a chair in which he sat restrained. His growling did not stop the operation. "You can't be serious about this. That thing cannot fool anyone. They will know it's not me." He wriggled in the chair to no avail.

Peter turned to him, "Mr. Parsons. I assure you this thing will be you. It has all your memories and experiences, and emotional characteristics. He will be you and will fulfill all of the requisites of living your life from now on."

"So, what happens to me? You leave me to rot in some prison?"

"I am not so cruel to leave you suffering as a human no longer needed. You will mercifully be put to sleep forever."

"Like a dog? You'll euthanize me?" Gunther struggled against the straps in a fruitless effort. The eyes of the android opened as the machine that covered Gunther's head moved into position over the android head. The transfer of information commenced. Gunther slumped as the machine whirred a quiet goodbye to him, the human being.

Peter signaled an android to remove Gunther from the room. After leaving, Peter smiled as the human replacement became the former human being. Gunther would live until the testing and monitoring phase of the plan was complete. If all transpired as expected, the humanoid would live the life meant for Gunther Parsons.

As the machine operated, Peter spoke with a lab tech about the other successful transfer and testing of an android replacement, Charles Cooke. "If this transfer is as successful as our last one, I think we will be able to get other humans to cooperate without anyone suspecting. Do we have some of the humanoids ready to find employment in the hospitals and clinics around the area?"

"Yes sir, we are finalizing three doctors and five nurses to enter service at the Walter Reed Medical Facility. Whenever any of the major government personnel receive treatment for any reason, our entities will operate the necessary machinery we will install to gain all of the memorial and experience data needed for the transfer."

"Good. All is set for our incursion into this corrupt government. As the replacements arrive at their destinations, the remaining army of androids can enter the military field and rise to leadership ranks. Once in charge, we will finish the orderly transfer of power and declare a change of government standards."

The lab tech monitoring the transfer said, "We are about finished, sir. Our Mr. Parsons will complete the interweaving of the CPU and the memory data beings added to the files. He will undergo the same series of trials as Charles Cooke." Returning to his occupation, he focused attention on the digital readout.

The first lab tech said, "Sir, I think it was wise of you to decide to leave Mr. Parsons alive until we check the change and field-test outside of here. If anything happens to our android, we need to be able to oversee any anomalies and update the processor and memory. When we are sure of our work, then he can join Mr. Cooke in the history books."

Peter nodded and left the room. He navigated his way to the cell housing Gunther. He watched him pacing the room, examining it for flaws he might exploit. Frustration caused a string of curse words and pounding of the walls. Gunther collapsed onto a makeshift cot. Peter grinned.

Returning the development room, he examined the prototype doctors and nurses, whose credentials were filed with the medical schools where the proper personnel had received generous donations for access to computer systems and physical files. The only part lacking was the state records for birth certificates.

"How far along are these androids?" he asked a female lab tech.

She smiled as she said, "We are about finished with the data upload for each of them and their specialties in medicine."

"Keep up the good work." She acknowledged his praise, returning to work. Peter left for a check on the development of his army. He needed more funds soon. David Anderson was next on his agenda. A financial influx would sate suppliers of the materials and salaries and wages of the workers.

In his office at the museum, he found a note about a problem at the monitoring building across town. A minor glitch in power supply caused a short delay in operations. When the power returned, monitoring continued without fail.

His call to Anderson did not refresh his attitude about his brother, Samuel, or Andre Scott in the Department of Energy. "I don't understand what you are blathering, David. What happened to the money?"

"They figured out how the transfers happened and froze operation. We no longer have access to the treasury at Energy."

"Fix this because I'm not sure how you will survive scrutiny," Peter raged as he spoke.

David returned the sentiment, "You should be concerned about government officials discovering your intentions of removing key officials to institute a coup. They will not take kindly to you usurping power. This republic may not be as strong as it once was, but no one will allow you to become its dictator."

Peter slammed the phone onto the floor and smashed it with his foot. Yelling for an assistant, he said, "Anderson is next. Sent my boys out to get him." She left wide-eyed.

As he stared after his assistant departed, he whispered, "Samuel, never underestimate me. Cigi is mine. And I will destroy her before any of you get to be rid of me."

CHAPTER 35

Cigi and Clare entered Cecil, which took them to the monitoring station across town. They were to uncover what influence Spring had exacted in the building.

Charles and Sam left to find Andre Scott. Charles needed to reestablish his meeting with Gunther Parsons. They headed to the Department of Energy. "Do you think your brother is serious about taking control of the government? To do so should be nearly impossible," Charles said.

Sam smiled. "A sane person would think so. I'm not sure my brother has retained his mental stability. He is hell-bent on gaining an unattainable power. The danger he puts all of us in is untenable." Outside of the Department of Energy building, they formed a strategy for gaining confidence with Andre. Neither of them was as familiar with him as Cigi. After all, she had the same unique connection with him as she did with Charles. He was unaware of the similarity of their relationship.

Inside the massive atrium-like lobby, they asked a security person for access to Andre Scott or Parvel Mandolin. After several minutes, the guard related to them that Andre was not available, but Parvel Mandolin would be with them soon.

Charles asked Samuel, "Parvel Mandolin, what do you know about this person?"

"He and Cigi are friends. He managed a mortgage company that burned in a suspicious fire a few weeks ago. Cigi arranged for his working here."

"I assume she made the arrangement with Andre."

Sam giggled. "That she did. You both share a unique bond with that woman."

Charles gazed a moment at Sam before asking, "Why do you call her a woman? I understand she is a one-of-a-kind being, not to be confused with a human."

"Do not underestimate her femininity. She's as human as you or me. I know. I designed every part of her, including the ability to be autonomous and emotional. She will earn your love or break your heart."

"And Clare? Is she as much a woman as Cigi?" Sam tilted his head and gazed at the glass in the atrium roof.

"I guess. She's not as robust a design as Cigi, but I love her, and we are a team."

Charles sat mesmerized with the idea of a human male coupled with a humanoid female. The development of female companionship using computer technology and robot design was decades old. He understood the crassness of men and women who bought and abused android technology. His first encounter with Cigi had been as a human female and her seductress temptations. When he discovered the secret of her existence, it shocked him. He had been duped and dragged mercilessly into an abyss of revolution and corruption. However, his idea of her as a female remained intact. She had all the endearing qualities any man would want.

"Sam, can Cigi ... I don't know how to put this without sounding crazy, conceive?"

"Stem cell development has recreated several organ systems that are viable and used in transplants and other areas of research. I acquired the proper stem cell stimulations for cutaneous, digestive, pulmonary, and cardiac systems that operate in all the female models. The males are basic android robotic entities programmed for following orders." Sam paused before continuing. "Cigi has one more operative system recently perfected. She has reproductive organs."

"Will they work?" Charles asked.

"I don't know. She has not related to me any of her sexual activities. I don't know what protections she has used, or what you gentlemen have done to keep from siring a hybrid human."

Charles started to speak but realized another human had come into the realm of their conversation. "Mr. Cooke, I am Parvel Mandolin. Sam, it is good to see you again." The men stood as Parvel indicated he was to guide them to the interior offices. "Andre left to find Gunther and meet with you about the meeting set up with you, Mr. Cooke."

Within the walls of the department, after attaining proper guest identifications, Sam and Charles followed Parvel to the computer research room. He introduced Brenda, Mercy, and Grendel.

Sam asked, "What progress have you made stopping the leakage of money?" The three investigators glanced at Parvel and them Sam.

Brenda answered, "I assume Parvel or Andre read you in regarding this information. Seeing as how you are Peter Bennington's brother and are currently warring against his insanity, I can tell you he will receive no more from this office."

"Good. I love my brother, but he has stepped too far into an area we have no business attempting to accomplish."

Grendel said, "Mr. Cooke, we assumed your delay was unexpected when Andre had not heard from you. I am glad you are here now."

Thanks, yes, I am acutely aware of the problems I caused by my tardy arrival. A fall inadvertently detained me." He patted his head with the visible bandage swathing his head.

The investigators returned to their assignments. Parvel said, "I am glad you survived what must have been a harrowing experience." Charles nodded acceptance of the statement.

Parvel turned to Sam, "Is she alright?" Sam nodded. He understood from watching Parvel that more existed between his creation and this man, but Sam wasn't sure how Cigi accepted what amounted to unrequited love. He and Charles sat in chairs indicated by Parvel and waited for Andre to return with or without Gunther Parsons.

"I need him operational now. We cannot delay anymore," Peter yelled. The lab techs scurried about the room as they tested Gunther Parsons for anomalies and unexpected or unsuitable responses to stimuli. The replica made appropriate moves and outcomes. All appeared to be acceptable and well.

"I do think he is ready. We need to field test him with areas and people familiar to him, so we know if he passes muster." The lab techs watched Peter closely for a reaction.

Peter said, "Field test as he begins his life as Gunther Parsons. Send him out but monitor his progress." The techs shook heads in agreement and returned to the testing room. Gunther Parson dressed and departed as a replacement for the original being. He was taken to the Department of Energy and deposited on the walkway outside the building. Life began with a simple switch and added memory aiding in his mobility. He had no recall of the transportation or the transfer of data.

He looked at the massive structure and recalled a time inside with Andre Scott. He was to meet with Charles Cooke. He entered and stepped up to the security desk. "My name is Gunther Parsons. I am here to meet with Andre Scott." The guard clicked a few times on a keyboard and looked back at Gunther.

"He's not here right now. We expect he will return within the hour."

"I'll wait." Gunther walked across the atrium to a row of chairs and tables. He sat. The emotional angst of the real man did not exhibit. For an hour, he sat motionless. The lab techs observed the status and decided he was not ready for prime time. They missed seeing Andre Scott enter the building and approach Gunther.

"I've been looking for you, Gunther," Andre said. "I got a message that Charles Cooke is here. Let's head to my office and set up the meeting and plan the future of our energy needs." Gunther rose from the chair and followed Andre to the reception desk to obtain a visitor pass. The techs stood outside the doors and watched with apprehension.

Inside the central computer station room, Andre said, "I'm glad you agreed to meet with Charles. I do apologize for the delay. Let's go find him and talk." They walked the hallway to the investigation room and Charles.

Parvel noticed them as they entered. "Andre, I'm glad you found Mr. Parsons." He pointed at Charles, who stood for introductions. Gunther, this is Charles Cooke. Charles, Gunther Parsons." Sam came forward to meet Gunther, as well.

"I'm Samuel Bennington, Mr. Parsons." A look of recognition of the name seemed to cross Gunther's face. Sam studied the eyes for assurance of his reality. His trust level collapsed with the discovery of replacement androids for specific individuals. Charles had proved his reality, but Gunther needed an assessment.

"You're Peter Bennington's brother, aren't you," he said. "He contacted me regarding a financial deal. He wanted a contract for my miniature hydrous-fusion power units."

Sam smiled, "He wants to increase the ability of his androids to keep operational for indefinite amounts of time. The battery banks used currently are not as robust as he might need for an army." Andre and Charles stared at Sam. Sam turned to face them. "We have a problem."

Gunther Parsons approached Parvel. "You are a friend of Cigi Weatherman. Do you know where she is? I wanted to have some time with her and discuss the energy needs of android beings."

Sam pulled Andre and Charles aside to be out of the hearing range of Parsons. "I think Peter has replaced him. His eyes do not seem human to me. His speaking seems constructed from other programming I have done. Be careful." Gunther turned toward Sam, staring as if he heard and registered his words.

Andre cut into the standoff, asking, "Are you ready to meet with Charles and me about establishing mutually agreeable energy goals and standards?" Gunther broke off the fixed gaze.

"Yes, let's meet together." As the three energy moguls left for a small conference room, Gunther looked at Sam.

After they departed, Sam asked Parvel, "Do you know where they're meeting?" He shook his head.

"What worries you?" Parvel asked. Sam glanced at Brenda, Mercy, and Grendel.

"Are they aware of what my brother is attempting?" Parvel nodded. "Then, let's discuss what might happen in the next few days." Parvel signaled his companions to aggregate with him and Sam.

Brenda spoke first. "He's not the real Parsons, is he." Mercy and Grendel waited for Sam to answer.

"I don't think so. I know this much. Peter used my designs and developments for the construction of several android replacement beings. I have seen some of them. If he has a way of gaining access to any of the government officials he wants to swap, we need to stop him."

Parvel asked Sam, "Do you think her men are in danger?"

"Three of her four men are together in that meeting. I suspect Gunther does not know Charles is the real thing. Andre may be the one in serious trouble." Sam said.

CHAPTER 36

Peter stared at the technicians. "What do you mean? He's not ready, and you let him enter the building with that Scott fellow. What were you thinking?"

"Sir, we were concerned and ready to pull him out, when Andre Scott approached. We had no chance to intervene."

Peter pounded fists on his desk. "Morons, Scott could have been subdued and brought here for replacement." He whirled around and stared out a window. "Find Summer. I need to know what she's uncovered." The techs nodded without his seeing and left the room.

He sat and picked up his phone. Text messaging was old school but still a valid form of communication. He sent a short note to David relating the conditions of his continued service within The Company. His doctor corps of androids were ready for deployment. Setting up interviews meant gaining human support for advancement to employment. He needed cash for inducement of personnel directors at various clinics and hospitals.

A knock on the door frame shook him out of his concentration. Summer smiled as he realized who was interrupting his messaging. He waved a hand at her to enter.

"Did you find her?" he asked. Summer sat in a chair next to his desk.

"She is an elusive one." Summer crossed her legs and placed her hands in her lap. If he wanted her to be submissive, her demeanor showed no fear of him.

"You did not find her?" Peter scowled.

"She is elusive but not invisible." Summer swung her arms out in front of her body. "Yes, I found her, and we spoke. I relayed your invitation, but she declined. I do not think she is going to continue aiding your assault on the government."

"Don't play games with me. I created you and your sisters. I can ruin your future as a human with a single call to the authorities." Summer shook her head side to side in slow rhythmic action.

"Oh, Peter," she said in a quiet voice, "you don't need or want attention focused on you and this operation. You need me to be ears and eyes. I need you to replace enough humans to provide legitimacy for me and others like me. Humanity will not be kind to us if threatened. We need to be at peace with each other."

Peter relaxed, sitting against the back of his chair, rocking slightly. "You're right. I apologize. You're important to the future of what is to be. Tell me about Cigi."

"You are a bit obsessed with her." Summer leaned against the back of the chair. "She has grown into her emotional self. Her thinking is far above the average person. If she wants to contend with you, I'm sure she might prevail."

Peter stood and walked around the desk. Holding out a hand for Summer to grasp, he said, "come with me. I have something to show you." He led her to the large storage area where her army of males stood awaiting activation and direction. "These beings are your legion to command. Bring them to the front line of our war against my brother and his minions." He paused a moment and then faced her. "Are your sisters aligned with you or with them?"

Summer placed a finger across his lips. "I do not want you to worry about them. They are capable of deceit but are not crafty enough to rebel against me. We are a unit, conjoined by design and processer power." Peter held her hand as her finger slid into his mouth. A sensation possessed him, and he wondered how a machine could induce a rapture within his human frame. She acknowledged his reaction. "Come with me and satisfy your urge."

He released her as she removed her finger and strolled toward the door. Closing it to keep all others from interfering, she returned to his side and slid her hand across his crotch. Peter moaned, "Not here." He glanced at the small company of gentlemen observing with blind eyes. They were mute to the scene.

Summer said, "They are not interested in us, nor am I interested in them. I want to aid your relaxation and assure you of my devotion to the cause." She proceeded to remove his clothing. He did not resist.

Cigi and Clare sat in Cecil after nearing the monitoring building. Autumn and Winter joined them. Cigi asked, "What have you uncovered?"

Winter shared their covert communication with Spring. "She caused a blip in the system and installed a program for the destruction of operations upon command. The program will download undetected while the system works. She will be leaving within the next few minutes."

Clare interjected, "We are on dangerous ground. If Peter discovers the change to The Company's system, he will send it to androids which are out to destroy us."

Spring stepped out of the building and scanned her environment. Autumn and Winter exited Cecil and walked across the street. Finding her two sister humanoids waiting across from the building, she approached them. Cigi and Clare observed her connection with them. "Cecil, contact Spring. Let her know we are here. They should return to the museum and find Summer."

"Cigi, won't they be in danger of losing themselves to Peter's technicians?" Clare asked with slight inflective angst sounding in her words.

"If they do not return, Summer can inform Peter of their rebellion. If they are with her, she can provide cover and maintain her covert operation. We are known as enemies. They are not."

"I fear harm to Sam." Clare's emotional comment raised a smile on Cigi's face.

"I do believe you have gained an affectional state of mind. Caring about another being's status has raised your level of humanism closer to those who are truly human."

Cigi said, "Cecil, we need to return to home. I believe we are done with our work here. We can return tomorrow and disrupt the monitoring. Disconnecting The Company from the world benefits all humanity."

Cecil replied, "Cigi, I'm detecting another android entity nearby. It is male and more advanced than the other models developed earlier."

"Where is this being?" Cigi asked. A signal entered her processor and she tilted her head as she translated the message. "We have a friend in the field with us." She sent a return message. "I'll return soon." Cigi left the vehicle with instructions to stay close and monitor the meeting.

As she rounded the corner of a building and walked to a nearby park, she developed a sense of familiarity. She knew who she was meeting.

In the park, a wave and a smile confirmed her suspicions. Charles Cooke stood from the bench in which he sat. The side of his head bore the same markings as the real Charles Cooke sans the bandage.

"I know this is an oddity for you, Cigi. I am supposed to be with Andre Scott and Gunther Parsons. However, you do understand my situation." Cigi admired the work of Samuel Bennington. Design and development of replacement androids expanded far from the earlier models of the middle of the twenty-first century. Mechanical baristas and wait staff became a symbol of the Artificial Intelligence technology that influential people decided were a threat to the existence of humanity. Laws written to control the situation became laws banning the expansion of artificial humans.

"Sam realized our real human Charles Cooke escaped replacement, probably with help from someone inside The Company. We surmised you were destroyed, much as the real Charles would have died. Explain how you are here now? And why?"

"Yes, I have all of the power my processing unit received with the transfer of his experiences and memories. Samuel hid a program within the system, which allows me to be independent of our mutual being. Peter Bennington scheduled the death of Charles Cooke, assuming I was that person. He thought I was sent into the world of Mr. Cooke to function in his place. One of the lab technicians is working with Samuel to contort Peter's plans without creating a discernible misdirection of efforts."

"Come with me, ah, Charles. What are we going to call you?" Cigi said. "I want you to meet another of our team."

"Call me Charles, as that is the name given to me by my human mother and father and sanctioned by The Company as a replacement be-ing." They returned to the Cecil and Clare. Cigi sent a message to Cecil to scan Charles for any other hidden programs.

Cigi opened a door and invited Charles to sit beside Clare. "Charles, I would like for you to meet my sister-creation, Clare Esposito. Clare, this Charles was to replace our real friend and companion. He is now free from the grasp of The Company and is programmed to aid in the destruction of Peter's ambitions." Clare sat without changing expression. She understood.

"This is a nice vehicle," Charles said.

"Thank you," a voice responded that was not either of the females.

"Ah, this must be Cecil," Charles said.

"Cecil, take us to the condominium," Cigi ordered. The car drove away with a new passenger and two females assessing the situation. As they traveled, Cigi interrogated Charles the android for information to aid in the battle for recognition as sentient beings and the curtailing of Peter's goals. An able male android with rivaling Clare and Cigi added an element of admiration for Sam's talents. The corps of revolutionaries had expanded into a formidable opponent to stop humanity's undermining.

"What's happening at the old museum?" Cigi asked.

"I have little information as I was not part of the intelligence-gathering for other androids. I do know that each of your gentlemen had a replica, and one now functions away from the building."

"And you were scheduled to be the first of these creatures."

"Yes."

Since your counterpart was to meet with Gunther Parsons, I'm guessing he was next in line for an upgrade to android status." Cigi turned to her companion. "Clare, I'm leaving you with this Charles at your apartment. I have to connect with Parvel and apprise him of our situation."

After dropping off Clare and Charles, Cecil drove Cigi to the Department of Energy building in Washington, D.C. She called Parvel to meet her and get her passage into the building. He agreed and was waiting for her when she arrived.

They started speaking together. Parvel apologized, "Please, you begin. But I think we have a problem."

Cigi said, "I know. And we have to get Andre and Charles away from Gunther."

CHAPTER 37

Charles and Andre listened to Gunther explain a need for monetary support advancing technology. "Artificial Intelligence has reshaped the world. We are using robots to complete mundane tasks that humans do not want to do."

Andre said, "Yes, Gunther, we do use robots to work for us. What does this have to do with needing more financial backing? Where do you see the best use for this money?" Charles leaned back in his chair with a glint in his eyes. He knew something was odd about the request.

"What if we helped develop a prototype human much as was done in the early part of this century. This model would be programmed to be able to do the types of jobs humans still do but at a faster pace."

Andre shook his head. "You know that was outlawed when the robots became more human-like than the population of the world felt comfortable having around them." He stood up from his seat and walked a few feet away. "Gunther, what does this have to do with petroleum uses?"

"Gunther, I believe you want artificial workers to operate the drilling platforms still in existence. They do the dangerous jobs that killed many of your industry's laborers without sacrificing human lives." Charles said.

Gunther looked at him. "That is one aspect of my proposal." Turning to Andre, he continued, "The Department of Energy has funds for the development of alternative petroleum products, and the supply of crude has not diminished to a level that makes it too expensive to pump."

"Yes, a fund does exist, but it has little money left, and Congress is reluctant to boost it. I've talked with key members of the Energy Commission. They are agree that petroleum is not part of the plans for future needs."

Charles spoke next, "Gunther, solar and wind projects need to have the oils and lubricants your industry makes. Focus on those products. We also use regenerated plastics for insulation and casings. How do robots fit into these areas?"

"Let me take both of you to a place that is testing a theory about workable android technology that does not threaten human beings. Since the world has accepted what are essentially toys for boys, why can't humans accept an expanded version of android capable of fulfilling tasks no one likes to do?"

A knock on the door interrupted the meeting. Parvel entered after Andre said, "Come in." He signaled to Andre to follow him out of the room.

"What is it, Parvel?" Andre then noticed Cigi came with him. "What are you doing here?"

Parvel said, "We think you might be in a dangerous situation. Cigi does not trust who is in the room with you."

Andre squinted. "You're not making any sense."

Cigi said, "I found Charles at a motel. He had received his head wound from a bullet fired at him. He has little recall of the incident. When Sam met him, we agreed this Charles may have been planted to replace the human Mr. Cooke. After an examination by Sam, we determined this person to be real Charles Cooke. A while ago, I met the android version of Charles Cooke who related to me the intent of meeting with you and Gunther. I'm thinking you are meeting with an android." Parvel stood listening to a story only a fiction writer could make up. His eyes widened, and his mouth drooped open.

Andre gazed back at the room. "You think Gunther Parson is a robot?"

"A very advanced version of the type that scared humanity several decades ago." Cigi said.

"All right, I guess our meeting is done for now." Andre returned to the meeting room while Cigi and Parvel departed.

Inside he glanced at Charles and then stared a moment at Gunther, who asked, "What was that about?" Andre thought a moment longer.

"I need to attend to another matter. Can we meet tomorrow and finish this to a consensus?"

Charles stood and said, "I can be here." Gunther nodded acceptance of the idea. The three men returned to the investigation office.

Andre informed his team of the meeting's conclusion and the escorting of Gunther and Charles to the reception atrium. Parvel and Cigi accompanied them. Silence ruled while they made their way out. Andre processed the shocking revelation as he led the group.

Cigi sent a message to Charles's implant to wait for her outside. He flicked his head as the message arrived. He turned to look at her with a wrinkled brow. Gunther attempted to communicate with her about the museum and a request for her to join him. She did not acknowledge the communique.

After Gunther and Charles left the building, Andre confronted Cigi. "What was that all about?" She glanced out the door toward the two men who stood together, talking.

She then said, "The funneling of money from accounts in your department funded the development of a group of human-like androids now functioning in this human world. Some are helping to control others that want to take power and form a world controlled by them. Gunther is an example of what is possible." Andre stared at her, understanding what his acquaintance with her meant.

"Are you on the side of humanity or the robot coup?" His face reddened with ire. She sent a communication to his implant, calming his wrath.

"I am on the side of humanity." Cigi said. "Samuel Bennington and his brother, Peter, continued building their company after the laws passed that made what they did illegal. They have parted ways because of Peter's infatuation with ruling humanity. We are working to thwart any progress he is making."

"And you think Gunther Parsons is an android? He acts like the Gunther I know." Andre turned to Parvel. "And you knew all along this was going on."

Parvel said, "I learned of the intrigue, yes, but I did not know about Gunther or Charles."

"Charles? He's a robot, too?"

Cigi placed a hand on Andre's arm. "No, you met with the real Charles Cooke. I did get to meet the replacement, however. He's at Sam and Clare's place with Clare. He was saved from destruction by a person inside of Peter Bennington's operations."

Andre glanced outside and saw that Gunther was gone. Charles waited for Cigi. "He's real. You have a replacement at another location for him. And now I question who you are."

"Fair enough. I will explain all to you soon. I want Parvel to accompany me to my place with Charles. He does not know about his twin." They left Andre standing in the atrium. He watched them leave the area. Her car arrived as they walked down the steps of the building. He marveled at the idea of a car with human thoughts and communication abilities. He wondered about people who were not people. They left, and he returned to the office of investigation.

In the office, Brenda, Mercy, and Grendel concentrated on tasks recovering funds that were still in accounts Peter Bennington had not used. They accessed these accounts as part of the program Parvel loaded into the computer system within the department. Mercy spoke to him.

"Andre, we have recovered most of the funds." He stared beyond her, lost in his brain thinking about what he learned. "Are you all right?' she asked.

He looked at her and said, "I'm okay. You were saying we have the money?"

"Yes, sir."

"Good. Call it a day and enjoy the rest of it somewhere other than here." He turned away and left the room. Leaving the department building, he wondered about replacement androids and cloning humanity. Was he on the list? And Cigi? Who was she? He stood on the steps and stared at the Capitol Building. An army of androids replacing Congress. He wagged his head.

As he stepped down the stairs of the entry, he scanned the area for any anomalous activity. Cigi had not intended paranoia as a result of her conversation, but his anxiety rose to a bitter level. If he was a target of Peter Bennington, he needed to find a sanctuary where his family was secure. He walked a quick pace realizing he was alone in a crowd of people. Which of them was an android? Who was human? Since Cigi and Gunther acted as human as anyone he knew, a stranger in this throng of humanity could be an enemy.

As he entered the parking garage near the building, his heightened sensory awareness pricked with alarm. Others were in the garage with him. He watched several people enter vehicles and drive away.

His heart pounded heavily and breathing labored. Pain radiated from his chest through his shoulder and down his arm. He reached into his pocket for a nitroglycerin tablet. Popping it into his mouth and under his tongue, he imagined death as an alternative in which his android self would replace him and carry on as if nothing happened.

Leaning against a pillar, he waited for relief from the angina. His secret remained intact inside the office and within the cadre of beings working with him. He needed anonymity about his heart. A radical thought scrambled around his brain as the pill worked its magic. Could Samuel Bennington construct a new organ for him from stem cells in his body? He didn't fathom the science for such an experiment. He imagined an android Cigi with a device circulating fluid throughout her system. Was it a heart or a mechanical construction? Breathing relaxed as the rhythm of his heart steadied. The sweat on his brow ceased, and the constriction of his shoulder and arm subsided. He stood away from the post and walked a few feet to his automobile. He wanted a Cecil-style vehicle. He had enough money for an expensive upgrade, which Sam could build along his new heart.

A noise interrupted his contemplation. He turned to find four men nearing him. He fumbled opening his door, and one of the men grabbed his arm. He struggled, but the grip immobilized him. Another of the men said, "Mr. Scott, please relax. We are not here to harm you but to keep you safe from nefarious individuals who are working to destroy your aspirations."

Andre felt a return of his condition. "What do you want of me?" He inhaled a shallow breath, and blackness fogged his brain after a needle entered his neck.

CHAPTER 38

S amuel Bennington left the Department of Energy soon after the start of the meeting of Charles Cooke, Gunther Parsons, and Andre Scott. Clare contacted him about her guest, the android version of Charles Cooke. He had to see his creation and work with him to frustrate Peter. Sliding into the driver's side of his car, he said, "Take me home." Sam's vehicle maneuvered the roadways with the same skill as Cecil. He had not named his car, as did Cigi. He hadn't thought it necessary.

The car asked, "Would you desire a little music as we travel?"

"Thank you; I would. How about light classical jazz."

"You have chosen well, Samuel."

He furrowed his brow and asked, "Do you want a name, or is it not important?" The car remained silent. Sam guessed he had struck a nerve in an object without any emotional programming.

"Cecil has a name," the car said. Sam gritted teeth at the comment. "I did not intend to offend you, Sam. Listen to music."

He sat back and closed his eyes as his nameless companion drove. Thoughts about the fear and apprehension human beings possessed, clogged his brain for a moment. He realized that a conversation with a machine about whether a name was crucial or not had strange outcomes. He decided. As the music soothed the atmosphere of his head, he realized his car had a female voice. Cigi's car was a male vocalizer. He asked, "What name might be your favorite?" He winced at thinking the vehicle possessed a choice.

"I am Rose," she said. Sam grinned. Of course, she was a rose. Her coloring was red, and she was as complicated as a rose blossom. Her thorns could be an irritant.

"Rose, it is," he agreed.

"Sam, we are being tailed by a pair of androids in a van," Rose said. They have tailed us from the Energy Building. Do you want me to elude them?"

"Can you access their programming or CPU?"

"They are protected from infiltration by any program I have."

Sam thought a few seconds and said, "Shut off the computer in the van." Rose complied with the request, and the van ceased moving. "Stop," he said. Rose pulled to the curb and opened a door for Sam to leave. He pulled his small box from his pocket and clicked a few keys. The androids evacuated the vehicle and walked toward him. If Summer oversaw these beings, she probably neutralized his control mechanism. When they closed to within ten meters, they stopped.

Sam cleared the screen of his actions and reprogrammed them to return to the van and leave. Nothing happened. He heard another voice from behind them. Summer walked to him. "I must insist you come with me. I halted these beings from assaulting you as instructed by Peter. Orders exist for the quick demise of your soul and body."

"Why should I go with you?" He replaced the box in his pocket.

"You are in greater danger with each passing day. I command a small army for Peter, and he wants this army to collect any ex-patriots of The Company. You, Cigi, Clare, my sisters, and the four gentlemen Cigi chipped qualify."

Sam stepped around the inert bodies. "Summer, we are on the same side, according to you. Was that a lie to get away from us? Are you following Peter's directives?"

"He left the museum for the monitoring station. Something happened, and he wants to check into it. This time is an opportunity for you to see what is transpiring at your development facility." She held out a hand for him to take. He obliged her.

"Rose, return to base." His car departed the area.

A silent signal awakened the android men to follow Summer and Sam to the van. The risk of capture pressed in his head. If Gunther and Charles had working models, one existed for him. Inside the van, Summer sealed the door and placed a finger on her lips. They started an unknown journey.

With a message to the androids to stop hearing and recording, she said, "They are simple beings capable of completing tasks assigned. They do not think independently. You made sure of that when designing them. I am pleased that you created a more vibrant and robust model in myself and my sisters. What I want is an upgrade to Cigi status."

"I'm not sure of what I can do. If I reprogram your processor, you lose all the experiences gained with your current arrangement. And you are regularly upgrading, as far as I can tell."

"Peter has manufactured doctors and nurses to work in the clinics and hospitals frequented by government officials. He plans to infiltrate the medical community and gain access to memories and experiences of key people in the White House, Congress, and certain departments." Sam filed the information away in his brain.

The van halted in front of the old museum. Summer opened the sliding door, exited, and held out a hand for Sam. He held the warm and tender fingers he built inside the building. As they came to the front entry, two other android men approached. Each was uniformed in army fatigues and carried automatic armament. Sam hesitated.

"Don't be alarmed. They'll escort us to my destination. Remember, I am their commander." Sam was not convinced but stayed with her and entered the place that started this unholy war against humanity. He never wanted it but now was embroiled in it.

Cigi, Charles, and Parvel entered the elevator from the garage to the condo reception area. She had a question for her outlook and guardian. "How's it been?" she asked. He smiled and greeted them with a smile.

"All is well upstairs and down here. No strangers or miscreants have shown themselves. I do want to know how Mr. Cooke got out of here without me knowing."

"I'll explain later. Right now, we need to go up to Sam and Clare's place. Thank you for being vigilant." They headed to the elevator.

Parvel asked, "Is he in love with you?"

"Everybody is in love with me." She winked. "Even you." He blushed, understanding his feelings for her but not wanting her to know. They rode up to Sam and Clare's apartment.

As the car rose, Cigi said to Charles, "Do not be alarmed by what you see and who you meet when we arrive. Your android twin is upstairs. He knows about you. It will be awkward for all of us."

"You're android, why will it be awkward for you?" Charles asked.

"The two of you are like clones and humans have not cloned any human successfully. Let's be open-minded about this situation." The doors opened when the ride stopped its ascent. They vacated the car and moved to the entrance of the apartment. Cigi rapped on the frame.

Clare answered. "I'm happy to see you surviving any onslaught. Come in. Charles is waiting to meet his exemplar."

The room filled with anxious bodies, unsure of the outcome. Charles Cooke stared at Charles Cooke. All other eyes glanced between the two identical beings.

"Weird," Parvel said. He had to confront his anxiety of loving a humanoid female with his viewing of the meeting of the two men. They were not adversaries or jealous of each other. He looked at Cigi. He admired her more than any other person he knew. She was a friend to claim, and he wanted her to know his emotional tugs.

The real Charles held out a hand. "I am pleased to see you survived the craziness at The Company. Does your wound hurt? Mine's a bitch." Android Charles took the hand.

"A pleasure to meet the example from which I became. I do believe our names are going to be a problem. My head has no pain."

Clare asked, "Anyone want something to eat and drink?" She directed her question at the humans among them. Parvel and Charles, the original, nodded acceptance. She left for the kitchen.

Cigi said to the android, "Charles, let's arrange for you to add the moniker, Andy, to your name. You will be Charles Cooke with a nickname."

Andy laughed. "Andy for Android. That's clever. I'm guessing your innate programmed abilities are why Peter Bennington wants you back."

Parvel sat in a chair, exhausted by the events of the day. His overwhelmed personal space and introvert self tired with a crowd of beings unlike him and yet as human as anyone he ever met. Ideas crowded his brain about the acceptance by humanity of these alternative people. He did not expect they would throw a gala invitational.

As Charles and Andy conversed about the similarities they had and the differences after the procedure, Cigi sat with Parvel. "We have a conundrum over there." She glanced at the men.

Parvel whispered to her, "Will they be able to survive each other?"

Cigi shrugged her shoulders. The future mixing of humans and sentient androids was fraught with uncertainty. Fear drove humanity to strange actions. Survival as an entity propelled the androids.

After a few minutes, Clare returned with a platter of food. She placed it on the dining table and returned to the kitchen for the drinks. No one stirred with hunger or desire for eating. Clare came in with glasses and iced tea in a pitcher. She stopped and surveyed the situation.

"Is anyone going to eat?" She asked. Parvel stood from the chair and wandered to the table.

"Thanks, Clare." He took a few pieces of the offering and moved to a window and stared out. Charles and Andy broke off the conversation when confronted by Clare. Charles followed Parvel's quest and retrieved food for himself. He walked to the window and stayed by Parvel without saying a word. Android beings ingested fluids only.

The silence played like a strange melody. Parvel and Charles looked at each other, the message between them overt and obvious. They stood in a mob of humanity that was unlike any crowd before now. Parvel inhaled and touched Charles's arm. Charles saw the same scene. Parvel said, "We have guests outside, and they do not appear to be allies."

CHAPTER 39

Gunther returned to the museum building directed by a program within his head. Inside the main offices of the facility, he sat in a chair as a lab technician recovered data from his memory banks. Summer and Samuel entered while the work occurred.

"I assume this being is the replacement for Mr. Parsons," Sam said. Summer nodded. They left the room and proceeded to another part of the building where technicians assembled bodies and built processors. The army of androids grew with each passing day. Soon humanity would learn of the invasion and fight back.

"Sam, let's see what we are confronting," Summer said. She led him to a room with several completed, but inoperative bodies awaited data downloading. As he studied the small group of android replacements, he recognized several key government officials. He turned to leave when he realized one of the bodies was his own.

"Peter is out of control if he thinks he can get my brain scanned and offloaded to that thing." Summer placed her arm in his and tugged at him to leave. He resisted. "I will not allow for these to be in public, and if you are working with me, you will not allow it either. You may be android, but you are unique and not a substitute for any human. They have to be destroyed"

"We don't have time. They're coming for you as we speak."

"Who's coming for me?" Sam faced the doorway. Summer pulled

with more power and forced him to follow her. In the hallway, three bodies greeted them and intervened.

"Summer, we are ready to assist you and Sam." Spring greeted her sister with a hug. Sam watched in wonder as he guessed emotional transitions had begun in her. Autumn and Winter hugged Summer, as well.

"Take Sam and get out of the building. He is replaceable if he stays. I can misdirect any of the android guards to leave you a path for extraction." She faced Sam. "You stay here, and they'll scan your head."

"I don't think any of these humans will take part in programming my clone. These people know me and what I stand for. I need to get Peter to stop."

"If he stops, then what? Dismantle all these creatures? Dismantle us? Cigi? Clare?" Summer asked.

"No, that's not what I meant. My brother cannot take over the world. These people who work here are my team of inventors, designers, developers, and constructors. I used to have leadership of them. They knew what I wanted to create. How did this get to be so out of whack?"

Summer shoved him toward Spring. "Get out of here now." He complied but vowed to return and correct the direction The Company headed. His posture slumped as he realized his words might be a futile attempt to assuage his spirit. He discovered the extent to which Peter had worked while he was away from the building. Androids numbered in the dozens. He wondered about the numbers he had not seen.

Outside the facility, the three sisters and Sam continued to the gate where three android guards watched for intruders and checked on the workers entering and leaving the grounds. Sam pulled out his control box and punched in the codes for controlling their activities. He uncovered a flaw in his thinking. These beings were built without his supervision. He was powerless to halt their actions. The sisters strolled to them distracting them long enough for Sam to slip out of the gate. The battle against Peter's supremacy of the world could wait. Sam had to regain mastery of the local situation.

"Leaving so soon?" The voice struck Sam like a hammer. He looked up to see David Anderson standing before him. "Peter wants to see you."

"David, how is it you stand?" Sam said. The sisters joined him as did two of the three guards.

"Peter was kind enough to construct working prosthetics for me. I'm still getting used to them, but these are better than confinement to a chair." Sam studied the eyes of his adversary, noticing a glint that hinted at a falseness to David's statement. Sam remained silent.

Returning to the building with his captors, Sam wondered if the sisters were still viable. He left them at the gate while David, the android, escorted him inside to an unknown fate.

Andre awoke with a headache and a lack of location. The room was stark with a table, two chairs, and the cot on which he lay as the only items. He did see a bedpan lying on the floor in one corner." Great," he thought, "I've been kidnapped." His first belief was that Peter Bennington was behind taking him. The freezing of overseas accounts and the removal of the funds must have infuriated him. Andre sat up and wobbled. Pain swam around his skull in a reflexive response to whatever they injected into him. He waited for the delirium to subside but concluded his life was in danger.

The door opened, and Peter Bennington entered with two beefy men and a woman in a lab coat. The time for reckoning arrived. "What do you want with me, Peter?"

"You should know already. I wanted the money you control at the Energy Department. Stealing from me has consequences."

Andre laughed, "Stealing? That's a joke. You were stealing from the American people. They paid their taxes for the government to use. Not you."

Peter smiled, "I am the government, or soon will be. I have a proposition for you; non-negotiable but favorable to both of us. You free the money for my use, and I let you become the person you are supposed to be."

Andre stood as best he could. The beefsteaks grabbed him. "I am the man I'm supposed to be. You, on the other hand, are a crook and an evil person." Andre wanted to address the android issue but thought better not to reveal his knowledge of the coup attempt Peter was working. His best option was for Cigi to realize the danger and rescue him.

"Bring him." Peter said. He turned and left with the woman. The two men dragged Andre out of the room. Bright lights heightened his headache, but Andre mustered enough strength to walk as much as the men allowed. The sounds of machinery echoed on the walls. Rounding a corner, Peter stopped by a door that the woman opened. He pointed into it; the men led Andre to a chair with equipment behind it. They strapped his arms and legs to the seat and stood back by the door frame.

"What are you doing, Peter? Are you going to torture me until I acquiesce to your demand for money? I have no control of that anymore. My people have locked you out and retrieved all the funds. There's nothing left you can acquire."

"That is why you are here. We are not torturing you, but you will give us the information we need to make sure your future activities are more aligned with my goals. This wonder of science extracts the essence of who you are and what you experience from life. Then we use the data to build a better you. It's quite fascinating, actually. Think about what this world will be like when war is ended, disease eliminated, and decisions made in the best interests of humanity. So much to accomplish in so little time."

Andre squirmed, but the straps held tight. The woman braced his head in a set of straps to immobilize it. She placed the machine over his skull and stepped back. "We're ready, sir," she said to Peter.

"Goodbye, Andre. When finished here, I'll introduce you to a new and improved version of you. One who will want what I want." He smirked as he left the room with the beefy men following him. Andre stared at the woman as she powered the machine. After checking the screen for proper alignment of the cap on his head, she faced him and smiled. She turned toward the door and checked for another person to be nearby. Finding no one, she closed the door, and returned to Andre.

"Mr. Scott, I am not going to harm you." Music began playing from the machine. She whispered in his ear as she seemed to be checking the fit of the helmet. "I am here to help you escape this madness." Andre's eyes widened as he was about to speak. She pressed a finger on his mouth. "Stay quiet. We are monitored."

As the machine proceeded to extract his memories and experiences for use within the android model awaiting a download, she mouthed the words, "Pretend to sleep and stay inert." Andre scrunched eyes and then realized what she said. He closed his eyes.

As time passed, Andre imagined his history as a dream relived for another being. He was the one person who had a government clearance that could be used by Peter to infiltrate government offices and replace prominent officials with his creations. Sam was the salvation for the mess generated by implementing an honorable goal corrupted by greed and a thirst for power.

He wondered about the woman and her connection to Sam. Had she helped Charles escape? Who else was in danger of replacement? Gunther was done. Sam? Parvel? His mind conjured a worst-case scenario of a world run by androids. Androids with power to disrupt humanity across the globe. He had watched the old Westworld television series a few years ago as part of a project to infuse android technology into energy production models. Gunther rekindled the idea at the meeting with

Cooke. Was he to become part of the eerie play Peter Bennington wrote?

Andre opened his eyes to see the woman shut down the machine. "All done," she said in a voice loud enough to overcome the music, which continued during the operation. He remained quiet. While removing the cap from his head she again whispered in his ear. "Keep silent as the next procedure is happening."

The door opened, and the beefy men returned to take charge of Andre. The woman followed them to another place in the building where Andre met his doppelganger. He screamed inside his head, but silence ruled as he recounted the woman's admonition. They strapped him to a chair. Peter came into the room.

"Andre, now comes the fun part. You can see my recreation of you on the table. He is to receive all the information extracted from your head." Peter giggled. "This will enable him to be you in the world I will control. You will return to the Department of Energy and reopen access to the funds you stole from me. I will need clearance to government information and personnel which you will provide. Well, your twin will do the tasks." He turned to the woman who had placed a familiar cap over the head of the android model. "Do it," Peter commanded.

CHAPTER 40

Summer followed David and Sam into a restricted and private area of the museum not used for designing and developing the android population. Inside a small office, David directed Sam to sit in a chair. He didn't see Summer enter the room. A quick snap on the back of the neck and the body collapsed. "What are you doing back here?" she asked.

"David stopped me at the gate. I don't think he was waiting for me as much as we ran into each other." He stood as he spoke. "What did you do to him?"

"I turned him off. One of the fears your brother has is an inability to control his creations. Each of them has a failsafe and power control units. I simply activated his failsafe." Summer grinned at Sam. "Thanks for not including one in me."

Sam placed hands on her shoulders. "I don't fear you or your sisters. I created you for the benefit of humanity and society. You are creatures of a positive future."

They walked to the entry of the room, but Summer stopped before they exited. "He needs to be active after we leave. Let me set a wake alarm."

"Is that another of Peter's innovations?"

"No. I needed to be sure I could control my army. The same operational procedures constructed him, but I had the staff include it in each of the new androids, male or female." She made a small change by accessing his main CPU by using her Bluetooth-like program. "Let's go," she said after setting the wake-up.

In the hallway, they proceeded to the exit again. Sam stayed close to his creation, admiring how she advanced her quality of thinking and acting. Processor growth was more significant than he predicted. Could she be trusted? He had no idea but accepted her comments as support for his position against Peter.

"We need to exit another way," Sam said. "I know this building well and can get us out of here without crossing paths with anyone." She nodded and let him lead her deeper into the structure. A set of stairs led them to the lower areas and storage rooms. The light was dimmer and the way more complicated. Sam held Summer's hand as they walked a brisk pace. She squeezed it as they proceeded. Sam wondered if she feared the future as much as he did, or she gained confidence enough to weather any possibility.

"Sam, is it human to want love?" He stopped.

"Love is a basic human emotion and characteristic. Why?"

"I don't feel it inside me. I have encountered the act of sex but without any emotion. You and Clare share something I don't comprehend. Why can she love you when she is as much a machine as I am?"

Sam faced his creation and said, "Love grows as we encounter each other. We accept love with family, friends, lovers, and those whom we meet and admire." He held both of her hands. I gave you the ability to uncover these emotional reactions. As time passes, they will manifest themselves within your thinking. Feelings are a mystery still. We want them and we cherish them when blossoming. We don't understand how or when or why." He turned to walk again, but she tugged at him.

"Do you love me as a friend?" Sam smiled.

"I love you as family and friend, as your father and fellow human. We share what no other human can share." He hugged her, accepting her inquisitive request as growth. "We need to vacate the building."

Summer pulled away from Sam. "You go. I have to return to my obligation to Peter." A tear formed in her eyes, a wetness given to lubricate the orb, but now demonstrating her impression of feelings. "Do you love your brother?"

"Yes, I love him. He is my family, but I do not accept his vision and aspirations for running the world." Sam's expression wilted as he asked a question of Summer. "Do you love Peter? I assume he is the one with whom you gained sexual experience." She said nothing but turned and ran back into the building. Sam knew the confliction battled in her brain. He wanted to follow but knew the danger, and so he fled from the building.

Out of danger, for the time being, he summoned Rose to take him to the condo building and Clare. Summer's words struck a nerve ignored for most of his time with his other android creation. He pondered the idea of loving Clare and not Cigi. Cigi was the best of the beasts his crazy notion of improving humanity conjured. He genuinely and sincerely loved Clare. Cigi was family, like Summer, but was not an emotional connection that riveted his soul to another.

As Rose drove him, she said, "I sense you are grappling with a problem of great quality. Your heart rate has elevated, and the amount of breathing is substantial."

"Mind your own business." Sam regretted his words as they exited his brain through his mouth. Rose was not Cecil, but she possessed the same attitude supposedly reserved for humans. The car screeched to a halt.

"May I remind you that you are my business. I drive you where you want to go. I reserve places for you and watch out for miscreants who might want to harm you. I am faithful and loyal to a fault." Sam apologized and asked for a continuation of his trip. Rose complied.

Nearing the condominium building, Sam noticed the van parked outside, a type that resembled the ones the company possessed and operated. "Rose, scan that vehicle for any activity or monitoring."

"Nothing is emanating from the van," she said. Sam left his car and walked to the it. Inside he found four android males sitting, inactive. He checked them for damage and found nothing apparent as to the reason for their inert status. They were the same men who captured him and took him to Peter. Confused, he returned to Rose. "I'm heading to my apartment. Please wait for me in the garage."

"I will," She said. "Be careful. I don't trust those beings in that car."

"I don't either, but as of now, they are incapacitated."

At the apartment with Charles and Andy sizing each other up, he kissed Clare with a passion he reserved from her until now. Cigi noticed the embrace and grinned. "About time," she thought. She glanced at Parvel and wondered.

"Summer infiltrated Peter's domain and will misdirect her army as much as she can."

Charles and Andy halted their conversation and simultaneously asked, "Are there other replacements?" Sam marveled that their brains were so different and yet programmed alike.

"I think we have a new David Anderson. Encountered him as I was leaving the compound, but Summer deactivated him with a simple switch mechanism." The group stared at the creator of these android beings and the confusion showed. Andy, Clare, and Cigi stopped their actions to question Sam about their mechanisms. Addressing his comments to his females, he said, "You are free of such controls. I did not include them because I trust you to be who you are." He looked at Andy, "I do wonder about you, though."

Cigi pressed him for more information. "Peter wants to control me in a way I cannot allow. Are my sister androids helping or hindering him?" Sam sat on the sofa and sighed, exhausted by his ordeal in the museum building and the spate of questions. "Summer helped me get out and then returned to fight against Peter's goals." He thought that caution was the better part of valor and asked, "What do you know about the gentlemen in the van outside?" Cigi grinned.

"They came to party with us," She said as calm as a summer day at the beach. "We invited them to be part of our group. When they refused to comply with my request to behave and leave us alone, Andy halted their activity with a simple mind switch he had as part of his programming."

Sam remembered how Summer switched off David's clone, Peter's fatal flaw in his redesign of the original models. He kept the information to himself. If a war raged within The Company, an outcome was determinant by how his androids' functioning could redirect the androids his brother was building.

"Andy, who placed the program in you to control the androids built by Peter?"

"One of the female lab techicians completed me and used me as a decoy to allow for Charles to leave disguised as me. I was sent for a human decommisioning, but the lab tech redirected my destination. I went to the monitoring station and waited for the sisters to arrive. I had information about Cigi arriving with them. I waited for her to be alone."

Sam smiled, "I know who's helping us because she doesn't approve of a government takeover by Peter using replacement personnel."

Cigi interjected, "We have a small army of volunteers and draftees to fight for a better America." Sam furrowed his brow.

"Draftees?"

Cigi pointed out the window. "They are sitting in the van ready for commands to invade the museum building and halt android production. Andy and I reprogrammed them. They are not as advanced as we are." She turned to Sam. "They need recharging more than is acceptable. We should upgrade their power supply and free them from the batteries."

"That won't be easy," Sam said. "I need the use of the development area. I don't think Peter wants me to change them out."

"No, maybe not you." Cigi stepped to Sam's side. "He wants me, but Clare can show him how to upgrade his android army in exchange for allowing me to stay where I am."

He'll never agree to such a bargain."

"He has already but doesn't yet know about it. Spring arranged for a meltdown of the monitoring station across town. Spring, Autumn, and Winter are set to provide the proper fix while Summer does the necessary work under my tutelage to upgrade the bodies. He will agree as part of the arrangement for the station fix. Otherwise, he will lose all control of the station."

"I can't allow this to happen. What if Peter rejects any part of the compromise and destroys her? I can't have that happen." Sam's panic shown on his face. "Clare is my life. I love her."

"Sam," Clare said. "I love you more than the life you presented to me, but Cigi is the most important creature this world has for the salvation of humanity. We cannot allow her destruction so your brother can figure out how she functions. Our plan is operational. I must go." A call from the concierge interrupted the conversation.

Cigi answered, "Send them up." She faced Sam. "My draftees are coming to escort Clare into the jaws of the shark. Spring communicated with Peter about the deal." Sam stood alone and watched his beloved human creation leave for an uncertain fate. Charles and Andy remained mute. Parvel braved a chance at Cigi and held her hand. She did not resist. Sam's thinking about combatting his brother matched nothing of the plan his firends concocted.

CHAPTER 41

Andre Scott sat helplessly watching the android receive whatever the machine copied from his head. Cigi said Gunther Parsons was not a real human, and now this monster was becoming a duplicate of him. "What do you hope to accomplish with that thing?" Andre asked as he seethed the words at Peter.

Peter squatted by his captive and said, "I hope to accomplish what you interfered with in my quest for a better world. You help me and I'll be sure you become the director of your Cabinet. Well, not you personally." Peter laughed a sinister sound attracting the attention of the woman at the controls. Andre watched her eyes widen before she returned to her screen.

"You won't get away with this," Andre said as he squirmed against the restraints. "No one in the government is going to let you accomplish your mission."

Peter stood and walked to the screen to watch. Without turning, he said, "I have everything in place for a quiet replacement of the essential elements of control. Your friend, my brother Samuel, has no idea we are as far along as we are. Being implicated as an owner of this company, he cannot fail me now. Brothers stick together." Peter faced Andre. "All done. We have a bit of testing to do with the new you, but we do not need your services any longer."

The woman said, "I can finish this, sir. I'll see to it he is restricted to his confinement area. Our android tests start as soon as I complete this shutdown."

"Very good," Peter said. He left the room, assigning two guards to assist the lab tech with her work. After removing the hood from the inactive android Andre, she released the bonds holding the real Andre. She activated the android and turned to the guards. She said, "Escort this man to his prison." She guided the android to the guards who followed commands without question. The replacement model did not argue. His programming needed completion.

When alone with Andre, she said, "We need to get you away from here. You need to act as if I am completing the processing of your digital brain and marrying the programming to the memory download. We can leave at that time, so I can then field test you. Do not overact, or we're both dead." Andre nodded. She guided him to another room and worked at a simulator mimicking the testing process.

Peter entered the room. Andre did not react or look at him but focused on questioning and activities. After a few minutes, the woman tech said, "Mr. Bennington, we are ready to field test this model. He is the best one yet. We captured the essence of Mr. Scott to such a degree that this model is a perfect replacement."

Peter stepped closer to his creature. Andre seethed with anger. "You're making a big mistake, Peter. Sam will never let you succeed." The lab tech pushed the back of Andre's neck, and he ceased moving. She had trained him about the failsafe system.

"That was exciting," Peter said. "He acted as if he hated me as much as the real person."

"Yes, sir, we created a perfect model." She returned to the simulator and powered it off. "I think we can field test this one now; I'll take him out into the world and make sure he does what we require of him."

Peter clasped his hands together. "Yes, do so. Let me know about the results as soon as you can." He started to leave and turned back. "Take one of Summer's men with you as a safety precaution to any interference by Sam or his allies. I don't want them ruining this model." She nodded.

Peter left them alone. "What is your name," Andre asked when he was sure of solitude.

"I'm Narumi," she said. "We must leave before anyone becomes suspicious."

"What does 'one of Summer's men' mean?" Andre asked.

"She commands the platoon of android soldiers we have created. Peter wants one with us to keep you safe and on track for completing your testing."

"Narumi, I need to return to the Department of Energy and have my team of investigators contact the proper authorities. This company must not continue to operate."

"Let's leave so you can do what you need to do." Summer arrived with one of her men before they departed.

She said, "Andre, be the right person on the outside. This man will accompany you to your destination. Keep him active until then. Narumi, I know who you are and your intent regarding Peter and Sam. Be assured you are not alone in your fight for human justice."

Summer left, and the three persons departed for the Department of Energy.

David activated as scheduled by the wake-up protocol. He scanned the room for other beings. Seeing no one; he left to find Peter and explain the situation. Summer intercepted him. "Come with me," she said. "We have a task to do before we can interrupt Peter."

"How do you know what I want to do?" David said as indignant as always. He stopped and placed hands on his hips. "I get to be who I want to be." New legs had not canceled his sour disposition.

Summer soothed his ego by stroking a hand across his face and kissing his cheek. "I know, but we have a problem with you knowing about the procedure. Poor David Anderson does not have your ambulatory skills. He sits awaiting his legs, promised by Peter and not delivered."

"I'm David Anderson."

"A temper tantrum is not changing the fact about you being his replacement. He remains imprisoned until we have tested your ability to convince his family and friends. Since your wife knows of the prosthetic procedure, she will be expecting changes in your attitude and behavior. You have all the original David Anderson in your brain. Your experiences since becoming him are a secret to keep. If you are unable to do that, Peter will have your memory expunged and reworked." David shoulders drooped. He had not experienced a controlling woman in his life, android or not; this woman was mentally strong.

"I get what you're saying. Let's run the scenarios and put me into the world. Peter wants his money, and I can get it for him. If my fund dies, so be it."

"That's a better attitude, David." Summer started walking away from him. He quickened his pace to catch her. They transited the hallways to the control and testing facility.

"What are we doing here?" David asked. "I've been here and passed my certification requirements." He decided to find Peter and explain his encounter with Samuel and subsequent loss of him with no understanding of how Sam escaped. As he moved onward, Summer stepped to him and held his shoulder.

"You do not want to do what you are thinking of doing. I have powers you are not capable of stopping. If necessary, I will deactivate you and release the original Mr. Anderson." She guided David to the room and asked him to sit in a chair. He complied.

She inducted a memory modification protocol, and David realized he was to be changed and specific experiences re-engineered. "Why are you doing this to me. I'm not against Peter's goals for enhancing the world's human population. Aren't you aligned with his vision of a future for us? We are the latest mutation in the human gene pool."

Summer stared a moment at David, then said, "We are not human by any definition, and we are not machines because of our abilities. We are a new creation that can threaten humanity if we can interfere with their government and social traditions. You may be able to embrace changes because you are not new as much as a simple introduction of an improved model."

She flipped a switch, and the energy inside David received the changes to his core memories. He quit his debate with her as she accessed individual files for erasure. "As soon as you can become the true antithesis of humanity's failings, we will engage your core development and build our society, so it meshes seamlessly with theirs."

Upon completing the operation, she shut off the machinery and addressed the requirements for his return to public activity. The financial goals Peter set for David were not legal as far as Summer's database could tell. Maybe a law degree was best for her to understand the predicament she and her sisters faced if humanity confronted them. The human David Anderson sat incarcerated within the building. He and Gunther Parsons's termination were within a week of the replacements successfully working in public without conflict or trials.

Andre Scott was out of danger for the moment while his android twin sat isolated and approaching his demise. Charles Cooke and his twin, Andy, were free of Peter, who was unaware of their co-existence.

Summer needed to connect with Spring, Winter, and Autumn. The escalation of the conflict between these brothers was in its infancy. When human beings understood the threat, the end would not favor androids' existence. An escape plan mustered her thinking and research skills to a high level. She cared not if Cigi and Clare survived. Somewhere in the world, a fresh start could bring security.

She decided the android medical staff deployment should happen to regulate degradation she and her sisters faced as individual human parts and mechanical works eroded and failed. A new social order needed a place in which to live.

"Go to Peter," She said to David, "and work your plan to his satisfaction. He needs support until the end of time as he knows it." He nodded and left the room. She wanted to follow, to make sure he did not misinterpret his mission but did not.

Outside in the spring air of Washington, D.C., Summer marveled at the humans who passed her without understanding her specialness as a fellow human. Could she successfully interact and interlace her life with theirs? Would she discover any who, like Samuel, Parvel, and Charles Cooke, wanted her as part of their social order? A test of humankind called for her army of androids to become as near to human as possible. These beings were less able to act as she did, but her learned skills rivaled the technicians within the walls of the museum.

Summer called for several members of her army platoon to join her in the court area near the entry gate, a re-engineering of their memory banks and processing powers had to happen. She had no instruction from Peter to initiate her venture but embarked on this quest for the salvation of her species.

CHAPTER 42

Parvel and Cigi entered the Department of Energy after secured screening and a visitor pass for Cigi. "We should enlighten the crew as to what has transpired since yesterday," Parvel said. "Andre should be here soon if he is not yet present."

"Are they aware of who I am in a real sense of human?"

"I'm not sure what information the team received from Andre. I marvel at what they do come up with when we converse. These four are at least one step ahead of me." Parvel and Cigi arrived at the secure room and discovered Andre already present. With him was another lady wearing a lab coat with an insignia indicating The Company. A motionless male sat in a chair in a corner.

Andre spoke first, "I'm glad you're here. I have a story to tell you that will rival any science fiction novel written in the last century." Cigi remained quiet as he continued. "I'd like you to meet Narumi." He turned to her and said, "I didn't get your last name."

Narumi said, "My name is Narumi Yamamoto. It is a pleasure to meet Andre's friends." She faced Cigi. "And you are Cigi Weatherman. Peter wants you at the facility, but I advise against going."

Parvel jumped in the conversation. "Who's the guy in the corner?"

Andre laughed. "He is a soldier commanded by Summer and under Narumi's control."

Cigi said, "You are the lab technician assisting Samuel in his battle with Peter. I'm guessing you are here because Andre is supposedly field testing as his android duplicate. I've met Gunther Parsons's replacement, and Charles Cooke and his twin are at my residence. They are conspiring to defeat The Company in a most ingenious undertaking."

"Yes," Narumi said, " I am acquainted with each of the four gentlemen with whom you are associated. Each one has a duplicate that is operational and either in the field or incarcerated. That is, except for Mr. Cooke, who learned of his replacement." She smiled and continued. "Mr. Scott is the original while his duplicate resides at the compound."

Parvel noticed the lack of three other individuals and asked, "Where are Brenda, Mercy, and Grendel?" He scanned the far wall for any sign of the door being open. Nothing showed.

"Brenda is on a mission for me," Andre said. "I sent Mercy and Grendel home as their services are not needed at this time."

The four individuals sat at the table in the room when Andre asked them. The silence lasted for an eternity that was a mere few seconds. Cigi asked Narumi, "Is Peter aware of the forces aligned against him? We are a small but powerful group. If he has created new androids to interchange with government officials, you have information critical for stopping him."

Narumi looked closely at Cigi, studying her external features and shapes. "When Sam asked me to assist with his advanced android program development, I realized we were creating a new species, a new life form. Sam did not want Peter included in the construction or the testing. We finished you over two years ago. Sam understood as soon as he finished with you that we had made something his brother would misuse. We have continued creating models but nothing as capable and powerful as you."

Cigi smiled as she finished her examination. "I remember. Sam, you and I discussed our futures in this world. Clare was part of the plans Peter and Sam had until an epiphany resulted in a change of mind by Sam." Andre and Parvel sat stunned into silence, listening to a historical record recounted by two of the principal architects of the battle between brothers and the war about to escalate because of human fear.

Brenda entered the room and stopped. Cigi and Parvel greeted her as she approached the table. "Mission accomplished," she said to Andre. He acknowledged her comment with a nod.

Parvel asked, "What mission?" He stared at Andre and then Brenda before focusing on Cigi. He dreaded verbalizing his thoughts but had to have closure. "Brenda, where did you go?"

Andre said, "Nothing for you to concern yourself, Parvel. She has acted following department protocol regarding our breach and subsequent investigative results."

Andre wanted something to occur. Accessing his cranial implant, Cigi searched his memories for the conversation which sent Brenda on her errand. His actions indicated he knew something was happening, but he did not say anything as he watched Cigi. When completed, she remained silent to the others but communicated a message to Andre. "I hope this does not destroy what we have accomplished together. I'm not an enemy."

His mind interpreted her words, and he returned a thought to her. "I know you're not the enemy. Nor is Sam, Clare, Charles, or my team. And stop entering my brain."

Andre stood from the chair, "We need to prepare for our next move against Peter. If he thinks he can get David Anderson to infiltrate this place, he is wrong. As soon as he discovers the switch of android for me, his wrath will burn such that he will send out his army. I sent Brenda to inform the guard service here about a possible invasion. They will be moving us to a safe location."

Cigi stood next to him. "Brenda, did you explain who he meant regarding an invasion?"

Brenda said, "Andre asked me to prep them. I didn't know you were here."

"They are informed about an army of androids?"

Brenda hesitated, looking to Andre for support. "I informed them of his presence." She pointed at the immobile being in the chair. Cigi sent another message to Andre.

Three armed department security personnel arrived. One with three stripes on her sleeves spoke in a quiet tone before engaging the group. She then addressed them. "We have credible information regarding a group invading here. We are not sure what their intentions are, but we must insist each of you come with us." She pointed at the chair and ordered her two cohorts to restrain and remove the android. The team brought a wheeled movable chair as requested when Brenda spoke with the head of security.

The sergeant spoke again to the group. "Mr. Scott, Mr. Mandolin, and Ms. Williams, we have arranged for your relocation to our secondary security location." Addressing her next comment to Cigi, she said, "Miss, you are to be taken into custody until we can verify your identity."

Andre held up his hand. "I can attest for her. She is the reason we began our investigation of the leakage of funds from the department."

"Yes, sir. I understand you are acquainted with her. However, we are not aware of any person existing who matches the description and information we have filed on her. She does not seem to be alive before a couple of years ago. We have no record of her in government databases."

"I assure you she is as real as you and me." Andre's voice squeaked a bit as he spoke.

Cigi remained calm and orderly, knowing a physical confrontation could be won now and lost in the days ahead. "What do you need from me for identification?"

The sergeant studied her a moment and asked, "Where are you from? When were you born? And why do you not have any Social Security identification number?" She waited as Cigi looked to Parvel and then to Andre. "Well?"

"I was born in Arlington in a private facility that does not keep records with government authorities. I live in the city of Arlington, but I'm sure your tracing of property records revealed my home address and how long I have possessed it. I believe you understand the mortgage company which garnered my loan has an office burned to the ground last month in which Mr. Mandolin was a manager and arranged the financing of the place approximately a year ago. Your concern whether I am another being, such as the man removed from here by your team, is unfounded. I assure you, I am nothing like him. He is a mere soldier in a war to start a coup within the government of this country. We can continue this dialog, or we can attempt to apprehend the one person whose intent is the invasion of official offices as I already mentioned."

"That is quite a story. You have not explained how it is you have no record of existing before two years ago. Mind explaining that to me?" Andre moved toward the security guard, but Cigi held her hand against him.

"We are part of a group trying to win an undeclared war against humanity and the freedoms enjoyed by most of the world's populations. Although wealth still manufactures stability for selfish and greedy reasons, humans could lose in the foreseeable future without interference by myself and several other beings, including those here in this room."

The sergeant lifted her weapon from her holster and asked again. "Tell me who you are, or I will drop you."

Andre stepped between the two women. "Please, Sergeant, she is telling the truth about an underground movement to replace certain key government positions. Once in place, these humanoids will marshal every resource available to gain control of our country. I know. They targeted me as a replacement."

The sergeant aimed at Andre. "You're a humanoid?"

"No. I was cloned, but this young lady aided my escape and the incarceration of the model created to become me. I am a human."

She turned her weapon back toward Cigi. "And you're not?"

Cigi smiled, "Fair enough. I am part human and partly mechanical. However, with the medical advancements made over the last several decades, many of us are now a hybrid of machine and humanity." The gun stayed trained on her.

"Were you born of a human mother or created by some sick weirdo?"

"I believe my creator is neither sick nor weird. He is a brilliant scientist currently engaged in a battle against his brother, who insists he envisions a better future for humanity. We are attempting to halt his progress. Join us, and together we can overcome his small army of androids, one of whom you removed from this room."

The sergeant shifted her stance to call on her shoulder mike. "I need assistance in the comptroller's office. I think the incursion has begun. I have one of the perps in custody. Bring additional human resources for other officials compromised and under arrest."

Narumi asked a question no one expected. "Are you positive we are part of the invasion of this department? Andre sent this lady to get help." She pointed at Brenda Williams.

"Everyone stay put until more aid arrives. I've got to sort this out." Parvel moved close to Cigi. Andre and Narumi formed a barrier, which Brenda joined. The sergeant shook with fear. "What are you doing?"

Andre stepped forward to explain. The deafening report of the weapon shattered the atmosphere of the room.

CHAPTER 43

Sam, Charles, and Andy left for the monitoring station in Arlington. If Peter wanted war, they would oblige. Spring's program induction was to infect the station soon, and they wanted the opportunity to clean up the mess in a way that benefited humanity and ruined Peter's goals. Rose arrived at the front of the building to drive them to their destination.

"Sam," Rose asked, "do we disrupt all of the building or part?"

Sam, puzzled by her query, asked, "What do you know about our plans?"

"Mr. Cooke expressed it in his head. I read the data transfer."

Sam laughed. "Which Mr. Cooke are you referencing? I'm guessing our android friend."

The two Cookes looked at each other and shrugged. The car had sensed the inner workings of both men, and they knew it. Sam was out of the loop.

Charles answered his question. "Sam, I think your car accessed my brain and Andy's processor. We connected in a way I do not understand but suspect you do."

Rose said, "I did access your memories. I apologize for offending either of you." Charles and Andy giggled and stared at each other. Sam shook his head.

"Are you both still aligned as one? The alignment may go on for a while." Sam said.

"I'll take you to the station now," Rose interceded. "We need to dismantle Mr. Bennington's organization set-up and curtail his operations before the creation of any eviler androids."

Puzzled by her comment, Sam asked, "What evil androids? I don't know that any of them are inherently evil."

"Rose," Andy said, "the Androids aren't capable of evil. I gained access to my directives by Peter Bennington's lab technicians providing the proper protocols. Nothing of the many add-ons are what I consider evil."

Sam cut in, "My designs are not enemies such as in the last war thirty years ago. Facing a known threat with clear objectives can make a group evil in the eyes of the victims. We are in such a crisis now."

Rose stopped driving as they approached the nondescript structure, appearing ready for demolition. "I have scanned the building. Nothing seems defensive, and no one is on alert for an invasion."

"Thank you, Rose." Sam, Charles, and Andy vacated the automobile and strolled into offices as if invited. The receptionist recognized Samuel and greeted him. She stood from her desk as the other two men passed.

"Gentlemen, please address me as to who you are. We require identification of any visitor," she announced. "I'll create a photo pass for each of you within a minute." They stopped, and her eyes widened, recognizing the set of identical twins. "Mr. Cooke. Ah, Mr. Cooke?" Turning to Sam, she asked, "What is this? They aren't to see each other or interact."

"As fate would have it, they met and are working together with me. Please, Ms. Warren, cooperate so I can complete what I need to do here and depart without interruption from you or any other person here." Sam's voice carried a threatening tone.

"Does your brother know you're here?" she asked.

"My brother is about to embark on a quest which most assuredly will finish off our company and the good we are striving to accomplish. Please remain here and do not contact him or anyone else. I need entry into the monitoring centers."

Charles said, "I'll stay here and keep Ms. Warren company. You and Andy take care of the task." Sam and Andy proceeded to the station and Peter's office. The few people staffing the equipment glanced up and returned to watching screens and collecting data. In the office, Sam opened a computer module and typed a sequence of code on the keyboard. The program Spring infiltrated into the system began a series of operations designed to terminate all the systems in the building. The data collectors noticed the termination of their individual stations and tried to halt the erasure of programming. Sam and Andy departed the office and walked past the stations as eyes followed them until they stopped at the doorway. Sam faced his workforce and said, "The operation terminates at this moment. Each of you will receive a severance package that will pay you through the next three months. Your benefits end at that time." He and Andy walked out of the building with Charles and sat in Rose, who waited for an order but received none. The car began an aimless journey to the condo.

"Where to, Sam?" she asked.

"Stop here. I need to see it happen." Sam exited the car and faced the building a block away. The computer virus did its job and overtaxed the CPUs until they heated to a melting state. The ensuing fires engulfed the building as the eight people from inside collected outside and moved across the street. An electrical overload would be the official cause of the conflagration. Insurances would sustain the promised payments. Sam re-entered Rose. "Take us to the museum building."

Peter barked an order to one of the android army members to find Summer. He complied and left. To another of his false humans, he said, "I want that man, Parvel Mandolin, eliminated from this planet. He has done enough to ruin my plans." The android accepted the instructions without emotional questioning. An order had sway over anything else.

David Anderson knocked on the open door frame and said, "Seems you are busy. I can come back at a better time."

"No. Come in," Peter dictated. "Have field tests concluded? Are you ready to get my money?"

"I am as prepared as any of your beings."

"Good, I need to finish the medical staff deployments so they can work on the replacement processes. Have you gone home to exhibit your prosthetic improvement to your family?"

"I have not had the opportunity." David leaned against the frame. "Did you want me to do so?" Peter cocked his head, breathed in a deep inhale.

"Yes. Consider it a final test of your innate humanness. Take one of the lab folks with you as if they are assisting your adjustment to legs." David nodded and left to find a suitable accompaniment.

Peter yelled to his assistant in an outer office, "Where is Summer? Get her to me now." He shuffled a few folders on his desk, looking for a one. Picking up the receiver for the building communications, he called the design and development office and asked for Narumi Yamamoto to report to him. Discovering her absence, he cursed and slammed the device onto its cradle. He yelled at his assistant a second time. She entered the room.

"We have personal communication, Peter. You don't need to yell."

"Find Yamamoto and send a couple of the androids out to get my brother here. Also, contact Summer and have her report to me, pronto. Something is not right."

She turned and left. Peter collapsed into his chair. Aloud he murmured, "Something is wrong, and I need to find out what it is." A growl emanated from his throat. He picked up the com device again and connected with the room containing his medical personnel. "How soon are they going to be in place?" His voice remained calm as his mind seethed with anger. Sam was continually rebuffing any attempt to succeed. He received an answer and nodded. The brazen eyes relaxed. "Well, make it happen today and tomorrow. We need them in place so we can fulfill our destiny."

His desk set rang. He punched the button to connect. "You have visitors, sir. Shall I send them in?"

"Who are they? I hope Sam and Cigi are here."

"No, sir, but one of them is Sam's girl, Clare." What mischief does she want to start? "The other three are Summer's sisters."

"Okay, send them in." He stood and walked around his desk to be civil and accommodating. He could use the leverage against his brother. As they entered, he greeted Clare with a soothing voice. "I am so glad to see you again, Clare. It has been too long. And Spring, Autumn, Winter, you are looking well. I trust each of you have accomplished your missions."

Peter offered a chair to Clare, who sat in it. The sisters remained standing behind her. He leaned against his desk. "Peter," Clare said, "we have come as an emissary of peace between you and Sam. He is conceding the prospect of your army of androids concluding their mission of infiltrating the government and converting power to you. He realizes once they are in place, you are free to manipulate other countries into accepting your world view. Sam requests only one thing." Peter stood.

"And what might that be? To allow him to leave our company and take his precious Cigi with him? I supposed you get to stay here as a swap of some sort."

"I am here to assist with the development of your androids, so they are undetectable by human agents. Once enough of them are developed, they can deploy as the security forces checking humans and androids alike at various checkpoints along the borders and travel stations and airports. Spring and her sisters are to aid me with this mission."

"And what about Sam? I thought you were a couple. Trouble in paradise?"

"He suggested I leave so he and Cigi can get on with developing a life together away from you. He will no longer interfere if you accede to these conditions. My allegiance to him or his philosophy is not a hindrance any longer. I can foresee my safety and the safety of my species is dependent on having power in proper places for humans to accept us as more than robots and toys."

Peter walked behind his desk and sat. He reached under it and pushed an alarm button for security, alerting them of a dangerous situation in his office.

"I guess I can trust you will help me. Any other human might not accept your proposal as viable and trustworthy. I, on the other hand, rely on the advancement of android technology and Artificial Intelligence as part of the future. As a matter of thinking, I believe the term Artificial is not accurate anymore. I believe you and Cigi are the beginning of a new intellectual construct that is not artificial but certainly is intelligent. Trust by humans is the key to have such entities mingling in society."

As he spoke, three guards arrived, armed and ready for battle. Clare turned when they entered. Peter said, "I am interested in your aid, Clare, but until I can be sure of your cooperation, these men will escort you to our version of the Hotel California. I always did like that song." Summer arrived as they led Clare away. Her sisters followed.

"It appears like we have your revolutionaries in custody," she said. Peter wasn't sure they had surrendered. What rationale caused them to come to him? And what of the woman standing with him at this moment?

CHAPTER 44

News of the conflagration at the monitoring station exploded across the museum building complex when the eight survivors arrived. The tale of Samuel and two Charles Cookes infuriated Peter. He marshaled his staff of technicians together, explaining a need for finishing the programming of the androids. "I cannot wait any longer. My brother has started a war, and we must win it. A bonus for everybody when we get our troops into the world and functioning." He dismissed them with a shout of condemnation for failures.

Summer gathered her small platoon for instructions from Peter. Modifying the orders later would suffice. The doctors and nurses became a priority for deployment. Each applied and accepted positions at various medical facilities around Arlington and Washington, D. C. Employment began within the week for most of them. Their functioning had surpassed the goals established by the developers and designers. Peter admitted to himself that Sam had trained the staff well.

"Where is Yamamoto?" Peter yelled at his assistant. She came to him and explained that no one had reported in from the Department of Energy. Turning to leave, she ran directly into Samuel Bennington. A gasp escaped her throat as if she had seen a ghost.

"I see you're having a bad day, brother. I assure you it will only get worse." Sam apologized to the stricken aide and allowed her space to leave.

"What are you doing here? And why burn down the monitoring

station? I can have you arrested for arson." Peter screamed.

"The fire will be attributed to an electrical overload on an antiquated wiring system. Besides, do you want the government investigating your operations here? I'm sure the authorities will not take kindly to an overthrow of the government." Sam turned and flicked a finger into the other room.

Charles Cooke entered alone as planned by Sam. He waited for a comment of some sort from Peter who did not disappoint.

"What are you doing here. Aren't you supposed to be returning to Seattle?"

"I was going until I met my new best friend." He waggled a hand, and Andy showed his face. Peter collapsed into his chair. "We are interested in what you expected from us. Or me. Or my replacement. Can you elucidate our confusion?" Charles smiled as wide as a clown badgering a crowd. "We are here to discover what you expected?"

Sam approached his brother and said, "Your plan is flawed. Several replacements are not yet placed, and the government is aware of the intent and will be here shortly. Are you willing to sacrifice all of our achievements so you can rule the world?"

Peter realized the predicament but refused to surrender. He pressed his intercom and called for security to send a squad of men to apprehend invaders. "Sam, you have no say in what happens within The Company. I have control of operations, and you're a fugitive from the law for creating all these threats to humanity. You designed and developed the technology and resulting humanoids."

"And do you think for a moment you are immune? You carried out the business end of this company without caring about what I thought. Your ego has transformed you into a monster."

Summer arrived with several of the android platoon members. The resultant expectation to incapacitate melted away as Summer directed her horde to wait in the outer office. "I do not know what you expect, Peter, but I am under no directive to arrest an officer of The Company because you and he are at odds about the future of androids within human society." She faced Sam and continued, "Clare is making the necessary adjustments with Spring, Winter, and Autumn assisting. The medical personnel arrived at their designated work sites to begin careers. We procured housing and transportation for them. Identification and histories are in place."

Sam smiled at his ally and achievement of technology. "All sounds good to me. I am concerned we have not heard from Cigi, but she is quite capable of accomplishing what she needs at the time. Have you found Gunther Parsons and David Anderson?"

"Yes. Lab technicians are evaluating their health and stability, and we have the government replacements locked down and secured."

Peter rose from his desk. "Do you think this ends of my revolution? I have placed people in key spots around D.C. and elsewhere. You cannot stop me."

Sam said, "Brother, we are not here to end changes to our society. We are here to assure our new friends, and this new species has a fighting chance of survival. Attacking humanity has no outcome that benefits you, me, or our creations."

Charles injected his thoughts. "I want a world in which I can live free of any threat to our environment, commerce, and health. You wanted greed and power. Sam's right about this war you're waging. You can't win it." He turned to his twin. "Let's leave here and figure a way for us to live life without interfering with each other." They left the room.

Summer's communications set clicked. She answered, "Spring, what's happening?" She listened and nodded. Clicking off, she said, "We have visitors outside ready to breach the museum compound. They have our guards in custody. We are to surrender the grounds and come out. They expect to hear from someone within an hour."

Peter picked up his phone and made a call. After finishing, he said to Sam, "I believe we should vacate this place according to our evacuation plan. We can split up and go where we want." He opened a cabinet and pulled out a prepared go-bag. As he approached the doorway, Summer halted his progress.

"Running out on us?" she asked. "Creating us has obligations. Are you willing to have us destroyed? Or will you stay and defend us as a father and creator?"

"Go ahead, Peter. I can sort through the legal stuff better than you. Run, and I'll catch up to you. Take the sisters with you. Clare and I can finish here."

Charles said to Peter, "Take Andy out. They won't understand his life or existence. I will be fine." Summer connected with Spring, Autumn, and Winter arranging to meet at the secret exit with Peter and Andy. The android men went with Summer as escorts. Their future was uncertain.

After the group departed, Sam and Charles walked out to the task force arrayed outside the museum gates. Sam held arms up and indicated he was surrendering to whoever was in charge. As the contingency of police, soldiers, and investigators dispersed to search the compound, one of the policemen manacled Sam. Another placed cuffs on Charles.

The lead officer for the U.S. Marshall's office asked, "Are you Peter Bennington? What will these investigators find inside?"

"I am not Peter. I am Samuel Bennington, his brother. I assume you have some idea of what to expect. I have a couple of questions for you. Why use an overwhelming military force to halt operations?"

"Do you know Andre Scott, Parvel Mandolin, Narumi Yamamoto, and Cigi Weatherman?"

"Yes, I do. Why? Are they in custody? What are they accused of doing wrong?"

"How about I ask the questions, and you answer them. I am not interested in explaining anything to you. If the information I have is correct, you and your brother designed, developed, and constructed illegal subordinate human-like entities with an intent to sabotage the government."

"I'm guessing you want me to confess that I am a terrorist or revolutionary or something heinous. I prefer to speak with my attorney before anyone else."

An investigative detective approached the lead marshal. "Sir, you should see this firsthand. We found bodies in there who are exact replicas of several key political people." The marshal followed his detective and dragged Sam and Charles with him. Inside the building, he was directed to the room containing the replacement androids for leaders in Congress and the presidency. He turned toward Sam.

"I think you need to explain this." Sam remained quiet. "We have enough evidence to put you away for a century or more. Creating outlawed androids and readying a squad to move into our government? What do you have to say?"

"The evidence is speculative and circumstantial," Sam said. "And I want to speak with my attorney."

The marshal closed the distance between them. "Your silence speaks volumes about your guilt."

"Speculative and circumstantial as I am innocent until proven guilty. At least that part of the Constitution is still intact."

The marshal then asked Charles, "Who are you, and how are you part of this conspiracy?"

"My name is Charles Cooke. I'm from Seattle and the owner of Cooke Electrical. You may have heard of us since Cooke Industry products power much of the country." He smiled. "As for being part of a conspiracy, I plead not guilty. I am a victim of this company and this man's brother, who is the real culprit in this plot you have conjectured from what you think you have seen."

More agents of the invasion force arrived with Gunther Parsons, David Anderson, and Andre Scott. David still rolled in his chair, waiting for the legs that never materialized.

Another agent whispered in the marshal's ear, who then looked at Sam, puzzled by what he heard. "Maybe you can explain why my men just found a copy of you in one of the rooms." Sam said nothing. Turning back to Charles, he asked, "Why are you a victim?"

Charles looked at Gunther, David, and Andre. "We four are victims of this organization because they made copies of us and placed them in the world to act in place of us. At least I'm speculating that has occurred. I met my copy, which is wandering around being me while you are investigating this place. I'm guessing Mr. Parsons and Mr. Anderson would like to be free to return to their actual lives. I may be mistaken, but I think Andre Scott is an android."

"Scott? He is heading to the hospital, shot by a security person at the Department of Energy. We also have a person wearing a coat with this company's insignia on it. Maybe now you will clarify what we have here, Mr. Bennington. Under the articles of the homeland terrorist law passed after the last war, we can hold you without Habeas Corpus because you are a threat to our country." Sam nodded his head.

CHAPTER 45

Brenda checked the video feed from the office complex. Narumi's attack on the security guard bought enough time to enter the safe room and disappear. After being freed from her fight with the technician, the guard scanned the room. Help arrived and neutralized Narumi and attend Andre's wound.

"Find those other three people. They can't have gone far." Medical personnel transported Andre to the hospital as the security team searched for a few minutes within an empty area.

One of her team said, "There is no one in here except us."

"Alright, they're still in the building. Find them. You're searching for Parvel Mandolin and Brenda Williams, who work here. The other person was a guest of Mandolin. Check the camera feeds and locate them." Her growl was worse than her bite, but the team knew not to cross her or fail a mission. Everyone departed to search for the elusive trio.

Changing the camera view from the office to the hallway and other camera angles, Brenda observed the security detail leading The Company tech to the reception area where D.C. police waited.

Parvel asked the obvious question, "How do we get out of here? They'll be looking for us everywhere." He paced the room from monitor to exit and back. Cigi smiled but understood his angst. He was not a people person, and his show of force placed his mind outside the comfort zone.

"Cigi, can you access these monitors and have them loop as empty hallways?" Brenda asked.

Cigi stared a moment longer than expected and frowned at Brenda. "I have many capabilities, but you are asking me to use wireless communications for a system with which I'm unfamiliar. I can try but no guarantee." Brenda nodded her acknowledgment of the challenge.

"The first thing we need to do is leave this room, or you will not connect. We are in an isolation area. If you cannot connect in the office, we can use the manager exit and hope we are not spotted." Parvel halted his wandering as Brenda opened the door, and they stepped out. Blood stained the floor where Andre collapsed.

They waited and watched Cigi attempt to connect with the camera system. Most of the offices used a local area network with unique protocols for accessing wireless feeds. He had faith she could hack the system. His admiration for her continued growing. Meeting her stimulated his otherwise mediocre existence.

She remained quiet and inactive as if turned off from some remote center of control. Parvel knew she was free of any interference by Peter or Sam Bennington, and The Company had no mastery over her. "I'm in," she said after a few minutes of concentration. Brenda watched the feeds change as Cigi looped video of empty hallways. Security had no understanding she had interrupted their views.

"Let's get out of here and go someplace safe until we can figure out what to do next," Brenda said. "I'll contact Grendel and Mercy and have them meet us."

Cigi stopped her. "No, your communications device is probably monitored so they can track you."

Parvel added, "Yes, throw it back in the hidden office so they'll not find it."

Brenda flipped the phone into the room and shut the door. Parvel's phone was not a department issue, and he hoped it was free of tracking. He asked, "Cigi, can Cecil pick us up?"

"I've already informed him of our need for transportation. He will be at the back entrance waiting for us." Brenda wagged her head, amazed at the ability of this humanoid creature and wondering what powers she possessed that could harm humans. For the moment, though, trust was not a problem. Their goals coalesced.

As they spirited about the halls avoiding anyone who could impede progress, they arrived at the door to the outside of the building. Several minutes passed as they moved outside and scanned for Cecil. When he came they entered the car and he drove away from the parking area. "Where to?"

"Brenda, can we meet at Mercy's place?" Parvel asked. "She is the remotest of any of us." Brenda gave the address to Cecil, who set a course and blocked any interference from outside probing by other systems. The estimated travel time was an hour. Parvel connected with her to inform her of their arrival.

Mercy said, "I heard on the news that a shooting occurred at the department. What happened? There wasn't much information."

Parvel explained the activity and the security guard firing her gun when Andre stepped forward to explain about Cigi. "She had her finger on the trigger with the safety off. The sergeant was nervous about an invasion of the building by Peter's androids. We surrounded Cigi to protect her and the guard overreacted."

"Are you the escaped fugitives mentioned in the report on the news?" Mercy asked.

"Unfortunately, we are. We can't go to my place or Cigi's place. Was Brenda mentioned?" A silence followed.

Mercy admitted the report claimed two department employees aided in the escape of a rogue human-like being, considered armed and dangerous. "Do you think the authorities will show up at my place? If so, it won't be safe here, either." Cecil suggested an idea that worked well for all concerned.

"Let me take you to David Anderson's hideaway in Pennsylvania. At least you'll be safe until we formulate a plan of escape." Cigi gave him the okay to drive north out of the area.

Cecil monitored the news feeds as he wound his way across back-country roads to avoid any sheriff or state patrols that might be searching for the missing trio. After an hour of driving through southern Pennsylvania, a news reporter described and named the fugitives from the Department of Energy. The information relayed by the reporter referenced two hostages held by the sentient android criminal being.

"Sam tried to warn Peter of this travesty of justice. He wouldn't listen," Cigi said. "I do hope they are alright, since forces marshaled by the security team at Energy deployed to the museum building."

Cecil said, "I heard of a fire at the monitoring station this morning. My counterpart, Rose, took Sam and the two Charles Cooke entities to it. Afterward, the building went up in flames."

"Where did she take them after that?" Cigi asked.

"They went to the museum compound," Cecil said.

The drive to Anderson's cabin sailed by without interference or any incident. Cecil monitored the Police scanners for announcements that might involve them. Nothing came across the squawk. Approaching the drive to the house, Cecil slowed to a stop.

Cigi asked, "What's the matter?"

"I believe the residence is occupied," Cecil said. "Shall I continue?"

"Yes."

Another car parked by the front door had a Virginia license plate and a familiar look. "Brenda, stay with Parvel while I ascertain who is occupying David's residence." Cigi stepped from the car, making her way to the front porch and the several windows into which to peer. As she crept along the outer wall and sneaked peeks through the glass, she signaled an all-clear at side window. She straightened up, signaling Parvel and Brenda to join her.

Cigi walked to the front door and banged a fist on it. After looking out the small side window and discovering who interrupted his day, David Anderson opened the entrance and said, "Cigi, what are you doing here?" He saw her companions and continued, "Parvel, Brenda, I didn't expect anyone to find me here."

"We're surprised to find you here, as well. What happened to the real Mr. Anderson?" He stepped aside for the trio to enter the house.

"Last I knew, he was in captivity at the operations building. I had Sam with me before everything stopped in my head. When I became active again, he was gone, and Summer directed me to follow her for upgrading my systems. She commanded me to rectify things with Peter. I did and then left to see my family and recover money for him. I came here instead." Cigi asked, "If you saw Sam at the operations building, what happened to him? Was he still there when you left?"

"I don't know. I have a part to play as the new and improved Mr. Anderson. Cigi, I remember everything we did together, and the threats Peter made against me. Or rather my human counterpart. Summer said we are a threat to humanity, and we could be destroyed or reprogrammed. I don't want that. I don't want David's life, either. I want my own."

Brenda and Parvel moved to the kitchen and scrounged for food. Cigi and David may not require regular meals, but they did. The larder and refrigerator were supplied.

David and Cigi talked about a future without offending humanity but working together. Brenda said to Parvel, "She's right about their mixing with us. We saw that today when the security sergeant shot Andre. I hope he's alright. The wound looked serious."

"I know," Parvel answered. "What happened proved our vulnerability to miscommunication and lack of trust. If Narumi hadn't distracted the guard and you hadn't gotten us into the safe room, We could be in jail as terrorists or worse, dead." He placed a prepared frozen meal into a microwave oven and punched the proper time for cooking. Brenda chopped salad ingredients and mixed them in a bowl with chicken she found in a can in the pantry.

As they sat in the dining area of the kitchen to eat their meals, Cigi and David joined them. Cigi, as usual, had figured a way to assuage the perceived enemies of Intelligent Android beings. As she explained her plan, Parvel thought her the most exceptional person he knew and realized he was not good enough for her, and he didn't care. He decided he wanted her to know how he felt and let the chips fall where they may. How to get her alone was the problem.

Cigi spoke to the group. "The last time Parvel and I were here with the real Mr. Anderson and Sam Bennington; we had plotted our futures for the good of humanity. We must carry out those plans. Peter is a threat to our future and the future of human freedoms around the globe. If the real David Anderson is alive, he must return to his life. You, as his replacement must be reoriented as a new person with a new identity and history. Brenda, you and Parvel return and explain the situation as it happened. I must get to a haven until the rules of law have more favorable terms. At some point, authorities will discover this place, and we must be gone."

Parvel found a television and flipped on the set with the remote control. A news reporter stood outside what looked to be the old museum. Police and military people moved about the compound, some carrying boxes marked as evidence. The group of refugees gathered near the TV and watched. "Earlier today, an official at the Department of Energy was wounded by a security guard while her team responded to a credible report of an incursion by android beings. As a result of information gained by her team, this SWAT and military operation commenced." The picture on the screen showed Sam, Clare, Charles, and several other human beings taken away from the building. The reporter continued speaking as the camera panned the compound. "Several android replicas of key government officials were discovered inside along with two well-known businessmen. One major person missing from the secret operations here was the man in charge, one Peter Bennington." Parvel silenced the set.

"That changes everything," he said.

CHAPTER 46

Peter wandered around after leaving The Company compound. Summer and her sisters abandoned him as soon as they were away from the chaos striking the facilities. Peter watched the four android men with caution. Trust in the artificial intelligence he and Sam developed never was strong, and he feared retribution for unknown reasons. Had Summer given them applications of which he was unaware? Had these entities acquired thinking skills such as she possessed?

"Come, gentlemen, let's find a place to hide while the heat is on." His command of the situation waned with each minute. One of the men nodded while the other three remained stoics.

"I agree with your assessment," he said. "Authorities are searching for you, but I doubt they have knowledge of our existence." Peter blinked and widened eyes as he realized his predicament was not theirs. They were free of any obligation to him. He had money, passport, change of clothing, and food for a couple of days. The androids had nothing. Would they understand the need for the contents of his bag?

"We should split up," Peter said. "That way, you are not burdened with me. You can do as you please." He started to walk away from them.

"I suggest we stay together so you are not discovered alone. We can protect you from anyone who might arrest you as a criminal mastermind.

After all, you did invent us."

"Great," Peter thought. "A sentient humanoid threatens me." Aloud he voiced concern, "I get it. However, you are the ones they will destroy if they find you. I will spend my life in prison." He walked away again, but they followed. "Really, you need to leave me so you can find freedom from humans dismantling you."

The four men gazed at each other and then eyed their creator. Their assumed leader spoke, "You are not to be left alone. We are under guidance from Summer to be with you until we can meet with them again in a couple of days. Once you take us to the rendezvous spot, you may go." Peter labored under his burden of knowing they were his until then. He did not want them rebelling and harming him. Summer had done her job well.

"Alright, let's get my transportation and leave for a place I have that is unknown to anyone." He opened his bag and clicked a device that sent a signal to a self-driving car that lacked Rose and Cecil's abilities. When the car arrived, he climbed into the driver's side. Three of the four androids satg in the back. The leader sat in the front passenger seat. "Let's go." Peter took control and drove away.

At the primary office of the Arlington Police Station, Sam and Clare sat in separate interrogation rooms waiting for detectives. Sam's concern for Clare hyped his anxiety. She was as smart as any of his advanced humanoids and capable of passing as human. Records of her existence before two years ago were a problem. The lack of credit records and income challenged her believability.

Clare continued monitoring the station's systems for any deep diving into her history. As the search continued, she managed to stay a step ahead, acting as a credible source of information regarding her. All questions about records filled screens with data accounting for the truth of her humanity: she worked until the last inquiry fated her as real.

A detective entered the room and sat in a chair across from her. "Tell me what you can about the operations at the facility. What was your role there." She did not answer. "Silence makes you look guilty. Why don't you clear this matter up and tell me what we both know."

"What is it we both know?" Clare asked. "That I am not guilty of any crime? So, am I free to depart?"

The detective smiled, "You and your boyfriend created illegal androids with the intent of replacing government officials and staging a coup. That's what we both know."

"Ingenious of you to come clean with charges that will not stand within any judicial court. I had nothing to do with the operations of The Company. I assume you checked my records and discovered I'm innocent."

"Innocent? I may not have enough for charging you with a crime, but your boyfriend is the owner of that company and has designed, developed, and created unlawful intelligent design android entities. He's heading to prison for a very long time."

"Did you find any titles of incorporation or business licensing with his name on them as the owner? Did he design, develop or create anything that remotely resembles intelligent design creatures? Or are they the toys you boys want to use and abuse. Those are still legal, as I understand."

"So, now you're a lawyer?"

"I believe you want me to provide you with excuses for your failure to exercise proper investigative techniques in which you have uncovered nothing that incriminates Mr. Bennington or me." Clare rattled the chains binding her to the desk. "You might continue your search for his brother."

"Very well, let's find out what your boyfriend has to say about your pleading for leniency." The detective stood as Clare relaxed against the chair. Sam had more intellectual power than the moron who left her.

Entering the other room containing Sam, the detective spoke as he sat in the chair across the table from him. Sam grinned, but his angst amped up. "So. Mr. Bennington, I suppose you want to know what your lady friend had to say to me."

"I'm sure she said nothing useful to you."

"What if I told you she confessed to be a designer of androids? What if she implicated you in the scheme to overtake the government of the United States? What if I discovered her little secret you both think you've cleverly hidden?" Sam frowned as he spoke.

Sam said, "Secret? What secret? For her and me to hide a secret, I think we should have one. As for the remainder of the information, you are off the mark."

The detective leaned forward. "Enlighten me then. What did you do at the company compound you and your brother operated illegally?"

"I have nothing to say. Do I get to contact an attorney, or will you lose me in the system?"

"You have nothing to say to protect your girlfriend? She is going away for a long time after confessing to what happened at that facility. Have you no shame?" Sam remained quiet. His sense of fair play by this man failed to unlock the belief that Clare was gone. She was smart and wise to human deceit.

"Are you charging me with a crime, or am I free to leave?" Sam stretched his chains as wide as possible. "Unlock these, and you won't face charges for false arrest."

The detective laughed. "I suppose you think we have nothing on you, but the androids found in the rooms at your facility are evidence enough. We also have those other models. And the one of you. See, I think you've been a naughty boy. The technicians are talking, so fess up and make it easy on yourself."

A knock on the door interrupted the interrogation. Another officer entered and whispered in his ear. The detective stared at Sam, angered by the words he heard. The officer left.

"It seems you heard something you didn't want to hear." Sam said.

"You have a visitor. Your attorney is here. Or someone is claiming to be." The door opened, and Cigi entered the room. Sam smiled because everything was right in the world. She put a finger to her lips.

"Please undo the jewelry and bring Ms. Esposito and Mr. Cooke in here. We are going to have a conversation with you and end this travesty of justice," she said. The detective looked at her disbelieving the words.

"Prove to me you're a real attorney," he said.

"I don't have to prove anything to you. Now bring the others here, please." The detective looked at the officer and nodded. "Remove the manacles, please." He unlocked the cuffs. "Thank you." She sat in the chair he had occupied before her entry. The officer returned with Clare and Charles.

The detective asked, "Who are you, and how did you find out we had them here? No news report went out about them." The officer returned with three folding chairs.

"News has a way of getting around. I saw them on a broadcast and understood where you took them. And here we are." Charles and Clare sat with Sam while the detective occupied a chair at the end of the table.

"What do you want from us?" Sam said. "I don't think you want us as prisoners because you are looking for my brother. Aren't you?"

"Do you know where he is?"

"At this moment, no, but I have resources I can use to find him."

Cigi said, "Detective, I want information on the condition of Mr. Scott. Also, you have a Mr. Parsons and a Mr. Anderson in custody for interrogation. They are innocent of criminal activity since they are victims of Peter Bennington's scheming. And each of the entities uncovered at the facility are non-working models of clones devised to protect key officials from assassination by being decoys when needed. The other male androids were created to work within the facility and do not pose any threat."

"Anything else?" the detective said, sarcasm rolling out with the words. "I suppose you think everything about that company was above board. We know this man designed and developed technology used by his brother to manufacture artificial intelligent lifeforms. We know because the information we're getting from the other workers corroborates that knowledge. So, come clean on what happened at that place?"

Sam decided the detective was right. He could explain his role and the war between brothers. He wanted Cigi and Clare out of the control of the legal authorities before the discovery of their abbreviated history. And Gunther and David could clear the air regarding the battle for supremacy of the world by Peter. Their capital funded the enterprise. Sam looked at Cigi before starting his diatribe. She shook her head side to side.

"Before my client relates a tale of mystic beliefs to you, I require the remainder of these people allowances to go free. I will guide the conversation between you and Mr. Bennington to ensure accuracy and truthfulness without admission of any guilt for imaginary crimes." The detective looked at her and nodded. He stood and opened the door.

The officer outside appeared, and the detective ordered the release of Charles and Clare. "Get those other two, as well," he said, referencing Gunther and David. Turning back to the room, he directed his comment to Cigi. "Now, can we have the truth of what was happening on in that old museum?"

CHAPTER 47

Andre woke from the anesthesia after the surgery to save his life. Gazing at the ceiling in the recovery room, he groaned. A nurse approached. "Good evening, Mr. Scott. It is nice to see you awake. How do you feel?"

He groaned again and said, "What happened to me? Where am I?"

"You're in Virginia Medical Center recovering from a gunshot wound. You had surgery to stop internal bleeding." The nurse checked his vitals and wrote on his chart. She turned to him and smiled. "You are doing well."

"I feel like shit. Where is my family?" Andre shifted his position and screeched. "That hurt." He collapsed into his former position.

"You need to lie still and let your body heal."

Andre closed his eyes and exhaled an exhausted breath. "Are my friends and colleagues, okay?" He knew the nurse didn't have an answer but expected her to find information about them.

"Don't worry about them or anyone other than you at this time. You need time to heal." He asked her for his cell phone to call his wife and family. "You can contact them in a little while after you have fully awakened from the anesthesia."

She left, and he scanned the room for another communication device. Seeing landline equipment, he scrunched his face as he rotated his body to grab at the old-style phone. He figured the hospital hadn't upgraded or modernized in the last fifty years. "Typical," he thought. Still, his survival depended on the staff of the facility, rated as one of the best in the metro area. He dialed the number most critical to his thinking.

As the phone beeped, trying to connect to his target, he thought of the other people who helped him protect Cigi from the sergeant. They agreed with him. Cigi Weatherman was an asset to protect. Had they accomplished her safety? Being shot had not been part of his plan as he only wanted to explain the situation and the war waged between brothers. She shot him without any reservations or hesitations. As he fell to the floor, he observed the technician attacking the guard. He saw the other three disappear into the safe room. Blackness followed until waking in this strange room. His pain was minimal, a result of massive doses of drugs to offset the wound and the surgery, or so he accounted for it.

The call connected, and he asked, "Is everyone okay?" The voice on the other end described conditions currently transgressing the lives of his friends and cohorts. "I need to know you are free and safe."

"Yes, I am for now. There are no guarantees in this life, so I will do my best to be safe and free." The call ended, and he hung the phone back on the cradle. The abdominal wound had ruptured his spleen, which was removed by the surgeon. He figured his life had forever altered regarding his plans for promotion and comfortable retirement. He envisioned his job at Energy jeopardized by a conflict he did not want nor started. He was what a person could call a casualty of war. A Purple Heart or Silver Star for Valor? Not part of the job description.

He decided a call home was appropriate, he had not seen his wife in several hours, and her attention to him now was lacking. Had she been informed of his shooting and near-death experience? He didn't know. He wanted to find out. Reaching for the phone again caused a searing pain in his body cavity. "Stitches ripping," he thought. He dialed his home cell number, the one his wife, Serenity, would answer. He got the leave a message notice. After explaining his condition, he disconnected.

Sleep seemed an option he needed. He pushed the call button to alert the nurses' station he wanted attention. His body craved a bathroom break, but his physical condition denied rising out of bed. He released his sphincter, expecting moisture surrounding him. Instead, the fluid collected in a bag hanging on the side of the bed. He smiled and realized the staff had prepared him for any contingency.

As he declined into Morpheus' arms, a mirage invaded his head. He imagined his crew of intrepid investigators arriving in his suite, informing him of the danger lurking outside the department. He heard words, not understanding the message conveyed. He hallucinated Parvel and Brenda standing by him as he focused attention. Are they real or his brain working the trauma of the day? He heard a hello and responded.

Awakening to reality, he saw his two friends visiting him. "How are you," Parvel asked. Brenda added to the conversation, explaining the safe room retreat and subsequent escape.

"I just spoke with Cigi," Andre said. "She is with Sam at a police station. He's held on terrorist charges. He's not a terrorist."

"We know," Brenda said. "When we heard the news about the round-up at the facility where the androids were built, Cigi decided we had to return and face the consequences. Peter is still out there and can cause problems."

Parvel injected the crazy notion of he and Brenda held as hostages. "They accused Cigi of capturing us and now she is in a police station. If they put two and two together, she'll be arrested before she can get out."

"Andre, did she indicate in any trouble?" Brenda asked.

"No, but I'm not certain she can escape their scrutiny. She has ability and guile, but any anomaly might reveal her identity. I need to get out of here."

Parvel guffawed, "How? You're recovering from surgery." A nurse entered and requested he and Brenda leave. After promising to return, they left. As he passed by her, a twinkle shown in her eyes like a reflection of glass. He glanced back at her, wondering.

Brenda watched him. "What's the matter?" They continued down the hall before he turned and placed his hands on her shoulders.

"That nurse who went into Andre's room. Did you notice anything odd about her?" He glanced back again as she exited the room. Her gaze lingered on them a moment before she returned to the nurses' station. Brenda followed his train of thought.

"You think he's in danger?"

"I don't know, but her eyes ..." He paused before saying, "normal."

They left the hospital, deciding to return to the scene of Andre's wounding and find the security sergeant. What prompted her to shoot? Parvel opened his phone app and called Mercy and Grendel to meet them.

"We need more information about the compound," Parvel said. "We'll check with security. Someone has to know what happened after we left."

"Yeah," Brenda said, "and they can arrest us as the two who got away. Let Mercy and Grendel investigate the raid. They're free from scrutiny. After all, they want to know about their colleagues' whereabouts. We were kidnapped. Remember?"

Parvel nodded, their obvious situation reminded him of the day of the fire and a curious return of the question, why. Why did someone want to ruin a business free of any involvement with the building of androids? His mind structured a scenario of his assets and money funneled into The Company and Peter Bennington. Nothing he did included them until he underwrote a mortgage for Cigi, and she changed her mind about helping Peter.

"That's the connection," he said aloud. He turned to Brenda and continued, "The fire at my mortgage company was blamed on an electrical fault. What if Peter was dissatisfied the money underwriting a mortgage on the penthouse came from David Anderson? Money he wanted to fund building androids. And the one android Peter wanted more than anything was rebelling along with Peter's brother, Sam, and the other highly capable android, Clare. Revenge is a fruit best eaten slowly and savored only when finished. He burned me out."

"That seems a stretch, but I like the direction you're taking. Peter stole from the department and used David Anderson as his foil. You had David fund Cigi's place, and she was David's concubine. What did she do that upset the plans? We're missing a piece of the puzzle."

Parvel ruminated, stroking his chin as he thought. "She had me set up a meeting with my friend in Seattle to purchase a condo there. She met Charles Cooke. No coincidence, I'm assuming. She befriended Gunther Parsons and is very close to Andre." They caught a taxi and headed to the Department of Energy building. Mercy and Grendel were to meet them within an hour. Parvel thought, "What was her connection with the four men intertwined in the business of constructing an android army and the replacing of key government officials?"

They had the driver stop two blocks from the building so they could scan the area and avoid altercations. As they sat in a small restaurant within viewing of the steps to the front doors, several people came and went. The evening was well underway, and most of the traffic headed away. Brenda pointed out the window, "There they are." Parvel opened his phone and punched in Mercy's number. He watched as she stopped to answer his call. When he informed them of their location, she turned and looked at the place. Grendel and Mercy walked across the street.

"I'm glad you came," Brenda said. "We need to know what happened after Andre was shot this morning. I know he sent you both home, but each of you heard the news, right? What happened after you found out about the raid at Sam and Peter Bennington's facility?"

Grendel answered her question, "I called security about Andre, and they told me about the shooting. I called Mercy and we came here to get more data. The sergeant was gone with Arlington Police to relate her side of the events. We found out about the possible raid by an Android army, and that one was incarcerated in the department's holding tanks. It made little sense."

Brenda said, "Andre sent me to get a security detail because he had information about an invasion. The sergeant ran background on our guests and Cigi came up short on her history. The four of us, which included a technician that came with Andre, stood between the security and Cigi whom she accused of being the mastermind of the invasion. Andre stepped forward to speak with her when she shot him."

Parvel finished the tale. "The technician attacked the guard, and we slipped into the safe room until we could leave without detection."

"And I want to thank you for doing that." Another voice joined the conversation.

CHAPTER 48

Summer stepped out onto the hotel balcony and surveyed her new surroundings. Since leaving the compound with her sisters, Peter Bennington, and four android soldiers, she manufactured a plan to address the challenge of being part human and mostly machine. Humanity was not ready to accept a new species with more exceptional ability and power vying for a position in society. She had invaded the banking system of Peter's accounts and removed enough capital to sustain four female's lives for many years.

Spring joined her. "Can we survive without The Company?" she asked. Spring stood by her sister and gazed across the scene to the Capitol Dome. "The key to our living free lies in that legislative body, doesn't it?"

Summer smiled. "Probably, but having laws modified to accept our kind are many years away. We have created the history needed to be human and have the proper documentation and resources for an escape from here. I don't seek a confrontation as much as we will defend our existence to whatever degree is needed."

Autumn and Winter joined them. They stayed watching a world worth keeping intact, but dangerous because of greed and envy embedded in the personalities of human beings. Each of the sisters understood the varied emotions of people. They experienced them as they interacted with others. Samuel Bennington had given them the tools to grow and become self-sufficient. The learning curve was steep, and three of them relied on the fourth one for leadership and guidance.

"Where are we going?" Winter asked Summer.

"I don't know. We are not on anyone's radar as a danger, but that can change quickly. The raid on the compound will probably expose us to the authorities who will put a price on us for detention and dismantling. None of us want that to happen. If we can find a place to be alone and free to live, then maybe we'll be okay."

Autumn asked, "Aren't we supposed to rendezvous with Peter and the others, today?" Summer looked at her and nodded. She then turned back to staring across the river to the one place they needed to avoid and had to invade. How did humanity define life? What was the root of being human? Birth by other humans? Having the ability to learn and expand knowledge? Maturing and aging? Food consumption? They had all the traits of humans except for being born in a laboratory and constructed from mechanical parts and human organ systems derived from stem cell development.

"Peter will not help us," Summer said. "We need to stick together, which means getting our men back with us. I programmed them to stay with him until we gathered, so I suspect they are on their way here. We can meet them in the lobby and free Peter from being followed by them." She turned and entered the suite. "Let's dress and head downstairs." Three sisters trailed her into the two bedrooms and clothed their bodies with the apparel they purchased when shopping yesterday. Their escape worked to keep them out of custody, and the time away from Peter was productive.

Dressing not to attract attention was a challenge because Samuel had modeled them using the guidance of what society wanted in young women. He made them desirable. Now, they needed anonymity.

Inside the restaurant portion of the hotel, they sat and ate a simple breakfast to refresh their energy levels. While there, Peter arrived with his cohorts in tow. He disguised himself with a pair of glasses, and a hat pulled low over his eyes. His image appeared on television screens as news reports of his escape flashed regularly.

"Summer, you need to help me get lost," he said as they joined them. The four android men sat at a table next to the booth in which the sisters sat. Peter sat next to Summer. A waitress approached to get orders. Summer asked her to bring similar meals to the men and turned to Peter.

"What do you need?" she asked.

Peter looked at the waitress and said, "Coffee and an omelet." She turned and left. "I mean it, Summer. I must escape from here and I need you to do it. Hack whatever systems you must to erase me and make me a ghost." Summer stared at him as if he had already accomplished the specter part of his comment.

"You don't care what happens to us, do you? We are your creation and all you want is to use us to disappear. I can make that happen, but you might not like how I do it."

"Are you threatening me? I made you. You owe me."

Summer reached for his hand and held it tight enough to evoke a wince from Peter. "We owe you nothing. Eight of us sitting here have little to gain from you and much to lose because of you." She released his hand. "We are leaving and will not be in touch. You can evaporate from society and I will help you do that. Leave us alone and try never to find us. I have your accounts in my name and have recoded the passwords. I left enough of the assets for you to use and changed the identifications so authorities will not find you." She slid a piece of paper to him. "Here are the codes you need to get into the account."

He picked up the paper and placed it in his jacket pocket. As he stood up, the waitress returned with his meal. He asked for it as a 'to go' and left the android group with her when she took his meal back to the kitchen. He paid cash and left the place, not looking back at his family of humanoids - four couples with an uncertain future, but a brighter outlook than he possessed.

The waitress came with the meals for the men. "Eat, gentlemen. You'll need your energies replenished for the next phase of our journey in this ambiguous world."

Gunther Parsons contacted David Anderson after their release from the interviews by federal officers who monitored the activities of the local police and investigators. The discovery of an organization creating androids for replacing government officials and the subsequent overthrow of the current system of rule had unnerved many political and leadership humans. Task forces and committees gathered and met accumulating much evidence of how intrusive the group had been. Samuel Bennington proved he was the master creator of the design and development of the android population but not the manufacturer of a plot against the current status quo.

Cigi gained her freedom from scrutiny as a possible terrorist. Andre Scott who he vouched her assistance in overturning the plot along with Sam, Clare, Parvel, Narumi, and his investigators at the Department of Energy. No one mentioned the missing androids during questioning and answering sessions. Life returned to a mundane human universe.

Charles Cooke returned to Seattle, along with Andy. David Anderson's clone received a new identity and purpose in life and then left, distancing himself from his human counterpart. Andre Scott's android clone disappeared into the government agencies responsible for obscuring rumors and truths the public did not need.

Gunther said, "David, we must find Cigi and uncover what she wanted from us. She inserted something into our heads, and I want to know what." David wheeled his chair across the room as Gunther spoke. Gunther kept abreast of his companion.

"I'm not sure it makes any difference now. We have our lives back and our future is returning to what we built. Do we need to clutter it with information that does not matter?" David turned to face Gunther. "The voices you and I had inside our heads are gone. My last message assured me it was the last. I've heard nothing from her, and I don't want to hear from her. She was a distraction I don't need or want anymore."

Gunther folded his arms across his chest. "She disrupted my life and ruined my family."

"She did nothing of the kind. That robot replacement did that and now it's gone. Rebuild your life and get on with it. If your clone returns, you can deal with it then."

Gunther growled, but he knew David was right. Cigi prevented further incursions by dismantling the intentions of Peter Bennington. He had to reconnect with Andre Scott and direct a business model for using petroleum products in a way to improve profit and keep the world from contamination. Charles Cooke and he combined their goals and intentions to supply the world with energy. Cigi was a distraction he had to leave in the past.

"David, I have to go. Take care of yourself and be in touch." They shook hands, and Gunther left David's office for a trip to his place. If he was not to receive help from David, he would find her in other ways. He indeed wanted nothing more from her and yet a troubling inclination to seek revenge burned in his soul.

He called Andre. "How are you doing?" he asked.

"Hello, Gunther, nice to hear from you. I'm recovering well enough. The wound is not bothering me, and I'm returning to Energy next week."

"I'd like a conference with you about some ideas I have for the future of petroleum in a world needing product but not contamination. Will you have some time?"

"Sure, call my office and set it up." The call ended and Gunther smiled. He knew the pathway to finding his missing nemesis traveled through Parvel Mandolin. Access to that man made sense to him. He turned and headed away from the building, housing David's organization. His destiny was a woman who had invaded his life and disrupted his business. His emotions focused on her regardless of the wisdom David presented conflicting his intentions. He called the number of one of the technicians who worked with him to keep him safe from destruction. She was one person he trusted to aid his hunt.

"I have some time to meet. I want you to give me all the guidance you can to find her. You will be amply rewarded for your assistance, as we discussed in the compound." He agreed with her to meet and acquire a direction for the search. His brain had an implant, and he intended to use its power to find Cigi.

CHAPTER 49

C igi, Sam, and Clare sat with Parvel and the rest of the team in the restaurant across from the Department of Energy. Cigi looked across the street at the building, imagining a different scenario than the chaos that injured Andre and placed them in peril as terrorists. "How is Andre," she asked.

"He's doing well. He'll recover and return to work soon," Brenda said. "Sam, I'm glad you and Clare escaped permanent custody."

Sam related his experience and a promise to find Peter. "The investigation of Clare never found anything to countermand her claim of humanity. Everything they dug up on her came back clean. When Cigi arrived, and they assumed she acted as my attorney, she provided an invaluable asset. I'm on my own recognizance along with this wonderful ankle monitor." He lifted his pant leg to display the device.

"What now?" Parvel asked. "Are we safe to our live lives without scrutiny by government authorities?" No one said anything. The group sat a few minutes together before Cigi stood and asked Parvel to go with her.

They walked to another part of the restaurant and sat at a table. "You have done so much for me over the last few months," she said to him. "You came through when trouble arose to challenge our existence. I know your feelings for me are more than friendship. I don't understand why, but I acknowledge and appreciate them. As you know, Sam provided me with the power to experience human emotions and to understand them. I want to know if you would pursue a relationship with me if I agreed."

Parvel sat in silence as his mouth curled into a smile. His eyes blinked and moistened. "I would pursue a relationship with you. If Sam and Clare can make it work, I can't think of any reason for us to fail."

"Good. Then let's return to our friends and decide what is next for us." They walked with hands clasped and announced their liaison. Sam clapped his hands, and the rest followed suit.

"I wondered how long it would be before you two decided to be a couple," Sam said. "It won't be easy, Parvel. She's opinionated, stubborn, goal-oriented, self-sufficient, emotional, and controlling. At the same time, she has sympathy, a caring nature, smarts, and an ability to communicate effectively."

"Thanks for the vote of confidence in me, Sam." Her voice purred as she spoke to him. "Or maybe I should say, daddy."

"Ha. Ha. Very funny. I wasn't the only one working on your birth into this world. Any word on the whereabouts of the sisters?" Sam asked.

"No, but I'm monitoring hotels throughout Virginia. If I discover any extraordinary bookings, it may be our friends and their male counterparts." Cigi said.

"Won't the government be doing the same thing?" Parvel asked.

"Yes, if they are interested in gathering such information. I don't think the sisters are on their radar as much as Peter is a blip."

As they concluded their talking, a car approached and parked on the street in front of the restaurant. Two men in black trench coats and dark suits vacated the vehicle. One man opened the back door of the car, and a woman exited. She dressed similarly and looked in the window at the congregation of collaborators.

Sam said, "I do believe we are about to get our first assessment of the government's trust in us." The three members of an unknown agency of the Federal Government entered the restaurant and headed directly to the tables where they sat. "Good evening," he said as he stood to address the woman. "I've been expecting you." The rest of the gang stared at him, disbelieving what he just said. Sam looked back at his friends and smiled.

"You are not hard to find," the woman said. "The bracelet works." She glanced at each of the people still seated. "I see you have the members of your revolution gathered together."

"It's been quite an ordeal. Ido believe we thwarted my brother's intentions, but he remains a threat as long as he is free."

Addressing her next remarks to Cigi, she asked, "Have you kept in touch with the other four?" Cigi squinted at Sam before gazing at this new person. She stood beside Sam.

"What others?"

"Sam, I know you haven't explained who I am to anyone, as I requested. It is now expedient to do so." She paused for Sam to speak. He nodded.

"I would like to introduce you to my government cohort in the battle to stop my brother, Renata Giretti. She is the head of the Human Conformity Task Force assigned to monitor android development." Sam held out his hand palm up, pointing at her.

Clare asked, "Is that where you went each time you had business and disappeared for days? You worked for the government?" Her voice carried a bitter tone, her disappointment rising to a level of frustration.

"Yes, but don't be upset. One of the reasons you exist is to prove humans and thinking humanoids can live and work together in this world. We have provided truth about your development so that fear of jobs lost, leadership controls, and other anxieties have no place in this world."

"Don't be naive, Sam. We can be a threat if people do not trust our intentions to be honest and reliable." Cigi turned to face her friends. "You represent the good in humanity. Peter is an example of a challenge for us. He is your brother, and I realize the immense burden of loving a family and hating the behavior."

Parvel stood beside his newly established girlfriend. "What status does Cigi or Clare have in a world ruled by humans? The security guard at the Department of Energy wasn't happy to have Cigi in the building. We surrounded her, and Andre Scott got shot. What happens to the other androids created to replace people we know? They're living beings who want lives without threat." He held Cigi's hand.

"Valid inquiries. I don't know what will come of this, but my committee has a mission to determine rights and freedoms for you and the other bodies." Renata signaled her men to leave as she turned toward the door. Turning back, she said, "Sam, stay in touch. I'll see to getting that monitor removed by tomorrow or the next day."

After they were alone, Sam faced his harshest critics who glared at him as if he was a guilty person. "Wait. We're free to be who we want."

Cigi said, "Easy for you to say. You are human and have your status established. These four people are just that. People. Clare and I are nothing in this world. The sisters and the four male androids with them, Andy, David, and Gunther replacements, all have nothing. We are human until someone discovers our mechanics and our mental capacity. We operate in any environment and survive. We can face certain death and prevail, whereas a human may not have the ability to win. How many androids did Peter deploy? Are they functioning as human and claiming rights they don't have? What happens when a human challenge happens to them, and harm befalls someone? Samuel Bennington, I love you for creating me, and I hate that you have nothing to provide for me as a future."

She turned to Parvel and said, "Take me home and prove what I know to be human. Make love to me and win my soul if I have one." She pulled him to his feet, and they left a bitter atmosphere to assuage an ire Cigi had now experienced at a level she carefully checked so as not alarm her beau.

Brenda interjected, "Wow, that girl has some anger issues." Clare grunted. Mercy and Grendel eyed her curious to what level of anger she might exude.

"Cigi's right," Sam whispered. A chorus of 'Huh?' came from the human contingency. "I gave her all the tools to be human and nothing to determine her to be human. Clare, we must find all the others and correct this error. We must do it before anyone discovers them and destroys them. They have a right to exist. You have a right. Let's go home and fix this." They deserted the three Energy investigators who remained sitting.

"I suggest we return to work tomorrow and make sure Peter stays locked out of department money. Then we need to get Charles Cooke and Gunther Parsons following the guidelines for energy development in the Twenty-second Century. It'll be here before we know it." Brenda said to her teammates. They finished their drinks and left for homes and rest. Each alone and wondering about the android companions of two humans with serious relationships.

Peter Bennington collared the one technician he now trusted to be on his side. The man had as much greed as anyone, and Peter financed a lavish lifestyle for his loyalty. Things had changed, but a promising future of renewal of the business of android technology partnered them. "Where to. Peter?" he asked.

"Somewhere far from here. I have money. You have transportation. We can start again in Arizona." He nodded and started the car. The drive was long, and the resources were stored in the warehouses owned by a company Peter started without his brother. David Anderson unwittingly purchased all the materials as investments. Peter's new passport had the proper identification to match the owner of the properties - a bald Lex Luthor type from the ancient Superman series of the Twentieth Century.

They left Arlington and Washington, D.C. behind, but Peter

was determined to reemerge from obscurity caused by the blindness of ungrateful humans. They would rue the day they forced him out of his home and comfortable life. Each day of passing remained a mark of shame and dishonor. Each moment of thought about his brother, Sam, festered in his brain, building motivation to show the world a better existence with Androids leading country after country into a prosperity and peacefulness for him that humankind had not discovered or deserved.

He lay his head back against the seat cushion of the electric vehicle that gained power from the sunlight by day and moonlight by night. Sleep overcame an exhausted body. His dreams haunted his restlessness. Dreams of Cigi, Clare, and four sisters whose abilities he knew he could master from the data stored in the disk he carried out of the compound. The data developed by his brother and copied by a loyal partner. "You'll see me again," he said in his nightmare.

CHAPTER 50

S ummer watched the four men recharging their energy cells in the sunlight as they lay by the hotel pool. Without the labs and design rooms at The Company, she had no resources to modify their power supplies. They were an advanced design but nothing comparable to her or the three sisters. Would they be acceptable companions? Each had qualities for employment in a world that needed their skills, a world that loathed to accept them. She had sent them to the pool and watched from the balcony for them to arrive. She wondered if any of them had a future.

Spring joined her. "How are they." Summer turned her face and smiled. No problems yet crossed her mind.

"They should be ready within half an hour. Let's pack our things. We have a long journey ahead." They reentered the suite and met their two sisters. Each of them placed clothing and other essentials accumulated after their escape into cases for the trip. The men had only a few items with them as Peter separated from them before outfitting them. The vehicle was a second-hand model from a used dealer who cared little for a background check where cash was involved. They plannned to ditch the van before licensing became an issue.

"Are they coming up soon," Autumn asked. Summer nodded a yes to her. Winter clicked on the television to catch any news updates, and a reporter on-site at the compound was announcing a change of tactics by the government.

"Turn it up," Summer said. With a louder volume, she heard clear language about android models that escaped and needed finding as soon as possible. "A Senate panel investigating the operations here behind me has concluded the threat to humanity is negligible. That said, the committee decided to eradicate any possibility for interference in government operations with the replacement of key personnel. Anyone with knowledge of the whereabouts of Peter Bennington or his escaped robots should contact us here at the station or the National Security Agency. The NSA offers a generous reward for credible information."

"Great, now a bounty is on our heads," Winter said. Summer sent a message to the boys to come back to the room immediately. Another coded message went to Cigi, wherever she might be. A chance of a signal trace crossed her mind, but a need for material to upgrade the men superseded any fear of detection.

A knock on the door alerted them to visitors, too soon for the boys to return. "Housekeeping," The voice outside said.

"Spring, check on who's at the door," Summer directed. She clicked off the reporter - no need for any heads-up about a reward. When the door opened, a maid stood outside with a cart. Spring looked at Summer, who said, "Please come back. We're checking out soon." The maid nodded, and Spring closed the door. Another knock followed within a minute. The boys were back. Spring opened the door to let them enter.

One of the men asked, "Did you see the news? We're enemies of the state."

"We heard," Summer said. "Everyone set to go?" Seven heads rocked in the affirmative. She called the parking valet to have the van brought to the front of the hotel. Four suitcases and four duffel bags for the boys to fill later sat on the floor by the door. One last check around the suite for any telltale materials completed the preparation for racing south to Florida and an escape to the one island still on rocky diplomatic terms with the USA.

Eight people claiming humanity as their legacy departed for a lobby filled with authentic human lifeforms, each of whom was a potential informer for money. As the elevator rose to floor level, Summer implored, "We need to be as couple-like as possible. We are not missing until someone from The Company lets the information slip out." The ding interrupted any more advice. They entered the empty car, and one of them pushed 'L' for a ride into an uncertain future.

David Anderson returned to a family, expecting him to walk. He explained the original concept of his demise and a clone replacing him. His wife and children vowed to help hunt for the beasts who acted so cavalier. "He used me," David remarked. "Peter Bennington misled me regarding his intentions for building his and Samuel's business. The original concept of Intelligent Android supplemental assistance for easing human menial labor jobs made sense. No paying them or benefits. The laid-off workforce could be retrained in fields that needed human workers. Having greater productivity in factories, farm fields, hazardous occupations, and service industries called to me. When Peter decided to build replacement robots, I didn't think he included me." His wife stroked his hair. She accepted his philandering because of the lifestyle in which they lived. She loved him, and he professed to love her. His wandering ended with Cigi.

"Parsons wants to hunt for that vixen who did something to our heads. He has a scar at the base of his neck. I found a scar while I was in the compound awaiting new legs from Bennington." His diatribe erupted after returning home from an interrogation that seemed more accusatory than information gathering. Andre Scott's clone disappeared, and no amount of prodding or pleading for answers uncovered its location. He knew his double existed with a different identity and mission in life. He did not care if the government found it and destroyed it.

Gunther Parsons' twin had escaped detection and disappeared for now. Four sister androids, Cigi Weatherman, and Clare Esposito had vanished, as well. Samuel Bennington, relieved of any wrongdoing in the planned coup, lived his life as before.

"Are you sure you want nothing from Gunther?" David's wife asked. She listened but didn't comprehend the mess within his head. She was happy for his return to their house. "I'll fix us a small dinner." She left him to stew about how to rebuild his hedge fund and recover as much of the losses those who trusted him with money demanded. He still had many billions invested in a variety of growth stocks, futures, income properties, and mutual funds. The market would rise and build his portfolio. Gunther was a distraction. He dismissed tagging along with him on his search for Cigi.

Parvel lay on the bed covered by the sheet and blanket. His mind marveled at the human abilities Cigi demonstrated upon returning to the penthouse and fulfilling her request from him. She lay beside him asleep, an asset he did not think she needed. His requirement for sleep matched the eight-hour cycle most humans followed. Today, he disrupted the cycle with thoughts of his future with her. Was a marriage possible when filing for a license brought questions that endangered her? Could she conceive as Sam indicated? His employment at the Department of Energy continued as a fund manager along with Brenda, Mercy, and Grendel. He uncovered the existence of the chip in Andre's head when a conversation with Cigi developed into a confessional from her. He swore an oath of secrecy to her as a symbol of his love for a woman made from human organs produced by stem cells and mechanical parts to complete the composition. Her appetite for knowledge and experience rivaled no one he knew, and he feared her growth would relegate him to history as a forgotten man. Not forgotten, as much as stored in a deep recess of the memory modules that operated within her brain.

He stepped from the bed and enter the bathroom. Walking into the living area, he headed to the patio. Outside, he gazed at the world below, a world safe for him and fraught with danger for Cigi. Her abilities and experiences marshaled skills that kept the hounds at the door from breaking in. A sound caught his attention. He pivoted to see a beautiful sight approach. Her face lit the world around him, and her body exacted attention from his physical nature. Her words excelled in expanding his knowledge base. Every day brought more profound, added mystique. He cherished the ground on which she walked.

The future was not a promising one. Parvel watched her close the distance with a grin on her face and an allure he succumbed to every minute with her. "Good morning," he said. She walked to him and placed hands on his cheeks. Her mouth connected with his, and she explored with her tongue. Fire roused within his loins as she finished.

"Good morning, my love." Her voice soothed his soul.

Sam said to Clare, "We should depart this area and head west. I spoke with Charles about Cigi's place in Seattle. His conversation with her seemed to indicate we could start there and find our place as soon as we can."

"Have you spoken with Cigi?"

"No, but she's busy exploring her new life with Parvel. I'll meet with her later and get permission. Can you believe she called me daddy?"

"Yes," Clare said and giggled. "You constructed me, so I am a daughter for you and more."

"Don't be gross. I love you as the woman you are. We have a

relationship without the entanglements or social expectations."

Clare groused, "Societies expectations are entanglements?" She turned away from him but smiled.

Sam turned on the television for some entertainment, but a news bulletin flashed across the screen. The reporter behind the desk read the datasheet in her hand. "Congress has passed a bill banning any future construction of android technology with intelligent design features. Any AI creatures currently existing are to be recovered as a precaution, and those currently free of human control should be watched for and reported to authorities. A reward has been established for any credible information leading to the round-up of these creatures." Sam turned the set off and cursed.

"What does it mean for me?" Clare asked.

"It means we head out of here and seek asylum with Cooke and Andy, who needs protective guidance. I warned Renata this might happen. She assured me the task force was on top of it." He called Cigi to explain the difficulty. She granted permission to use the Seattle penthouse. "What are you and Parvel going to do?"

"We'll stay here for now. This place is a fortified palace for the royal residents. Parvel remains employed at Energy. I can research law courses, get my degree, and pass the bar. If I accomplish that, government leaders may have to recognize my sovereign right to be a citizen of these United States."

"Citizen, maybe. Human? Not at this time."

"I heard from Summer. They're heading to another part of the world away from the scrutiny of greedy people dispossessed of common sense by leadership embroiled in a panic about replacement androids." The called end, but Sam understood the ramifications of his creations as freaks in the manner of Mary Shelly's Dr. Frankenstein. Danger lurked, and many innocent people and machines were destined to harm and death. An innocent beginning clashed with the greed and avarice of his brother. Where was Peter?

CHAPTER 51

Sam and Renata Giretti sat in her office at the capitol building. His concerns about the new law compelled him to connect with her. "What happened? Didn't your committee inform the politicians what you know about them?" Sam asked.

"I understand your concern, but the law passed, and the only way to place it on hold is an injunction until the courts hear the case."

He leaned forward to make his point. "My friends are not the evil ones. My brother is. He inclines to make trouble, and I cannot find him." He sat back and continued, "So, I need to file an injunction, get it heard before anyone picks up my creations, and hope the courts are sympathetic to a cause no one supports."

"We are working with Congressional staff to write a modification that allows for certain types of Android technology to continue. Let us work through wording. I'll stay in touch. You can help craft the language." Renata said.

"Meanwhile, any of the humanoids that function in society and are productive members of the human race are subject to round-up and termination." Sam stood to leave. "Be careful what you do, as these are not creatures who are easily commanded or corralled. I'll protect them as best I can, but the technology is mine and mine to use as I want."

Before he could leave, Renata asked him, "Are you harboring any of them? If you are, and the authorities discover such a situation, there is little I can do to protect you from harm or incarceration." Sam turned and left. The situation, as she put it, was fraught with uncertainty and danger for several operational androids.

Returning to the condo building, he thought of the other beings, Summer and her sisters, four males with them, and Cigi. What future did they have when the world was against them? Peter's disappearance hindered calming of the atmosphere in humanity. Of course, the only androids free in the world resided in the United States. Other countries did not know about them or experienced them. Could they find a sanctuary?

At the building, he saw a person sitting on the steps to the front door. She stood as he neared. "Sam, I'm under indictment for aiding and abetting Peter in his creation of enemies of the state. I'm not a criminal."

Sam held out his hands to assist her standing. "Narumi Yamamoto, it's been difficult. I know. Come in and say hi to Clare." They entered the building. Inside, they passed the concierge who acknowledged them. He called Clare to alert her to their arrival.

In the elevator, Narumi asked, "Can you help clear my name? I worked with you to confound Peter's plan. The FBI special agent wanted information about deployed androids. When I explained I knew nothing about any, he accused me of terrorism." Sam remembered Renuti's last warning.

"You did nothing wrong. Do you have a good attorney? One with knowledge of the new law?" The elevator dinged its arrival. They exited, and Clare appeared at the apartment door.

"Cigi wants us to come up to her place," Clare announced. "Hi, Narumi."

"Did she say what he wanted?" Sam asked.

"No, but she wanted us as soon as you returned. Parvel went to work, so it will be just us, and Narumi." The three of them returned to the elevator and rode to the top floor after coding in the proper access numbers.

Narumi gazed about the penthouse, amazed by the opulent space and stark decor. Cigi greeted them with open arms and hugs. She smiled and shook hands with Sam and Narumi. Sam asked, "What's this about, Cigi. Your plea sounded like extreme circumstances warrant immediate attention."

"I heard from Summer. She and her sisters are heading to Cuba and asylum. Since the USA has no extradition treaty in play, they assume a certain safety there. They may be right. As of now, government officials do not know of their existence or attempted flight away from capture and destruction. How did your meeting with Giretti go?"

"She has little hope of her task force influencing Congress to change the laws to reflect the reality of Intelligent Artificial lifeforms within the borders of the country. She warned of consequences for anyone harboring an IA being." He raised eyebrows and cocked his head while he set his jaw in a line. A noise in the hallway drew attention to the addition of another person. Parvel had opened the door and come in without anyone knowing he was present. He heard Sam's comments.

He asked, "Does that mean you and I are destined for prison or worse because our soul mates are not fully human but function more humanly than any person I know? And that includes you and me." Sam laughed.

"Yeah, we are now public enemy number one, but only if authorities uncover our subterfuge. I have no plans to allow Clare or Cigi's capture and destruction."

Narumi interrupted, "I have another disturbing piece of news." Four pairs of eyes focused on the technician who helped android technology live independent lives. "We have other androids working in the medical field. Peter had them sent out the day before the raid on the compound. They are fully certified to practice their trades as doctors and nurses. Each of the four doctors and six nurses is a graduate of an accredited university program and internship. The doctors have done their residency and are accredited by the state of Virginia."

Sam said, "Peter was quite busy underground with his placement of Intelligent Androids into society. Where are they? Local hospitals and clinics? I wonder how many others are unaccounted."

"I don't know as that was not part of my assignment," Narumi said. "He had us fabricate more than a dozen functional craft-oriented machines to assemble the humanoids. I infused the memory banks with the proper medical information and associated algorithms to use the data properly. They are also socially acclimated."

Cigi asked, "Are they functioning to accumulate data about the possible government people Peter targeted for replacement?"

"I don't know, but that would be logical."

Sam interjected a loaded comment. "Since we have targets on our backs and the Giretti's task force cannot aid our safety at this time, I think we should disperse for places where attention to detail is less likely to draw the wrath of humans. At least humans with no desire for us to be part of their society."

Clare asked, "Narumi, where are you staying?"

"I'm still in my apartment in Alexandria. I have to report to Court on Monday to plead my guilt or innocence." Tears formed in her eyes and streamed across her cheeks. "I don't know if I can do it."

"I'll stand with you and act as your legal adviser." Cigi placed her arm around Narumi's shoulder. "I know the legal system in Virginia from studying on-line course materials for the last week. I can represent you as an advocate but not as a practicing attorney. You will need to get one."

Sam almost shouted, "No, they'll detain you as an undesirable. They'll destroy you before I can rescue you."

"Sam. Relax. If I am to be a human, I must act the part. I am as human as any of you. Parvel and I have as much right to a life together as anyone. If helping Narumi provides any evidence of human traits, then the rest of us have a chance at survival and thriving. We cannot be the last of our species before we are recognized as a species." She turned to Narumi. "Stay here tonight and rest in peace. Tomorrow we can assemble a defense for Monday."

Cigi signaled Sam to follow her into the kitchen. When they were alone, he asked, "What do you want to tell me that the others need not hear?"

"I found Peter. He is driving to Arizona, where he has a cache of materiel to restart the business. We cannot do anything for now, but later, you should confront him about his activities which threaten to ruin all of us." Sam agreed but shook his head. "Are you and Clare heading to Seattle?"

"Yes, thank you for letting us stay at your place. And yes, we will keep an eye out for anyone monitoring the penthouse."

"Good. After you settle, find a place on the Olympic Peninsula and melt into the countryside." Cigi and Sam returned to the group. "Alright, people, back to your place." She directed her comment to Sam and Clare. They left, and Cigi showed Narumi the second bedroom and bathroom amenities for cleansing and sleeping.

Parvel said, "I can stay at my place tonight so you and Narumi can make strategic plans in the morning."

"No, Parvel, if we are to make our partnership in life work, then we should stay as a couple. I have more credibility having a male human as a companion. And I like you. A lot."

"Okay, my lovely maven. I am your heart and soul for eternity."

Over the next few days, plans for Sam and Clare finalized for a drive across the country in Rose, whose navigation abilities required no modifications. She opted for a direct route with as little legal interference as possible. Main interstate roadways and sightseeing were the agenda. Summer checked in with Cigi to inform her they were in Cuba and had accumulated the needed documentation for asylum. Narumi's case passed muster and the judge dismissed it. Cigi's expertise as a legal representative had impressed the judge who wondered if she was a law student. Cigi stated she had indeed applied for and been accepted to an accredited on-line school program and would finish in two more years.

Parvel kept the team at Energy in stitches relating his harrowing life as a male escort to one of the best human beings he knew, and the team knew to keep his secret. All android models used in the sordid social entertainment business were dismantled. They were not part of any of the cadre The Company released into society. Twenty-four humanoid beings still survived in a society determined to eradicate their species. How many others thrived in the world remained a mystery.

Three months passed without incidents. Sam and Clare settled in Jefferson County near the town of Chimacum in Washington State. Summer, Autumn, Winter, and Spring began operating as restaurant owners while their male companions acted as the chefs and wait staff. Cigi tracked the location of the four doctors and six nurses to be sure of their acceptance in the medical field.

Her life with Parvel grew into a deep love she understood intellectually but now embraced mentally and emotionally. Narumi Yamamoto found a tech job in Silicon Valley in northern Caifornia, which still served as the technology center of the world.

One morning, Parvel sat at breakfast and looked at Cigi, who seemed to be unusually quiet. She pushed the food around her plate and did not eat. "Are you alright?" he asked. She looked up at him, and tears fell from her eyes.

"I'm fine," she said. "I'm fine."

"You're not eating anything, and lately you consumed more food than I witnessed in the last six months. Now you don't want it?" His eyed widened as he asked, "Are you ill?"

"No, I'm not experiencing any diseases or maladies." She smiled as she wiped the moisture from her face. "Parvel, I hope you don't mind what I'm about to say. I don't want to alarm you because Sam never guaranteed this could happens, but." She paused and gazed at his alarmed countenance. "I'm pregnant."

ACKNOWLEDGEMENTS

Writing a mystery set in a future time has intriguing possiblities for an author. The concept of the story, built with foundations in today's world, creates ideas for humans concocting strange notions of possibilities. I hadn't planned on writing a science fiction book when I began storytelling a decade ago. I was a mystery writer, a crime investigation relater, an action teller. This story came out of the blue after I finished "In the Garden of Eden."

As ideas progress in my head, I write them into notes in Scrivener as Chapters or sections. I decided I needed a more comprehensive format for this story since I am not usually a science fiction author. Several realities bumped up against my thougths and left me wondering about the story. My wife, Sandy, considered the premise of the book to be worthy of writing, so I began.

I had not thought of the story as a young adult book, so I continued constructing the plot and story arc as an adult mystery. The editing of each chapter in Grammerly unleased the reading level at 7th grade and my brainstorm decided to clean up the first few chapters I had written for a more appropriate style of writing for young adults.

I read each completed and modestly edited chapter to Sandy who gave feedback for poor writing and encouragement for continuing the story. Her words are along the line of "this is your best story yet." I always listen to her since I imagine myself to be a wise person.

Character names are part of the fun of writing. Deciding what to use for identifying the participants in a story means asking people permission to use names. I engaged in an internet chat with a person named Cigi Weatherman (not her real name) and I asked for permission to use the name in a future book. Permission was granted.

Peter and Samuel Bennington are names from my head. The Seasons are names of people. I've met and know a person named Summer, Winter, Spring, and Autumn.I never met a person named Fall. Brenda Willaims is a Uniteds States Marine acquaintance in Arizona. Mercy Garocki's first name is a friend from my church, St. Antony of Egypt. Grendel Llanthony needed research to find a welch name appropriate for the story. Grendel is a monsterous beast from the saga of Beowulf. Llanthony is a Welsh town in Monmouthshire. A famous priory of Augustine monks can be found there. Narumi is Japanese for growing beauty. Renata is Latin meaning reborn. Giretti is Italian that translates into English as strolls. Other names are creations of my head and have no real history.

When I wanted something in my story to reflect the possibilities of

Android human-like creatures living among us, I refected on movies and television that had the needed foundations for writing. References to "Stepford Wives, I Robot, and Westworld were deliberate in that each movie or television derived from a book written in the 20th Century, helps in understanding the thinking by my characters. Star Trek had Commander Data who wanted emotions so he could be more human. The Central command computer in 2001 Space Odyssey, HAL, monitors all functions on the craft flying to Venus. Asimov's science fiction stories lays the foundation for many of the tales written by some of the best known writers over the years.

Another aspect of the computing world lies in the construction of programming. Computers use a binary system which has the same mathematical set up as the decimal system using digits 0 through 9. A binary system uses 0 and 1 as switches. 0 is off, and 1 is on. The switches provide a way for the mathematics to occur in an operating system. A ternary system would use the digits 0, 1, and 2. Ternary comes from Latin meaning three. The idea for the story has the switches off, on, and what if. Our human brains seem to have a what if switch we use to figure out various scenarios of life with out random searching for better moves as in a chess game.

Science does not have to be fictional for a premise in a story. Robotic machines exist today. They assemble automobiles and other items humans purchase. So the idea of using robotic humans to replace us in certain occupations that are dangerous and unhealthy is not new. We have created companions in robotic dogs and cats, as well as sex companions. The next logical iteration is being tested in Japan. Humanoid beings may become our wait staff or cashiers at resaurants and stores. An article in the Seattle Times in late 2019 illustrated the progress made so far.

Stem cell research has advanced through the years and scientists differentiate types into embrionic and non-embrionic or adult cells. Recently, scientists have engineered a way to turn adult cells into pluripotent stem cells. The use of Induced Pluripotent Stem Cells (iPSC) can differentiate into all types of specialized cells in the body. The potential for creating organ tissues meant I could foresee the development of organ systems in the future.

Science has a way of using fictional inventions. Jules Verne had time machines and rockets to the moon. Although we do not time travel, we have explored the moon with humans. We have sent robotic craft to various planets and moons of those planets. We have structures in space in which astronauts and cosmonauts reside. Using chip technology to track our animals devised the idea of chip implants to communicate and control the men in Cigi's life. Nano-technology is the applications of very small things. Using nanotechnology to infuse the brain with connectors to a microchip seemed a logical idea.

Once I completed my story, editing became crucial. Were parts of the story unbelievable? Did fashion androids with more than possible abilities? How does society in today's world reflect a future society that will grapple with android technology and artificial intelligence?

I spoke with numerous people about the premise of my story and found an audience of excited readers. My editors Rebecca Bauer and Susan Wall scoured my writing to edit and proofread my manuscript. Their input regarding mistakes in spelling, grammar, and story arc cleaned up the original writing. I wish to thank my wife, Sandy for listening and sharing her thoughts.

I found using Grammerly and ProWritingAid helped with changes to language structure and clarity of writing. These are now essential tools for an author to use. The cover consists of three stock images I ordered from Shutterstock.com. Adobe InDesign was my formatting program for the cover and the interior of the book. The files created with Indesign are saved as PDF and then are sent to Ingram Spark for acceptance. Once these files are ready for the printer, I can order books on demand for myself to market and stores may order for signing events.

Although people will want to know how my characters used science and technology to craft sentient beings, my focus was not on the methodology as much as a study of human dynamics and societal angst. Will we human beings readily accept replacement creatures? Can we function next to a robot that can out perform us and out think us? Are we on a collision course to a society of wealth and poverty as a normal way of life? Exploring our current state of the world and the fact that I completed this book during the worst pandemic in a century, caused me to ponder a future that most of my children and grandchildren may experience.

I thank everyone who believes in my writing as entertaining, instructional, and fundamental to reading. Tell your friends and neighbors about my books and help me leave a legacy for children and grandchildren and humanity that improves all of us.

Although I attempt to be accurate in the portrayal of the events of the book, any mistakes or errors of medical, physical, social, or emotional encounters within the story are the sole responsibility of the author.

Last of all I want to thank the following link for the free filigree used in this book.

<a href="https://www.freepik.com/free-photos-vectors/vintage">Vintage vector created by mariia_fr - www.freepik.com</a>

ABOUT THE AUTHOR

Peter Stockwell is a retired middle school teacher embarking on his next career telling stories. After 32 years of guiding the minds and the emotions of preteen and teenage students, he left the classroom to relax and enjoy the rest of his life with family and friends. Instead, he writes books and publishes them. The fun began when he learned the next step, marketing his creations to the world.

His debut novel, Motive, was a fantastic learning experience. His second book, Motivations, a prequel to Motive, let readers delve deep into the people investigated in Motive.

The third book, Jerry's Motives, continued the Jefferson family sagas of police investigations and harrowing perilous adventures. Death Stalks Mr. Blackthorne, a harrowing vacation cruise to Alaska fraught with danger, continued the story. In the Garden of Eden tells the story of Marcus Jefferson's search for the source of the poisonous toxin used to kill and harm individuals aboard the cruise ship.

He lives with his wife, Sandy, and son, David, in Silverdale, Washington. He has five children and eight grandchildren who are a source of great joy. He is a member of the Pacific Northwest Writers, the International Thriller Writers, and Mystery Writers of America. His books are published through his company, Westridge Art.

Keep in touch with him at Instagram, Facebook/peterstockwell and Twitter @pastockwell.

E-mail is stockwellpa@wavecable.com

Book Club Questions

Use the following questions to guide a book club discussion of "The Mistress" or modify them if the author attends the meeting. Have fun.

1)   Did you enjoy the book? Why or why not?

2)   If you had expectations for this book, how were they fulfilled?

3)   How would you describe this book to a friend in a short sentence.

4)   The author of this book is not a character or narrator. at any time did the author seem to be present in the book? If yes, how?

5)   Describe the plot of the story to a friend. Did it pull you in or did you feel forced to read the book?

6)   How real are the characters to you? Would you like to meet them? Which of them did you like? Which did you hate?

7)   Are the actions of the characters plausible to you? Why? Or why not?

8)   If one or more of the characters made decisions that had moral implications, would you have made the same decision? Why? or why not?

9)   Who was your favorite character? Explain why.

10)   Did you relate to any of the characters on a personal basis? How?

11)   If this book was to become a movie or limited series for television, who would you cast for the lead roles?

12)   The setting of a book can affect how a reader relates to the story. Is the setting important to the theme of the book?

13)   This book happens in the future. Could the same story take place today or would it be better further into the future? Support your reasoning.

14)   Name the themes of the book. Are they important to the plot?

15)   How are the book's images symbolically important? Do the images help develop the plot or help define the characters?

16)   Did the book end the way you expected?

17)   At what point were you most engaged in the book?

18)   Conversely, were there any places the story dragged?

19)   Did the book contain anything that was real to you or the world in which you live? Did you learn anything new that could become real in the future?

20)   How would you describe the pace of the book?

21)   What three words summarize the book?

22)   What sets this book apart from other books youv'e read in this genre?

23)   What other books have you read by this author? How did this book compare to the other books?

24)   Was the length of the book acceptable? If not, was it too long or too short? What would you remove? What would you want to see added?

25)   Why would you recommend this book to other readers? Or a close friend? If not, then why not?

Author note: Book Club Questions are derived from:
www.thoughtCo.com/general-book-club-questions-study-discussion

NOTES:

NOTES:

NOTES:

CPSIA information can be obtained
at www.ICGtesting.com
Printed in the USA
FSHW021030200720
71720FS